ROMAN'S RECKONING

LUCAS LAMONT
MM ALPHA/OMEGA MPREG

ROMAN'S RECKONING

THE CHRONICLES OF FATE BOOK 1

Dedications:

This book is dedicated to any artist who desires to have their voice heard for the first time. Don't give up on your dream and stay true to who you are. Your story, in whatever medium you choose, is good enough. The world without art is black and white. Let your color shine through and make this a better place.
I especially want to dedicate and say thanks to the following:

> To "J" – for giving me the opportunity to be your partner for 14 years for which I didn't deserve and for helping me grow my artistry to what it is now

> To "A" – for being the most precious gift in my life and harnessing a strength that is beautiful and will change the world

> To "M&D" – for unconditional love and always supporting me as your son

> To "MMP" – for your dedicated friendship and love which lead me to a journey I didn't know I was going to take

To "C" – for being an intellect and giving me the fist bump I needed

To "JMP" – for shaping my world and opening a door

To "L" – for telling me to jump

TABLE OF CONTENTS

Characters	Classification	Age
Dr. Jacob (Jake) Erricson (Sur)	Alpha - Type 5	45
Adrian (Omarro) Erricson (Veo)	Omega - Type 5	41
Roman Erricson	Alpha - Type 6	24
Ryan Erricson	Beta	18
Rixen Erricson	Omega - Type 4	18
Dr. Dustin Cavenbelle (Sur)	Alpha - Type 4	40
Alec (Froyer) Cavenbelle (Veo)	Omega - Type 4	39
Andrew "Drew" Cavenbelle	Alpha - Type 4	22
William (Berncrest) Cavenbelle	Omega - Type 3	24
Mikaél Cavenbelle	Omega - Type 5	17
Matthew Whitmore (Sur)	Alpha - Type 5	39
Terrence (Bastian) Whitmore (Veo)	Omega - Type 5	39
Peyton Whitmore	Omega - Type 5	20
Siro LaCroix	Alpha - Type 5	24
Garrace Huntington	Alpha - Type 4	18
Nico Hallen	Omega - Type 4	23
Laycin Vaughn	Beta	18
Dr. Paul Birowack	Beta	55

Glossary

Pre-Wolf Era – the previous existence of humans evolved from primates and also the only existence of the human female gender

Wolf Era – current time, existence of male humans evolved from *Canis lupus* (wolves)

Rank – The biological make-up of a wolf-descendant: Alpha – Beta - Omega

Blood-Type – a categorial gene system to determine purity of the strongest genes ranked 1-5 in Alphas and Omegas

The 6th Blood-Type – An evolutionary anomaly in top tier Type-5 Alphas

Pup – a wolf-descendent child from birth to age 9

Adolescent – a wolf-descendent child from age 10 – 15

Natural Adult – a wolf-descendent man from ages 16 and older

Legal Adult – a male of age 18 and older

Sur – formal title given to an Alpha father

Veo – formal title given to an Omega father

Post Education – beginning of adult and specialized education of 4 Levels in two-year cycles begin at age 16

Contract – Legal requirement to form an official relationship bond including commitment, evaluation of assets, reproduction, and authority

Fated Mate – a highly sought out bond indicated by primal phero-mones to connect with one specific mate or "Fate" for care, love, and reproductive purposes

Heat – a 4-month cycle for Omegas at peak fertility where the womb drops for insemination

CHAPTER 01:

A Dinner of Obligation

Roman tapped his hand and foot while ignoring the muffled conversations that hummed throughout the elite restaurant. His occasional exhales of displeasure sent subtle waves across the candle flame glistening inside the crystal holder resting in the table's center. If the mood lighting were any darker, shadows might actually engulf his parents' disapproving faces as they observed his apathetic posture. Making a scene in this ostentatious and overpriced restaurant was not only unacceptable but also grounds for a scarlet letter in the metropolitan city of Tauris.

"I don't think it is too much to ask for you to show a little more enthusiasm here." Roman's Omega father, or Veo as they are called, swirled the remaining gulp of white wine in his glass before downing the ineffective elixir. His unmoving eyes pierced the soul of his now 24-year-old son who was acting like a clueless pup. Even though his Veo's eyes rarely ever looked at him that patronizing way, Roman did not change his behavior.

Instead, Roman ran his fingers through his newly primped and trimmed blond hair, a regular habit when he left his discontent unspoken. But with the now vocal displeasure taking place in the restaurant, Roman felt compelled to answer his Veo.

He sighed. "I'm fine." A lie and a poor one at that.

Veo's eyes shifted to the left where he heard another family laughing and enjoying the hypnotic piano notes playing to elevate the restaurant's ambiance.

"Try to be grateful, Roman. This is an opportunity most alphas kill for. This behavior is nothing more than a petty protest." His teeth gritted against the glass he angled toward his face, forgetting the glass was empty only seconds ago.

"Adrian..." his mate, Dr. Jacob (Jake) Erricson, replied in a familiar tone.

"Jake, I'm looking for support here. The Whitmores will be here any second, and there is no need to start this engagement on the wrong foot. After all, this was your idea."

"I agree..." Jake attempted.

"Then just support me on this one." Adrian's eyes caught the attention of the waiter finishing up an order at a nearby table. Catching the waiter's eye, he gestured to his empty glass. Too much was at stake to lose his cool.

Jake's sympathy drifted toward his son in a way which silently agreed with his mate's observations. Roman typically deferred to his right-minded Alpha father, or Sur as they are known. It was easier to connect and communicate to his Sur, for Roman himself was also an Alpha, a rare one at that.

Roman was a Type 6 Alpha, the rarest of all humans on the planet. It put him on the highest peak of Mount Olympus, so to speak, and yet, even Zeus himself would be jealous of the status Type 6 wolf-descents possessed on Earth. This formal introduction to his soon-to-be contracted and contrived Omega mate was nothing more than a demonstration of Roman's status in public, showing him off like a shiny, one-of-a-kind car. A few patrons already recognized him and his family. The occasional looks and whispers reached their table when conversations among the family ceased.

"They should be here," Adrian said, breaking the silence at the table as the waiter soothed his ears with the sound of the wine refilling his glass.

Jake's head swayed to his left as he zeroed in on the guests-to-be entering the door. "I do believe that's them," he replied, slowly standing as he recognized the fellow Alpha elite he'd known for over ten years.

Matthew Whitmore's eyes beamed like the proud celebrity he was, hearing the gasps of fellow restaurant guests as he passed them. He led his son to the table slightly lit from above as if Wolf-God's light shone upon the Whitmore family.

"Dr. Erricson," Matthew spoke, shaking his hand with enthusiasm.

"Please, call me Jake tonight. I suspect the formalities should calm themselves considering we'll all be family. Might as well start now if you're okay with that. I don't wish to assume."

"Not at all, as long as you're comfortable."

"Good." Jake gestured to his mate who joined him standing at attention with his usual bright, welcoming aura.

"Matthew, it's wonderful to see you again," Adrian's attention turned. "Terrence, it's been too long."

Terrence was Matthew Whitmore's Omega mate. His permanent judgmental expression was juxtaposed to his bright smile. Typically, Terrence's dark facial features were hard to read against his bright white skin and glistening green eyes. But the Erricson family had mingled long enough with the Whitmores to correctly distinguish his mysterious emotions. Tonight, Terrence had every reason to celebrate with a delightful disposition.

"Adrian, always a pleasure." Terrence turned slightly to locate his son behind him.

With hand outstretched, Matthew gazed at his own son, his diamond in the rough. "And you remember our son, Peyton."

Peyton's cautious gaze made eye contact with Dr. Erricson, now presented as Jake with permission, and he offered a mild handshake.

He repeated the same formal process with his Omega, Adrian, then quickly glanced at Roman, his Alpha-to-be, before scanning the room, exhibiting his shy and submissive personality.

"Of course!" Jake replied. "Peyton, you've grown into quite the handsome young man. And I hope you remember our son Roman."

Jake and Adrian stared at their son now standing beside them, ready to observe the opening act, hoping Roman would at least play the part if he couldn't find it in his heart to genuinely build the crucial connection needed for the next chapter in his life.

It was Peyton who started the conversation. "Nice to see you again."

Peyton took the moment to study Roman. His eyes were beautiful—not to be outdone by any other physical feature he possessed. Roman's shoulders were strong and held up a nice, white, buttoned-down shirt tightly fitted with tan pants against his well-formed body. Finally, Peyton looked to the beautiful curvature of Roman's lips for a subtle reaction.

It was apparent both boys were holding their cards close to their chest. Unfortunately, Roman's scent said it all. Although he smelled beautiful like rain in a lush garden, a natural scent Peyton could see himself getting used to, Roman's scent was muddled by anxiety and, if Peyton was not mistaken, a hint of frustration. Peyton's head fogged with a mixture of nerves and excitement in this novel arrangement. His disappointment settled in once he noticed the Alpha—no, his Alpha—wasn't reciprocating the same pheromones.

After what felt like minutes, Roman finally brought his hand out to show good faith in his attempts to be enthusiastic. The handshake was gentle and warm by comparison to any formal, business handshake. After all, this wasn't supposed to look like a business transaction; this was a contract for love. Or at least, a consolation prize of what was assumed to be love.

"Wow," Roman replied. "I can't believe how much you've changed in what...two years?"

"Not quite that long. It was the opening of the new science lab for your Sur, I think," Peyton replied with a slight smile while taking his seat directly across from Roman.

"A worthy investment, indeed," Matthew interjected. He informally toasted the moment with his sweaty water glass while wearing the killer smile he used to seal any business deal. No doubt he planned to exercise it tonight.

Jake smiled and bowed his head slightly in gratitude for Matthew's compliment. "Thank you. But of course, we all know the state-of-the-art laboratory and all its success rests on your funding. It's Wolf-God's blessing for any scientist and doctor to know they can do research to better the human race with such generous benefactors and allies like yourself." Jake returned the toast back to him with his wine glass.

The blatant compliment was no surprise. Everyone at the table acknowledged this truth at once with silent approval. The entire Whitmore family was loaded with money and confidence which went back generations. Their business was heavy machinery, mainly for drilling and excavation. Every time a new search for a natural resource went underway, odds were the Whitmores were bound to come into a lot of cash, nothing less than seven digits.

Parental focus volleyed back and forth like an audience watching a tennis match between their two sons, all the while holding their breaths. Both Roman and Peyton knew immediately what their parents were doing. They all hoped against all odds their sons were fated to each other. The scent of the primal pull was said to unite the natural bond mates together for the rest of their lives in a way which could never be duplicated with anyone else. It was quite the gamble for Fated Mates to meet in a public restaurant without having the initial imprint done prior. A lot of pressure would have been put on Roman to control himself, to avoid sexually courting Peyton in the restaurant while his primordial desires pushed all decorum out the window.

With enough time to confirm everyone's disappointment that they were not a Fated pair, the night resumed. Soon, the Whitmores were served their drinks, dinner orders were taken, and both sets of parents engaged in separate conversations, forgetting both of their sons in the process.

Now was the perfect time for Roman to really evaluate his betrothed. Immediately, Roman considered Peyton's young age, not to mention his even younger-appearing complexion. It wasn't a conversation he was ever willing to entertain with his parents, but he always knew he'd chase a younger Omega over an older one. A strikingly younger Omega satisfied his tastes, and surprisingly, Peyton sated him in way he didn't feel possible. Peyton was indeed a beautiful young man; a Type 5 Omega didn't come with anything less than stunning beauty. His rare dark auburn hair was layered and short, and his eyes were a rich gray with scattered silver specks. Although he was an Omega, Peyton had inherited his Sur's soft, medium color complexion.

His appearance showed almost identical features to his Sur Matthew, indicating where his looks were headed in the next twenty years. It was a welcome thought when Roman realized he would be satisfied if Peyton were to appear like his father later in life. Not that Roman would be so shallow to base his happiness on outward attractiveness alone, but the uncomfortable position he was currently in tonight made it easy for his mind to wander to such things.

However, Roman also noticed clear differences. Peyton had never grown to be as tall as Matthew nor even Terrence. He was average compared to his Sur's statuesque height which commanded a presence. Terrance's height was shorter but not by much. As a matter of fact, height wise, Peyton stuck out at the table. Roman and his Sur were Matthew's height; however, his Veo was the tallest tower out of all of them.

But to Roman, height was trivial compared to Peyton's overall presence. His scent was pleasant: a full-bodied vanilla with a hint of citrus, but Peyton's nerves were getting the better of him, and his scent tasted like anxiety laced with excitement, and dare he reveal, lust. Roman couldn't help but wonder if Peyton's internal glands were pulsing slick at this new revelation. If they were, he couldn't smell it, well-masked by other less enticing scents.

The 24-year-old watched as Peyton studied all the items on the table with his shoulders down and posture slightly hunched. His overall demeanor demonstrated submission. If he was a wolf, he'd be on his back whimpering with a tucked tail. Roman envisioned him in school reading a book in a corner while all the other boys socialized and roughhoused. Some Low-Type Alphas found this attractive and exploited the submission to every corner of the relationship: conversations, decisions, money, and sex. These Alphas displayed their dominance early in courting to show confidence, strength, and protection skills. It was needed in order to get approval from the Omega's parents; it was also a precursor to how the relationship would continue to play out behind closed doors. But High-Type individuals, which they both were, abandoned this primitive and fundamentalist practice years ago. To be Type 3 or higher in the modern world was to assume families were more interested in equality, support, and status versus brute force and survival skills.

"Forgive me, Peyton. I have to admit I don't know a lot about you," Roman finally said.

"It's not a blaming kind of situation," Peyton replied calmly.

"Right. So," Roman briefly searched for the standard courting questions, "what things do you like to do? What interests you?"

Everyone else at the table casually eyed the two, trying not to be noticed, continuing their own conversations.

"Reading comes to mind first of all."

"What kind of books?"

"I'm not into novels, really. I've been reading a lot of computer science manuals and gaming textbooks."

Roman hesitated. "That's cool. What games do you play then?" Roman had potentially found a topic to be equally passionate about. Although not a couch potato by any means, he did enjoy getting lost into gaming sessions with his brothers and friends on the sport offseason.

"Oh, I don't play games. Sorry, I could have been more specific. I'm working on building my own game."

Shocked and intrigued at the same time, Roman replied, "That's...amazing! Wow. An action game, RPG, what?"

"No, nothing like that. Online enhancements for educational support. In essence, I'd offer mega-corps curriculum licenses for gaming apps to increase basic academic skills for a population struggling with traditional instruction."

Roman's shoulders relaxed and his excitement bottomed out. He was genuinely supportive and impressed by his ambitions. Unfortunately, Roman's stereotypes for Peyton were being validated right before his very eyes. "Neat." It was the only response he came up with at the time which expressed disappointment. How was he going to relate to that? Peyton didn't comment on the crestfallen interest. "Are you interested in any outdoor activities? Sports, hiking, the beach, hanging with friends?" Roman knew at this point it was well-mannered and expected of him to keep the conversation going so Peyton could avoid any impending embarrassment.

Peyton thought for a second before responding. The next round of questioning wasn't going to prove to be any more fruitful. "I guess I spend a little time outdoors; I'm not a shut-in. But I don't get involved in any specific physical activity. I don't typically hang out..."

"Peyton," his Sur cleared this throat, "why don't you tell Roman about your studies?"

Peyton's eyes moved to his Veo who gently rested his chin on his hand while cupping his cheek. A hint of encouragement broke on his face, urging Peyton to show his worthiness of this great opportunity.

Peyton exhaled slightly. "I'm Level 3 in my studies and hoping to finish early this year."

"Impressive! Especially at the young age of 20!" Jake exclaimed, nodding to his son Roman, trying to visually remind him that Peyton was talking to him and not his father.

A blink and a forced smile later, Roman replied, "What is your specialty?"

"Business Analytics and Entrepreneurship." Peyton's entire persona lit up and he bounced lightly at his accomplishment. It was one of the few areas of his life he boasted about and rightfully so.

Roman, although academically gifted, did not choose to fast track his education like Peyton. At 24, Roman was adequately finished with his peers in post-adolescent doctoral studies for his career in patient care. With Peyton anticipating his finish on Level 3, and early to boot, he was approximately two years ahead of traditional schooling.

Roman couldn't help but wonder if Matthew and Terrence considered the inevitable exposure to the explicit content of their obligated reproduction rituals when they chose to accelerate their Omega son's adolescent learning. Then again, Roman remembered when he was 20, he showed his younger 14-year-old twin brothers everything from his assigned reproduction curriculum. But Roman knew Peyton didn't have siblings, and he didn't appear to be the type who had friends who could desensitize him to the details of pheromone-induced arousal, Omega heats, knotting and insemination, and the gory details of birth.

"You have quite the ambition," Roman replied. Both Omega parents nodded and glanced at one another, pleased with both their sons' attempt. "I'm finishing up my studies to be a doctor, myself."

"Just like your Alpha father," Matthew connected.

Roman's hand picked up his luminescent tumbler filled with his own poison, whiskey on ice, and waved his wrist to swirl the ice cubes. "No. My dad's a scientist," Roman politely corrected. He lifted his glass to get the watered down 80-proof into his mouth to avoid revealing his annoyed expression.

Roman's Sur interrupted, "I am a doctor." He grinned, knowing exactly where this conversation was going.

"No. A doctor is someone who sees and treats patients in the here and now. A scientist is someone who observes variables to see if treatments can be approved for doctors to use."

"I see patients. I treat them." Jake beamed, loving every moment of playfully getting under his son's skin. Jake tilted forward to see his Omega mate's expression.

Adrian stared back, shaking his head while smiling. "They do this all the time." Adrian leaned toward Terrence, giving him the "I don't know what to do with them" face.

Terrence winked and nodded back, amused at watching an Alpha son and father playfully quarrel with each other, an experience never afforded to him since becoming a parent of such a demure Omega child.

Just then, as if listening for a cue, three staff members approached the table to deliver the entrées and refill drinks. Delightful cuisine smells engulfed the room; the sounds of silverware, glasses, and cloth napkins replaced chatter for a few moments. There was something about the meal that released everyone from the dense anxiety surrounding the table. Natural interests and conversations became regular soon after.

Peyton's eyes continued to stay bright, especially when he kept Roman in a steady volley of conversation. When he smiled, Roman couldn't help but smile back.

Adrian and Terrence noticed the boys' successful discussions first. Looking at each other, they were almost telepathically communicating, as most Omegas do, that the need for chit-chat was over. When the dessert menu was passed around, Adrian took it upon himself to begin what inevitably brought them here in the first place.

"So," Adrian lifted his fourth half-emptied glass of wine to his lips, sipped, and continued, "I will be the first one to say here tonight that this is a great opportunity for both Roman and Peyton to begin a beautiful life together while also merging two exquisite bloodlines, or at least, that's what my mate tells me." Others joined in Adrian's laughter.

Terrence smiled. "We have no problem with the blood test proving Peyton's Type and lineage, of course."

"The same." Adrian gestured with his raised glass.

Matthew's scent became stronger, an Alpha signal indicating he was ready to show off his "pack" or family to the Erricsons. There was no question, even with the Whitmores' unlimited finances and social status, who really had the upper hand. Even with the progression of Omega equality and security with being a Type 5 Omega, nothing beat out an Alpha Type 6, and everyone at the table knew it. Unfortunately for Matthew, the Type 6 Alpha wasn't him.

"The fact is," Matthew began, "my mate and I couldn't think of a better contractual pair for the next century. These boys together could easily usher in an outstanding Type 5 generation, and perhaps maybe even another Type 6 Alpha. Both boys come from outstanding, consistent Type 5 bloodlines, are intelligent, determined, financially solvent, attractive, have a great network of support from well-respected members of the metro area, and have their priorities in order."

Everyone beamed at the table for his short speech like it was a symphony of success—everyone except Roman.

"You mean like the priority of finding a mate before it's socially looked down upon?" Roman cleared his throat after the terse comment. The alcohol he kept luring down his throat gave him courage.

Everyone else's joy dimmed as it Roman stole Matthew's thunder. If this wasn't a public courtship to his son, Matthew would have come down on him and criticized Jake for not teaching his son how to respect a seasoned Alpha, especially a rich, powerful one such as himself.

Adrian huffed. "Here we go..." He sat back in his chair and smoothly pressed his fist up against his lower face, his thumb to his lips like he was getting ready to bite his fingernail. His mind flashed back to the car ride here in which an argument on precisely this topic had caused the attitude spillover when they first entered the restaurant.

In the end, it was Peyton who paid the ultimate price for the comment. He understood. All understood. This whole arrangement had been done because one of the rarest Alphas in the world couldn't find his Fated Mate—and that rare Alpha was Roman. In a typical Low-Type, an Alpha aged 24 without a mate wasn't cause for social alarm. But Roman wasn't typical, and he certainly wasn't a Low-Type. For the sake of his family, status, and vitality of his potential offspring, Roman needed to let go of the fantasy afforded to every other Alpha of finding their Fated Omega in exchange for an acceptable contractual obligation orchestrated by their parents. Peyton was that Omega; Peyton was that contract. In addition to Peyton giving up his own dreams of finding his Fated Alpha, his anticipated Alpha had let it slip that he was not interested in this contract.

Terrence looked at his obviously slighted son and fought the urge to rub his back like he was a pup and not a fully grown adult.

Matthew decided it was time to once again swoop in and be a superhero. "You know, Roman, we all get it. Every father knows their child is the most precious and highest priority in the world. I know it won't matter saying that to you right now, but the moment you become a father, you'll know."

All expressions flickered with hope—all except Roman.

Jake chimed in, "He's right, son. Being a parent is the most amazing experience you'll ever have. It trumps everything: your money, your career, and even your status."

"Now, that's not to say your status doesn't matter," Matthew cut in. "I mean, we all know there's a lot of pressure being a Type 6 Alpha; I can't even imagine. No one here can." Terrence and Adrian nodded to affirm his claim. "Everyone here at this table has hopes and dreams their Fated Mate will present themselves, and I'm telling you right now, it's a beautiful thing when it happens—damn near stops the heart some say."

Roman squinted. "With all due respect, sir, is this supposed to help?"

"What I'm trying to say son is life waits for no man. Several Alphas give up the chance to long term bond with any mate in the hopes they find the right one."

"Almost 30%," Jake added.

Matthew continued, "As parents, we love you to death. But a determined Alpha like you needs to recognize procreation is just as important as all the other accomplishments you spend your life working toward. Now, I'm sure with your dad's specialization in science, I don't need to school you on the safety risks of having a pup the older you get. We wouldn't want Peyton in his late 20's or 30's trying to birth a baby. The success drops considerably. And I know Peyton is enthusiastic about this. He's a realist, always has been, maybe even too much. Procreating with you means he wants to produce offspring he can be proud of in the best way. Being bonded with a close family means everything. Now, I apologize; we didn't do enough to court the both of you together over the years. So, if it's the process alone you are angry at, that's understandable. But hindsight is 20/20. For Peyton to do this now means he wants to care about you genuinely and not take advantage of you like some complete stranger would. If that's not the beginning of true love, I don't know what is."

Roman at this point couldn't stand to look at Matthew any-more. *Love?* The contract hadn't even been signed with the lawyers, and yet Matthew was already a year down the road assuming their consummation and pregnancy would automatically equal intrinsic love? After a long uncomfortable silence, Roman knew he had to break it with a cold hard truth. "Intrinsic love doesn't happen with contractually bonded mates. The science supports that. This completely robs both Peyton and me of the chance everyone else sitting here experienced."

"Actually..." Matthew attempted.

Terrance gasped. "Matthew, don't—"

"It's okay, babe. I got this." Matthew paused. "Terrence and I aren't Fate Mates," he confessed.

Terrence shifted in his chair, hoping others in the restaurant couldn't hear the confession. Even though he assured himself no such leak had occurred, he closed his eyes and bowed his head in shame.

Peyton sprang to life in a way he hadn't yet done tonight. He looked shocked and betrayed all at once in the moment. "No. That's not true. You've told me all my life..."

"We know," Matthew cut in. "I'm sorry. Lying to you is not something I'm proud of—we're not proud of. But I love your Veo more than I could ever love someone else. Please let that be a testament to what it means to be truly bonded." Matthew directly looked at Roman. "It. Does. Happen. And it's not something science is going to show you. It's faith."

Peyton laid both arms on the table to steady himself from the warped reality his parents disclosed for the first time in his life. It was counter intuitive, but Peyton stared at Roman to signal the need for Roman to comfort him, the only person he wanted to trust at the table.

Matthew continued, "I see it in my son's eyes, and I know his true scent. This is not a ruse; this is not a trick. He's on board because he wants this for every right reason there is. Somewhere, we got our wires crossed. Our family clearly misconstrued expected nerves for passionate enthusiasm. We see it now. But the question still remains: are you onboard for a mate who truly wants this and has a family who is thrilled in caring for you both? Or are you needing a different path, and if I can be frank, a potentially discouraging path at this point in your life? We're not a Low-Type family; we're not going to force you into a contract you don't want. The choice is yours."

Damn, Matthew is good. Really good, Roman thought.

All eyes were on Roman now. He took his rightful time to reflect on the evening. Inside his mind, he already admitted Peyton was undeniably beautiful and fell under his idealistic age. And Matthew presented quite the valid points. Did he wrongfully assume Peyton's initial insecurities were permanent? Why was it so hard to believe his entire persona couldn't change once he was comfortable with him? His personality was gentle, not necessarily a trait he'd want in a friend, but for sure a trait he'd desire in a bond mate. The hardest part to ignore was the truth: Roman was upset. This arrangement fell into his lap quickly considering everything. In addition, there was going to be some difficulty in finding commonalities. Was that clouding his judgement in accepting an otherwise amazing offer? Perhaps. With one final look into Peyton's warm, glistening eyes, Roman spoke the words he swore he'd never utter tonight, "I want to try this. I really do."

The crushing weight of emotion lifted so fast it gave a strong sense of being light-headed and damn near knocked everyone out of their chairs.

Roman's Veo quickly grabbed his hand and squeezed while his eyes were on the verge of pulsing tears of joy. Peyton's Veo couldn't hold back the urge anymore, and he reached out to warm his son's back and glided his hand back and forth to affirm the beautiful decision. Both Surs just stared at one another, barely believing the words Roman spoke. Together, the Alphas exhaled with pride and pined for celebratory cigars.

Finally, there was Peyton with a quickened breathing pattern and smile which went on for days, curing depression of any soul.

Roman zeroed in on him with a satisfied expression and took in Peyton's strong and true scent—the vanilla and citrus intoxicating. He reached across the rectangular table and gently laid his hand on top of Peyton's. At that moment, Roman experienced the pleasure of a deep inhale of the scent of Peyton's slick moistening and collecting outside his body originating from his presumably virgin insides. Roman's narrowed glance confirmed to Peyton he scented his slick.

Peyton blushed rose red.

Roman smirked and nodded his head, giving Peyton his silent approval and rapt interest.

CHAPTER 02:

A Tale of Three Brothers

After a long silence in the car, Roman's Veo spoke only one sentence to his son in the lonely backseat. "I'm proud of you."

His Sur glanced at Roman in the rearview mirror for a reaction or response but was offered none. They had decided not to discuss the rollercoaster of events back in the restaurant.

The rush of the evening faded. Speckled reflections of street-lights revealed moisture on the car from fog and gentle rain. The glimmer struck every drop on the back passenger window. Roman wished he could have seen the ocean water beneath the bridge, but the moon refused to show its bright face tonight. Maybe it was a good thing; otherwise, he'd find himself losing control and howling continuously as his body morphed into his ancestral wolf form.

A ridiculous claim.

Motion feature films depicted convincing cinematic interpretations of wolf-descendants born with the ability to shift into an animal. It was similar to the creation of vampires—nothing but farce.

He mindlessly watched each streetlight pass as they neared the hills where the elite cowered in safety from the underprivileged Low-Types of the inner city. The separation was political more than anything else. Tonight, Roman didn't feel like evaluating politics, socioeconomic status, educational privilege, or Blood-Types.

Reaching the uphill driveway was relief. The security of knowing he was home in his familiar estate house meant he could hide away in the comfort of his room and not think about contracts. Then again, there was no way his brothers were going to let him off the hook without getting the full rundown of the evening's events.

Opening the door before his parents helped Roman begin to relax. The high-vaulted ceilings and bright yellow light from chandeliers and recessed bulbs warmed him. His steps were quiet on the dark gray floors that complimented the much lighter walls. However, the moment was short lived when he saw his brothers in the kitchen, both giving him "You're going to tell us everything" grins. At times like this, it would be difficult to deal with even one brother, but twin brothers giving him the same look was downright overbearing.

His brother Rixen hunched over the kitchen island with his short blond hair just above his ears and natural highlights emphasized by the lights shining down on him, making him appear like an angel. His smooth and vulnerable face was accented by ice blue eyes and full lips. The way he leaned on the counter lifted his thin white t-shirt, exposing the weakly tanned skin on his back above his khaki shorts. Rixen looked as if he could walk right into a surfer clothing store and be mistaken for a model or showy store clerk. The magazine on the counter before him appeared disheveled; Roman could tell he flipped through it only to pass the time.

Ryan, his other brother and Rixen's twin, stood on the other side of the beautifully designed kitchen island, one leg crossed over the other while he leaned his weight on the back of a bar stool. His white shirt was identical to his twin, but he complimented it with black athletic pants and white socks on his feet. Even though Ryan possessed the same smooth face and features as his twin, he was a tad more rugged and serious looking. This subtle difference made it easier to distinguish the two from each other. Ryan's body also had a stronger muscular build due to his higher dedication to working out, a hobby Rixen endured only because Ryan pressured him into joining. Both boys held their gaze on Roman, waiting for him to begin the conversation. When that didn't happen, Ryan decided to break the ice first.

"So?" His word drawn out.

Roman glanced at him, then to Rixen who copied his twin's expression. "What?" Roman couldn't come up with anything better. He heeled off his shoes, kicked them to the side where hard flooring met the carpet, and made his way to the den only steps away from where his brothers stood.

Ryan quickly joined and sat in the soft chair across from him while Rixen followed shortly thereafter, planting himself on plush couch next to Roman, feet curved slightly on the cushion which narrowly separated them. "Spill it, bro."

"It was..." Roman paused, angling his eyes toward the ceiling for a moment before resuming his eye contact, "okay."

"Just okay?" Ryan's next words were cut off as the door open and closed again.

Their parents walked through the hallway and into the open space where all three of their children sat. The awkward silence was a clear sign there was no invitation for them to join in. Taking the hint, Jake led his mate up the stairs to their bedroom. Moments later, their double doors closed, signaling to the boys it was safe to resume the conversation.

This time, it was Rixen who chimed in. "What was he like?" he asked in a soft tone, unlike his twin brother.

Roman searched for a compliment first. "He's cute. Quite attractive, actually. Other than him being significantly shorter, I'd say he could be a part of our family tree." Rixen's eyes widened while Ryan's expression was certainly disgust.

"That's a good visual." Ryan's sarcasm showed. "Not! Remember that when you're lying on top, getting ready to impregnate him."

Roman grimaced. "Thanks for that. I'm not saying it like I was hoping to have sex with someone who looked like my brother, you ass. Gross."

Ryan's gaze went to the right and into the dark, quiet fireplace with a blank face.

Rixen rolled his eyes. He was annoyed at this "failure to communicate" act which regularly happened when Ryan tried to orchestrate a conversation. This forced Rixen to step in and stop problems before they started, tonight being no exception. "Now, why am I getting the impression you're not totally into this 'cute' boy?"

Roman found Rixen's accurate intuition annoying at times, and yet, in time of need, it was very comforting. "Other than the obvious frustration I have over a contracted mate to begin with, he's not really my type personality-wise. We have nothing in common other than trying to find a mate. And you know how much enthusiasm I have for finding my Fate instead."

Rixen appreciated the honesty and empathized with every word.

Ryan, on the other hand, found the whole process nothing more than a whiny tantrum. "Just be happy our dads are fussing over you so much, Wolf-God!" Like Roman, Ryan didn't mind letting everyone know his views on the entire situation.

Roman was over Ryan's petty issues, and the feelings were mutual. Roman leaned forward for effect. "I'm not in the mood to argue with you tonight about whether or not Sur and Veo love me more than you, okay?! Right now, with the way things went tonight, I'd gladly switch lives with you in a second."

This was the most frustrating overused line Roman played on Ryan. It was a headache like nails scratching on a chalkboard. "You keep saying it, and yet you have no idea what it's like to be a Beta!" Ryan spoke tersely.

"Look, I'm not ignorant. You don't need to give me the rhetoric," Roman replied.

Betas faced that plight their entire life. Betas just existed—and not much else. They weren't given a Blood-Type like Alphas or Omegas because their reproduction was obsolete. Betas possessed no womb and no active sperm, an anomaly which plagued science since its recognition. No one cracked the code in DNA to successfully remove the sequencing for delivering a Beta child, therefore diminishing the 25% of the world's population who couldn't pass on their genetics. This also limited their selection of mates—not for reproduction—but for companionship. Alphas and Omegas rarely committed to Betas during childbearing years. Doing so would give up their chance to pass on their own genes. This left Betas to choose among themselves and commit to lower-stakes contractual agreements. Betas never found their Fated Mate; it was not genetically programmed into them to find one. To never experience the connection of a Fated Mate made being a Beta difficult to relate to.

"What? No biology lesson? How about culture lesson?" Ryan clapped back.

The other disadvantage was arguably more noticeable on a day-to-day basis. With the diminished ability to reproduce, Betas weren't held in high regard either. If parents had a Beta child and no other, they were typically content to love the child without reservations or conditions. But producing an Omega, or preferably an Alpha, meant that pup was the shining gold star and treated as such. Producing a sterile pup amid those who could reproduce lent itself to clear divisions of attention and care.

"You have my sympathy in some regard, of course. But you don't understand the crazy amount of pressure that's been put on me. I have to be the perfect doctor, the perfect athlete, the perfect student, and the perfect specimen for reproduction. Which by the way, is no longer my obligation since I fucked up in trying to find my Fated Mate. Being an Alpha is all together fucked up, not to mention being Type 6." Roman held the weight of his throbbing head on his fist as he leaned his body on the couch's armrest.

Ryan was having none of it. Roman's spiel only appeared to anger Ryan rather than connect with him. "Oh, you had to bring up that stupid bit about being an Alpha as if anyone feels sorry for you being the elite rank. Fuck you, too."

"It's true!" Roman defended. "Rixen and I are expected to assimilate into these roles while you sit back and get to decide single-handedly what you want to do with your life."

Ryan didn't want to admit to Roman the obvious benefits of being Beta. As long as Roman lived, Ryan had the freedom to live the life he wanted without expectation or responsibility. He'd be free to have any career he wanted and all the respect which came with it, be immune to the natural territorial wars Alphas loved to inflict on one another and on Omegas, and mate with whomever he chose, whenever he chose. Should Roman die before Ryan, he, by law, would inherit all power and control Roman was expected to have after their parents died.

This also included possession over Rixen if he wasn't Fated or contracted. And if Rixen was mated, his Alpha would have control over all his interests. Rixen would be the last to inherent any power even if, hypothetically, Rixen was older than his Beta brother. That was the burden all Omegas had to bear. But no one ever entertained the discussion of the expected future Omegas faced; it was just assumed, one of the few fundamental practices which stuck over the centuries.

The room fell silent for a moment with Rixen caught between his two stubborn siblings. Both were at an impasse. But with Roman being a true Alpha, the conversation wasn't going to end with Ryan having the last word, whether he was right or not.

Rixen finally piped in, "Did you make a mistake agreeing to this contract then with... with...?"

"Peyton," Roman reminded him. "You remember, don't you?"

Rixen squinted. "I think so? He doesn't come off as someone to remember personality-wise."

Ryan shrugged his shoulders in agreement. Peyton wasn't a standout.

"Tell me about it," Roman huffed. "I don't know if it was a mistake. He's all-in on this, and thank Wolf-God he is because I don't know if I can handle both of us having second thoughts."

Ryan decided he was going to attempt round three in the conversation. "Knowing you, and I do know you, I can't imagine you just sitting there nodding your head 'Yes' all the time while everyone else assumed you were okay."

Roman looked at his Beta brother and grunted, "Things definitely started that way, that's for sure. But like you said, I decided I couldn't be silent any longer, and I voiced my lone opinion."

"A trait shared by many Erricsons in this house," Rixen added, smiling.

Ryan looked at Roman, aghast. "Whoa, you got balls, bro! You seriously told the Whitmores you weren't interested right in front of their faces?" This is where Ryan thoroughly enjoyed his older brother—when Roman's attitude wasn't being used against him.

Roman took in the realization of Ryan's claim for himself and confessed with an astonished face. "Yeah. That's exactly what I did."

"And how did Sur not rip your face off?" Ryan was on the edge of his seat now.

"He didn't freak out, yell, beat his chest...nothing. I could sense him empathizing with me, actually." At the end of the statement, the camaraderie between the boys faded again.

"Favorite," Ryan muttered.

"Shut up!" Roman cast back.

Rixen intervened, "What did Veo do?" It was his turn to sit up and breathe in every word.

"That's the interesting part. He was about to blow a gasket. We had words in the car before getting to the restaurant and the fumes lingered throughout the entire night."

All three boys glanced at one another and silently acknowledged and agreed their dads oddly switched roles tonight. Adrian normally fixed all problems while Jake typically ruled the roost with words written in stone. But that wasn't how it went down tonight at dinner.

Ryan relaxed back in his chair again, shaking his head. "I still can't believe Dr. Jacob Erricson let his son question the approval of a contract which was already agreed upon in front of one of the most powerful Alphas in the city."

"Oh yeah, and that's another thing," Roman continued. "Peyton's dad is quite the charmer. He could sell a dominant personality to an Alpha if he wanted to."

"Is he just like when he's on TV supporting political candidates and social causes?" Rixen wondered.

"Yes, but a thousand times more in person. He just stares into your soul and casts a spell on you. He could probably force anyone to do whatever he wants."

Rixen stared at his Alpha brother, inhaling deeply as he prepared for the next question. "Did he force you into agreeing to contract?"

Rixen caught Ryan's eyes, looking for consensus on the thought or at the very least acknowledgement that it was an okay question to ask.

"I'd like to think not." Roman remained optimistic. "Both of Peyton's parents seemed as normal as they could be. I'd find it hard to believe they have any ill-will or ulterior motive to all of this. And like I said, I want this to work."

"You never said that," Ryan corrected.

"Then, I'll say it now: I do want it to work. I just need time to adjust to it and get over the fact that a Fate just isn't in the cards for me."

Rixen shot a look at Ryan with a smile which was all the acknowledgement Ryan needed. "So, what you're really saying is that you want to get shit-face drunk?" Ryan offered.

Roman's reply was instantaneous. "Oh, fuck yes." Roman jumped up off the couch and headed toward the fridge. The light from the open door shone into his soul.

The twins followed, grabbing as many bottles as they could carry and followed Roman to the bedrooms in the basement.

Roman was happy in that moment, knowing he had brothers to support his desires in getting the slight buzz back he had in the restaurant and then some. He was also thankful for the support he needed to get through this stressful life-changing time.

Brothers 'til the end.

<hr>

"Wait, wait, wait...wait." Ryan spoke like a broken record, barely able to balance as he stood on Roman's bed. "You're telling me he actually reads computer manuals for fun?"

Ryan and Rixen laughed loudly without a care while Roman tried to stifle them, controlling the heckling at his future mate's expense.

"Stop," Roman chuckled. "It's not funny." Hearing himself say the statement out loud made him burst out laughing again.

Ryan lost his balance and staggered clumsily on top of Rixen and Roman. Both slowly pushed him back up to a sitting position as they balanced their beer bottles in their hands.

"Dude, you sure know how to pick 'em." Ryan's joy seeped out as he tried to take another swig out of his drink.

"Ugh. Guys, what am I going to do?" Roman rubbed his face, trying to fix the blurry corners of his eyes. Every part of him felt heavy. He felt like his body could soak into the mattress if he let it. Laying on the bed sideways allowed Roman to tap his large feet in a pattern on the soft carpet below. Looking to the left, he saw Rixen's body in almost the complete complimentary way to his: feet and torso on the bed with his head almost hitting the floor. Roman observed him, amazed he was able to keep his four raspberry malts in his stomach in that position.

"You'll figure it out, Roman. You always do." Rixen sighed, trying to tap his brother on the head, completely missing and hitting the side of the bed.

Ryan mumbled words nobody could understand but Roman assumed it was agreeing with Rixen.

After a few pregnant pauses, Roman threw out the next random thing which came into his head. "Guys, I totally scented his slick in the restaurant." In an instant, all started guffawing like lunatics.

Rixen used his arms to try preventing himself from completely falling off the bed while Ryan's body vibrated in his attempts to catch his breath.

"Wolf-God, you are one nasty fucker," Ryan commented. Roman happily nodded in agreement as if he'd won some prize for experiencing a mating encounter neither of his brothers had. "What's it like knowing the Omega's wet over you?"

Roman sighed. "It's weird actually...and kind of hot."

"Awe, dude, don't be getting a boner in bed right now." Ryan grabbed Roman's king-sized pillow and threw it at him. Roman failed in his poor attempt to catch it while still being amused by the conversation.

Rixen slid his whole body back up on the bed and cradled his head in the hook of his arm, face turning somber. "So, what are you two going to do once the contract is signed? Are you going to leave?" Rixen's words burned the humor out of the room.

Once again, Roman found his twin brothers staring at him in an equal fashion, making it difficult for a stranger to decipher who was who. It was a question which always loomed in the background of all households when the firstborn found a mate. Making the decision to leave the den was logical and even natural. But giving up the comfort of the family he'd known for 24 years? That was the difficult part.

"Sur and Veo briefly discussed offering up an apartment in downtown overlooking the ocean. It wasn't discussed much after that. It's not entirely my decision, anyway. The Whitmores get a lot more say in this process now than they would have ten years ago. At least, that's what Veo said."

Rixen was the first to say it. "It's going to be weird without you here."

Ever so slightly, Roman could see Ryan's head drift up and down in response to Rixen's comment. But that's all he'd get from Ryan. "Look, I'm 24 years old. If I could have found my mate when I was 18, I'd have been gone while you two were still adolescents. And if we were a Low-Type family, odds are Sur and Veo would have kicked me out anyway and said, 'Sink or swim.'"

Ryan uttered, "Yeah, but you're not just the oldest—you're the Alpha. The household's going to be unbalanced without you. Nothing's going to be the same."

"I get that, but it shouldn't have been this way for this long anyhow. It's time to move on." Ryan gave Roman an uneasy look. Roman continued, "Hey, don't worry about me. Just wait until Rixen finds his mate in a year and leaves you here. Science says twins share a special bond. Here's hoping you don't spaz out when it happens."

Ryan's attitude shifted to macho. "I'm not worried about it; doesn't bother me."

Rixen's head tilted up toward his twin brother. Ryan glanced quickly at him, trying to ignore what was taken as a punch in the gut.

Rixen pressed, "But it's not like you're going to move out the day the contract is signed."

"No," Roman replied. "Typically, there's a grace period before the Omega's first heat after contract. The problem is knowing when that's going to happen. It could be next month; it could be three months from now. I don't know."

"But he should know," Rixen continued. "It's typically four or five months after his last one, assuming he's had his first one already."

"Wolf-God, he's 20. There's no way he hasn't had his first heat yet or a few heats for that matter."

"Then he didn't tell you?"

Roman exhaled. "It wasn't exactly the conversation starter at dinner tonight—let's just say that."

"Well, he should know. That's all." Rixen examined his nails while staring up at the ceiling.

Ryan interjected, "It's not like you know. You haven't had your first heat yet."

Rixen furrowed his eyebrows and his voice went monotone, "No, Dr. Erricson. I haven't." He sat fully upright and breathed life back into his words. "But I'm a ticking time-bomb at this point. Pretty soon, Sur is going to throw me in my room and bolt the door, so I don't get an emotional heat before my real one."

"And just who are you thinking about getting an emotional heat over?" Ryan asked.

Rixen's eyes shifted. "I don't have anyone in mind. I'm just saying."

Ryan wanted to press the issue but decided to let it be. Instead, he kept his attention on Roman who looked like his mind was going a hundred miles per hour. "Peyton's going to have quite the wake-up call when he's in heat for three days dealing with you as his Alpha. Try not to break him in half. The little virgin won't know what hit him."

"How do you know he's still a virgin?" Roman interrogated.

"Oh, come on, Roman! You know he is." Ryan snickered, getting another head shake from Rixen.

"Yeah, well, he's in good company then," Roman squeaked. His eyes studied the black and blue design on his comforter, refusing to look at either of his brothers who he could tell just radiated the "Deer in the headlights" look.

"No way!" Ryan exclaimed.

"Seriously?" Rixen added.

Roman finally looked up with a gaze innocent like a pup. "What? Is that so hard to believe?"

Ryan spoke diligently, "You mean to tell me, Roman Erricson, my 24-year-old Alpha Type-6 brother has never had sex?"

"Come on, Roman, even I find that hard to believe." Rixen began showing his true twin colors again.

"I'm not saying I haven't done anything. I'm just saying I've never...penetrated a guy before." This time Roman felt almost ashamed to speak. He couldn't count the number of times his Alpha friends talked about all the experiences and encounters they had with hot Omegas practically begging for them for a fuck. It wasn't that Roman wasn't interested; of course, he was. But whenever he thought about acting on it, Roman found himself stopping every time.

"But you've had a guy suck you off, right?" Ryan eloquently spouted.

"Yeah, that and more hand jobs than I can count. Even dick on dick stuff. But I've never 'Done the deed with my seed.'"

"Wow. I have to say: I misjudged you." Ryan smirked as if he was sitting on a throne equal to his Alpha brother who was six years older than him.

"What? Like you have?" Roman inquired.

"...Maybe."

Rixen glared. "Who the hell have you boned?"

"Who knows? Maybe they boned me?" Ryan teased with glee.

"He's full of shit, Rixen." Roman waved him off.

"My lips are sealed." Ryan made a lock gesture at his closed lips and pretended to throw away an imaginary key. "Now the only question left is who has Rixen let tear him open?"

"Ugh," Roman rolled his eyes.

"There has been no one, dick wad," Rixen defended.

Ryan grinned. "I bet I know who."

"Who? Tell me!" Roman belted.

Rixen shook his head with confidence. "No one. There's been no one."

"Kendal Jordan," Ryan shot back.

"Oh, what do you know? Did Kendal tell you?" As soon as Rixen said the words, he realized he walked right into a trap. Rixen watched both of his brothers simultaneously fall off Roman's bed from laughing so hard. Both of their faces were red from the lack of oxygen and yet nowhere near the deep crimson splashed across his own face. Ryan was the first to regain his composure.

"You slept with that Low-Type? Okay, okay. Now I need details," Ryan breathed while still grinning from ear to ear.

"No, I don't want to hear this," Roman indicated, shaking his head.

"You will hear no details of me sleeping with that 'Low-Type' as you put it," Rixen replied, trying to stay straight-faced.

"Kendal was a Low-Type sleaze who was looking to piss on every tire in the parking lot so he could call it his and you know it."

"You really don't have any tact in trying to get someone on your side, do you?" Rixen made the question rhetorical. "And no, I'm not telling you."

"Oh, come on!" Ryan pleaded.

Roman interjected, "I want to know how you and Kendal accomplished that without Ryan or me knowing."

"Yeah!" Ryan piggy-backed as he took a swig.

"Wait," Roman offered, "did this happen during the resort trip all our families went on down in Gemini?" Rixen didn't speak, which was the most obvious response he could have given. "Oh, Wolf-God, how? When? You were like 10 years old!"

"It was two years ago, and I was 16. Quit being dumb."

"Um, question still remains," Ryan said, finishing the last drink in his bottle.

"When Kendal and I wanted some alone time, we just came up with an excuse to not go out and do things with the rest of you like the hiking trips or a couple visits to the lake. I just came down with a lot of 'stomach aches' and 'cramps' on that trip." Rixen laid out the explanation smoothly like he was the clever wolf in sheep's clothing.

"Right, I remember those." Ryan blinked. "Guess we didn't know it was from all the cum he was pumping into ya."

Roman shut his eyes and groaned while Ryan was laughing too hard to see a pillow thrust against his skull.

"I can't believe this. I'm never going to be able to remember that trip the same way ever again." Roman rubbed his face, his eyes getting heavy with exhaustion.

"Hey, it's not like you were the one sleeping with him," Rixen pointed out.

"Ouch, that bad?" Ryan winced. "I should have guessed. Idiot didn't even know what he was doing. I think you could have done a lot better than him, bro." He quivered at the thought.

"He got better," Rixen paused, "after the third time." He stuck his tongue out and bit it. Now he was just showing off.

Roman gestured with arms stretched to the ceiling. "How are you not pregnant from this guy yet?"

"Duh! We just talked about this; I haven't had a heat yet," Rixen explained.

"Plus," Ryan added, "it helps that his family moved right after the trip."

"It wasn't right after the trip. It was a few months later," Rixen corrected.

Ryan grunted. "You would know."

"Speaking of pregnancy," Rixen pivoted, "that's what everyone's going to hope for right after Peyton's first heat after the contract."

"Yep" was all that came out of Roman's mouth as he slowly slid down the side of the bed, now using it as a backrest. His eyes zoned out to the corner where the floor met the wall, refusing to blink.

"Are you really wanting to have kids with this guy?" Rixen asked.

"I think," Roman paused for what seemed like ages, "I really want to go to bed."

The room fell to a silence it hadn't all night. In the stillness, there was a slight shudder of a breeze with a mix of wildlife fading in from the window. No one said anything for almost a minute. Finally, Roman broke his eternal stare to glance back at his brothers. Both were still sitting on his bed, mystically matching each other's expression of intrigue and concern. Unwilling to entertain the conversation further, Roman gave the look which said "I'm done"; his brothers knew it well. They slowly lifted their bodies off of his bed and tried gingerly not to knock over any bottles on the nightstand or floor, even though most of them were empty.

Roman sat on the floor, gently hitting his head against the mattress of his bed in a slow rhythm. That morning, Roman had been a young man determined to walk into a "business" dinner and politely diminish anyone's suggestion that he and Peyton should be contracted mates. A few hours later, he had turned into a newborn pup eating out of everyone's hands, willingly even. The act sealed the contract before anyone signed it. And now, in the few hours before dawn, Roman wasn't ready to come to terms with having a child, any child, with someone other than who was his Fated Mate. Even if that meant waiting another five years to find him.

He is out there. Isn't he?

CHAPTER 03:

A Heartbreak & Admission

"Why didn't you tell me?" Peyton's voice was barely above a whisper. At first, he wasn't even sure if it was his voice that spoke or if it was just in his head. But he caught a glimpse of his Veo looking at him and then over at his Sur, so he knew it had been out loud. Right now, he struggled with what hurt more: having to ask the question or having to listen to the answer.

On the opposite side of the city, in another posh and upward community, the Whitmore Manor suffered from the same silence as the Erricsons. But being a Whitmore differed from being an Erricson. The unnerving silence in the car ride home was followed by an even harsher silence at the grand hall dining room table. Although the room was filled with brilliant light, everything else was void of life. All the dishes and silverware were put away. The candelabra was bare. No noises nor smells emanated from the kitchen off to the side.

Matthew spoke first in a calm, unwavering voice, "We didn't want to disappoint you." Unfortunately, his son's face showed that wasn't a good enough answer. Matthew rubbed his thumb against the stubble on his cheek, the motion making an audible noise as he contemplated his next words. But he couldn't come up with any other explanation, so he felt there was no other choice but to say it again firmly, "We didn't want to disappoint you."

At one end of the large rectangular table, three out of the eight chairs were occupied by the Whitmore family. Matthew, the Alpha of the house, sat at the head of the table. His dinner jacket hung on the back of the grandiose chair, revealing his blue gray dress shirt. His collar and cuffs were unbuttoned, the fabric pushed halfway up his arms to his elbows which rested on the strong wooden table in front of him. His hands were lightly clasped together as he held his chin with his thumbs. His face was blank and unreadable, an expression rarely seen by anyone in public.

"Peyton," Terrence spoke softly, his hand facing palm down as if to reach out with an olive branch to his son, "we know how this looks right now, and we are truly sorry. But this doesn't change how much we love you, and it definitely does not change anything that has happened tonight."

Unlike his typically perfect and stoic public appearance, Terrence's expression was emotional and worn out. His once carefully slicked-back combover was now disheveled and damp. Perspiration marks dotted various areas of his shirt, turning his blood red dress shirt even darker. Terrence found it difficult to look at his son, opting instead to look at his mate, his contracted mate, not Fated Mate.

"Doesn't change anything?" Peyton scoffed. His gaze circled the room, feeling like he was in a stranger's home, suddenly feeling like a hostage in the very place where he grew up. *Who are my parents exactly?* "This changes everything." His mind returned to the moment Roman stood up for himself, claiming he wanted his Fated Mate instead. He remembered his own father there, performing one of the best speeches of life, convincing Roman he was making the right decision all under the pretense of being able to trust his Alpha father. Peyton's eyes welled up with stinging tears. "I feel so stupid."

Peyton sat across from his Veo, and to the right side of his Sur, looking down at the table and occasionally his own hands folded in his lap. He couldn't even remember the car ride home, nor how he got into the dining room. In the hurt and confusion, he almost forgot about the most attractive Alpha he'd ever seen saying he wanted to be Peyton's contracted mate for the rest of his life. But every time he kept hitting that word "Contracted," Peyton's heart sank and his mind raced. Anger boiled from his blood and steamed out of his gritted teeth. It all circled back to this moment. Over and over again, he tried to focus on Roman's beautiful face in the restaurant, just to have it all take backstage to his parents lurching disgustingly forward toward him at home.

"You're not stupid, sweetheart." Terrence touched his hand on the table, trying to connect with Peyton.

"Just leave me alone!" Peyton pushed away from the table with his foot, crossed his arms, and stared at a hallway he really wanted to run down.

"Your Veo's right, son. If this is about Roman, he's fine. He said 'Yes,' and he even said it with a smile. It's going to be okay." Matthew's tactics were a lot less effective on his son than on his constituents, but that never stopped him from trying.

"This isn't about him, okay? This is about me!"

"What is?!" Matthew gestured with both arms in exasperation.

Peyton looked at his Veo. "What do you think of me?" He knew if he was going to get any answers, it was going to start with him.

Terrence's eyes grew wide as his face angled. The question was left field at best. In a conversation involving his parents' mating contract, Terrence couldn't possibly see the connection to his son's demand. As he glanced at Matthew, it was clear neither of them knew where their son was going.

"What do we think of you? We love you! All of this tonight was for you. I don't understand." Terrence's voice grew weary. He held out his other hand for Matthew, who gladly squeezed it for comfort.

Matthew joined in on the sentiment. "Why would you ask what we think—"

"Why am I entering a mating contract at the age of 20?" Peyton watched both of his fathers. Like he anticipated, his Veo couldn't hold an honest face, while his Sur locked eyes with him as if there was nothing wrong. Naturally, it was his Sur who smoothly answered without missing a beat.

"We've talked about this already. We felt it best for your future. That's what we've always said." Matthew's eyes shifted to Terrence, who refused to look up at him.

"That's not entirely true. You've only been talking about this contract for a few months," Peyton corrected.

"Right. But even you have to know that parents think about their sons' futures way before they make decisions. It would be foolish otherwise."

"Exactly my point. How long have you and Veo been 'thinking' about putting me into a contract?"

Matthew's calm expression winced ever so slightly. As a businessman, Matthew was always three steps ahead of any problem. But as a father, Peyton never ceased to demonstrate Matthew was continuously three steps behind. "We started—"

"We've known for a long time, dear," Veo interrupted. His eyes were heavy, but they were honest. This time, Terrence was able to look Peyton in the eye. The more he did, the more Matthew looked away.

"How long?" Peyton asked, starting to get a feel for where this was all headed.

"Ever since you started showing signs of accelerating classes."

"What does that have to do with it? That's a great accomplishment for any person. I was 14. Why would that trigger thinking about a mating contract when I was 14?"

Matthew chimed in, "Being a great intellectual mind doesn't trigger that, Peyton."

"But leaving the social world behind does," Terrence followed.

Peyton's eyes furrowed. "Leaving the social world? I haven't been a shut-in. I still go to classes. I'm not always taking online courses."

"That's because the school doesn't offer every single course online. Otherwise, you know you would."

Veo's expressions were always hard for Peyton to ignore, intense and almost always soaked in depression and dismay. When his Veo was truly embodying those emotions, it was downright scary to watch. Watching his heartbreak broke Peyton's heart. "There is no basis for convicting me as an isolationist," Peyton defended.

"Name one of your classmates, not from your online class," Terrence demanded.

Initially, it seemed like one of the easiest questions to answer. No different than someone asking, "How do you tie a shoe?" or "How do you brush your teeth?" But seconds went by without an answer, and he realized just how hard the curveball was. He couldn't think of even one name of his classmates from his onsite classes.

"Fine," Peyton reluctantly agreed. "I sometimes go a bit overboard with the isolation. But I feel the requirements of life will keep me in check. I'll be regularly forced to work with people for the rest of my life; that's just how it works. It's no big deal!"

"'No big deal?' That's not 'just how it works'!" Matthew felt the rationale for tonight's dinner give him strength for the first time tonight since coming home. "Do you think I have been this successful in my career because I'm just 'forced to work with people'? Your Veo has social anxiety! Do you really think Veo accompanies me at every social function for my job because he loves the fact that I am 'forced to work with people'? Do you honestly think we walked away from that dinner tonight with a contract in our lap because the Erricsons knew we were 'forced to work with people'? For how smart you are, Peyton, sometimes I do wonder what rock you live under."

Peyton shook his head in disbelief. He stood, shoved the chair into the table, and glared at his parents. "You sat at that table tonight, begged me, then watched me spew all of my accolades to Roman and his family tonight. You sat there, proud of me like I could do no wrong. And yet, now you are going to tell me that for one of the biggest decisions in my life, I needed you two to hold my hand?"

"Was it, son?" Matthew countered. This time he stood up and stared down his son, reminding him who was Alpha in the Whitmore house.

"Was it what?"

"Was it really one of the biggest decisions in your life?"

"Of course, it was!"

"Well, we've told you how long it's been on our minds. Why don't you sit down and tell us some truth now? When were you going to make this decision for yourself?"

Peyton retreated from his Alpha father at the scent of his dominating pheromones. His Omega father looked like shattered glass, so to keep the peace, Peyton reluctantly agreed to sit back down. Peyton was forced to think about his father's consternation. He crossed his arms with a dramatic exhale. Of course, Peyton had thought about it all his life. What impressionable pup hasn't? What hormonal adolescent hasn't? What heated or pheromone-induced adult hasn't?

But the deeper Peyton dug beneath the surface of just knowing he wanted it, the more he realized it was the only part of his life he hadn't planned out. Everything else was calculated, prepared, and practiced for. But finding a Fated Mate? There wasn't a class for that; there was no textbook, and there was no research doctor who was going to entertain teaching a submissive anti-social Omega how to court someone. As much as Peyton wanted to be part of that 70% who found a forever mate, he was really scared he fell into that 30% Roman's dad mentioned at dinner—a statistic Peyton never took notice of until now.

"I...I don't know," Peyton confessed.

His parents exhaled, satisfied that perhaps he now knew what this was all for. The discussions over the previous months and the preparation for conversation filled them with hope. It was all to get Peyton to the next chapter in his life, perhaps the most important part of his life, a happy ending just like every other success he had.

Terrence exuded fatherly love and reached out his hand again. Peyton, after a few brief seconds, offered his own and let his father comfort him with his touch. "We know this wasn't the way you wanted to do this. Quite frankly, your Sur and I didn't expect you to go along with it so fast when we first brought it up. We were relieved but also shocked."

"Why did you agree to it so fast?" Matthew inquired, staring at his son with an open heart and bona fide interest.

"Because it's just like you said at the restaurant tonight: I'm a realist," Peyton confessed. "I guess I knew deep inside the whole Fated Mate thing wasn't in the cards for me. Not with how I was structuring my life anyway. I feel bad for Roman spending years trying to find his without any luck. I guess maybe I should be more thankful that I have parents who would do all this work for me to make sure I didn't suffer like that."

Tears never formed in Matthew's eyes like they did for Terrence; however, the emotional gratitude and bear hug was enough for Peyton to know his dad appreciated the well-reflected thoughts.

Terrence wiped his eyes as a sunrise of joy crossed his face, and he joined them both for a full family hug.

"So, are you the 30%?" Peyton asked.

"Sorry—what?" Matthew asked, letting go of his son. They returned to their respective seats, and once again, Peyton held their attention.

"Are you and Veo part of the 30% who never found a Fated Mate?"

"It doesn't matter. We found each other and had you. Why would think we're part of the unmated statistic?"

"I'm 20. That means you both were 18. No one gives up on finding their Fated Mate at age 18." Peyton received two immediate glances from both parents which reminded him the comment was hypocritical. "Okay, most people."

"Your father and I come from an older, traditional way of mating," Veo began. "Yes, as wolf-descendants, we all hope for our Fate to just show up one day. But that's hard. Really hard. Sure, there are stories of those finding success at formal courting events; we went to them. But finding a Fate is far worse than a coin-toss. And if you keep surrounding yourself with the same people, you'll never get there."

"So, you and Sur just gave up?"

"No," Matthew continued, "like Veo said, we had families who felt there were priorities in mates."

"You mean Types."

"It's definitely an important part of it, yes. The courting formals Veo was talking about? Those were by invitation to only Type 4's and Type 5's."

"Why?"

"That's just the way it is. It promotes strong vitality. Dr. Erricson would say it's all about the genes." Matthew chuckled.

"I still don't understand," Peyton said a bit dismayed.

Terrence weighed in, "Our parents gave us time to find our Fated Mate among a small pool of candidates. Some of those candidates did find their Fates at those parties, and it was beautiful to watch."

"It was frustrating to watch," Matthew interjected. Peyton laughed.

"Okay, yes, it was frustrating. Excruciating," Terrence admitted. "But our parents didn't want us to have our lives controlled by waiting for this special bond to just show up one day. Were they a bit rushed in their thinking? Oh, absolutely."

"Parents back then wanted it over and done with, Peyton. And we knew that was wrong. That was why we stepped back, way back, and watched to see if you felt like it was something you wanted to pursue."

"And then I didn't," Peyton spoke.

"Yeah," Terrence agreed, "you didn't. So, your father and I talked about how we'd go about this."

Matthew continued, "I had one of those philosophical mortality discussions with Dr. Erricson last year. He was mortified to think Roman might never settle down with a mate. And I have to confess, I shared my same fears with him."

"You two had a little too much to drink that night I think," Terrence patronized.

"Alex said we were just fine. I take a bar owner's word as good as Wolf-God's." Matthew nodded.

"An Omega owning a bar," Terrence muttered with disapproval.

"Anyway..." Matthew refocused.

"So, that's how Roman and I came about?" Peyton interrupted.

Matthew nodded. "Based on what we already knew about him and what Dr. Erricson knew about you, we all agreed this was the match everyone could be satisfied with. And I may not notice the things your Veo does, but I did notice the glimmer in your eye when we first brought up being mated with Roman."

"Or let's talk about how you looked when we told him Roman agreed." Terrence grinned, teeth shining.

"But Roman didn't agree. That's the impression I got tonight."

Matthew sighed. "I still defend the notion I didn't know Roman had any reservations on this."

Peyton turned to his Veo. "Did you know?"

Terrence shook his head. "No. I think it was just cold feet. It's not an easy decision. He still had stars in his eyes, baby. It's so hard to get someone to shake those out. I wouldn't be surprised if he's still hurting over it a little bit."

"Yeah, I don't blame him," Peyton agreed.

"Once again," Matthew announced, "we are very sorry for not telling you the truth of how we came to be. It was not something we wanted to share with you: the idea we weren't given a decision at all. We wanted you to have one. And we hope you understand you had one this entire time."

Peyton paused for a moment. "I did. And I do. And I'm sorry. I love you both." Peyton stood up and hugged his family one more time. His relieved breath transformed into a huge yawn which both of his parents found contagious.

"Clearly, it's time for us all to go to bed," Matthew declared.

"Yes, let's all go to bed and relax tomorrow. Monday you have school. And then, Tuesday afternoon, we meet with the lawyers for the contract. Roman will be there, too."

Peyton's heart skipped a beat. "That was fast! Wait, I don't remember that being discussed tonight."

"It was already planned. Remember, we thought tonight was going to go off without a hitch." Matthew grabbed his suit coat and waited for his Omega to grab his.

"I still can't believe I'm going to be mated with a guy like Roman, a Type 6 no less."

"Don't sell yourself so short. You're a strong Type 5 with an immaculate Blood Type percentage, and Roman needs to be equally grateful for you, too."

"Why?" Peyton asked.

"He may be one of the most sought-after Alphas, but he's still a Type 6."

"What does that mean?" Peyton felt his Sur touch his arm, slowly guiding him to hallway.

Matthew continued, "I suppose it's not something you'd learn in a school textbook yet. Type 6 Alphas can't find a Fated Mate. It's a fault in their genetics. Roman was always destined for a contractual mate." All three Whitmore family members began their journey to the bedroom corridors, Peyton in front with Sur and Veo behind him.

"Huh," Peyton let the fact soak in. "Do you think Roman knew that? I didn't get that impression at dinner tonight." Peyton's parents gave each other a cautious glance. Like many tricky conversations, Terrence let Matthew do all the talking.

"I'm certain he had some clue, Peyton. Just dreamer's denial. That's all."

"You better go to bed right away, Peyton. Have a good night, sweetheart," Terrence cooed.

"You too," Peyton replied.

Peyton shut the door to his cozy bedroom and dove onto his inviting luxurious bed. He was on the verge of being a contracted Omega to a crown jewel of an Alpha. And yet, Peyton took his Sur's words to heart. He was equally desirable. Just because he was shorter and less athletic didn't mean he was a lost cause. Roman did express a need and desire for Peyton to socialize more. Peyton decided it was something he'd let Roman help him slowly acclimate to. Sports? Not so much.

Peyton would, however, love to watch on the sidelines as Roman played a rough game in the hot sun with equally competitive Alphas and Betas. Peyton imagined Roman staring at him from afar, making sure he was watching as Roman removed a sweaty shirt and threw it aside. The sun would kiss every inch of his exposed skin, every bead of sweat glistening as it ran down his muscled torso.

Not wanting to forget anything about that evening, Peyton suddenly got up and found his diary on the desk. In it, he started recording every detail of the night—the good ones anyway. Then, he went on to describe Roman himself: his face, hair, lips, smile, his laugh.

Lost in the moment, Peyton's mind tried its best to recreate Roman's scent. Remembering in part how he smelled like rain, he lifted himself and opened a nearby window, taking in a generous breath. With eyes falling slowly closed, he inched his way back to his bed to lay down.

He imagined Roman on top of him, wanting him. Instantly, Peyton's breath quickened, and his skin heated. The excitement made his insides vibrate and pulse. When his hand stroked his neck down to his nipple through his shirt, he felt his slick begin to bead on the outside of his body. Peyton remembered Roman smiling once he discovered the scent. The memory shook his attention back to reality, and his eyes opened. He couldn't get his clothes off fast enough, throwing them off in all in directions toward the floor. Before he began his occasional ritual, he grabbed a soft towel from under his bed and laid it under his hips.

On his back, he leaned up against the decorative bedframe and observed his hard length outlined by the soft white cloth of his underwear. A clearer outline of his cock head was visible due to the fluid soaking all around it.

Omegas were notorious for producing copious amounts of liquid from every sexual body part—a turn-on for insatiable Alphas begging to ease their pain and bring pleasure to a vulnerable Omega in the throes of a burning heat. It was no surprise when Peyton massaged the area covering the entrance to his insides that his slick soaked his fingers and began dripping. He brought it up to his face, inhaled his own scent of citrus-infused vanilla and licked the few drops off his hand.

The sensation on his tongue began sending his primal instincts into hyper drive. Not wanting to play around anymore, he tore his underwear off and heard his cock snap back on his lower stomach with a thud, spewing out pre-seminal moisture. He instantly tested himself by pushing a finger deep to his insides, massaging his slick glands, and when satisfied, he added a second alongside it. Even though the pleasure was his own, he dreamed as hard as he could for it to be Roman instead of him. The deeper and harder he thrust his fingers in, the more slick coated his hand and the towel under his body.

Slipping in a third and fourth finger, Peyton took the next step to imagine Roman shoving his big cock inside of him, destroying his virginity. Peyton moaned as his other hand stroked his hot hard member. Whispering sweet nothings aloud to himself as if Roman could hear him, his body overloaded with sensation. The feeling started in his core and instantly spread into the rest of his body. His testicles drew up, nipples hardened, and hole tightened around his bathed fingers. All at once, contractions on his neck, chest, hips, cock, balls, taint, prostate, and glands rocked him. It took everything in his power not to scream his ecstasy. His first release came from his cock vibrating in his hand. Heavy spurts hit his skin with audible noises, dousing his neck, chest, and stomach in his hot semen. The second release came from inside. His glands and his prostate worked together in unison as they performed heavy contractions on the four fingers deep inside him. Slick dripped out of him like a running sink, passing his knuckles and soaking the towel which was doing little at this point to hold all the liquid coming out of him.

After his short self-love session, he cleaned himself up and lay on his bed. The wind sweeping in from his window returned the sweet smell of rain inside as it moved the hot scent of orgasm out. An image of Roman smiling stuck in his mind's eye. Never losing focus, Peyton let slumber take him, and his smile drifted into the deep memories of his brain and heart.

CHAPTER 04:

A Study of Ranks

Mikaél Cavenbelle carried his textbooks to his last class of the day. His short black hair bounced in a wave in time with his purposeful stride. Light blue eyes searched for Room C136—Dr. Birowack's Level 2 Class: Wolf Ranks 101. Behind him, his best friend Laycin Vaughn did his best to catch up.

"Dude, can you slow down a bit?" Laycin pleaded.

"I can't be late for Dr. Birowack's class, especially on the first day. My Sur will kill me!"

"I'm sorry. I didn't think the line at lunch would be backed up that much."

Mikaél located the door to his salvation. He peered into the classroom where a generous number of students were listening to Dr. Birowack speak. As he listened in, Mikaél sighed in relief as he heard the doctor struggle to pronounce student names. He opened the door with Laycin huffing on the back of his neck. The door creaked and everyone glanced over. After the awkward entrance, they found the only two remaining desks in the room right below Dr. Birowack's nose.

"Ah," the distinguished doctor sighed, "you must be Mr. Cavenbelle."

Mikaél's eyes widened as he worried that his father had given the professor the complete rundown of his son. "How did you know that?"

"With age comes an intelligent sense of smell. In addition, I can distinguish between over two hundred men in a closed room and scent their Blood-Type in a matter of seconds." He stroked his long silver beard while his new students stared at him in awe.

Dr. Birowack was the head of the world-famous genetic lab at Tauris Medical Center, but he also taught a few classes as an adjunct professor at Ashershire Preparatory to help usher in the next generation of scientists and educate the general population. Everyone knew he was a brilliant man, but they had no clue of the power he claimed to possess.

"Wow," Mikaél breathed, trembling slightly, "you can really do that?"

He felt Dr. Birowack's gaze lock down on him. His fierce green eyes accompanied by a pair of busy salt and pepper eyebrows burned in his skull. The creases around his eyes and in his forehead indicated a dominance Mikaél had no idea a Beta could possess. His heart caught in his throat.

"No, that's pure nonsense. You make it easy when your name is right there on your notebook."

Mikaél sighed, face blushing as the rest of his classmates giggled and snickered. After catching his breath, he looked down at the yellow-colored notebook and turned his head sideways in awe. "Uh, sir. My name isn't on this notebook."

"Good observation, Mr. Cavenbelle."

"Then how—"

"Young man, I've worked with your father for almost ten years and taught your brother. Do you honestly think I don't know who you are?" Dr. Birowack smirked.

This time, the flood of embarrassment stuck. More laughter and comments buzzed around him, including from his friend Laycin, who was enjoying himself way too much at his friend's expense.

"And you must be Mr. Vaughn." Dr. Birowack pointed to the center of Laycin's face with a black remote control.

Laycin straightened. "Uh, yes sir."

"I'll spare you the magic tricks and just tell you I know because you are the last name on my roster I haven't checked off. Do please remind yourself and Mr. Cavenbelle to be on time to my class from now on. You may be adults, but you are still adolescents to me. Understood?"

Both gentlemen resolved to be on their best behavior. Mikaél never considered himself a fool, not that anyone could tell after his first impression. Blood pulsed in his head, and brow sweat accumulated at the tips. He gingerly opened his notebook to the first clean page and tried to make himself invisible.

Laycin, on the other hand, took the moment in stride and settled comfortably in the wood-backed chair. His long legs stretched and remained in an inclined position as he tapped his pen on his notebook.

"Wolf Ranks," Dr. Birowack began, "refer to what?" His arms stretched out to his students, waiting for a volunteer. After only a couple hands showed their interest, he decided to focus his attention on Mikaél once again. "Mr. Cavenbelle, can you tell me?"

Mikaél straightened at attention and felt a lump in his throat. "Ranks refer to biological disposition. They are the Alphas, Omegas, and Betas." Mikaél gazed at Dr. Birowack who sat on the corner of his desk with his arms crossed. He studied him but made no effort to affirm or contest him. "They represent how we will contribute to society."

"Such as?" Dr. Birowack pressed.

"Instinctual response: dominant or submissive personality traits, social position, expectations and responsibilities, and role in reproduction."

"Can you tell me about them in regard to their rank?" Dr. Birowack stood as he pushed a button. A large screen slowly descended from the ceiling.

"Alphas instinctually show dominance. They are expected to be members of strength in both mental and physical ability. They typically are leaders, bosses, people of influence. They provide protection and a path for the rest of their family or 'pack' as some say. Omegas show submissive personality traits and seek safety under an Alpha. This comes from the primal instinct to protect the womb since Omegas are responsible for childbirth. Omegas typically hit the glass ceiling when it comes to professional advancement, legal, and personal rights."

"I'm certain your sociology professor would love to hear your soapbox on rank rights, Mr. Cavenbelle, but I'm just interested in science. Now, tell me about the Betas."

"Betas serve no reproductive role, and because of this, they aren't ranked in their Blood-Type; however, they are used as safeguards for Alphas and Omegas. They support where they feel they are needed or wanted. This makes them great for peacekeeping in the home or civil service professionally. They can also serve as a surrogate Alpha, but once again, they can't reproduce."

Dr. Birowack stared off into the distance and then out to the rest of the class. He walked over to the front where Mikaél and Laycin sat. "Tell me, Mr. Cavenbelle. Did your father tell you all of that?"

"No, sir."

"Are you just that interested in genetics?" He rubbed his beard.

"Yes, sir."

"Why so?" Dr. Birowack asked, his head turned slightly.

"I want to be a father one day."

"And tell me, which rank do you want your pup to be? Alpha, Beta, or Omega?"

Mikaél blinked. "I don't really care. I just want him to be healthy."

"That would be foolish of you then, Mr. Cavenbelle," Dr. Birowack stated.

"It matters?" Mikaél asked, surprised at his professor's claim.

"Of course, it does. It means everything."

Mikaél glanced at Laycin who was biting his lower lip to keep from laughing. "Why?" Mikaél felt like his world was falling apart.

Dr. Birowack leaned down. "That is why you are here. That is what you are going to find out." He walked over to the door and shut off the lights, leaving everything in a dark haze. In a few seconds, a bright presentation popped up on the video screen reading: Wolf-Ranks 101. "Be prepared to take lots of notes and take them fast. I don't like to repeat myself. There are two tests during the semester. Fail them, and you fail the class. Any questions? Good." Dr. Birowack continued, "Now then, ranks were determined long before we humans were here. Our ancestors were wolves and needed ranks in order to protect and preserve the pack..."

***

"It's not funny, Lacyin!" Mikaél snapped. The ride home was unbearable. He wanted to crawl into a hole and live there. Or in this case, crawl into the trunk of Laycin's car. It was hard to hear his best friend's continuous laughter, but even harder to see his massive expressions of elation. "You can stop now! Any time! I swear to Wolf-God—"

"Okay, okay, okay," Laycin huffed. There was silence for just a moment before Laycin was back at it again, grinning ear to ear, jolly hysterics emanating from his diaphragm.

"Ugh. Will you just pull over and let me out then?" Mikaél picked up his shoulder bag, indicating he was seriously considering just bolting out of the car going about 80 down the highway.

"OKAY!" Laycin giggled. "Man! He ate you up and spit you out. He Beta'd you bad!" Laycin's surfer voice was usually entertaining until he used it like this—the slow, painful accentuation of uncomfortable situations. Thankfully, he was nice to look at. Laycin's gray eyes sparkled. His light brown hair was very similar to Mikaél's: soft, straight, and flowy. But his hair was a bit longer, barely staying out of his eyes and ears. He had puppy dog lips which were drying out a bit from air whipping past them in their top-down red convertible. At the age of 18, he was only five months older than Mikaél, but Laycin had a complexion which made him appear older than he really was.

"Shut up." Mikaél gave Laycin the death stare.

"Damn near cut your dick off."

"If you value your impotent balls at all, you will stop now."

"Okay!" Laycin drew out one hand off the steering wheel while showing the "Don't shoot!" gesture.

"Dr. Birowack is going to talk to my dad. I know it."

Laycin imitated an old man's voice in order to mock Mr. Birowack. "'That is why you are here. That is what you are going to find out.'" He chuckled again but was able to contain himself after a few seconds as he shook his head.

"My dad is going to kill me." Mikaél pinched the bridge of his nose and groaned.

"Man, you have got to chill out. It's fine. You said the old man knew you. He was just trying to shake you up a bit."

"Well, it worked."

"I have to say—I was proud to see you stand up to him in regard to the whole rank thing."

"I meant what I said."

"About Omega rights and you being a parent?" Laycin put on a pair of shades to block the sun currently ricocheting off the bright buildings as they neared the exit for Mikaél's neighborhood.

"Yeah."

"Why didn't you say 'Alpha'? Everybody wants an Alpha pup."

"I don't know. I'm Omega, so I guess I'm biased."

"You should have said Beta." Laycin smiled behind the dark shades.

Mikaél's voice huffed with humor. "Oh? Why is that?"

"Because Betas are cool. Betas are hot. Betas got it goin' on."

"I'll take your word for it."

"You should, Mr. Cavenbelle. You should."

"Can I ask you something serious?" Mikaél's tone shifted, and he spoke softly.

"Uh-oh. Don't like the sound of this." Laycin exited the highway and entered a well-hidden neighborhood. He tore off his sunglasses and looked at his best friend with curious sincerity.

"Do you ever think about your inability to have kids? Does it ever bother you?"

Laycin's brows shot up. "Think about it? Sure. Does it bother me? Nah. I'm good."

"Seriously?"

"Yeah. I mean, if I wanted to become a parent, there are other options. And that's assuming I want to settle down. I don't have the primal need like you Omegas do. Plus, it gives me all the freedom to become an awesome uncle to your screaming brats!"

"Uncle Laycin?" Mikaél laughed.

"Yeah. Or Uncle Gray Wolf! Master Wolf of the Universe!" Laycin balled up his hand in a fist like a superhero showing his stature.

"Uh-huh." Mikaél shook his head. Laycin's hot red ride pulled up in front of the Cavenbelle home. "Do you want to come in?" he asked.

"Nah. Not today. First day back got me all worn out, but I'll see you tomorrow morning."

"Alright. See you later."

"Bye."

Mikaél stepped out and watched Laycin back out. When he saw him whip out of the cul-de-sac, Mikaél sighed audibly, fearing the inevitable conversation with his parents.

Mikaél stepped into the foyer and stealthily closed the door. As he set his bag on the wooden bench, he slipped off his new white shoes and slid them under it. He listened with his left ear, trying to determine whether his dads were on the other side of the wall in the kitchen. Feeling as if he had a good chance, he stepped lightly on the wood floor and turned to the left. At first, the bright white kitchen gave no signs of life. The island in front of him complete with a large cooking range was empty, which meant Veo hadn't begun his elegant dinner prep yet. The hard cornered U-shaped countertops were lightly dusted with appliances, fresh flowers, and today's mail. His ears and sense of smell betrayed him. When he fully entered the kitchen, he observed both of his parents at the kitchen table in the far-left corner. His Sur was reading a newspaper, and Veo was looking over photo negatives and prints.

"Well, there he is," his Sur, Dustin, said, delighted. He folded up his newspaper and stared at his son with dark green eyes and his crooked smirk. "I was beginning to think Laycin forgot where we lived and got lost."

"You guys are way too quiet. And I hate how these large, tinted windows block the view from the driveway." Mikaél turned and walked back to the fridge, trying to find the lunch meat while conveniently hiding his grimace.

"Hmm, bad first day?" his Veo wondered, looking up only briefly from the fruits of his exquisite photography skills.

"No." Mikaél found a couple cold cuts, mayonnaise, and bread and set them on the island. "Just stressed."

"Hey, don't fill up on that. It's Pollo Bianco, tonight."

Mikaél shared similar features with Alec, his Veo. Even though Alec's hair curled, it was just as dark as Mikaél's. His skin had a natural olive tone with dark eyes and facial hair not shared with his son. But he did pass on a prominent slender nose, designer lips, and a dimple on his chin. The dimple wasn't nearly as visible on Alec due to a shadow of facial hair.

"How was your first day in Dr. Birowack's class?" Dustin asked, folding his hands in his lap. Alec looked up with interest.

"It was okay." Mikaél lifted the butter knife and spread sauce on two slices of artisan bread. He avoided eye contact, praying neither father would press the issue. He hoped that as long as he didn't make a big deal of it, they wouldn't.

"So," Dustin held a beat, "you don't know if you want an Alpha, Beta, or Omega pup?"

Mikaél dropped the butter knife on the granite island. He thought wrong. His eyes drifted to the side, then back to his parents. Both his Sur and Veo grinned at him as if they caught his hand in the cookie jar. "Seriously? How did you find that out?"

"It was on the news." Dustin's head tilted. His sarcasm gloated as Alec stifled a chuckle. Mikaél stared at his Sur with a deadpan expression, letting him know the dad jokes weren't going to be effective in the moment. "Dr. Birowack told me."

"Did he even wait five seconds after I was out the door to talk to you?"

"If it makes you feel any better, I called him for an unrelated reason. He just mentioned he enjoyed having you in class and thought you were quite astute and composed for being put in the spotlight on day one."

Mikaél narrowed his gaze as he found an empty chair at the round glass table. "In other words, you asked him."

"Yes, I asked him. It's not every day a boss gets to teach his employee's son."

"Isn't that a good thing?"

"Dr. Birowack will be all right. Do what you're supposed to do, and everything will be smooth from here on out. As long as you're on time, that is." Dustin stood and patted his son's shoulder.

Alec pivoted. "How does Laycin like Level 2?" He fiddled through a few prints and organized them into folders on the floor next to his chair.

"He didn't say a whole lot. He doesn't jump for joy when it comes to school. Which by the way, he's the reason I was late to Dr. Birowack's class."

"That's no one's fault but your own," Dustin interjected.

"Agreed," Alec chimed in, writing down notes and clearing off the table. "I'm going to start getting dinner ready. Are you joining us this evening, or is that all you're having?"

"I'll eat later. Just not a lot, I guess." Mikaél grabbed the second half of his sandwich and headed toward the hall. Before he left the kitchen, he stopped and turned around. "What about you two?"

"Oh, I'm starving!" Alec replied as he strolled to the kitchen island and put a large pan on the island's gas range.

"No, that's not what I meant. I mean, when you were pregnant for the first time, what did you want? Alpha, Beta, or Omega?"

Alec looked up, face serious. He turned his head toward his mate who shared the expression. After a beat, Dustin's face melted into a gentle smile which gave Alec permission to do the same.

Dustin replied proudly, "We wanted our children to be healthy and happy. We know we got the healthy part down, hopefully the happy, too."

"Why does Dr. Birowack think it's so critical to desire a specific rank so much?" Mikaél asked, tone discouraged.

"Because Dr. Birowack is about science, not family."

"So, what does science say?"

"Science says it depends what you're after."

"Like what?"

Dustin chuckled. "I'll let Dr. Birowack tell you that."

Both of Mikaél's parents went about their business as if Mikaél was never there. His Sur resumed his newspaper while his Veo began to set out several things from the refrigerator. Mikaél twitched his lips and began his descent down the wooden hallway.

The Cavenbelle home had a pitched cathedral ceiling complete with a lacquered wood design. Straight down to the end of the open hallway revealed a T: left was his parents' bedroom and right was an extra-large guest bedroom. But halfway down the hall and to the right began another hallway which led to the basement.

At the bottom step, a similar design was laid out. His older brother Drew had been out of the house and mated for over a year now, so his bedroom held only a few artifacts left inside. The left hallway led to what was now his own private bathroom and to its right was his bedroom. His parents rarely came down to the basement, so he had control of everything. Most of the time he claimed the right side of the basement like his personal condo. A large island fireplace was off-center which he could walk 360 degrees around. The farthest right had a den complete with home theatre and extra-large sectional couch. Feeling like he needed to destress a little more than normal, he shed his pants, standing in his underwear and the soft fabric of his dark pine t-shirt.

As he reclined, the cool leather felt great on his warm skin. He dug into his pocket of the pants he was wearing and pulled out his phone. He found a text from Laycin:

[Laycin: Did your Sur kill you? If you don't respond by tonight I'll assume yes]

[Mikaél: Yes. Consider me a corpse. ;-)]

[Laycin: Does that mean you're okay?]

[Mikaél: They're good. Overreacted I guess]

[Laycin: YOU? Overreact? NEVER!!!]

[Mikaél: Uh huh]

[Laycin: So]

[Laycin: Forgot to tell you ... I got a message from Garrace after lunch]

[Mikaél: ?]

[Laycin: Wanted to know if you'd consider going out again]

[Mikaél: Ha ha! Give you one guess as to why he asked you first ;-)]

[Laycin: Because he knew you wouldn't answer his text?]

[Mikaél: BINGO!]

[Laycin: So that's a no then LOL]

[Mikaél: What do you think?]

[Laycin: You're not one for second chances are you?]

[Mikaél: When they don't involve sleeping with someone else? Sure!]

[Laycin: Wait...]

[Laycin: You were sleeping with him?]

[Mikaél: No! You know what I mean!!!! SMH He wanted to though]

[Laycin: What happened with that?]

[Mikaél: Hayden. That's what happened. Barf!]

[Laycin: He slept with an Alpha? Damn.]

[Mikaél: Mhm good for him ☹]

[Laycin: You're better than Garrace anyway]

[Mikaél: Aww. You gonna take me out?]

[Laycin: As long as you're paying! Hehe]

[Mikaél: LMAO! Deal.]

[Laycin: Saweeet!!!!]

[Mikaél: Uh huh. Ttyl]

[Laycin: Later man]

CHAPTER 05:

A Closer Look at DNA

The Tauris Medical Center sat in the center of the city like a shiny beacon. A massive renovation and expansion made it the envy of institutions in several territories and states. Under Dr. Paul Birowack, an unprecedented dedication of medical research was underway, thanks in part to the Whitmore family's multimillion-dollar donation and support. Serving as his protégés, Doctors Jacob Erricson and Dustin Cavenbelle stood in charge of his most-prized studies—including unlocking the secrets of Type 6 Alphas.

"Jake," Dustin spoke while going through a clipboard of paperwork, "did the blood tubes from the lab come in this morning?"

Jake looked up from his blood accessioning labels for a quick glance at his partner. His mind, deep in thought and preoccupied, cooled his usually bright disposition. "Yeah."

"Ray says they weren't there." Dustin observed Jake's distant state.

"They're there; I know they're there. I did the blood draw myself and walked it down here." Jake pushed back, sending his wheeled chair soaring to a glass front refrigerator. He opened the door, pulled out the tubes in question, and handed them to Dustin.

"You drew Roman's blood yourself? When?"

"Before he went to school."

"How is he not bothered by you treating him like a science experiment?" Dustin asked, tapping his pen on the clipboard.

"Cash helps." Jake laughed.

"What does he think we're doing?"

"He knows we're tracking Type 6 Alphas and trying to figure out where they come from and what they can do."

"Just like that?" Dustin inquired.

"Just like that." Jake labeled the chilled tubes and placed them back in their racks. He set them back into the fridge, ready for processing. Sensing Dustin still standing there in an awkward silence, he glanced up again. "What?"

"I'm just shocked you tell him everything we're doing about Type 6."

Jake made a face. "You don't tell Mikaél what you do?"

"Not to that detail, no. I'm not sure he's that interested," Dustin replied.

"I'm in a different position than you, Dustin. Roman gets blood drawn once a month and comes here for a bi-annual check-up. I mean, Wolf-God, I convinced him to give a sperm sample on his 18th birthday."

"Glad I wasn't here for that conversation. How did you convince him to do that?"

"A new car."

"Damn! Are you serious?" Dustin's jaw dropped.

"He was already getting it for his birthday anyway. Two birds, one stone." Jake winked.

Dustin shook his head with amusement. "They can be bought so easy, can't they?" Jake didn't respond, still attempting to get work done. "Still, you have more guts than I do, I guess."

"What else would you have me say other than the truth?" Jake's voiced elevated with frustration. Dustin sensed the rush of the changing scent on his partner.

"We say nothing other than the truth, gentlemen." Dr. Paul Birowack stood at the door watching his best eye each other for perhaps a brawl. "The truth must always be spoken. But the Wolf-Devil is in the details. And those who search for the details will certainly find him." He walked in with grace and assurance. "Now, I do believe we can hold a higher decorum here with our institution's finest, or are we no better than the competitive interns on first floor?" His mere presence calmed the simmering waters.

"Sorry, Paul," Jake stood down. "Sorry, Dustin."

"No, it's okay. To be honest, you've been off all morning," Dustin replied.

"I don't think I've done a good job hiding it. That's for sure."

"What's going on?" Dustin asked, crossing his arms, his clipboard up against his chest.

"Roman's going to contract today. I'm meeting everyone at the lawyer's office after work today to go over it and sign it." Jake's eyes drifted to the large open window, looking down into a city clouded in gray.

"Ah." Dr. Birowack nodded. "The golden child is getting mated. How exciting."

"Wow! That came out of nowhere," Dustin exclaimed. "You don't sound excited at all."

"Oh, I am," Jake reflected. "I'm just not sure Roman is."

"He's not excited to be in contract with his mate? Uh, why?" Dustin found a chair of his own and swiveled up to Jake's worktable.

"He still believes his Fate is out there." Jake braced himself for the criticism.

Dustin's brows furrowed as he connected the statement. "Wait. You didn't tell him?" Jake grabbed a set of vials and began labeling them, ignoring him completely. "Hey, look at me." Jake turned back, tensed, and prepared himself. "I was just shamed on not being fully transparent with my kid, and here to find out you didn't even tell

Roman he won't ever find his Fate because his genetic code lacks the high-quality pheromone marker?"

Dr. Birowack interjected, "He did tell him the truth."

"What do you mean?" Dustin scratched the back of his head.

"Jake told his son he'd find a mate to be with for the rest of his life. And barring any hiccups, I'm sure this afternoon it will be true."

"With all due respect, I'm not sure that's the same thing as the truth, Paul," Dustin rebuked.

"The Wolf-Devil is in the details, Dr. Cavenbelle. Those who look for it will find him," Dr. Birowack reminded him.

Jake and Dustin exchanged uncomfortable eye contact. Neither one of them knew what to make of the situation. Both parents seemed to be chasing their own tails. And then there was Dr. Birowack, enabling every strategy in the playbook.

"What are the next steps, then?" Dustin asked Dr. Birowack with deflated enthusiasm.

"Hopefully, we will have our first reproductive test subject." Dr. Birowack gazed at Jake. Knowing the atmosphere of the room, he mentally prepared himself for Round 2.

Dustin realized he was late to the party again. He observed the glances between the two researchers and did a double take. "You can't be serious?" Dustin asked in emotional shock.

"Dustin..." Jake attempted.

"Is nothing sacred to you for the advancement of science?" Dustin felt alone and betrayed. He'd always felt up until now he was truly a partner in this Three Musketeers crusade for a better understanding of life. But it became clear Paul and Jake were having private meetings and conferences on the side. "Has your son even agreed to let us exploit his Omega's pregnancy?"

Jake stared at his friend and colleague who appeared alone and deceived. "I haven't asked him yet," he replied without blinking.

"Boy, if that's not putting all your eggs in one basket, I don't know what is. What about the Omega? Do you expect Roman to just usurp his mate's rights and force him into it? Plus, what's going to happen when the Omega's parents find out after the fact that we've been sitting on the sidelines waiting to guinea pig their son? This is just a lawsuit waiting to happen for misrepresentation. I mean, please tell me two of the most intelligent research doctors I know and respect foresaw these critical roadblocks."

"Of course, Dustin. That's what we do—look at all the variables for every decision we make," Dr. Birowack assured him.

"I don't understand then how you both seem to be so calm regarding this. You must have some strong confidence the Omega's parents are going to be okay with all this."

"Yes, Dustin, we do." Jake's voice was strong—too strong. It showed once again Dustin was out of the loop. But today was Dustin's day to show just how keen and intuitive he really was.

"I'm going to regret asking, aren't I?" Dustin sighed. Dr. Birowack stayed poised and emotionless. Jake pressed his lips tight and rubbed his sweaty palms onto his thighs, planting his feet hard on the floor while keeping balance on his swivel chair. "Who is the Omega your son is signing the mating contract with?"

Dr. Birowack walked down the open hallway. Several technicians and managers were working on different projects, appearing their best to show they weren't eavesdropping. "We need the room, please. Everyone, take a fifteen-minute break." The room fell silent, but no one moved. It was rare—no—inconceivable to watch Dr. Birowack stop productivity. Once again, without words, he communicated to his staff this was no joke.

One by one, they filed out the main door, all looking at Dustin and Jake cautiously, wondering if someone had died or worse—been fired. After the last employee exited and Jake was sure the door was secure, he saw Dr. Birowack's nod of approval to continue and divulged the heaviest news yet.

"My son is set to be a contracted mate to Peyton Whitmore—Matthew Whitmore's son."

Dustin's chest felt on fire, blood pumping a mile a minute. He felt as if someone had slapped his face and punched him below his sternum. Jake and Dr. Birowack were prepared for a banshee scream, but the lack of oxygen in his lungs prevented him from doing so.

"Well," Dustin spoke quietly, but the pause that followed was deafening, "if that doesn't beat all."

"Dustin, I'm sorry." The words instantaneously bounced right off of Dustin and back on to Jake.

"Paul, you can't honestly be supporting this?" Dustin asked in amazement.

"When going through the Blood-Type data, the Whitmores have an extremely high purity of Type 5 descendants in their history."

"How pure?" Dustin asked curiously.

"Most Type 5's purity rates fall between 60-80%. The expectation is these percentages will only go down over time, especially with Omega rights getting more liberal every year. Parents are allowing their sons to mate freely among the lower Blood-Types. However, there are some families who still follow the aristocratic practices of pure breeding, and the Whitmore family is proof of that, even the ancestors of Matthew's Omega mate.

"So, what's the Whitmore percentage? 80%?" Dustin guessed.

"93%."

Both Dustin and Jake's stunned expressions pleased Dr. Birowack. It was the superiority of his knowledge, even over his protégés, that kept his world spinning.

"Look, this is great and all," Dustin confessed, "but doesn't a Code of Ethics violation go off in anyone's minds here? Or am I on an island by myself?"

"Mr. Whitmore has been thoroughly debriefed on the situation at hand. He's fully aware and proud of his family's legacy. He knows we have a rare opportunity to make, quite possibly, the first scientifically recorded and researched genetic code of the obsolete purity of a Type 5 Omega and golden divergent Type 6 Alpha. The opportunity for his family to be a part of scientific history is invaluable, and he passionately agreed. And quite frankly, his monetary gratitude shows itself in spades."

"That's assuming everything goes smoothly. What if his son never gets pregnant or the contract never comes to fruition?" Dustin pointed out.

"We have quite the strong non-disclosure agreement. Should anything go wrong in this venture, Mr. Whitmore and his family have very little recourse," Dr. Birowack confirmed.

"Little is not zero. Going public alone could ruin us. And, no offense, Paul, but I have a hard time believing Matthew Whitmore listened to you discuss advanced science terminology which swayed him to agree to all this."

"He didn't," Jake broke in. "I did."

Dustin stared at his near stranger of a partner and shook his head slowly. "You never cease to amaze me, Jake." He reflected on the heavy conversation. In his mind, he saw Jake and Paul smiling at each other in satisfaction. His own invisibility was overwhelming. "Well, you two seemed to have this all figured out. I'm not sure what you need me here for anymore." Dustin's heart heaved, but he refused to let his emotions go further.

"That's not true!" Jake yelled.

Dr. Birowack intervened, "You are an integral part of this team, Dustin. This project needs your expertise, or it will surely fail—there's no doubt about that. Jake and I did not tell you everything because there was no reason to do so. If Roman hadn't been so generous of himself or willing to contract, the opportunity would have been completely lost to us—our research relegated to the sidelines while other territories across the nation and the world discover first-hand critical information. Nothing degrades a scientist or doctor more than having to read every discovery in the latest medical journal of someone else's success—especially when we're this close."

"Paul, I don't disagree with you. I'm just worried all these risks are making us lose sight of what our goal is."

"Then let me remind you, Dr. Cavenbelle." Dr. Birowack exhaled as he walked toward the large windows, staring at the traffic below with his hands behind his back. "Eight billion people from the origin of primates were nearly wiped out in a 100-year timespan. The virus attacked women first, effectively killing them off and with them any chance of offspring. And somewhere, somehow, Wolf-God gave us the chance to be in their stead. With men the only gender left, we have ruled this world ever since with the extraordinary power to reproduce and sustain ourselves. In another 100 years' time, the world's population stabilized at three billion. But the overall population is slowing down dramatically due to lower Blood-Types refusing to reproduce in the numbers our ancestors endured and from higher Blood-Types suffering from lower fertility, accompanied by birth rates with higher pregnancy-related deaths. That is why we are here, gentlemen." Dr. Birowack turned and observed the man's head held a bit lower and stared to the floor. "Even the slightest chance that a Type 6 Alpha can produce a new superior human with a spectacular gene profile, desirable traits, and reduce these reproductive issues means we should be taking every opportunity to better the generations who will come into this world long after we are dead. But that's only going to happen if you stick with us."

Dustin reflected, embarrassment washing over him. He felt petty and childish. Ever since entering this study five years ago, Jake and Paul had been nothing but good to him. The instruction and knowledge he'd received over those years were not only invaluable but also very promising that the work they were completing was indeed useful and applicable for a better future. Hearing Paul's words was a wake-up call to the importance of his work.

Dr. Birowack resumed, "Time is of the essence, Dustin. In the entire world, there are confirmed reports of one thousand Type 6 Alphas. Most underdeveloped nations shun and even murder them while other developed nations simply ignore their importance or prevalence. I am one of three doctors in the world leading this study, and I won't be around forever. Wolf-God knows I am on borrowed time already. When I am gone, I hope to pass this on to two individuals I know and care as if they were my own sons. I'd hate to know now that one of them doesn't want what they've spent the last five years fighting for. So, I need to know: do I have your confidence, doctor? Are you here with us? And will you be here with Jake when I need to step down from my life's work?"

Without hesitation, Dustin confirmed his loyalty, "Yes, Dr. Birowack, of course."

"And you, Dr. Erricson?"

"Absolutely, sir."

"Splendid!" Dr. Birowack beamed.

"Jake, I'm sorry," Dustin offered. "I wish I could have taken all this in objectively. I know you haven't or would ever keep me in the dark regarding our work, our baby—so to speak."

"I appreciate that." Jake answered. "And I do apologize. I know I can trust you with anything, and I should have with this."

"Wonderful, gentlemen!" Dr. Birowack spoke spiritedly. "Why don't I call the rest of the staff back in, and you two take an extended lunch somewhere nice to bury the hatchet, my compliments?"

"I wish I could," Jake lamented, "but I want to make sure Roman's blood sample gets taken care of, and then I want to head out a bit early today to beat the traffic for the lawyer's office, if you don't mind?"

"Of course, of course!" Dr. Birowack confirmed.

"Dustin, why don't you and your family come over for dinner instead?" Jake offered.

"Oh, not tonight. Drew and his mate are coming home. And this week is a bit crunched with Alec preparing his studio, I'm afraid."

"Is Sunday night out of the question?" Jake countered.

Dustin paused. "Sure. Sunday is great."

"Sunday confirmed and that will be you, Alec, and Mikaél?"

"Not Mikaél; he won't be interested."

"I think it would be great to for our families to meet. I've met your kids. Mikaél's never met my boys."

"Aren't your twins Level 2? I'd be shocked if they haven't."

"If they have, Rixen and Ryan have never said anything about it. And I know Roman's never met him."

Dustin gestured with a quick nod. "Alright. We'll make it a reservation for three then."

Dr. Birowack clapped his hands together. "Ah, see! There are my doctors."

Dustin and Jake smiled at Paul, then back at each other. The healing between the two had already begun. Jake began working with a smile and upbeat tempo and Dustin tapped his pen on his clipboard with his usual pep.

CHAPTER 06:

A Closer Look at a Contract

Jake rolled up to the parking space on location for his son's appointment. In the next space over, his Omega Adrian and son Roman sat in their car. "You ready?" Jake asked with cautious optimism as they all got out of the cars.

"I guess." Roman observed the building as if the sun was in his eyes.

Adrian pulled his son into a side hug and patted his back for comfort. "You do want to go through with this, right?" Adrian asked, trying to get the truth out of Roman's expression.

"Just nervous, I guess." Only a few nights ago at dinner, he was into this with a considerable passion. Later that night, he suffered from buyer's remorse. Today, he was conflicted. Outside the building, he felt tense and unsure of himself. He hoped more than anything that seeing Peyton again would revitalize those initial feelings.

As Jake walked up to his son, he could smell the nerves radiating off his body. "Just relax," his father whispered in a calm voice.

All three Erricson members walked into the building. The Whitmores' lawyer's office was on the tenth floor. In the elevator, his reflection in the closed doors showed his discontent. Roman readjusted his posture and expression to appear settled and confi-dent. The ding of the elevator startled him for a moment; it was a trigger for butterflies to go mad deep inside him.

Walking to the right, they could see Whitmores waiting in a foyer behind clear glass doors. The motion made them all look up and smile upon the Erricsons' arrival.

"Matthew," Jake smiled, shaking his hand firmly, "great to see you again. Sorry we're a bit late. I got off work a little later than I'd hoped."

"No worries at all." Matthew returned the enthusiasm, eyes twin-kling. "I hope you don't mind that we're meeting in my offices."

"Quite all right. Is your lawyer here yet?" Jake scanned the hallway.

"They're both in the conference room already. They said getting a head start meant less waiting for us."

"Sounds good." Jake studied Peyton in his tan dress shirt and navy blue tie, scenting his nerves and timid disposition. Then he looked to Roman which gave him his cue.

"Peyton." Roman stepped forward to give him a firm hug.

Peyton returned the favor, wrapping his arms under Roman's shoulders and pressing his head against Roman's firm chest. He felt Roman's heart rate increase. It pleased him knowing Roman's heightened emotions mirrored his. The affection felt very different from any embrace he received from his parents.

Terrence and Adrian both took a moment to observe their sons in the warm embrace.

"Okay," Terrence agreed, "I don't think we should keep the law-yers waiting any longer."

"Indeed," Matthew said, gesturing to the door. "After all, they're getting paid by the minute. We're not." The group laughed as Roman and Peyton unlocked their embrace.

All walked through the heavy, dark wood door into a first-class conference room. At the table, sat across from each other, two well-seasoned lawyers finished organizing of a stack of documents.

The families sat near each other while the Alphas sat strong next to their respective lawyers. In their ancestral state, this would be two wolves standing in the wild waiting to see who presented himself as more confident to lead the merging pack. But here in modern day, there were rules and decorum to follow. The law heavily supported an Alpha and his demands, but no contract could be signed without the Omega saying so. However, the Whitmores raised the bar in this community for what it meant to be successful, a blow to the traditional Alpha advantage.

Across from one another were Roman and Peyton, both feeling understandably out of place. Neither of them had ever been in this position before. But every man knew the goal in life was to only have to do this twice: once as a mate and once as a father depending on how many pups they had.

Pups. There was that thought again. Roman flashed back to an earlier conversation with his brothers. It was going to come up in the contract, not only by law, but by necessity. Contracts were known to go awry later when these things weren't agreed upon. Discussing it in contract was going to be awkward enough, but knowing the plan would be put into place? That pushed discomfort to a whole new level.

"Okay. Are we ready to proceed?" Whitmore's lawyer spoke first; it was easy to do since this was his turf. All in the room politely agreed and the dance of the Beta lawyers began:

"Let it be known on today's date, under the law of our state, and in the name of Wolf-God, we are here to merge the Whitmore and Erricson families under the Partnership and Copulation Agreement (or P&C) of #1 Alpha—Roman Edward Erricson—and #2 Omega—Peyton Reginald Whitmore. Do all parties, including their legal representation, agree this is why we are here?" All agreed with professional candor. A paper was placed before Jake, who courteously put it in the center for his family to see. "Do you, Roman, under the advisement of your parents Jacob Tyler Erricson and Adrian Asher

(Omarro) Erricson, acknowledge and find legally accurate the following considerations: name, birthdate, location of birth, current residence, rank, and Blood-Type?"

"Yes, sir," Roman replied.

Whitmore's lawyer asked for the blood draw results. Although Blood-Types could be confirmed through birth records, an added layer of protection to all families involved was a blood test signed, sealed, and delivered to the lawyers. Too many families committed fraud to secure contracts with preferred families for financial gain. Erricson's lawyer handed him the sealed envelope containing the confirmation of Blood-Type and bloodline.

"Okay. Yes, we have Roman who has been ranked an Alpha and Blood-Type 5 Accelerate overridden by a Dr. Paul Birowack to Type 6. Bloodline purity at 79%." The lawyer handed the paper to Matthew who showed it to Terrence. Terrence nodded as he slid the paper over to Peyton. Peyton's smile was big, like he'd earned the highest score on a pop quiz. He looked up at Roman who pushed his chest out a bit in his hot pink shirt.

Once the paper returned to the lawyer, and the questions continued. "Roman Erricson and family, the Whitmores are requesting a standard contract with rights and benefits outlined by the state and territory. Are you aware of and have you read the standard contract before you?" All three of the Erricsons acknowledged doing so. "Next, the requested provisions are as follows:

The Whitmore family is requesting the standard support funds for Peyton be a total of $1200 per month until his expiration. The Whitmore family agrees to the transfer of titles, any monies, or other items of value which are currently in Peyton's name as well the family assets after the expiration of Matthew James Whitmore and expiration of Terrence Cassius (Bastian) Whitmore to Roman Erricson. Should Roman's death precede Peyton's death, the Whitmore family requests all assets in consideration be immediately retained by any surviving Whitmore family members unless offspring are born. Peyton and his parents have consented to Peyton carrying offspring. They are agreeing to a minimum of one but are requesting no more than three pups in order to fulfill the terms of the contract. And finally, the Whitmore family is requesting Peyton and all off-spring born within the terms of the contract retain the last name Whitmore and avoid the legal default to the last name Erricson."

The Erricson family's shock was reality television gold. The lawyer held his best poker face as Jake mumbled a few expletives under his breath. Adrian grabbed his Alpha's hand, squeezing it to calm him down. All terms were pleasantly agreeable...except for the family name.

Roman glanced at Mr. Whitmore, then to his father Jake. "Dad, is he serious?" Roman blurted.

"Matthew, what the hell is this?" Jake demanded.

Matthew kept his posture firm but his voice soft. "It's a contract; it's business. We feel it is in our best interest to keep the Whitmore family name alive. Our name is very important to not only us, but also to the city, state, and territory we live in. We have no intention of letting our namesake perish because of some irrational dark-age rule which says the Alpha male deserves all the name and glory."

"Business? What about our family legacy? Are we nothing?" Jake stared at Matthew with awe and disgust.

"Now, Jake, let's not put words into peoples' mouths. It's just a matter of respect and honor to our family and the bloodline. As I'm sure you already know, our family is at a 93% purity rating for Type 5. I mean, by comparison to your family's 79%, it seems only logical."

Jake scoffed at the notion his family was somehow valued less by a lower percentage of purity. His animal instincts wanted to hoist Matthew by his neck and show him what it meant to be an Omega family coming into an Alpha's family. But he wasn't a wolf; he was a man, a man with human faults and weaknesses. His pride was being tested. Barely looking at his son, he tried again. "Then I'm sure we can come to some sort of negotiation. Peyton doesn't have to have Roman's name. We'll write it in the contract." Jake hoped this would suffice.

"It's not good enough, Jake," Matthew said, unmoved.

"What gives you the right to just singlehandedly say you get the namesake on the kids?" Jake clamored.

"It's the right all Omegas should have. An Alpha is a part of the reproduction process for an hour, two at most. An Omega's pain physically and mentally begins even before conception. They carry to a full term of six months and then risk their very lives to give birth. It's the least they should get." Matthew turned to Roman. "You'll understand this should you have an Omega pup of your own one day. Then you'll get to decide what you feel passionate about. But Peyton is all we have, and we're fighting for him. Your family gets the honor of knowing you'll pass on your coveted Blood-Type; we get the name."

Matthew's words, which were a comfort to Jake only a few nights ago, were like a fiery blaze burning down every good thought Jake had of him. He also saw Adrian give a look of despair, but the look was also laced with empathy which told him Matthew was hitting a homerun on Omega rights. Jake never anticipated the team Matthew would play against in war was his own family. Finally, he dedicated the moment to his son Roman, who looked like he'd been hit by truck. "Roman? What do you say?"

Roman witnessed a war and ceasefire on his family in a matter of moments, yet he hadn't even been invited to participate. All eyes in the room were upon him now. It was reminiscent of the moment when all wondered if he'd consider the contract in the first place. Now he was being asked to accept a rewriting of the playbook, one he never anticipated he'd have to address.

"I-I just..." Roman started, barely able to form a sentence. "Peyton, is that what you want?"

Peyton saw the unfairness in his mate's eyes. He imagined this whole process going so differently. Thus far, nothing was happening the way it should. Peyton didn't want all this negotiation and paperwork nonsense. He wanted to kiss his mate and seal the partnership in celebration. Peyton wanted to defer to Roman and his wishes, but he couldn't ignore his father's words. If his father's legacy was the only request asked of him, Peyton was willing to support him. "I would like this. Yes," Peyton said clearly. He observed his father's approval in his victorious facial expression.

Roman's face, on the other hand, appeared wounded.

Peyton wanted to do so much: hold out his hand for Roman to grab it, jump across the table and comfort him, say every right word when it all seemed wrong. Something. Anything. But he didn't. He stayed glued in his chair.

"Then we need to discuss the financial support," Jake countered.

"What about it?" Matthew glared.

"Did you honestly think no one was going to notice one of the most financially successful families in Tauris asking for $1200 in welfare?"

Matthew choked. "Welfare? Seriously, come on."

"What do you need it for?"

"It's the principle of it. It's what Omegas are entitled to." Matthew once again spoke in a voice which made all of Jake's objections seem uneducated.

"You get zero, Matthew," Jake said without hesitation.

"That's preposterous!"

"Fated Mate or contracted mate, you'll never get anyone in this city to agree to a namesake change and the amount of financial support you're asking for—I don't care if it's based on salary or not."

Matthew turned his head slightly and his eyes narrowed with amusement. He tapped his hand a few times and smirked. He now understood he wasn't the only successful businessman in the room. Matthew found himself at the pinnacle of compromise or another brawl. Before making a final decision, he turned to his Omega.

Terrence, who had gone through this entire intense display a silent observer, visually expressed his understanding. Without verbalizing it to Matthew, he had made the decision. "We'll accept that: the namesake for the forfeiture of financial support," Terrence confirmed.

"Mr. Erricson," Whitmore's lawyer cleared his throat and stared at Jake, "do we have an agreement on that last request?"

"Yes. We do." It was like knives down Jake's throat to say it. But there it was, his dissent silenced. Jake sensed Matthew's accomplishment in the scent he was giving off. The Alpha wolves had a stand down and the Whitmore Pack won more than what the Erricson Pack wanted to part with—money be damned.

The rest of the contract went by in a blur. Like Roman, Peyton was required to go through the ceremonial questions and confirm all his information to the Erricson family lawyer. The Erricson family's requests were textbook. Matthew's agreement to their terms made it seem like there were no requests at all. With the requests settled, it meant the hard part was over.

"Okay. Now then. Are there any other questions or requests?" The Whitmore's lawyer looked up and held the gaze of each individual in the room. Everyone was the same: anxiety high, breaths held, and eyes wide and observant. All was approved and cleared. Or so everyone thought.

"A termination clause." Adrian Erricson's voice broke the silence, only to be followed by another Earth-shattering silence. All eyes, ears, and opened mouths fell in his direction.

"A what?" Matthew asked in disgust.

"Dear, what are you doing?" Jake asked in a whisper.

"Yes, what are you doing?" Terrence repeated sternly.

"We want a no-fault clause in case this does not go as planned." Adrian spoke with a firm tone.

The demand was unheard of. A mating contract was sacred, the most serious bond one could make. Breaking any mating contract lent itself to the ultimate public scandal and criticism for an everyday citizen. To break with another well-known and respected family carried dire social consequences, a penalty Adrian wanted to circumvent.

Terrence came alive in a way he rarely ever did. He jumped up in a defensive posture which border-lined threatening behavior. A once kindred spirit, Terrence pointed his finger squarely between Adrian's eyes. "This is a slap in the face to any contract and the divine process it stands on!" His voice was gruff and authoritative.

Matthew looked as if he'd seen a ghost while Jake stood up near his Omega, ready to physically defend if he had to, which made Matthew also stand alongside his own.

Peyton's hand was over his mouth in shock the minute he felt the table shake with his Veo's momentum. Roman's knuckles were white as he gritted his teeth, ready to spring into action to protect his own beloved Veo. And yet, through all of it, Adrian sat there still, face unmoved as if he'd complimented the family with affection.

"Doing this is nothing but a means to an end," Matthew said plainly.

"No," Adrian replied, "this is business. Perhaps everyone should have one. This contract is avant-garde as it is; let's show just how serious we are."

"This is cowardice!" Terrence stressed.

"You're wrong. This is showmanship for just how serious we'd take a contract. Nothing to lose, nothing to gain. Unless you feel this is just all a ruse."

"We don't think that," Terrence replied.

"Neither do we," Jake affirmed.

Matthew huffed a couple of times while tapping the outside of his hip with his fist and staring at the ceiling. "Fine. Add it in."

Terrence gasped. "You can't be serious," he pleaded.

"Do it," Matthew commanded.

With Jake leading, all slowly returned to their seats. Terrence contrived a calming breath and looked at his son. Peyton held a forced smile, and this time, he reached out his hand to comfort his Veo.

Jake whispered into his mate's ear, "I am so turned on by you right now." Adrian hummed politely as to not appear boasting or bragging.

"I'll just add that here." Jake's lawyer wrote down the addition with an unwavering professional tone. "Just sign here and here, and we'll get copies made."

"I can do that right after this, if you want to stand by," Matthew's lawyer replied. Jake nodded as he triumphantly signed his name. Adrian followed and pushed it back over to Matthew, as was customary. Terrence followed. He looked up at Roman, trying to appear as natural as possible.

The contract made it to Roman, and he saw the signatures. He looked at the overwhelming bleached white page with its dark writing. Here was the point of no return. The process was a page out of a horror movie, his disappointment ruining this expected celebratory tradition. Roman took in stagnant oxygen and breathed out.

As he signed, he thought, *This is the worst of it. Happiness awaits me shortly.* He looked up at Peyton who was equally distraught, a comfort to him knowing his emotions weren't overreactive nor out of place.

As the paper met the middle of the table, his hand was complimented by Peyton's on top of his, and his heart skipped a beat.

Peyton relished the few seconds his hand sat atop Roman's. Somehow the simple touch assured him victory was near. Seeing Roman's deliberate handwriting on it made him smile. After the final pen stroke, it was done. It was here: Roman Edward Erricson and Peyton Reginald Whitmore were contracted mates.

"All right," the Erricson lawyer sighed. "I think we are good. We'll wait around for the copies." He examined the temperature of the room. "If all parties are interested and willing, at this time, a few moments are usually given to the newly paired to be on their own. We can leave them in the room if you'd like?"

Looking for any sign of disagreement, Jake spoke first, "I'm okay with that."

"Same here," Matthew added.

The room cleared, and with it went all the rich antagonizing pheromones the families exuded. Peyton looked at his new Alpha, his mate, his partner. A slight color flushed his cheeks. "Hi" was all he could manage, unsure of what to say or do next.

"Hi," Roman laughed back. Roman observed his new Omega. The excitement expressed by his mate was charming and undeniably sexy. It was hard to believe the young man in front of him was his, and he Peyton's. He felt as if he could shake himself awake, and all of this would have been some sick joke. But time passed slowly, and no such extra burst of consciousness occurred. The genuine excitement was lost to him up until now. He slid his chair back slightly and pushed off.

For Peyton, the mere sight of Roman getting up to walk toward him sent pheromones rushing throughout his body and his breathing quickened. On weak legs, he stood mere inches away from his Alpha. His breath brushed over Roman's soft shirt. Unsure of what to do, he glanced up at Roman, who slowly put his hands on Peyton's shoulders. He ran them down Peyton's arms, and he felt his body shake. With an uncomfortable stretch, Peyton lifted his mouth to Roman's.

Roman's eyes approved, and he kissed Peyton; his lips were soft and electrifying. Peyton had never experienced anything like this before; he involuntarily inhaled and kissed Roman back with confidence. It was sweet, slow, and cautious.

Peyton felt a brush of sadness when Roman disconnected, but he didn't want to feel as if was too eager or needy. Unfortunately, his own body betrayed his calm face as he felt the blood rushing and pulsing in his reproductive organs. Peyton felt his shaft lengthen in his pants while insides churned fresh slick, waiting for Roman's next move.

Roman sensed all of Peyton's wants and needs. He held back any subtle urges he had in order to wait for an authentic moment to go further. For a show of effort, he pulled Peyton in for a deep embrace. Stroking Peyton's hair and the back of his neck allowed Roman to breathe in that scent of his which was starting to become familiar to him. It was strange for Roman to feel what he was in those moments.

When they both heard the knock at the door, Roman was the first to let their embrace go. As he did, the connection drifted. It faded farther away as Peyton distanced himself. Peyton gave him one last look and smile for the day which he reciprocated. As Peyton returned to his father's grasp, the magnetism was weak and insecure. His gaze fell back to the now empty room which appeared sterile and impersonal.

CHAPTER 07:

A Cavenbelle Celebration
& Criticism

Mikaél sat at the kitchen table reviewing notes from day two of his studies. However, his focus was on his anxiety as he mentally prepared for the arrival of his older brother Drew and his mate. Mikaél loved his brother and his brother-in-law Will, but with Drew being the only Alpha son and the oldest in the family, Mikaél always felt second fiddle in the household when Drew was present. Having Drew and his mate gone for a year gave Mikaél a sense of connection and value previously absent in the house. But as the minute hand on the clock moved higher, Mikaél felt his own presence shrinking—even without his brother there.

"Mik," his Veo spoke, "what's wrong? You seem a bit preoccupied."

Mikaél scrunched his face, thankful he had his back to his father who was pulling a roast duck out of the oven. "Fine."

"Come on, now..." Alec used his best parental voice, setting the pan on the counter.

"What? I'm fine." Mikaél used his most convincing voice.

"I think you can handle your brother being here for one evening." Alec saw his son's shoulders tense.

Mikaél turned to the side, exposing his profile. "I know. It's just, every time he..."

"It will be all right, Mik."

Mikaél sighed. This conversation had played a thousand times, like a broken record. Nothing could be said which he hadn't heard before. He faced the window, waiting for headlights to light up the driveway.

Dustin stepped into the kitchen. "Wow. Smells great." He marveled as his mate continued working on the side dishes. "Do you need anything? Another hand or something?"

"I'm good. Just get your son ready. He looks like he's going to an alternative rock concert."

Dustin eyed Mikaél with disappointment. "Hey, you should clear off the table. They're going to be here any minute, and you're not even dressed."

"What's wrong with the way I look?" Mikaél sat there offended by the comment.

"Change" was Sur's only word.

Knowing he meant business, Mikaél slapped his books on top of each other and pushed the pile back in his bag. Lifting it on his shoulder, he made his way down the hall. As he rounded the corner, Dustin shook his head in amusement.

"Don't push it, Dustin," Alec warned in a calm tone.

"What?"

"You know how he feels."

"He'll be fine." Dustin brushed it off as he darted around the room, making sure everything looked presentable.

Alec exhaled his own defeat; his attention was needed elsewhere. It was like the Harvest Moon meal in here with all the rich smells, serving trays, and cloth napkins. Stepping back from his nearly finished masterpiece, he gazed at it all with approval, giving himself a pat on the back.

Mikaél walked back to the foyer when he heard his brother-in-law finishing his conversation with Dustin about how his parents were doing—emphasizing how both he and Drew had seen them this past weekend. All casually watched Mikaél walk in with his gray sweater and damp hair. On his face, he wore a half-hearted smile. Drew was the first to make a move for a "bro hug."

"Mik! Good to see you," Drew called in a deep voice. Mikaél stood there, unmoving. "Come on. Don't miss out on this." Drew basked in his own spotlight.

The first thing Mikaél remembered about his brother smacked him in the face—literally. Drew's considerable height pushed his muscled chest into his petite brother. It was like hugging a brick wall.

Drew possessed very similar facial features and hair as Mikaél. The only difference was Drew's dominant facial structure which came naturally from being an Alpha. His large body frame was barely contained by his white shirt, tucked in by a black belt. Drew's essence was that of an Alpha's too, very of the Earth. The scent was spicy like cinnamon but calmed by a wave of tea leaf. Mikaél's childhood flashed in his mind as he got a strong whiff.

He released himself and repeated the action again with Will. Thankfully, Will's embrace was tender and gentle, which fit everything else about him.

Will's face was larger, forehead longer, body skinnier, and height taller than even Drew, but he was a gentle giant. His blue eyes and translucent skin made him approachable, but it always left Mikaél with a feeling that he was sensitive to the touch as if he'd break. His hair was newly cut with sharp buzzed edges going down on both sides of his face. He wore a loose faux vest shirt with black, gray, and red patterns paired with expensive dark blue jeans. Mikaél secretly enjoyed Will's scent, a sea breeze with a drizzle of cantaloupe syrup.

As he inhaled deep, he must have forgotten just how pronounced the scent was because today it was downright pungent.

"Hi, there." Will sparkled with glittery teeth and a soft persona.

"Good to see you both," Mikaél replied to his brother's earlier comment. There was no faking the statement at this point. Having Will there soothed his anxiety for the time being.

"Well, let's not stand here. Come on in." Dustin gestured his family into the kitchen, the proverbial gathering place.

Drew and Will automatically walked to the bar stools at the right side of the kitchen. Behind it sat a rarely used carpeted patio. Dustin leaned on the empty part of the island not owned by the gas range, taking in his son and son-in-law.

Upon seeing them, Alec walked up and embraced them with gusto.

After his hug with Will, Mikaél swore he saw a wink go from his Veo to Will. But it was so quick and nonchalant, he didn't think to investigate it further. Mikaél stayed in the kitchen hallway near the oven which was keeping the side dishes and bread warm.

The initial conversations were small talk: "How are you doing? How is work? How is school?" Afterward, a few comments and jokes about politics set the evening in motion. Mikaél mostly watched unless spoken to, rocking back and forth on the balls of his feet. Looking to his far left, he saw twilight in the distance. Any other time, this view would be breathtaking, but tonight it was a sign that time was moving very slowly.

"Are we hungry?" Alec asked with anticipation.

The whole family sat down at the kitchen table. Dustin and Alec sat across from each other as heads of household. Mikaél managed to get to the table quick enough to get his favorite seat facing the scenic windows. The chair next to his left stayed vacant as Will chose the chair across from him, and Drew sat next to Will on his left.

The smells from the duck, seasoned potatoes, and freshly prepared vegetables filled the air and combined with the soothing warmth of freshly baked bread. Dustin went around and filled each wine glass with Pinot Noir, giving a gentle glance to each person as he did.

Mikaél found the food and drink comforting; it gave himself something to do and focus on instead of his awkward stares at Drew who was, no surprise, controlling all conversation.

"...and that's when Dr. Chase said he'd take me on as an intern for his human physiology studies," Drew announced. "Of course, I assured him he was making the right choice." He pressed his large hand against his rock-hard chest as he lifted his glass with the other to take a satisfying drink.

Sur and Veo gasped with pride. "I knew you'd do great things." Dustin beamed as his attention shifted to Alec. "Didn't I tell you he was going to do great things?"

"That's fantastic news," Alec affirmed.

"A toast," Dustin held up his glass, "to hard-earned and well-deserved success."

Mikaél almost missed lifting his glass as he tried to finish the bite of food on his fork. But he did just in time and played along. However, when the wine touched his lips, he found it difficult to tilt the glass back down.

Dustin noticed immediately. "Whoa, let's take it easy on that."

"What?" Mikaél asked, trying to play coy.

"Just because you're 18 in a few months doesn't mean you get to drink to your heart's content. You'll become an inebriated fool," Dustin corrected.

"So, in three months, when I'm legally able to drink, I can become one then?"

Dustin gave his son a look which meant not to press the issue.

Drew, with his mental high, felt like he should keep the momentum going. "Dad, it's not like the lightweight can handle much. One more and you could roll him up and lay him out on his bed and wouldn't see him until tomorrow morning." Drew grinned.

"Drew," Will uttered, giving his mate a look.

Drew readjusted his posture. "So, Mik, how is Level 2 going?" Drew asked like it was a peace treaty.

"It's Level 2. I can't imagine it's changed in the few years you've been there," Mikaél replied.

"Does that mean Dr. Birowack is teaching you then?" Drew inquired.

"Yep."

"Has he picked on you yet?" Drew laughed.

"I don't know if I'd say that," Mikaél defended.

"Oh man, the first day I walked into Birowack's class…" Drew took another opportunity to talk about himself and the whole room gladly gave him every bit of attention.

Here we go, Mikaél thought. He grabbed another roll from the breadbasket and prepped it with butter, occasionally looking up to pretend he had never heard the story before. If there was one particular downfall of Drew—Mikaél thought there were many—it was how Drew loved himself so much he assumed every word he said was ingenious, like a highly skilled improv comedian. Thus, Mikaél usually suffered déjà vu every holiday, including Drew's birthday. Like clockwork, the repetitive format of Drew's performance was a success received with laughs and ear-to-ear smiles.

"…so, basically what I'm saying is, Dr. Birowack is a wealth of knowledge. Do what you're supposed to do, and you'll learn amazing things, Mik," Drew finished.

Mikaél forced a look of content.

"I am just so proud of you." Dustin grabbed his son's shoulder with his left hand and shook him proudly. Then, he noticed Will with a generous amount of food on his plate and wine glass untouched. "Will, are you doing okay over there?"

"Hm? Oh yes, thank you."

"It doesn't look you've eaten a lot."

"I'm just taking it slow tonight." He turned to Alec. "It's all very good." Alec nodded in thanks.

Dustin continued, "Do you not like the wine? It doesn't look like you've touched it."

"I'm actually going to hold off the wine until dessert. I brought one with me I've been drinking for awhile."

Drew shook his head. "Don't try it. It tastes like shit."

"Drew!" Will gasped, mildly entertained.

"What? It's true!"

Alec cut in, "I, for one, can't wait to see what you brought for dessert."

"Don't get your hopes up," Will replied. "It's more like what we bought."

"Really?" Alec frowned. "I thought you loved baking. You always make something really good."

"I just haven't found the time or energy lately." Will looked down at his plate. Drew rubbed his neck.

Dustin chimed in, "I understand. Two fairly new mates just out of school, balancing jobs, their relationship. It can be a lot. I remember when your father and I first started together. Mated bliss usually gets you through the first month." He winked at Alec, signaling a joke.

"Eh, maybe more like two weeks," Alec corrected, proud of his words. He lifted himself off his chair and started clearing the table.

"You should have had Mik bake us something. I'm sure he had the time." Drew ate the last bite on his plate.

Will assisted in changing the focus. "Can I help, Alec?" he asked eagerly.

"No, I got it," Drew insisted.

Will exhausted the energy he was saving to get up. He smiled at his Alpha as he strutted himself into the kitchen with a pile of dishes.

"I can help, too," Mikaél added, not to be outdone by his older brother.

Loud dishes, running water, and cupboard noises drowned out a casual conversation between Will and his Sur-in-law.

Alec asked Drew if he would wash while Mikaél dried. Although Drew agreed, he gave Mikaél the "Yeah right" face, which meant Mikaél was washing, and Drew was drying.

"So, you holding down the fort?" Drew asked, looking at his younger brother, wondering whether or not he had eaten in the last month.

"I guess. Things are uneventful around here for the most part. Veo's got an exhibit coming up soon." Mikaél handed him a clean, wet heavy serving plate to dry.

"Yeah, he said that. Will and I should be there. How is Laycin?"
Mikaél ridiculed, "You care?"

"About him? No. You? Maybe a little." Drew smirked.

"Why?" Mikaél chose to concentrate on the dishes rather than give his undivided attention to his brother.

"You look miserable."

That made Mikaél look up. "Uh, thanks? Can't imagine why."

"You don't even look like you're here tonight."

"Hm. I haven't noticed." Mikaél played it up with sarcasm. Drew was going to have to work harder than that to get the rise he wanted. "Anyway, mated life still going good?"

Drew looked at his brother in awe. His question was authentic and considerate. He decided to answer back in the same way. He rubbed his eyebrow. "It's...life-changing. It's one thing to know you have a Fated Mate out there, and it's quite another to know he's in your bed every night safe and happy. And that's great..."

"But?" Mikaél was listening carefully at this point.

"Everything is more...adult."

"Ew." Mikaél's face scrunched.

"Not like that, dumbass." Drew searched for the right words. "One day, you are in your room watching T.V., bullshitting on your phone, eating nothing but junk food, smelling like you need a shower, going out with friends, staying up until dawn. And then... bam! The next day you are responsible: you clean up, you stay presentable, you spend your time making the most of it, and use every waking moment pleasing your mate."

"Yikes. How...enticing." Mikaél handed Drew another large plate, breaking his reflective trance.

"I know how it sounds. My words are bad. You're better at using them. Always have been."

"Wow! A compliment! Didn't know you had it in you."

Drew's face lit up. "Yeah, I guess mated life softens you a bit, too. Makes you rethink other priorities, too."

"Like?" Mikaél handed him the last glass.

"Trying to be a better older brother?"

"Uh-huh." Mikaél stared down at the sink, trying to find any rogue pieces of silverware. After none were found, he let out the dirty water and flushed it with the tap. This was all the distraction he needed to not engage in this sorry attempt of an apology seventeen years in the making.

Drew's face soured. "That's it? That's your response to that?"

Alec looked over just for a moment, trying to gauge whether or not he needed to be referee.

Will noticed Drew's arms open and palms up as if he'd unfairly lost a game.

Mikaél sensed eyes staring in his direction, and he dropped his voice lower. "Who is this 'Being a better brother' really for? Me or you?"

"Me? What do you mean is it really for me?" Drew looked perplexed.

"Oh, stop it, Drew. Of course, it's about you." Mikaél found a clean towel and dried his hands. "It's always about you," he muttered. Mikaél saw his Veo set out dessert plates and found it a perfect getaway to find the fridge, opening to reveal a multi-flavor cheesecake.

"Ooo, that looks nice," Alec gushed. "Okay, Will, I forgive you for not making a dessert."

After the joke subsided, plates, silverware, and Riesling were distributed. Will got up and pulled the mysterious wine he had been holding for dessert out of the decorative bag which held the cheesecake.

"You need an opener for that?" Alec asked, ready to get up and help.

"No, no!" Will insisted. "It's a screwcap anyway." Will got a couple of strange looks from Dustin and Alec. Walking back over, Will rejoined the rest of his family at the table, bringing a glass of his concoction with him. Drew, on the other hand, bit his lip and pretended like the comment was never said.

"Wow," Dustin said. "Not only does it not have a cork, but the bottle also doesn't even get brought to the table. This must be a pitiful wine," he joked.

"You want to taste it, Sur? Take a walk on the wild side?" Drew egged on.

"Quite the invitation there. How can I resist?" Dustin replied dramatically.

"Oh, come on. This way I can have another person to heckle him with."

Will stared at his father-in-law, practically jumping at the opportunity to give it to

him, smiling like it was going to be quite the entertaining result.

Dustin held out his hand like he was getting ready to taste a piss-poor attempt at a potato derivative. But to play along, he sniffed the glass first: plain, neutral, nothing exciting, though the smell did seem off for a reason he couldn't put his finger on. After one college-try, he attempted to think of characteristics as it sat on his tongue. But the words didn't come right away.

"And?" Alec asked.

Dustin's face showed true efforts in a guessing game. "It hits okay at first; I'm not feeling like I've been poisoned." He laughed. "After that, it disintegrates to nothing. But something is off with this." He sniffed the glass again. "Does this even have alcohol in it?"

"No," Will replied firmly, satisfied as he looked at Drew.

Drew himself looked oddly void of emotion. He didn't do his usual frat boy, overdramatic slam; he just sat there waiting. Dustin looked at his son and son-in-law trying to figure out the puzzle box.

It only took a second for Alec to connect the dots as an Omega easily does. His eyes grew wide, and he inhaled with elation, looking at both men for some sort of signal his intuition was right. When Will cracked a smile first, he knew his sense of smell was right all along.

"Oh. My. Wolf-God!" Alec exclaimed, body shaking in excitement.

"What?" Dustin asked, still not in on it. "Is Will going sober?"

Drew rolled his eyes. "No, dad! We're pregnant!"

Joyous thunder radiated off of Alec.

Dustin barely registered the words as the inner jubilation grew. "What? Really?" Dustin yelled. Now he got it.

Simultaneously, Mikaél observed his parents jump up to give their expecting sons a hug. After hugging one, they exchanged and hugged the other. Mikaél wanted to get up with the same emotion, but his heart hardened in the moment.

"I knew it; I knew it! I could scent it when I first hugged you. How far along are you?" Alec rambled.

"Eight weeks in. We're expecting delivery in January."

"How wonderful." Dustin turned. "Mik, get in on this family hug," he insisted.

Mikaél did as he was told. The five them completed a not-so-co-ordinated hug. The pheromone jumble was a bit of a headache. His plastered smile showed clear cracks and fractures.

Drew noticed and had the gumption to exploit it. "Are you okay, Mik?" He tried reading his younger brother. "In shock, right?" Drew's nerves radiated down his back.

"Yep. In shock. Congratulations," he said to Will. Will smiled back in thanks.

Mik stood back and waved his hands back and forth at hip level, hitting his hands together in casual fists when they met in the middle. Not wanting to fake it anymore, he turned and walked to the other side of the kitchen which led to the connected outdoor patio. He opened the door and stepped onto the wooden planks, breathing the fresh air and facing the generous backyard and never-ending tree line. This side of the house was technically a walkout basement, so he couldn't see the scenery in the now pitch-black sky.

As expected, everyone stared in an awkward silence. Some knew while others had no clue why Mikaél walked out, much less refused to share in the moment.

"Excuse me." Alec sighed as he chased after his younger son. Behind him, he could hear Dustin repeat congratulatory sentiments. He found Mikaél leaning on the railing. His body was lit from the generous light radiating off the kitchen through the French doors. "Mikaél Alexander, this was really not the time!"

Mikaél shut his eyes. "Look, I tried. I can't do it."

"Can't do what? Be happy for your brother? Hold up being selfish until at least after they left?" His Veo was usually calm, riding a smooth wave like he belonged in a generation of hippies. But not now. Now, he was a commanding parent.

"That's what I've always been asked to do! 'Mikaél, can't you just stand there and be proud of your brother's honorary academic awards? Can't you just stand there and be proud of your brother's athletic awards? Can't you just stand there and be proud of his stature, cleverness, presence, his status as first born, his Fated Mate, their unborn child, his status of being the Alpha in the household?'

That's what I've always done! It's always about him. When does it stop?!"

"You stopped it tonight! That's for sure," Alec clapped back.

"Look, you and Dad can turn a blind eye and live in La La Land, but I can't. I'm sick of it."

"Do you honestly think we don't care about you? You're smarter than that," Alec patronized.

"I think you and Sur are more than happy showing off Drew like he's a trophy and have no problems with asking me to dust and polish it when there's a chance he might not look perfect." Mikaél looked at his Veo, hoping something he said sank in.

"Look, I get it. I grew up with two Alpha brothers in a family of six. I wasn't even the youngest, and I still got the shaft. That's just what Omegas deal with," Alec revealed.

"So, what does that mean?" Mikaél asked flabbergasted. "That this is okay?"

Alec paused and stared at the little bit of grass illuminated about twenty feet below him. His tone changed drastically. "No." A pregnant pause again. "No, that's not what it means." This time his gaze went out to the stars trying break the blackened sky. "I tried to have a conversation like this with my Veo once." Alec hinted at a smile as he went down memory lane.

"What did Grandpa Veo say?" Mikaél inquired with curiosity.

"Not much at all really."

"Why?"

"Remember I said I tried. This was thirty years ago. Times were different then. My Veo wasn't going to entertain a conversation like that. He had four pups in an eight-year timespan. Giving a spotlight to an Omega child with two Alphas and a Beta as siblings? It was never going to happen."

"So, what did happen?"

"I endured it. Didn't have much choice. I knew if I had an Omega pup of my own, I wasn't going to take the same approach. I'd like to think I didn't, no?" Alec's face appeared vulnerable. He was ready to take the criticism should Mikaél say he was doing wrong by his child.

"I am tired of feeling like I've been ignored."

"I don't think 'ignored' is the right word. Your brother has a loud and commandeering personality. And I have to admit, Sur does little to tame him."

"You think?" Mikaél snorted.

"I notice these things. But I also know you, my Omega. You are quietly passionate. I'm confident if you could write, paint, or read your emotions to someone who cared to listen, you'd be leaps and bounds over your brother. That's why you and I mesh so well. We're both like that. Will is a bit like that too. He couldn't be an A-type personality like your brother. Drew couldn't withstand that."

"Yeah, but the difference between Drew and Will is I like Will," Mikaél gruffed.

"See?" Alec's face drew into a smile. "I think you and Will have a lot in common. I know he's found his voice by now. But you? I think you're still working on it, babe. You should talk to Will about it sometime. See what he has to say."

"Right. When am I ever going to find a time to talk to Will long enough to have a conversation without Drew breathing down his neck?"

Alec turned to see a shadow blocking the light coming from the house. "How about right now?"

Mikaél whipped around to see the gentle giant walk out to the patio, his footfalls pronounced. Alec patted Mikaél's shoulder softly before walking back in, leaving Will and Mikaél alone.

Although he was gracious for the opportunity, Mikaél felt the need to clear the air first. "I apologize for what I did in there. I really am happy for you and Drew. I think you'll both make great parents."

Will shone in his ethereal way. "I know you are. And thank you. I appreciate that. I think you'll make a great uncle, too."

Mikaél looked at Will's kind and beautiful face, almost dangerous. Then his eyes wandered down to the noticeable puff of fabric around his stomach. "That's why you wore that sweater, isn't it? To hide any sign of a bump."

Will nodded, impressed by his connection. "You got it."

"When Veo said he smelled it on you when you first walked into the kitchen and winked, I started to wonder if I did too when I met you at the door."

"They say another Omega is always the first to know. Alphas apparently are good with it as long as it's their own Omega. Otherwise, they mostly mistake it for an onset of heat."

"I bet Drew loves that." Mikaél imagined Drew guarding Will with a baseball bat in a grocery store or down in Tauris Square.

"He's the protector, that's for sure. Not that I need protecting." Will stood up straight to emphasize the fact he wasn't a pushover physically. He rubbed his stomach for a moment like an expectant Omega.

In doing so, Mikaél wondered if he was a pushover emotionally. "There's something I've always wanted to ask you."

"Of course." Will listened in with an open ear and open heart.

"I know they say the pull of a Fated Mate is tremendous, but do you think if you weren't Fated to my brother, you'd still love him the way you do?"

Will grinned; he was entertained by the question which truly fell into the category of "Gross, you like my brother?" He spoke, "Believe it or not, being Fated and being loved are two different things."

"Really? Everyone describes it as the same," Mikaél spoke, clearly unconvinced.

"People describe it the same way because the feeling is intoxicating. No one categorizes it as different because they don't want it to be different."

"So, what's the difference then?"

"Being Fated means Wolf-God has given you someone special in the world to be your mate and have the desire to procreate," Will said succinctly.

"See, that's where I have trouble. That doesn't sound different to me at all," Mikaél defended.

"It's very different! Think about it. We're descendants of wolves. Wolves form packs, ranks, and yes, even take mates to make certain they survive. That's fate; that's what we all do. But a wolf never lived to be 60." Drew softened his tone. "A wolf never built a house, made clothes, cooked a meal, provided for education and luxury, championed for rights, celebrated birthdays or holidays, or wondered who would be there unconditionally until death. That's what love is for."

Mikaél was lost for words. For once tonight, someone was speaking his language. "I knew there was a reason why I liked you."

"And this is the reason why I like you. I could never have this sort of conversation with your brother." Will gave a goofball face which made Mikaél laugh.

"Speaking of, you didn't answer my question about being with my brother."

Will's eyes reflected for a moment in the corners of the wooden deck where the light met the dark. He looked back into Mikaél's waiting eyes. "Yes. Even if I wasn't his Fate, I'd still love him."

Mikaél squinted his eyes. "Hmm. More power to you."

Will laughed. "Oh, believe me, there are days. There. Are. Days."

"He doesn't push you around or try to make you feel less of yourself, does he?" Mikaél sighed, comforted and unnerved that he was finally able to ask it. And yet, he didn't want to push onto Will all the memories he didn't like about his brother. It wasn't his problem.

"He definitely has an opinion or advice once in a while about his passions. But at the end of the day, he's only going to get so far with it. We're two different people, and we complement each other nicely in that way. And like I've pointed out before, if I feel slighted, he's only taller than me when he's on top of me." Will winked.

"Didn't need that visual." Mikaél's face scrunched. Will giggled, proud of himself for getting the reaction he wanted. Mikaél looked down at Will's stomach. "Can I..."

"Hm?" Will followed the dotted line from Mikaél's gaze. "Oh, sure!" Will lifted his shirt to reveal a noticeable bump in an otherwise lean, muscled abdomen speckled with a few beauty marks.

"Right now, there's really no difference. Just a pooch. When we told my Veo last weekend, he practically glued his hand to my stomach like he was going to feel it kick already."

"Huh. Neat," Mikaél replied.

The patio door made a noise again and a much broader silhouette stepped out. Drew held the door open with a cold, emotionless face. "Come on, Will. We're going to head out." His words were quick and directive.

"Drew, I'm..." Mikaél attempted.

"Save it, Mik. Some other time." Drew's eyes never lost sight of Will. His Omega sighed and gave Mikaél a big comforting hug, then squeezed his arm for good measure.

Mikaél's face cautiously looked back at his older brother who appeared to fall back into the brooding stance he knew all too well. The familiar feel of dominance and threat sent a chill down his spine. In retrospect, Mik realized it was this he didn't like about his brother the most, and everything else perhaps was his own hang up.

After his brother and brother-in-law left, Mikaél stayed outdoors, soaking in the breezy air just a bit longer. Without Will's words warming his senses, the air was colder, harsher.

CHAPTER 08:

A HIERARCHY OF SEX

"Got your tissues ready?" Siro asked, flexing his eyebrows. He didn't have to do much with his dark golden eyes. They already had that "bad boy" and "come hither" look. He could get anything he wanted with those eyes: a lucrative job with no training, a perfect test score without studying, a mate without asking, or someone else's mate without telling.

The inconsistent stubble on his chiseled cheekbones and chin held his 24-year-old Alpha face in the balance between a grown-up boy and a young man. Siro could swing whichever way he wanted. His brown hair was natural, though his blond highlights weren't, and he resembled a suave actor in the golden age of film, except for the few waves of hair falling gently over his forehead. His small tight frame was exotic, model-perfect, and to look at Siro was to see perfection. However, hearing him speak revealed his Achille's heel.

"Why? Are you gonna drop your drawers?" Roman teased, looking at his friend.

"Who knows? Maybe. Unless we're getting some stupid black and white shit with pictures of old guys in lab coats pointing at diagrams with metal sticks like we did back in adolescent school." Siro reached into his pocket, pulled out a piece of gum, and balled it up before shoving it in his mouth like a dog. He wished he had a

cigarette in its place, but that wasn't going to fly with Dr. Birowack—
nor any instructor in the school for that matter.

"And what are you hoping for exactly?" Nico tilted his head forward to better see Siro sitting to Roman's right. While Siro's looks
made a man want to kill, Nico's looks made a man want to love. Nico
could have walked right out of a romance novel with his wistful
expression. His hazel eyes were so moist with vulnerability, no one
could guess what was on in his mind. Although Nico appeared tall
and statuesque, he lacked muscular definition for a guy whose face
was like an oasis in a hot desert. Just a few lines defined a chest, arms,
and waist covered by a soft gray summer shirt. He loved working on
automobiles outside, a hobby which gave his skin a sun-kissed look
that contrasted beautifully with the whites of his eyes. His short
shaggy hair was roughly combed but naturally parted on the side.

"How about some hot muscle dick knotting some innocent
18-year-old hole bent over on a couch in a sketchy apartment?" Siro
gave a Wolf-Devil grin, waiting for his closest friends to react—and
react they did, eyes wide as they barely held back the laughter.

"Holy hell, Siro!" Roman whispered as the empty seats in front
of them filled.

"That was very specific. Did you watch that this morning?" Nico
half-teased.

"No." Siro paused, then winked. "It was last night."

Any other spot in the classroom and they'd have the disgusted
eyes of everyone else in the room looking. But luckily sitting in the
farthest highest elevated seats, they didn't have to test the theory.
No one ever missed this particular class; all the seats filled up early.

"So," Siro said, carefully waiting for Roman's defense, "when
were you going to tell me you got contracted?" He gave Roman the
"Yeah, I found out, you motherfucker" look.

Roman grunted as he stared down Nico—signaling he dis-
proved of his betrayal. "I don't know—in the year of never?" His
face whipped to Siro to return an equally fierce "Get real" look.

"What's up your ass?!" Siro replied, offended he was being treated so unfairly.

"Shhh! Wolf-God, keep your voice down. We can talk about this later."

"You're damn right, we're talking about this later," Siro assured him.

Right on time, Dr. Birowack entered the mini auditorium for his lecture. "Gentlemen, welcome to your last unit regarding sex and reproduction education for your clinicals." The room clapped at his dry humor. "Now I know, for most of you, this will be a review of content at this point, but we also like to mix this with genetics, so there will be some academic validity for everyone who considers themselves 'sexperts'—so to speak." The room responded with laughter and jeers. "In addition, this class will show you content no other class will see, and I plan to keep it that way. Therefore, all electronic devices go off. If I find proof any one of you leaked this to younger viewers, we're headed back to textbooks and stick figures for the rest of the year. You have sixty seconds to do so, starting now."

"Yeah, that's what I'm talking about," Siro sang as he pulled out his phone and gladly shut it off. Roman and Nico followed with not quite as much vigor.

"You are such a hornball," Nico commented.

"And what are you? Asexual? Please! I've heard about you getting your engine serviced regularly by different dudes. Oh, and your car too."

Nico stared, annoyed. "Yeah, I heard you have to do tally marks on the walls now because your bedpost was too worn down."

"Ooo, good one, Nico. Your daddy tell you that one?"

"Stop, you two! Damn!" Roman intervened.

Nico and Siro gave each other one last stare before giving Dr. Birowack their full attention. It wasn't as if they were enemies by any means, but "frenemies" had a nice ring to it. Without Roman as the glue keeping them together, they wouldn't be in the same social circle. Unfortunately for Nico, this was his only social circle.

Siro liked to hop around the different crowds which fully accepted him. What Siro liked about this threesome the most was neither Roman nor Nico came across as fake or pitifully trying to impress him for attention and approval.

Dr. Birowack introduced the content. His words were few because the film spoke for itself. With most students near 24 and in their final steps of education, nothing from this part of the lecture was new. As a matter of fact, several men in the class were already Fated or contracted. A few even appeared or scented pregnant. But this particular film had its value in being graphic and educational—a combination not available to any other level. It was a nice gift at the end of a long and tedious journey.

The real challenge of watching the film was not to get aroused to the point of it being obvious or worse—uncontrollable. Should a generous amount of Alphas start leaking pre-fluid and Omegas start producing slick in a confined space, this might as well be an orgy class from all the hormones fuming like the musty, unmistakable smell of gym locker room.

As the film started, it was quickly determined Siro was going to have to settle for a compromise. Both subjects in the film appeared in their late 20's. The Alpha was indeed a dominant specimen, muscular and driven, but his Omega was equally built and cumbersome. The only difference, of course, was the Omega being overtly submissive—downright slutty, to be frank. Since there was a goal, this wasn't going to be a leisurely entertaining film with gratuitous amounts of foreplay and extended fucking; however, the film intentionally did close-ups on some very interesting scientific responses to arousal. The first was expected: flushed skin and protruding pheromone glands in the neck from blood spreading to the reproductive organs in response to anticipated consummation.

During sex, a wolf-descendant's eyes dilated. The Alpha started first, and the Omega followed when he submitted—a clear physical sign of permission to move forward, other than the typical uncontrollable organ response. The next step was known but not discussed in casual conversation. Interestingly enough, both ranks produced slick in a similar way. But Alphas had such a different chemical make-up, the natural response was minimal in most. To have an Alpha produce comparable amounts of slick to an Omega indicated a severe biological fault resulting in inactive sperm.

Although both ranks produced pre-seminal fluid, an Alpha produced three times as much, including semen, during orgasm. Both were capable of multiple orgasms, and in an average copulation, there would be three separate orgasms with almost no refraction period needed unless the Alpha produced a knot. Once that happened, an Alpha's physical energy greatly reduced by comparison and required more time should another session follow.

Watching these very visible and dedicated body responses in both ranks was a hypnotic spell. No one shouted; no one whispered. The Alpha in the film triggered a very generous response in his Omega. Sounds of his moans became deafening at times.

The smell of pheromones in the room began to simmer.

Roman suffered more than most from this sexual agony, and it was visible to both Siro and Nico.

Siro reveled in his friend's discomfort, gratified to watch him squirm—karma for not telling him about the contract.

Nico's response differed drastically. His face was soft and empathetic. Roman noticed Nico's gaze in his peripheral, and occasionally, the two made eye contact, but Roman tried to focus as best as he could on the film. Nico took Roman's periodic glances as permission to do it more as a friendly reminder to Roman he was there for him.

Roman's leg bounced and his skin became very warm. He heard Siro sigh, a deep sexual growl which only exacerbated the problem.

As his leg became more audible, Nico pushed his leg over to touch Roman's, causing some initial friction. Roman slowed his leg to a stop and exhaled a couple of deep breaths, allowing him to not focus on the front of his pants beginning to tighten.

The film transitioned for the preparation of penetration. The close-ups at this point drew murmurs from the crowd which Dr. Birowack put a stop to quickly. In the film, the Omega laid on a long leather inclined bench. With his leg lifted with the assistance of the Alpha, the light reflected a ridiculous amount of slick covering the legs, testicles, and fully erect cock. Liquid dripped from both his urethra and anal opening, meeting in the middle of his taint and dripping down on the dark leather fabric, once again exploited by the bright shining lights. The Alpha's response to his proud work turned his movements primal. He dug three fingers into the Omega's hole without hesitation (a clear sign of foreplay not shown in the film) with an impressive inside view of the Omega getting his very swollen slick glands stroked so they gushed out more liquid. After extracting his large fingers, the Alpha rubbed the slick all over his chest and licked it, another animalistic response to later send the message to others he claimed the Omega as his. And finally, he inserted his very large erect member and began a rhythmic pattern.

Lightheaded, Roman felt his own pre-cum flex out of him. Knowing the sticky fluid was forming a small pool, he had to read-just in the seat. As he shifted, the air moved around him, and he inhaled a strong scent of Nico's slick. Nico must have sensed him inhale again, this time deeper and longer, a sign he caught the scent, because Roman noticed Nico make longer, stronger attempts to make eye contact. It was difficult, psychologically difficult not to engage him, but he managed.

In the climactic finish, another inside camera view of the Omega showed a swollen orb, a womb, drop above the Omega's slick glands. The Alpha's penis extended, sensing it, and began to hit it with force. Layers of the womb began to wear down, and with one more thrust, he was inside it. Returning to the outside, a view of the upper half of the Alpha's shaft expanded to an even larger size, and with one more thrust, the knot was formed with the Omega's internal muscles holding it. The final inside view showed the womb muscles contract around the Alpha's engorged head, and it pulsed several times before stopping: the insemination was complete. The film ended with a narrator explaining the knot would cause both Omega and Alpha to orgasm again in an interval to signal the slow decline of the knot—very slow actually. According to the film, it could take another ten to twenty minutes for the knot to subside, totaling an average of an hour-long session.

Suddenly, the film screen blazed white and the bright lights flashed on. Moans and groans came from every corner of the room. The entire room of men adjusted themselves in their seats from a rollercoaster ride they weren't prepared for, though no one stood up yet. It was an obvious sign there wasn't a dry man in a chair. Dr. Birowack changed the large screen, preparing for his presentation afterward.

"What the hell was that?" Roman asked, panting lightly.

"Looked like this morning for me," Siro said delightedly.

"You're not serious?" Roman replied.

"Of course, I'm serious. If I hadn't, I'd look like the two of you thirsty pups right now," Siro hummed.

Roman sighed heavily once more, rubbing his forehead where it met his hairline. A small amount of perspiration stuck to his fingers. He glanced back over to Nico who was hunched down in his seat a bit, looking back at Roman like he'd run a mile while dehydrated. Roman looked at the floor, reflecting on the constant soul stares Nico felt compelled to repeat during the film. He didn't want to read into it, so he gambled on the idea Dr. Birowack was going to ask them to take notes and pulled out a notebook from under his chair as a distraction.

"Any questions?" Dr. Birowack asked with a comedic deadpan face. He was met with a unanimous laugh from his class and continued his introduction.

Roman leaned over to Siro and whispered, "Yeah, I got a question. How come you made us watch this video first and then sit through the lecture afterward?"

Siro nodded. "Because he's a sick fuck like the rest of us."

"He's a Beta. What does he care?" Roman asked.

Nico joined in, "It's probably the punchline. He has no ability to procreate, so he'd like to see us all hot and bothered knowing we're not able to do anything about it."

"Who said we weren't?" Siro offered.

"Uh huh," Roman added.

"Now, gentlemen," Dr. Birowack addressed the class, "there are a lot of considerations one must go through before determining a mate. The first is to look at their Types. Now, who can tell me what they know about Blood Types?" A beat later, without even considering volunteers, he called on Roman. "Mr. Erricson."

Roman nearly flipped out of his chair. Nico gasped and Siro snickered under his breath. "Yes, sir?"

"Blood-Types," Dr. Birowack began, "or just 'Types' as people call them, refer to what? Can you tell me?"

Roman sat up at attention and gulped audibly. "Blood-Types refer to traits. The traits are scored on their strength and purity and averaged up to a number." Roman gazed at Dr. Birowack sitting on the corner of his desk with his arms crossed. The professor studied him but made no effort to affirm or deny his claims or even stop him from talking. "A rate of 1 is lowest, and indicates a pattern of less desirable human traits, closer to our primitive ancestors: the wolves."

"Such as?" Dr. Birowack interrupted.

"Lack of conformity to human and social norms, lower ability and drive to complete higher education, stronger emotional and physical aggression. But it also indicates stronger stability in pregnancy and birth rates."

"How about the other side?" Dr. Birowack got up as he pushed a button. Some notes appeared on the presentation screen above.

"A rate of 5, I guess, is self-explanatory. Typically shows strengths in intelligence and physical abilities. A lot of High-Types find success in business or celebrity careers. They've been patterned to be the closest to primate descendants. Unfortunately, when they do consummate, there's an elevated chance of complications during pregnancy and birth."

"Thank you very much. I did well in hiring your father," he boasted.

Roman groaned in his seat as he began to write down what appeared on Dr. Birowack's screen. Looking to his left, Siro was more interested in drawing phallic symbols. He leaned over to his left and whispered to Nico. "Dodged a bullet on that one." Nico nodded in agreement.

Siro caught wind of it. "Not yet you didn't." Suddenly, Siro raised his hand and in a loud voice asked, "What about Type 6?"

The entire room turned to face Siro with strange faces. But then, in their views, they saw Roman. Many of them put the name "Erricson" and his face together and realized why the question was being asked. Whispers made their way across the room.

Roman was about ready to sucker punch Siro. Instead, he gripped his pencil, one pulse away from snapping it in half.

"Ah, yes, I suppose we do have a celebrity in our presence. Tell me, Mr. LaCroix, what question do you want answered which you feel Mr. Erricson can't already tell you?"

"Yeah, is his disease contagious?" Siro joked. Several gentlemen around them approved of it, judging by their amusement. Roman's control ran out and his fist hit Siro's arm. Siro gave a decent reaction for being surprised, but his composure resurfaced quickly.

"I will dispel any rumor or misconception Mr. Erricson is some sort of deformity or disease. As a matter of fact, he's quite the opposite. He's the diamond in the rough, the needle in the haystack, and so much more. A Type 6 Alpha has the strongest genes for survival and aesthetics. They possess more natural abilities for knowledge, strength, appearance, health, and potentially reproduction."

The accolades left many of the students in awe. For those who already didn't appreciate Roman for who he was, they were enlightened to the point of admiration. Unfortunately, Roman's ears were deaf to any of the compliments.

"What do you mean 'potentially reproduction'?" Roman spoke up, gaining more attention in his direction.

"There are only around 1000 confirmed cases of Type 6 Alphas in the world. Other than knowing they can reproduce, not a lot of science has been dedicated to the study of Type 6 Alphas and their reproductive mates. Therefore, there is not much research on the benefits of their offspring."

Siro interjected, "So just have Roman here impregnate 69 Omegas then. You'll have all the research babies you want plus 1,069 Type 6 Alphas in the world." A few laughs were received, but the room started to die down, turning against Siro and his antics.

Roman grimaced. "Wolf-God! Shut. Up."

"Then I'm glad you are here, Mr. LaCroix, because you clearly have a lot to learn about reproduction." Now the laughs were at Siro's expense, and he relaxed in his seat a bit. "Although it is not impossible, you definitely won't find any right-minded person betting on the fact that—should Mr. Erricsons have, as you say, '69' offspring, was it?" Dr. Birowack looked amused as he continued. "That all of his pups would be Alphas. Well, clearly you can't have a Type 6 Alpha if you don't even have an Alpha to begin with. In addition, you may be interested in knowing that just because a Type 6 Alpha chooses to procreate, it does not automatically produce offspring Alphas to be Type 6."

Roman raised his hand. "Wait, really? But isn't that how genetics works? Those who have the genes have a greater chance than anyone else?"

"'Than anyone else?' Sure. One percent more, assuming the Type 6 Alpha mates with any random Omega. To mate with a Type 5 Omega raises the percentage a few points higher," Dr. Birowack replied.

"Bringing the total to what?" Roman asked.

"Add the one percent to one tenth."

"Seriously?" Roman's eyes grew wide.

"Being a Type 6 Alpha, Mr. Erricson, is not simply flipping over a card. There are 23 chromosomes to be passed on from each parent. To have any chromosome passed on be less than the integrity it takes to be a Type 6 Alpha means there won't be one—hence the scientific anomaly. No one knows what those numbers are; no one knows who someone has to be in order to produce a Type 6. In addition, those same parents can reproduce children who are not Type 6. Therefore, I have dedicated my life's work to the research."

"I'm aware," Roman replied, mentally prepared to recite the speeches his father gave him about what he and Dr. Birowack had dedicated their careers to.

"Then you must be aware, and believe me when I say this, because I never have, nor will I ever describe any student of mine this way: you are indeed special, Mr. Erricson. And it's in the way everyone wishes they could be, even if they don't say it out loud." The room was silent. All eyes were locked on his words, including Siro who had chosen to pay careful attention. Dr. Birowack spoke to all, "That will conclude class for today, gentlemen. Thank you, and remember, any hint of the distribution of the film, and your semester final will be you drawing your own diagrams."

Slowly, the class began packing up, conversations varying from highlights of the instructional film to Roman and his spotlight. Just as the students in the front headed toward the door, Nico stood up. "Dr. Birowack?"

He looked up. "Yes?" He squinted. "Yes, Mr. Hallen?"

"Is there a Type 6 Omega?" Nico asked.

All chatter stopped and movements ceased. Roman looked at Nico, who genuinely appeared to want to know the answer. He joined the rest of his class and gave Dr. Birowack his undivided attention.

Dr. Birowack's face lit up with amusement. "Ah, yes. Conspiracies. The fact that if one exists, the other must also. Like aliens from outer space, the monster under your childhood bed, people turning back into wolves, and decent airplane food, a Type 6 Omega is nothing more than myth."

Nico deflated. "It's just that simple?"

"Indeed. A Type 6 Omega needs not to exist. To categorize an Omega under the same criteria we do as Alphas would mean one expects them to have even more submissive traits or to have a prettier singing voice. No, Mr. Hallen, they do not exist." He squinted again. "I understand your disappointment at the news, Mr. Hallen. Therefore, if you must make an old curmudgeon say again what he vowed to never say at all, then I shall: you are special, too." The class enjoyed the comment and resumed their exit. "Good day, everyone."

CHAPTER 09:

A Warning Call

"Hey boys, there's a good tree over there. Why don't you two fuck like rabbits behind it?" Siro suggested like a smartass. The young men walked to the parking lot, following Siro to his car.

"Fuck off, man," Roman retorted.

"Easy, easy!" Siro stressed. "I'm just playin'."

"We're both over it, okay?" Nico voiced clearly.

"You two were quite the sight in there. I thought you were going to throw down right there and give the entire class a live instructional. I would have recorded it if Dr. Birowack didn't plan on making good on his threats about cutting us off from the videos."

"What do you suppose the incentive is, anyway?" Nico thought out loud.

"Eh, buddies of mine said there's a couple more videos like this he shows." Siro pressed the unlock button on his sleek black car, pulled the driver side door open, and threw his bag in the center of the backseat. Nico and Roman looked at each other uncomfortably.

Roman asked the unspoken question, "We have to sit through that again? Twice?"

Siro nodded with a pleased look plastered all over his face.

"Roman!" A young man with dark hair and even darker skin hurried over to the parking lot with his bag barely hanging onto his shoulder.

Nico recognized him instantly. "Hey, Julian!" He smiled.

Julian lifted his chin and acknowledged Nico only for a moment. "Damn. You guys must have run here."

"Just trying to get out of here before the lunch hour traffic." Roman tapped his textbooks alongside his hip. He glazed over Julian's bright expression and focused on the crowds beginning to file out of Ashershire.

"Crazy film, huh?" Julian's voice trembled.

"It was...something." Roman laughed uncomfortably.

"A masterpiece!" Siro added as he puffed on a cigarette.

Julian shifted his weight with his shoulder bag. "I was wondering if you were available sometime in the next few days for a study session? Maybe get something to eat afterward?"

"Uh-oh." Nico let the words slip from his mouth.

Julian glared back.

Roman's nerves hit his stomach. "I'm sorry, Julian. I have study sessions already set up with Nico and Siro."

Julian's expression fell. "I see. Well, maybe just dinner sometime then?"

"I'd love to," Roman slowly drew out, "but—"

Siro cut him off. "—the celebrity Type 6 just went into contract. He is now," he flicked the butt of his cigarette toward the grass, "unavailable," he exhaled.

Julian nodded and accepted defeat. "Congratulations to you and yours."

"Thanks," Roman returned while holding back every desire to tackle Siro in the parking lot.

Julian finally returned his attention to Nico who was poorly pretending to be busy on his phone. "See you around."

Surprised that Julian was talking to him, Nico barely got a word out before he saw Julian pivot and hastily walk back toward the building with the same pace.

Once Julian was out of sight, Roman growled. "Was that necessary? Did you really have to talk about the contract?"

Siro played innocent. "What? I only said the truth! Now get in the car before we get stuck in the parking lot!"

Roman bit his tongue, unsure whether or not he could choose his words carefully enough. The last thing he needed was a stranger overhearing opinions about his contract which could be misconstrued as negative. Instead, he let Siro enjoy his moment and opened the door to let Nico crawl in the back before he sat in the front passenger seat, beside the enemy.

Siro drove a few blocks down from the campus, passing rows of cars lining the streets. It was lunch hour; and building after building was dedicated to different restaurants. Normally, they visited a burger bar after class, but today, they changed it up for some traditional rice noodles, egg rolls, and fortune cookies.

The restaurant didn't have a terrible wait, but it was enough to let them take in the surroundings. The ceiling was industrial: large vents, filters, beams, and long lights floated down to light the cherry wood floors and dark leather booths. The booth lights were sconces decorated in deep red patterns. Unfortunately, during the day, it was hard to see the real effect they were capable of until the evening. To the right of the cash register, a huge glass plate separated the customers from a loud line of professionals making seafood rolls and steamed dumplings. After they ordered, they filled their drinks and found an open booth in the back corner with a city view of the street. Roman took the moment to relax, looking forward to the food he was about to eat. But the moment wasn't meant to be.

"Now, ya bastard. Confession time. Spill it," Siro demanded, pleased he could say such things to an equally powerful Alpha. Nico watched as he sat next to Roman.

"Okay," Roman huffed. "I am now in a contract with Peyton Whitmore, the son of Matthew Whitmore."

Siro choked on the long drink he was taking of his dark-colored soda. "The fuck?" They were the only words he could get out before going into a full coughing fit. It was a lie to say Nico and Roman didn't enjoy watching him suffer.

"Problem?" Roman asked innocently.

"Are you crazy?" Siro gasped.

"Not more than usual. Why?"

"Dude, I'd sooner die than get into a contract with that shithead!" Siro's eyes were big and searing. He was serious.

"Peyton isn't like that. He's..."

"Don't get stupid on me, Roman! The guy's dad..." Siro blanked, then snapped his fingers. "Matthew! He's psycho! And his creepy Omega isn't any better." Siro peered around, paranoid a Whitmore spy was listening in.

"His Omega? Terrence? He's harmless!" Roman defended.

"Wolf-God, you know his name?!" Siro whined.

"Siro, I'm in a contract with his son. What did you expect me to call him? Mr. Peyton's father?" Roman shook his head, showing Siro he was being stupid and no longer making sense.

"I'm telling ya', he's bad news." Siro pointed his finger at Roman.

After a dramatic pause, Roman asked, "So...do I get to hear the reasons why or do I just have to accept the words of the prophetic ghost who disappears when I blink?" Roman took a sip, noticing Nico's grunt of pleasure at the comment.

Siro growled. "Yeah, laugh all you want."

A waiter came by and delivered food to the table. Nico and Roman prepared to dig in, napkins ready and chopsticks in hand.

Siro moved slower than a snail, still trying to silently communicate to Roman.

"Seriously, Siro. What?" Roman threw down his chopsticks and pushed his food aside to give Siro his undivided attention.

"Okay. You know Wolf Run, right?"

"The new development up north? Yeah. So?"

"Do you remember what it was before the development?"

"You mean, what's still there? It's a preservation. Natives say it houses some of our oldest ancestors."

"There's only two-thirds left of it now."

"Hmm," Roman connected. "Let me guess: Whitmore?"

"Now, you're using your head." Siro pulled in his food and took a few bites, signaling for Roman to do the same. Nico sat there silent, eating contently, occasionally enjoying the view of the ever-changing traffic.

"If you're asking my opinion of it, no, I don't like what happened. It's horrible. The whole preservation should have been kept intact, even at the expense of..." Roman paused.

"Your father-in-law?" Siro pointed out. Nico turned, waiting for Roman to finish.

"Yes," he murmured, "my father-in-law." It was hard for Roman to say it.

"The issue is that's the least of your problems," Siro added.

"There's more?" Roman said sarcastically.

"On one side, you have all the activists and tree huggers like you and Nico shouting at Whitmore to abandon the project." Nico and Roman both glanced at each other, disapproving of his comment. He continued, "But on the other side, you have other competitors trying to get in on the action."

"Siro, Whitmore doesn't build houses. He goes after mineral rights so companies will use his equipment."

"Right you are. So, use your brain power. Who else would be at play?"

Roman thought for a moment. "Easy. Whoever owns the mineral rights. It's either private landowners or the government. But it's a preserve. That means the government owns it."

"See, that's what everyone originally thought. But come to find out, private ownership backed all the way up to the preserve because the government didn't invoke eminent domain when the laws were stronger under conservative control of the legislature. It's rather funny; who the hell wants to live out in Wolf Run? Right?"

"Tauris grew too fast. It's one of the fastest growing cities around. But that doesn't answer the question nor tell me why Whitmore is such a bad guy."

"Shut your hole and listen then," Siro said, putting down his fork. "On the right side is the ocean, to the north is the mountains, and the preserve runs east to west. The government agreed to give up the preserve against the prairie because they claimed it was less consequential. But it was up to the developers to get the major landowners out of there. And not just out of there—out there their way."

"What do you mean?"

"Everyone knows people get rich off of selling minerals to the government, but the second-best lucrative business is who gets it out of the ground."

"Enter Matthew Whitmore," Roman said.

"If Whitmore gets all the landowners to agree to selling the rights directly to the government, the government will use Whitmore's company to do the digging. That's how he makes all his money: government contracts. But if the property owners sell directly to development companies..."

"The development companies get to choose who they want to excavate the land," Roman completed, taking a big swig of his drink.

"Bingo! Private developers aren't going to use Whitmore. He charges premium. And besides, he doesn't need them. The government has him on speed dial. But there were fifteen landowners back then who had to sell their rights. And in the beginning, none of them did."

Nico chimed in, "I remember that. All the news showed them with picket signs right off the highway. One by one though, they all caved. Obviously."

"That's not a surprise, Siro. Whoever got them to finally sell gave them a price they couldn't say no to."

"No. Not 'whoever.' The government. In the beginning, they all said no to them. Ironically, in the end, that's who they ended up selling to."

"So, the government gave them a better bid, Siro. What the fuck?" Roman was restless.

"The government? Really? They'd never do that. The private sector will give them a better deal every time. Besides that, two of those landowners never agreed."

Roman's brow furrowed. "Pretty sure they did, Siro. The neighborhood would have never been built, and the media would have loved to continuously show them fighting 'the man.'"

"You don't think Whitmore has the connections to make certain only good things get said about him?"

Roman sighed. "So, this is what it's about? What are you claiming he did?"

"Well, one landowner randomly turned up in the hospital, and another was found dead supposedly from a heart attack."

"Oh, come on!" Roman roared.

"Yeah, that's a bit crazy, don't you think?" Nico added.

"I'm not sure how it happens, but I don't think Whitmore is one to get his hands dirty. He probably hires a hitman or something. What I know about this city is whatever Whitmore wants, he gets. He doesn't take no for an answer. I know you're his family now or whatever, but I hope you don't ever fall into feeling like you have to do something he wants you to do."

The words hit Roman harder than they should have. He flashed back to a very convincing Matthew Whitmore at dinner and again at the lawyer's office. But then he also remembered how when his own father flipped out on the Alpha, Matthew sat there unchanged. Then there was the freak out Terrence had right after Adrian mentioned the addendum. Both of Peyton's parents had walked out of the contract meeting heated. It was the silent awkward stares of both Siro and Nico which brought his mind back to focus.

"No. There's been nothing like that."

"Good." Siro sighed. "Because I'd hate to see what it's like for you to be on their bad side."

Roman's eyes lit up. "Wow, Siro. I didn't know you cared."

"Ditto on that," Nico said, pushing his empty plate out.

"Look, I understand if I come off a bit harsh, but I always fight for the weaker man who gets bullied for the plain fact they're weaker."

Roman decided to let go the notion that Siro had put him into a "weak" category—a foolish comment considering Roman's strength could overpower Siro's with ease. "With that in mind, how are you so connected and passionate to all this?" Roman asked.

Nico shared while finishing his drink, "His dad was one of the fifteen people who sold his land." Both Roman and Siro looked at him with amazement.

Siro spoke, "How the hell do you know that?"

"What? I've worked on your dad's truck. He likes venting." A light bulb went on. "Ah, that's where you get it from."

Siro looked at Roman. "My Sur always said, 'Whitmore rewards those who follow and punishes those who don't.' I suppose you know the benefits of that."

"You mean the contract?" Roman asked.

"No, the research medical center your Sur works at."

Roman's facial expression revealed his shock. "Huh?"

"Don't you remember the last election? Whitmore backed that corrupt candidate who promised to develop Wolf Run. In one of

Whitmore's disgusting speeches, with his creep Omega by his side, he gave thanks to all his supporters and promised to give back to the city which, in my opinion, he robbed blind and got rich off of in the first place."

"And you're thinking..."

"Your Sur's medical center. That was the gift!"

Roman groaned. "Can we switch to another topic? I'm done with this."

"Whatever, man." Siro held his hands up, defensive and annoyed.

"I got one," Nico offered.

"Thank you!" Roman delighted.

"What's Peyton like?"

Roman considered. "He's shy. He doesn't like really any of the same things I do, but I know he likes me—a lot!"

"Sounds...great?" Nico replied.

"I mean," Roman reflected, "he's adorable and kind. I like him, too. But now that you mention it, he definitely comes across as if he submits to his Sur a lot."

"Wonder what he'd do to his own son if he crossed him. Probably kill him."

"His only son? I doubt it." Roman shook his head.

"Whoa, Whitmore's only son is an Omega?" Siro replied, aghast.

"Mhm."

"You sure you want to go through with this? Are you giving up on finding your Fate, then?" Nico inquired.

"Contract is already signed, so I know it's going to happen." Roman laughed. "As for your second question, I guess he's not out there."

"That's too bad." Nico looked at Siro, who mirrored his expression.

Both had heard enough from Roman to know continuing the conversation was pointless. There's only so much a person can say to a friend who remained steadfast in a decision—good or not.

CHAPTER 10:

A Blow to Brotherhood

Ryan heard a knock on his bedroom door, a courtesy understood in the household to avoid stumbling into extracurricular activities by another family member—learned the hard way. "Yeah?"

The door opened to reveal Roman, his face showing he wanted to talk. "Hey," he muttered.

"What's up?" Ryan's voice was louder than normal as he attempted to hear Roman over his headset as he played a well-crafted open world video game. After Roman didn't answer right away, he looked at his brother now sitting on his bed with shoulders slumped forward. "Hey guys," Ryan spoke to other online players through a microphone, "I'm going to head out. Catch you later." He paused. "Yeah, yeah. Chill out." After closing out of the game, he took his headset off and looked at his brother. "What's going on?"

Roman's mind played through all the different events from the day he could possibly speak about. He chose his extreme experience in Dr. Birowack's class as an ice breaker, turning his frown upside down. "Got to experience the sex video everyone anticipates today."

"Oh, damn!" Ryan replied. "I've heard about it; is it as raunchy as they say it is?"

"That and more if you ask me. Though Siro appeared desensitized to it."

"No surprise there." Ryan smirked. "But I'm going to assume that's not what has you so down in the dumps. Otherwise, I'd think you'd walk in here whistling."

"I don't know about that," Roman replied. "It's not like you can jack off while watching it; I bet it gave everyone blue balls. Not exactly a pleasant feeling."

"Hm. Good point. I wonder how long the bathroom lines were afterward."

Roman's eyes widened. "Well, I wasn't going to stick around to find out. But you're right. That's not why I'm here." Roman took a few moments to gather his thoughts. "I told Siro and Nico about Peyton today. Actually, I told Nico who told Siro to be more specific."

"Ah, how'd they take it?" Ryan asked.

"Nico didn't say much. He's worried I guess, but that's just how he is. Siro, on the other hand, had quite the opinion."

"There's the shock of century. Did he give you hell for it?"

"Yeah, but not for the reason you might think," Roman pointed out. "Siro wasn't bothered by Peyton. In fact, I don't think he even cares. However, he had quite the opinion on his Sur. Damn near went on a rampage."

"Why?" Ryan asked, confused.

"He gave me some ridiculous story about how he thinks Whitmore kills people in order to get clients to support his business instead of his competitors."

Ryan blinked. "Wow! That's...that's something."

"Right?"

"What put that psychotic idea in his head anyway?" Ryan stood up and moved from his gaming area to the bed and put his back against the headboard, sitting and supporting himself on his soft pillows a couple feet away from where Roman sat.

"Come to find out, his dad was one of the landowners pressured into selling land for the Wolf Run development. Siro appears to be on some sort of justice crusade."

"Huh?" Ryan looked at him, not knowing anything of the heated topic.

"Nothing," Roman said.

"I hate to ask," Ryan started, "but does this add another mark against your new husband?"

"Please don't call him that," Roman snapped.

"Sorry, sorry. Went a bit too far," Ryan apologized.

Contrary to the once known term of endearment, "husband" was a derogatory term wolf-descendants chose to drop, among others, to show separation from primate-descendants who put negative connotations and forced beliefs onto others. The word carried with it social expectations which didn't apply: the existence of a female entity, social norms decided by gender, and a modern equalization which did not recognize the hierarchy system of ranks: Alpha, Beta, Omega. Another example was religion. Across the world, all human life believed in Wolf-God and his pack who protect the humans and animals who roamed the Earth. There were no sects, dissentions, or interpretations from those beliefs since the natural instincts of the ranks were programmed into every human.

Roman knew there were flaws in the wolf-descendant system. Omegas still felt repressed based upon the automatic waiving of property rights to Alphas as well as the negotiations of producing offspring and the control of abortion rights. All were designed to protect the survival of the species and give a succession to offspring in the event of an Omega death which carried a discouraging rate of pregnancy-related deaths.

"It's okay." Roman sighed, knowing his brother didn't mean any harm in his poor choice of words. "I can't get over the fact that whenever I talk about Peyton, my mood just drops."

"You still struggling with whether or not you made a mistake?" Ryan surmised.

"It's crazy to think I'm supposed to spend the rest of my life with someone I've only seen twice. I just need to be with him for a while and spend some quality time with him."

"Which is when?"

"Tomorrow night."

"Ah. Good luck to you." Ryan gave a salute.

"Thanks." Roman looked around and noticed someone missing. "Where's Rix?"

Ryan huffed sarcastically. "Oh, he's out finding himself with his new sport."

"He's still invested in this volleyball thing?" Roman was equally perplexed.

"Apparently. He's held out for this long. Stupid."

Roman glared suspiciously. "Stupid? Why? Because it's something you wouldn't do?"

"It's a stupid game of 'Keep it up.' If he did fútbol or something, I'd consider investing some time with him."

"Couldn't someone make the case it's just a silly game of kickball?" Ryan refused to answer. "You know, I said this whole separation thing was going to be a problem."

"That's not what it is!" Ryan growled.

"Are you sure?" Roman stressed.

"Yes!"

Pushing the already cracked door farther, Rixen came in a tad sweaty and fatigued. He watched innocently as Roman and Ryan stared at each other uncomfortably.

"What?" Rixen asked.

Roman stood and began his getaway out the door. "I think I'll sit this one out." He could feel Ryan's glare on his back as he disappeared. His feet pounded the stairs back to the main floor.

"What's going on?" Rixen asked suspiciously.

"Nothing," Ryan brushed off.

"Oh, okay then." Rixen stared at his twin, giving him a face indicating he believed him like he believed the Earth was flat.

Ryan looked out his bedroom window. "I don't know why you're doing this dumb sport."

"I'm not having this conversation again." Rixen dismissed him, turned around, and headed to his room.

"Come on, Rix. Wait." Rixen ignored him. "Wait!"

Rixen attempted to close his bedroom door to signal an end to the conversation; Ryan refused, catching it before it slammed. Rixen, of course, was not surprised by his action.

"Why can't you just support me for once?" He threw his duffel bag on his bed and removed his shoes by kicking them at the wall, hearing Ryan speak to his back.

"I support you!" Ryan defended.

"Yeah, when it's something you like or find worth in. I don't need your permission to play a sport because you don't like or don't want to do it."

"The bigger point is you hate all sports," Ryan pointed out.

"Uh, since when?" Rixen inquired, turning around finally to face him.

"Since I could barely convince you to even work out; not to mention, I still have to coax you into doing it."

"So, I changed. I'm allowed to do that."

"Since when?" Ryan snapped.

"Ever since I decided I wanted to find some part of my own identity. Now, I found myself a new sport, some new friends..."

"New friends?" Ryan's head jerked back a bit. "Like who?"

Rixen bit his lip, regretting his comment. He stood there, running his hand through his moist hair, wondering if he really had to continue. But it was too late now to stop. "I mean, Garrace is there. He helped persuade me to join." He turned around and unzipped his duffel bag, pulling out his clothes to find something else to focus on.

"And I'm glad you have someone to invigorate you," Ryan thought a bit on how he wanted to finish the statement, "...even if it is Garrace."

Rixen turned around, offended by the comment. "What's that supposed to mean?"

"Nothing other than he acts like Wolf-God's gift to man. He just slithers around like a snake trying to find his next lay. He's silent but deadly because he's not overt about it."

Rixen showed his annoyance with the comment. "He's not like that; he's really cool and actually a little sweet." He walked slowly to his dresser, finding the lounge clothes that would give his muscles a rest from the typical tight shirts and snug pants, hoping Ryan found his comments inconsequential.

"Sweet? Ugh. You sound just like the rest of them."

"Whatever." Rixen pulled off his practice shirt. The air in the room exacerbated the sweat sticking to his body. Stretching his arms up, he walked out of his bedroom toward the bathroom to take a shower.

That's when Ryan saw them. As Rixen walked by, he noticed a pattern of red indentations in half-circle markings on the tops of his shoulders. Before he could comment, he saw Rixen's back. It revealed several red splotches which crept up to the middle of his shoulders. The higher up the red marks were, the darker they were with the highest mark practically purple.

"Whoa, what the fuck, Rix?"

"What?" Rixen turned around. Ryan grabbed his shoulders and turned him back around with force, getting another good look. "What are you doing?!" Rixen demanded.

"What is wrong with your back? You have marks all over you. Damn, are these nail marks? And man, that looks like a hickey if I ever I saw one." Ryan felt a heavy numbing sensation in his stomach as a lightbulb went off in his head. "Rix, who the hell is sinking their teeth into you?" Ryan waited—and waited some more. One thing Rixen was never good at was lying or covering up his facial expressions in a poker game. "Rix. Please tell me this isn't Garrace."

Rixen kept his silence and held Ryan's gaze only for a moment until he couldn't any longer. His next move was staring at the floor. Anxiety flooded his body, and he felt his heart beat out of his chest. And still, he stayed silent.

"What the actual fuck, Rix?! Please tell me it's not him!"

"I can't," Rix whispered, daring to look back at his brother seething with anger and disappointment.

"Of all the people. Why him? WHY HIM?" Ryan's voice was strong and harsh. Rixen could smell the anger pheromones coming off him. His own body began to shake, starting with his hands.

"Why do you care so much?" Rixen attempted to reach Ryan's vocal tone and volume but didn't get there, nor did he really want to. He didn't want this conversation vibrating up the walls, causing others in the house to listen in or dig later for information.

"He's a sleaze, for starters." Ryan crossed his arms in a showing of his parental personality. He was downright shaming his brother.

"He's not like that. He's respectful. He's considerate of my feelings toward the matter."

"Feelings toward what?"

"That I'm not interested yet in going public with our relationship." Rixen grew more confident. He mirrored his brother in his commanding stance.

"Relationship? Ha, how convenient. So, basically, you've just given him a free pass to have other quiet flings he doesn't share with the public. Why do you care about not wanting to go public? Are you ashamed of it?"

"No, I wanted to avoid conversations like this!"

"Ah-ha, so you are ashamed of it! You just don't want to be ridiculed by everyone because they'll just validate everything I'm saying."

"No, Ryan. Just you. I don't want to hear this from you!" Rixen pointed his hand out with finger extended.

"Me? Why me? I'm the one person in your life you should be able to say this all to. I'm your brother!" Ryan's frustration grew as he dared to think he was being slighted by his twin, his kindred spirit, his constant.

"And yet, Ryan, you're not! You are the most judgmental person I have in my life. No one hurts me the way you do. It hurts in the way you look down on me, and the things you are willing to say to me! And the worst part about it is you don't even know you're doing it!" Rixen's eyes wavered, and he felt his tear ducts vibrate. He fought to hold in the small drops of emotion.

"You're better than him, Rix. Of all the people you could have chosen to screw around with, you chose the worst person we know. The guy should be submerged in a vat of penicillin or wrapped in a body condom."

"That's not funny!" Rixen replied.

"It's not a joke! You know it's not a joke. Damn it!" Ryan started to breathe heavily. "I don't know how else to put it, Rixen. You. Are. Better. Than. Him. So much, it's not even close!"

"You know, I seem to remember not too long ago we had a conversation where you said Jordan was the worst person to sleep with. I mean, what are you going to do, Ryan? Follow me around the rest of my life interviewing and scoring every single mate I meet?"

"Now, that's not funny." Ryan glared.

"Yeah, well, guess what, Ryan? It's not a joke either."

Ryan tapped his foot, thinking, searching for some way to make this better, to keep his brother from making a mistake. "Think about this, Rixen. Convince him it was a fleeting thought, just something you wanted to try, a one-time thing. He does this crap all the time. There's no way he'd fall to pieces over it if you ended it now."

Rixen threw his hands up. "You are so ignorant. Do you honestly believe this was a one-time occurrence?"

Ryan's eyes shifted in thought. "Okay...how long has this been a thing?" At the same time he regretted asking the question, he also felt the insatiable need to know.

"Every night since volleyball started." Rixen stared his brother down, almost pleased to say it.

Ryan could barely process the words he'd just heard. He reflected on the timeline. "A month? You've been sleeping with him every single practice for a month?"

"Yes. Yes, I have."

"How is that even physically possible?!" His amazement raised his voice again.

"Practice ends at 4:30, the arena clears out soon after, and we find a dark corner backstage in the theater. We have to avoid the locker rooms—it's just not feasible. Too much traffic. And if we stay too much later than 5:30, the school gets suspicious of loitering." Rixen stared at the floor again, hating himself for revealing so many details. But what did it matter now?

"Wolf-God, that is the most disgusting thing I've heard yet. You have sex for an hour? There's no way he can knot you in that amount of time with the expectation you two wouldn't get caught."

"He doesn't knot me; he pulls out. And we don't do it for an hour. Quit being dramatic. Believe it or not, we spend most of the time talking and enjoying each other's company."

Ryan felt an impasse. His brother was infatuated in the worse way. Every piece of respect he had for his brother shattered into pieces, and he didn't foresee healing from the wounds they inflicted any time soon. "This is the craziest thing you have ever done, and you don't even see it. You can't even look at everything you know about him and see you're just going to be discarded trash."

"Stop it."

"You think you're fucking special? Well, let me be the first one to tell you—you're not fucking special. You're fucking stupid. That's what you are!"

"Stop it!" Rixen's face turned red. Any chance of him holding himself together was quickly fading away. His eyes pulsed and the mist started blurring his vision.

Ryan wanted his words to hurt, just like Rixen's words did in how much he disregarded everything he was saying, like he couldn't trust him. Instead, he chose to embrace the words of a player, a rat, a scuzball. "I don't want you anywhere near me! You reek of him. You are nothing but a slut and an idiot."

"Ryan, quiet! Please!" Tears escaped, strong enough to dodge his face and fall straight to the floor. "You don't mean that!" His voice trembled.

"Screw this. You know what? I'm done. You want to be his bitch? Go for it. You're going to be the laughingstock of everyone, and I can't wait until it happens."

Rixen's uncontrollable pain warped quickly. Like an angry adolescent wolf, he leaped forward, pushing Ryan with a force he hadn't expected.

Ryan stumbled back considerably but never lost his balance to any sort of consequence. With a fire in his eyes, he rushed forward.

Even though Rixen anticipated it, Ryan's force felt ten times harder on his chest, and within a second, he was on the floor with a thud radiating pain from his pelvic bone halfway up his back. Both of their faces and breathing patterns matched in ferocity, blood red in the face and heavy.

Ryan stood over him, waiting for Rixen's next move, but it never came. With his intense pheromones spewing out, Ryan could have been mistaken for an Alpha in that moment.

The clear difference between the two was Rixen's lower lip trembling and his voice beginning to whimper. Like Ryan, Rixen's pheromones expelled with equal intensity but his was pure hurt. He didn't know what else to do. His body froze like concrete, and he forgot how to move. Suddenly, the door to the upstairs vibrated and then opened.

"What's going on down there?" The voice was their Veo, filled with concern.

It took all the energy Rixen had left to bear, but he successfully calmed his voice, removing the tremble enough for him to say, "Nothing."

"Are you sure?" Veo asked.

Rixen winced and shut his eyes in pain. Physical pain, yes, but emotional pain even more so. "Yes, I'm sure."

After what seemed like forever, the door quietly shut again. After the sound cleared, Rixen breathed even heavier, holding out to the very last possible second before crumbling emotionally.

Seeing his brother in this state, Ryan's face softened and the realization of the damage he had inflicted began to settle in. "Rixen...I..."

"Just go away," Rixen whispered, turning his body to the side first, moaning from the pain, dull and constant. He felt Ryan's arm trying to lift him, but he pushed it away. After finally getting up on his own, he limped toward the bathroom and shut the door forcefully.

Ryan stood there a moment, reflecting on his own actions. Not just the physical ones, but the emotional ones too. He had shamed his brother and hurt him to the point to where there was nothing left. In an instant, he hated himself with a passion. Hurting his brother in this way was never what he thought he'd do, especially over something like this. He wanted nothing more than to comfort and love his brother. But he didn't know what to do. With his own emotions overtaking him, a tear began to fall, and he wiped it away as he headed for the cowardice of his own bedroom.

Rixen's back went flush against the bathroom door as if he were trying to prevent his brother from entering. He only looked at himself in the bathroom mirror for a second to see his red eyes. Stepping into the shower, he gladly let the cold water attempt to cool down his heated face and body.

As the water warmed, he shivered, in part due to the drastic temperature change, but also as the shock of what had transpired set in. His brother hated him in a way he never felt before. All the childish fights and even the silly arguments in the past year were a distant cry to what just happened. In all other instances, a day went by before they called a truce, sometimes even without speaking. But he remembered how Ryan spoke with a hateful tone which hit harder than the pain of the floor. All the nasty words broke a chain, a bond, and he worried whether it could come back together.

The single episode wasn't the issue. It was all the connections he could make to his brother's philosophy on how he should live his life in the exact image of him. Having an opinion was one thing, but Ryan's goal was to make him suffer and force him to become less of himself. Rixen wanted the brother he thought Ryan was capable of being: the supportive, helpful, caring, fun, and connected person.

After Ryan's second judgement of who he slept with, he couldn't imagine a positive scenario in the future: either he'd continue his sharp unrelenting approach or ignore him all together. Right now, he didn't know which scenario was worse.

Gingerly, Rixen felt his back. It was tender to the touch and no doubt bruised. The physical pain reminded him of the emotional pain, and he leaned forward to rest his head on the tile below the showerhead, letting the now hot water hit his back. Finally, he let his emotions go in a howl of tears in the safest place he knew no one could hear him.

Both Ryan and Rixen were out of sorts at dinner. Everyone noticed, Veo the most suspicious because he had noticed the prior disturbance in the basement.

Roman was the only one who ventured to ask what was going on. They both denied any issue, but it was a transparent lie; however, no one wanted to address the potential drama during the meal.

The worst part of it all was watching Rixen move stiffly while walking and try not to wince. It was crushing to watch him sit down and stand up from his chair. That got an instant comment and inquisition from Veo, garnering everyone's full attention. Without even looking at Ryan, Rixen played it off as a volleyball injury during practice. Veo even tried to coax Rixen's shirt up to see just how bad it looked.

The thought of seeing it made Ryan's heart speed up rapidly. But in some miraculous spell, Rixen was able wiggle his way out of having to produce the result of the assault.

Ryan knew the instant it happened, he would rival any attempt Rixen could make in a physical brawl, and in that moment, he wanted Rixen to know it. He also reflected on the words he had said. He had always made disparaging comments and even empty threats one expects from brother to brother, but nothing like this. It was pure, out of control rage like an abusive Alpha showing his rogue Omega what happens when he doesn't submit. It was disgusting to make the comparison and even worse to know it was true; he felt the power and regretted every moment afterward. There was actually one thing Ryan acknowledged he did say right: Rixen did deserve better—a better brother.

Deep into the night, Ryan laid in his bed, tossing and turning as he reflected on the evening after the falling-out. Turning on his side toward the wall of Rixen's room, he heard his brother crying himself to sleep. Ryan put his hand up against it and felt the stinging sensation return to his own eyes.

CHAPTER 11:

A Date for a Date

The next day, Roman felt like someone died in the house. Both Ryan and Rixen stayed in their rooms all Saturday. Usually, they were off galivanting on some adventure to explore an uncharted park, people-watching at the beach, running to specialty stores, trying out new restaurants, battling on video games, or hanging out with their posse.

Roman tried Rixen first, who was easier to interrogate. He observed him sitting on his bed with his reading glasses staring into a small pile of chapter books spilled on his bed. The attempts to talk to him were like talking to a wall. Equally, in his own room, Ryan lost himself in his video games at his desk.

Any other day, he'd press both of them to figure out what fight they clearly had, but today was the day he was going on his first official date with his new mate. Roman and his Sur took cues from Matthew and were content to do so. Roman was tired of his inconsistent feelings toward Peyton and was more than ready to shake them off.

Nerves followed him all day; as the hours ticked by, the more apparent they became. It was hard to eat, engage with his friends on his phone, watch mindless videos online, work out, anything! Nothing eased the anticipation; the day was murder.

Dinner reservations were at 6:00 at an equally swanky restaurant as where they first met. So, when 4:00 rolled around, he vigorously showered, shaved, and made it to his room to figure out his clothing.

Roman wanted to show Peyton just what kind of Alpha he was. Therefore, he tucked his generous assets into a tight set of seductive underwear, accenting the curves and bulges just right. The fabric felt great on his newly shaven cock and heavy sack. He ignored visualizations of Peyton too much while staring into the mirror in order to prevent any premature stains or time-consuming shenanigans before he left.

Before he dressed in his light blue dress shirt accented with a dark blazer, he studied the rest of his reflection. Roman possessed defined leg muscles all the way down to his ankles. A light spread of hair covered both of his legs. His stomach had a few lines of definition which protruded better when he flexed or worked out. His upper chest was defined a lot better, also covered fully in an equal layer of light hair. Two quarter-sized nipples sat low on his pecs, currently aroused from the cool temperature of his room.

Tonight, his face was fully smooth again just like his first meeting. His green eyes and dark blond hair sparkled from the ceiling lights. After dressing, he shone like a new penny. He was ready.

Nothing was ever simple with Matthew Whitmore. In addition to deciding the time and place of their date, Matthew wanted to meet Roman's Sur there to have what he called a "pre-date meeting." Both Roman and Jake rolled their eyes at the idea but went along with it. They both suspected this had to do with the part of the contract not discussed in the lawyer's office: the next steps in deciding how and when Roman and Peyton should move-in together while also discussing their parents' wishes for consummation.

While driving to the restaurant, Jake decided to tell his son the whole contract with the Whitmores was becoming unorthodox, including the fact Roman was going to have to taxi with Peyton to drop him off at his house and then use it to get back home since Jake's presence was "required" tonight.

In general, the advice from all parents to their newly coupled sons was always helpful to any couple willing to hear it, but Matthew came across as requiring approval for every decision as if he was the mob boss in charge of their relationship. Maybe there was some validity to Siro's allegations of power and submission. The most frustrating part was Peyton's lack of voice in it all. Roman didn't have a clue about what he thought.

When the driveway up to the restaurant stopped at valet parking, Roman knew this wasn't the place he wanted to be. Sur read it on his face but gave him a comforting smile, signaling it was going to be okay. Under the entrance awning stood a gentleman in a formal suit not too different from a castle guard. He greeted Roman and his father and watched them enter.

The restaurant, hidden from the outside by tinted windows, was brighter inside than expected. It required only two of the largest chandeliers Roman had ever seen in his life to light most of the room. The only other light came from a rather impressive effect of lighted glass on a wall housing the 5-star kitchen. Mid-level was a large opening about twenty feet wide with a view into the kitchen. If they wished, patrons could sit near the area to get the best views of chefs from around the world in all shapes, sizes, and origins with large white toques. In addition, they could experience the first scent of the flowing aromas and hear the hustle and bustle of edible artwork being served on white plates with golden trim.

Jake walked up to the host who asked for the reservation name. Knowing better, he spoke the name "Whitmore" versus "Erricson." Instantly recognizing the name, the host led them both to a quiet corridor. The short hallway revealed more private booths with tapestry drapes for optional privacy as if patrons needed to discuss something confidential or illegal.

In the third booth sat Matthew and Peyton. Matthew settled for an enthusiastic handshake and shoulder tap for a hug.

Seeing Peyton's smile warmed Roman, and he decided to start the evening off right with a gentle kiss on his cheek and a firm hug. Roman sighed, sensing both their elevated auras.

"Gentlemen!" Matthew announced. "Glad to see your shining faces. For me, it's been too long. And I can only imagine how these two feel about it." He winked at Roman to indicate some sort of man code which communicated an understanding of obvious sexual urges any young couple must be chomping at the bit to release.

"We've been looking forward to it, of course!" Jake returned.

"I hope you two don't mind the location back here. I know it kills the ambiance a bit, but these booths provide a nice private atmosphere I think these boys will appreciate."

Boys? Roman thought. *Is that what Matthew really thinks of us? Two hormonal boys wanting to experiment with playing house? Not two consenting adults beginning our lives together?* Maybe this was the missing piece to it all: Roman and Peyton might always live in the immature shadow of Matthew who had solved all of life's issues in his unprecedented wisdom without having touched the age of 40 yet.

Peyton followed up, "I like it; I think it's a good start."

Roman's expression to Peyton's forward comment was that of welcome surprise. "I'm glad; I agree."

Jake smiled with his eyes. He gestured for Roman to sit next to his mate in the cozy space facing Matthew and himself.

A waiter in a bright white shirt and black pants with hair slicked all the way back took the drink orders. All ordered some variation of a cocktail. After their waiter arrived again, Matthew led the table conversation from small talk to what he was really good at: business.

"I know this wasn't quite how any of you thought tonight would start, but I'm grateful you entertained my idea."

"Oh, no. It's no problem at all," Roman assured. He snuck a look at his father who took the hint, enjoyed the inside joke, and lifted his drink to his lips to hide any offensive expression.

Jake joined in a second later. "You said you wished to discuss something?"

At that moment, Roman felt his hand being squeezed below the table. It made him jump slightly. Turning to his right, he saw Peyton somewhere between joy and anxiety. It was all he needed to know exactly where this was going.

"There's no way to really say it lightly. Peyton is about two weeks away from his next heat."

It was a natural reaction for everyone other than Matthew to show some level of discomfort. The conversation was a natural part of life; however, the lack of warning made it more comparable to someone exposing themselves at the table without a care of who witnessed the act.

"I see." Roman didn't have experience with this. Sure, he found himself with Omegas who tried to seduce him into taking care of their heats for them. But Roman was able to withstand the siren's song when it came to desperate propositions. In reality, he only was exposed to so much. Rixen never talked about his heat because his hadn't developed yet, and whatever Veo did about his was well-hidden and never discussed. With their parents' bedroom located on the second floor of their home, all events were private—as they should be. Knowing textbook information about heats was very different than having a real, applicable conversation about them.

"With that mind," Matthew continued, "Peyton mentioned, and I agree, building a physical relationship before it happens is important so when the heat strikes, you'll know how to get him through it."

By no surprise, Peyton felt the most embarrassment wash over him. Peyton's father made it sound so antiseptic; he was a doctor giving a prescription of sex. And what if his heat wasn't so close? How long had his father planned to hold out before trying to give him and his mate quality time together? This didn't even address how they'd begin their new life together.

Jake's mind filled with confusion. "You want them together from the necessity of knowing how to deal with a heat?" Roman and Peyton were both internally thankful Jake said what they both were thinking.

Matthew's face was offended. "I think it's in the best interest of both boys. A heat is a very painful and an emotionally scarring process if not taken care of properly; it is a cruel burden of being an Omega. When they are left to themselves, help has to either be medically provided to block the hormones which trigger it, or a medical professional brought in to use tools to physically relieve the pain as much as they can. But everyone knows it's not anywhere near the success of the real relief an Alpha can provide. I'm sure you know that, Jake."

"Of course, I do," Jake defended. "I'm just of the opinion, with them being mates now, they'd be entitled to such benefit, regardless if Peyton was anticipating a heat or not."

Matthew paused and stared into his drink. To the rest of them, it appeared as a calming technique to prevent him from lashing out. "I admit I'm very protective of my son—to a fault. I'd be foolish to not realize the disservice I am doing by not letting them spread their wings before now. Sometimes, a father needs things like the natural occurrence of a heat just to see how important it is. As much as I want Peyton to take the suppressants, there are too many negative side effects. But I'll never know the potential shame an Omega can feel by having a stranger, although medically trained and trusted, take care of needs required by the true care of a mate. I saw it all over Peyton's face for three cycles. He needs what is owed to him, and that is to be with the man he's going to spend the rest of his life with."

Somewhere in the creative part of his mind, Roman imagined the restaurant being full of patrons giving Matthew a standing ovation for another successful speech to a crowd who waited on his every word. It was very refreshing and comforting to know Matthew was now taking this seriously. Roman envisioned, for a moment, Terrence talking to his mate about the matter. *Was it Terrence, his Omega, who convinced him to do this? Or has Matthew really turned the corner himself?* Regardless, the fact of the matter remained—this was nothing more than orders from a controlling parent. To dwell or fight on the issue was petty and pointless. Roman needed to move on and thank Wolf-God for the new development.

"So..." Roman gathered his nerve. "When do you anticipate this happening?"

Matthew looked strangely at Roman. "I thought tonight would be a great opportunity."

Roman's eyes widened. Peyton himself began giving off the scent of nerves and displeasure. Roman knew this was not meant for him personally. It was apparent Peyton's own father cared little for his son's pride and worth.

"Wait," Jake interjected, "we discussed how this night would go. We'd drop them off here for their night, they'd taxi back to your place to drop off Peyton, then Roman would come back home. Are you suggesting Roman stay at your place and simply leave after consummating their relationship?"

Matthew's head danced in the memory of his own insistence. "No, I thought about that too. That's why, if you'd consider it, I made a reservation this evening at the Water's Edge Hotel. I wanted to respect the boys' privacy without having to worry about the para-noia of prying eyes."

Roman inhaled and turned to Peyton. It was subtle, but he saw his mate wince and drop his body just a bit lower than it was before. Roman could also feel the heat radiating off his body and smell his salty perspiration.

Only Roman's admirable strength kept him from flipping out. Behind the backs of the Erricsons, Matthew had orchestrated this entire night. Roman, and to a certain extent Peyton, were nothing more than puppets. Roman wanted nothing more than to get up and walk out, taking Peyton with him under the wing of his own Sur.

Jake himself sat there in awe. He felt the slow disintegration of a once proud partnership he had with Matthew Whitmore. The man who championed the pairing next to him had gone rogue, cutting him out of every decision. But criticizing the process now only hurt Roman and Peyton. As the waiter came by with menus, Jake saw the desperate opportunity he needed. He looked at his watch in the overdramatic way to try and make it appear as a genuine oversight.

"Matthew, I think we should consider heading out so the men can have their night."

Matthew took in Jake's words and realized he was right; it was time. "I agree. I believe that's best." Matthew stood up, taking one more look at Peyton and giving him a cautious nod before he pro-ceeded to give Roman a strong Alpha stare. "Roman," he acknowl-edged. After a tug on his suit coat, he began his exit as Jake gave a gentle wave to both and followed.

The initial shock of it all didn't leave right away; there was a stunned moment which took some time to subside. Roman looked down at Peyton, who was still sitting to his right, his expression concerned as he wondered how Peyton was dealing with the last twenty minutes.

Peyton, almost jittery, stressed about how all this was going to hit Roman. Was this going to be a casual meal between friends like an uninspired blind date or a celebration for a new mated couple? Peyton knew what he wanted, but it all rested on how much patience Roman still held for his family. "I'm so sorry; I wanted to tell you this so badly. I wanted all this to go so differently."

Roman's eyes softened. "Listen. We're going to make the best of this. This is our time, not our parents'. We're going to make the best of this and do whatever comes naturally—no expectations—no judgements. Okay?"

"I just fear this has all gone wrong and that—" Peyton cut off as Roman's hand brushed along Peyton's cheek. His face brightened.

"As much as I love being here next to you...would you mind if I..." Roman pointed to the empty seat across from them. He wanted the ability to look at Peyton and converse with ease. Peyton thoroughly understood and gestured openly in approval. After sitting in his seat, facing Peyton, he settled into how a date should begin. "Now, how about we take a look at these menus?" Roman suggested.

"That sounds great; after that ordeal, I think I could eat an entire page of this menu." Peyton's eyes widened in sarcasm. He felt his comfort return, revealing more of his personality. Looking at Roman without the overbearing oversight of any parental figure was a dream come true. He started to shed the adolescent mask he wore in front of his Sur and began to show the person he wanted to be for Roman.

The menu selections were divine but a bit hard to decipher. There were culinary terms throughout the descriptions no average person ever discussed. So, when Roman chose his menu item, he based it on the general idea. He let Peyton order first: pan-seared swordfish. Roman ordered a filet of beef. After the waiter removed the menus and put a second round of drinks in front of them, Roman continued the conversation.

"There are so many things I want to say, and yet it's hard to find a starting point."

Peyton pushed gently. "What comes to mind first?"

"Honestly, wanting to know what it was like for you after the contract signing."

"Oh," Peyton choked, "interesting to say the least. I knew my Sur was going to play hardball. But even so, I didn't think it was going to happen the way it did, and I let them both know in the car ride home."

"Really?" Roman's interest grew. "Like what? What caught you off guard?"

"Sur told me of the courtesy in me keeping my last name; that particular conversation was communicated to me as non-negotiable. I knew the part about how many offspring were going to be approved." Peyton blushed a bit. "It must have been a conversation our dads had earlier. Anyway, I didn't know he was going to demand the kids carry the Whitmore last name. I was floored."

Roman was perplexed. "But when I asked you what you wanted…"

"I know, I know," Peyton interrupted. "I don't know if any of the words which came out of my mouth in that room were my own or an automated computer. When your Sur got my father to negotiate, I wanted to stand up and say, 'How about we give up the names instead?' but by that time, I felt my input was unwanted, even by my own parents."

Roman nodded with understanding. "I can't say I felt any different." Roman paused. "Can I ask you something?"

"Of course." Peyton smiled, excited Roman dared to dig deeper.

"Is your Sur…is he always like that?"

Peyton's face grew serious; it wasn't an unexpected question. "My Sur," Peyton looked up, looking for the right words to fall into his head, "has been a hardworking perfectionist my entire life, and in the last ten years, he's had a steady group of followers telling him he is the perfect businessman and family man in the public eye. But the more he gets absorbed into rhetoric, the less difference there is between how he treats Veo and me compared to his business partners."

"Our contract seems to be his next business venture," Roman criticized.

"You're not wrong. Interestingly enough, I've never seen him handle a situation in this way ever since I can remember."

"What? The control?"

"No, that's very him. What I mean is: he's scared. At home, when I hear him talk to Veo, he's stressed. I mean," Peyton shifted in his seat, "I've seen him stress about work. It's loud, insulting, and authoritative. He puffs out his chest like he's on an Alpha quest or something. But he acts totally differently about this."

"How is that?"

"He thinks out loud to himself and rambles solemnly. It's hard sometimes to hear him when he's near Veo. I can only imagine the verbal massacre I'd get if he caught me listening in. But I've seen him on his bed, holding his forehead, rubbing his temples, getting a neck massage from Veo, and it's all over worries."

"That's actually really sweet. It's comforting to know how he's doing this all for you. But I'm sorry—his approach is very off-putting."

"No, don't apologize. I get it. He's so protective of me; I always wondered if I was an Alpha if he'd be sitting back and watching me do what I want to do."

"There's another question I have."

"Please, do." Peyton really enjoyed the quality conversation. It was natural; it was attentive; it was pure. The light lit up Roman so beautifully. He wanted to take a picture and just stare at it, but he hadn't worked up the courage to do that yet.

"I'm not saying it doesn't happen or that there's anything wrong with it. But I'm only asking because of who your father is. Why are you the only child in the family? And wouldn't someone so passionate about continuing the family name want the chances of it increased with the possibility of having an Alpha pup?"

"You're not the only person to ask; even my parents get that question a lot. It's annoying really. I feel it puts me in the 'Oh, you have an Omega? I'm so sorry for your loss' category."

"Oh, no! Seriously, I didn't mean anything by it."

"You don't offend me, I promise. I knew where you were going with it." He saw Roman relax, his back hitting the booth. "I asked too. Almost everyone I know has two kids or more—not that I know a whole lot. And the only other person I know who is an only child—it's not for a good reason."

"Is that the same for you? Is it not a good reason?"

Peyton's eyes reflected on the conversation he had with his Veo when he was still a pup. The words sounded just as serious and vague today in his head as when he first heard them. "Veo said I was a challenge from the start. The conceiving, the pregnancy, and the birth. Nothing came easy. The most details I got out of either of them were that, on the day of my birth, there was a high chance neither Veo nor myself were going to come out of the hospital alive."

In a quiet emotional tone, Roman spoke, "Oh Wolf-God."

Peyton shrugged off the shock of the moment. The reaction was all too familiar. "My assumption then was either my parents were deathly afraid of trying again or something happened to Veo where it's not a possibility anymore. It's a reality of how it all works though."

Roman stared at Peyton. The strength and vulnerability he had was beautiful and attractive. "I'm glad you're here."

Peyton's eyes glistened. "Yeah?"

"Yeah," Roman replied. Roman was about to continue, but soon after, the meals came tableside. The heated plates brought beautifully presented cuisine. Silverware with bright cloth napkins were handed out and drinks replenished for a third time. After a few anticipatory comments, both partook and marveled at their first tastes.

"Okay, my turn for a personal question," Peyton announced.

"Go for it," Roman replied, waiting for Peyton's best shot.

"When I met you last week, you asked me about my hobbies, and I completely saw it in your eyes, with every word which came out of my mouth, I was disappointing you in that regard."

It wasn't a deathblow, but Peyton's question did pack a punch. To his own detriment, Roman realized tonight the quiet personality he plastered onto Peyton also came with the misjudgment that Peyton was somehow inept—not academically, but in social intelligence. Either Peyton was much keener and more capable than he originally let on, or Roman had poor skills in maintaining a vague disposition when dealing with disappointment.

"Disappointed." Roman chewed on the word coincidentally with a bite of food. After swallowing, he continued, "It's not the word I'd use. Scared works."

"You? Scared?" Peyton didn't see that one coming.

"By all means, Peyton. You and I are on some blind date reality show setup for the fact we agreed to be mated before even seeing each other. This whole thing was a shot in the dark. I was worried we'd be incompatible. We'd move in together and find ourselves regretting the decision."

Peyton was impressed at Roman's ability to express emotions in such a deliberate and inviting way. But he already knew Roman carried with him maturity, sincerity, and quality conversation skills. To a certain extent, he reminded Peyton of his Sur without the pretentious façade.

"I know. The same thoughts went through my head." Peyton bit his lip. "But I'd like to think so far that's not the case?"

Roman smiled. "No, I don't think it is."

Conversations continued to the end of the meal. Roman discussed some more details of his family including his Sur's dedication to Blood-Types, although he left out the obsession of studying Type 6; that conversation was for another day. After asking for the bill, the waiter explained everything was already settled. To put the cherry on top, they ordered one hot apple dessert with vanilla bean ice cream drizzled in hot caramel sauce.

When the delectable treat was done, Roman assessed the restaurant. "Do you want to get out of here?" he asked with a soothing voice.

"More than ready," Peyton replied. As he got out of the booth, he stopped himself from walking down the narrow path back to the main dining room. "Before we go, do you mind if we take a picture together?" Nerves pushed up from his stomach.

"Sure!" Roman said enthusiastically.

Peyton pulled out his phone and attempted to hold it in a position which complimented them, but Roman's height made it more challenging than he expected.

"Here, let me." Roman assisted with his phone and held it up at a complimentary angle. Both smiled once for the first shot. As Peyton held his pose for an anticipatory second photo, Roman snuck in a kiss to his temple and took the second.

Peyton blushed and took the phone back to get a better view of the photos; both were perfect. He stuck the phone back in his pocket and stared at Roman for a second, trying to read his face.

"So, I don't want to suggest anything or make you feel uncomfortable, but do you want to go to the hotel? I have no problem going straight home. My Sur can deal with it." Holding a stoic pose was difficult; Peyton didn't want to come off as begging or laying a guilt trip.

"I think that would be nice," Roman said, staring into Peyton's eyes.

The ride to the hotel lent itself to discussions of the ocean. Roman was relieved to find that even though Peyton wasn't a connoisseur, he did have some fond memories of going to the beach a few times.

The hotel lobby showcased beautifully vaulted ceilings accented by an exotic fish tank that consumed the entire wall behind the check-in desk. Once announced, they were greeted and sent to a private check-in area. Since neither of them had luggage—a part Peyton's father didn't plan very well—Roman suggested they explore the boardwalk.

The opposite side of the lobby had French doors leading to a deserted pool area, and beyond was a generously sized overlook lit with decorative lamps. The oceanfront view echoed with the sound of the waves. The crisp salty air hit them; the night air temperature had dropped considerably compared to a month ago. With fall upon them, a nightly walk like this would only be pleasant for a few more weeks.

Near the water, a bridge connected a boardwalk shared by a few hotels. The longest stretch jetted straight out into the water with bright lamps, calming any nerves about safety. They walked out to the end and sat on a bench, enjoying the soothing sound of the water. Peyton settled in the middle and Roman went to his left, closing any gap between them which could have indicated a platonic rendezvous. They complimented the majestic atmosphere, enjoying themselves in silence.

Peyton leaned his head on Roman's shoulder, something he'd never dreamed of doing before. "Roman, I need to ask you something." Roman's head turned slightly to see Peyton's almost worried face, and he waited in anticipation. "I don't wish to make this a completely awkward conversation, but what are your thoughts about having kids?"

Roman was stunned but considered the question seriously. He turned his head to give Peyton his complete attention. "I want them if that's what you mean."

"It is. I'd like to think your parents weren't forcing you to have them in order to please them."

"No, of course not. How about you? Is that what you want or what your parents want?"

"I want them," Peyton reassured him.

"Why the question?" Roman's curiosity grew with the nerves which followed.

"My heat starts soon. I hate to bring it up like this, but my Sur does a good job of breaking down walls on any embarrassing topic."

Roman laughed. "Yeah, I agree. What is it you want to know?" The nerves hit the pit of Roman's stomach.

"Are we," Peyton paused, "using protection when my heat hits?"

Roman felt a bit light-headed. Before all this, Roman thought he was already an expert on being an adult. But the entire Whitmore family had forced Roman into realizing how little about it he knew. One week ago, he was legally mated, and tonight, he was having a discussion on his timetable to begin fatherhood. Roman decided to be an adult and answer honestly.

"I didn't think about it much. Everything else around it was taking center stage. Like you said, your upcoming heat does force the conversation. I'll say this: If someone had asked me when I was 16, I would have said not until I was 30. At 30, I could easily hear myself say I wish I had done it at 16. Now that I'm 24, I feel the time is right. I could see starting next year. So, long way to answer your question, yes, I'd see us using condoms." Roman evaluated Peyton's reaction. "How do you feel about that?"

"I agree right now is not the time. Although, if you had said it was, it would have forced me to reflect on what I was waiting for. I think it's hard to visualize when the perfect time is or what it looks like. All I know is being with a mate makes the journey less frightening and more pleasurable to think about. Not to mention, I'm glad to know I won't have to deal with a stranger inserting things into me in order to ease the pain. It's a horrible experience."

"You won't have to do that anymore." Roman leaned in and gave Peyton a tender kiss. When the quiet crashing of the ocean waves was overshadowed by their soft moans, Roman knew it was time to start walking back.

The large, impressive suite was accented with fresh flowers, a bottle of chilling champagne, two glasses, and a few chocolate-covered strawberries. Roman had to hand it to Matthew—he knew how to sweeten a deal he wanted done his way. He led Peyton to sit on the pearl white bed while he did the honors of breaking out the gifts.

Peyton selected one of the seductive delights and bit into the mix of bitter chocolate and sweet strawberry. The sensation was intoxicating when paired with the champagne. With the alcoholic buzz still lingering from the three drinks he had at the restaurant, it only took a couple of glasses to send him back to a rushing wave. The room was warm, making it easy to notice the atmosphere shifting: tightening, sparking, budding.

Staring at Roman sitting next to him, Peyton found it hard to focus on the words he spoke. Instead, his eyes traced the broad shoulders of his mate all the way down to the slender hips and noticeable bulge in his tight slacks. His imagination flourished, triggering unaccustomed pheromones in Peyton. As if the pheromones weren't enough to send him for a loop, his felt his inner glands begin to pulse slick deep inside. The wet sensation now seeping into his underwear pulled him back to reality as his nerves began to take over. He set his glass on the side table and felt his trembling hands push himself up to a standing position, wondering if he should wait in the bathroom until the hormones subsided.

"Are you feeling okay?" Roman asked, noticing Peyton's flushed skin. He stood up to assist Peyton, anticipating some sort of reaction to the food.

"Yeah, I think it's just getting warm in here. I just need a second to—"

Roman grabbed Peyton's waist. Peyton's entire body stiffened, his muscles tightening, breath quickening, and skin temperature rising quickly.

Staring down at his mate, Roman took in the flood of pheromones which began to perfume everywhere. He inhaled deeply and caught the scent of a rich vanilla and citrus compliment. This, however, was different. The smell was thicker, mustier, and more seductive. Suddenly, it clicked for Roman what kind of reaction Peyton was having. He felt a bit foolish for not recognizing it sooner. But in realizing it so late, the pungent aroma hit him hard and fast. Whatever power Peyton's body was using to entice him, it was working. With his arms already locked onto Peyton, he walked forward, pushing tight against Peyton's body. The deep kiss they shared made it feel as if they never stopped their embrace from the boardwalk.

Peyton glanced cautiously at Roman. He could smell the pheromones on Roman which told him he was getting ready to take control. For once in his life, he didn't know what was going to happen nor the outcome it would produce. All he knew for sure was the considerable mass of an Alpha hovered over his small body.

Not wanting protective layers between them any longer, Roman's hands began unbuttoning Peyton's shirt as his body fell to the bed. His panting increased as he exposed more of Peyton's white skin. But Roman kept himself at a slow, calculated pace. In the moments where the heated passion became predictable, Roman's mind became clear and aware.

"Peyton," he breathed. Roman was met with a moan in response. When he felt Peyton's eyes focus on him, he continued, "I don't want you to feel you have to do this."

Peyton appreciated Roman's words, but he didn't want to hear him speak. He thrust his head up and brought Roman back down to his lips. Peyton did want it. He focused one deep look into Roman's eyes. They were clear, green, and full. He was waiting for something he'd wondered about from his required reading on reproduction. Eye dilation was said to give mates the ultimate connection. But yet, the act was void. Peyton realized Roman was looking back at him in a heavy lust but nothing else.

And right now, he was okay with that.

Roman assisted Peyton in undoing his own pants. Peyton's eager hands finished the job. His hard cock sprang up and instantly a drop of pre-cum dropped down his shaft. He eyed Peyton, waiting for his next move; it didn't disappoint. Peyton's sweaty hands grabbed a firm hold and practiced a few long strokes. Roman moaned, and he felt his loins contract. More fluid left him, lubricating Peyton's hand as his thrusts quickened. Not wanting his first orgasm with Peyton to be like that, Roman pushed his hand out of the way, grabbed onto his mate's pants, and repeated the same motions. He didn't allow Peyton any modesty. Peyton's naked body sent the aroma of slick into the room. It made his own spine tremble.

Roman's large hand grabbed onto Peyton's member and reciprocated. Peyton moaned quietly, letting his mate's name escape his lips. With his eyes closed, he felt his vision flash brighter. In a matter of seconds, he felt familiar fires deep within.

Peyton pulled his head off the pillow and looked down at Roman stroking the both of them in tandem. The sensation built a pressure deep inside him which was getting ready to release. Peyton clenched his eyes as he felt a rush come over him. As he orgasmed deep, he felt slick spill out from his insides. Roman moaned as Peyton's cock grew even stiffer in Roman's hands. Seconds later, glands in his cock began their own rhythmic pulse, and load after load of hot seed escaped him, coating his chest and stomach. While in the throes of orgasm, he felt Roman's body grab his and spin him around, so Peyton was on top.

Roman felt Peyton sit up which gave him a full view of his body in a new light and angle. He was unblemished as if the sun never touched him. He observed Peyton's own cock—hard again as if he never had an orgasm—an enjoyable sight. Roman massaged every inch of Peyton's body as he felt Peyton involuntarily grind his cock up against his. While this seemed to suffice Peyton for the moment, Roman began to think about the next steps in this process.

As much as he viewed this moment as organic, Roman also couldn't ignore Peyton's father practically demanding this to happen so he could feel better about himself.

What kind of inquisition are we going to be subjected to? Has Peyton's Sur hidden a camera in this room so he can take notes and critique me on how he doesn't approve of my mating techniques?

Roman decided to let Peyton make the decision. To give Peyton some clue of his thoughts, he lifted Peyton's hips up and forward. Now, Roman's very sensitive cock was rocked tight against the center of Peyton's generous ass. Peyton continued his thrusts, pumping drops of slick all the way down to the base of Roman's cock, then to Roman's balls and into the sheets below.

Wanting to gauge his tolerance, Roman slid one finger inside him before inserting a second. Peyton's face showed no signs of pain, impressive since Roman's fingers weren't small. Assuming Peyton would take charge of the penetration, Roman let him orchestrate, but they didn't progress further. Roman wondered if Peyton was lost in ecstasy or unsure if he wanted to proceed. But Peyton's current movements were very pleasurable and beginning to become unbearable. A heat rose from his balls, and they didn't give much warning.

"Peyton," he panted, "if you don't stop..." He moaned more loudly with each motion. Not able to reach his mate, Roman didn't have any more power to hold out. As a natural reaction, he grabbed the shaft of his own cock. Peyton leaned forward one more time and pushed back, lining up his swollen hole against Roman's extended cock head.

In a muscled push and deep groan, Roman's cum shot out with audible impacts like pushing water out of a pressurized gun. Hot seed splashed all over Peyton's wet hole and down Roman's cock. Roman was all too happy to show Peyton just how much a heated Alpha could produce. Eventually, the orgasm subsided, and both he and Peyton were well coated on the outside of their bodies. Roman panted heavily, barely able to catch his breath. As he looked down, Roman saw his own chest covered in Peyton's second load. He then grabbed Peyton and met him halfway down, moaning deep into the Omega's mouth.

Roman saw Peyton smile and sigh with relief. Though he didn't say anything, Roman felt the sex was incomplete. Obviously, the penetration didn't go as he expected, but there was still an experience he wanted which he had never done before. After Peyton's face indicated he thought the act had ended, Roman surprised him by gathering a layer of his own cum on several fingers and began to fuck him.

Peyton gasped and whimpered in agony. He was sensitive to every motion. Semen felt very different from the natural slick he produced, leaving him in thralls of ecstasy. Having Roman stretch him open with his fluids made Peyton feel things he never had before; it was addicting. As the pleasure grew, he pushed back on Roman's hand. Peyton's expression spiked when he felt Roman's fingers press against his swollen Omega glands and prostate at the same time. The act sent him back to deep long groans he couldn't stop.

Roman's constant massaging caused blood to rush to Peyton's inner reproductive organs. If he was in heat, his womb would push down, preparing for impregnation. But right now, all he could focus on was feeling like a second heartbeat was happening inside him. When the sensitivity became too much, Peyton felt slick rush out like he'd never felt before.

In another orgasm, Peyton screamed as he felt his hole spasm. Roman egged him on with his own moans of approval, getting his hand covered in Peyton's clear slick. When the orgasm faded, Peyton thrust off Roman's fingers and collapsed on top of him. Sweat collected everywhere, but his sensations were numb; his whole body was. He felt Roman's strong arms wrap around him and plant a kiss on his forehead.

"Are you okay?" Roman asked, knowing he had sent his mate into sensation overload.

"I don't know how to describe what just happened," Peyton replied. "It was the most intense experience I've ever had in my life."

Roman spoke softly, "It was quite the experience for me, too."

"I'll have to memorialize it," Peyton panted.

"Hmm?" Roman lifted his head.

"I have a diary. I write down the best moments. With you, that's all of them."

"Glad to hear it." Roman paused. "Me too," he added.

Even though Roman responded quickly, his mind was going in so many different directions. The sex was satisfying, no doubt about that. But he had so many questions.

Did Peyton abstain from penetration on purpose? How does he feel about me after all this? What does he expect the next part of our relationship to look like? And finally, can I bear to tell Peyton he isn't everything I need?

CHAPTER 12:

A Crushing Cocktail Hour

Both Rixen and Ryan spotted the bright taxi pulling up in the driveway. When Roman stepped out, they watched every step he took as he approached the house. When the door finally opened, they rushed to the foyer.

"Boys!" Jake yelled, disapproval in his tone.

Roman was greeted with two excited lap puppies practically humping his leg. "Wolf-God, what the hell, you two?"

"What?" Ryan began. "You didn't honestly think you were going to get very far without having to spill your guts, right?"

"Hey!" Adrian walked over. "Give him a break, guys!"

"No way!" Rixen replied. Roman groaned and sidestepped to make his way to the basement.

Adrian crossed his arms. "You know, when you find your mates, you're going to want some privacy too—and be frustrated when you don't get it."

"What do you mean? We'll get it. Roman will be so focused on his mate, he won't care about us. He won't even be here."

"Phones exist, you know," Adrian snapped back.

"Good point. Gotta go!" Ryan said from two fleeing legs, Rixen on his tail. Without knocking, Ryan pushed his older brother's bedroom door open to the sight of him in his underwear getting ready to put on pajama pants and a white t-shirt.

"Dude! You both have to chill!" Roman grabbed his phone and lay on his bed, staring down at the two investigative cops in front of him.

"Sur didn't tell us until this morning where you were. He made us give up our phones so we wouldn't contact you," Rixen shared.

"You two willingly gave Dad your phones?"

"Otherwise, he said he'd take the power cords to the gaming systems," Ryan replied bitterly.

"Yeah, he wasn't playin'," Rixen added.

"Damn!" Roman looked at his phone. A new message appeared from Peyton. He opened it to see the pictures they took in the restaurant with a heart symbol below them. Not to completely leave him in the dark, he sent a smiling face back with the intention of messaging him later.

After a few seconds of dead air, Ryan tapped the side of Roman's feet. "Don't make us ask again, seriously." Ryan observed his brother. "Is that him on your phone?"

"Yes, it is." Roman turned his phone around to show them the pictures. Like moths to flame, his brothers gawked at the photo.

"Wow. Cute," Rixen commented.

"Nice!" Ryan stressed. "That's at the restaurant? How was that?"

Roman divulged the details, starting with Matthew Whitmore's stupid outline for the evening. His brothers couldn't get enough of that. Then, he discussed the highlights of the conversations between him and Peyton including the continuous rapport. Then, it went to the night's stay in the hotel.

"Basically, you followed Matthew's demands," Rixen concluded.

"That went through my mind too, but I promise it was more authentic than that."

"So, the chemistry went well?"

"If you mean the sex, yes. And I'm not telling you all the details of that. Sorry," Roman declared.

"I can live with that," Rixen replied. "Still, congratulations on losing your penetration virginity. Guess we can't poke at you for that one anymore. No pun intended." He grinned while Roman stared at his phone in silence. Rixen leaned in. "Did you do that?"

"I tried." Roman struggled to explain.

Rixen and Ryan did a double take to each other and then back at their brother, his face looking like he was preparing to rip off a sticky bandage.

"Roman, I haven't known anyone to have sex and physically fail at penetration," Ryan criticized.

"Thanks, asshole. It wasn't like that," Roman snapped back as his face turned red. His brothers continued to stare and wait. "I was there ready to do it. And it just didn't happen. He was on top of me, and he just didn't go through with it."

"Do you think he didn't want it?" Rixen asked.

"No. I mean, he was so open and willing to discuss everything else. I have to imagine he felt comfortable enough to tell me if he wasn't ready for it." Roman reflected once more, trying to crack the mystery.

"An Omega choosing not to have his mate penetrate him. That's not a good sign, Roman," Rixen criticized.

Now Roman went on the defense. "You don't know him, Rixen! Maybe not every Omega is like that. Besides, it's not like you've had any experience lately."

"Says who?" Rixen flared.

Roman blinked, caught off guard. "Seriously? Who?"

Rixen wondered for a second if he wanted to bring up the topic. He looked down at Ryan who was sitting on the bed giving him a nasty look back. "That's not important right now," he murmured. "So, what's next?"

"Oh," Roman deflated, "that's the next issue. You see, Matthew only 'allowed' us to do this because Peyton's heat is coming up in two weeks. I guess that's the next step."

"Wait. Peyton's Sur set the whole evening up because of Peyton's heat? So, this wasn't just to practice for the sake of practicing. This was an audition for the real thing coming up," Ryan laid out.

"I don't think you have to describe it as an 'audition,'" Roman replied.

"You know those last three days, right?" Rixen pointed out. "Unless it's an emotional heat. Then it's just the single event."

"I went to school too, you know. You don't need to remind of me of that."

"Good news is they're excused days for classes and work."

"There's that," Roman quipped, staring down at his phone, a signal for the end of the conversation.

Rixen sighed optimistically. "It does sound like everything is headed in the right direction. Soon, you'll feel the connection you need for your mate, and you won't have to worry about anyone choosing not to support your contract."

Roman looked up. "Huh?"

"Nothing," Rixen dismissed. He turned and left the room but not before seeing Ryan eye him with disdain—a look Rixen pointedly ignored.

Roman looked at Ryan, unable to ignore his crossed expression. "What's up with him? What's up with you?"

"It's nothing. He's just making another stupid decision." Ryan crossed his arms.

"Is he," Roman paused, "sleeping with someone?"

Ryan felt his hands tense up. "That's what I've been told."

"Not that I'm judging, but why is he always involved with a guy in one way or another?"

"He's starved for attention and approval, I guess. I don't understand him anymore."

Roman's head turned. "You seem out of it. Did you two have an all-out war a couple days ago? Because if you did, you don't look like you've recovered."

Ryan's face frowned at the memory of his heated exchange with Rixen. It still hurt as if it had happened a few minutes ago. "I don't know what's going on. He's like revolting against me or something. He's doing his own stuff, and he doesn't want to tell me anything anymore."

"You're not the easiest person to talk to, you know," Roman commented.

"I'm his brother!"

"So? I am too."

"It's a special twin bonding thing. You wouldn't understand."

"Sure," Roman sighed. "I'm taking a nap and not waking up until tomorrow."

"Oh, you can't do that," Ryan replied.

"Huh? Why?"

"Tonight is dinner with dad's friend or co-worker, whatever he is, and his family."

Roman moaned. "I forgot. Please no."

"Should be fun," Ryan added sarcastically. "At least we don't have school tomorrow."

"Gotta love Wolf Moon holidays!" Roman stretched out and yawned.

"You know it. Later, man!"

"Mhm. Bye." Roman looked at his phone one last time to see the pictures from the date as the last thing he saw before sleeping. He smiled with his head on the pillow and closed his eyes.

***

"Ryan, I need you to set the table!" Adrian demanded, prepping the night's meal.

"Veo, I've been cleaning all afternoon for this. Why can't Rixen do it?" Ryan attempted to deflect the order.

"Because Rixen is doing other odds and ends I told him to do, and now I'm telling you to do this." Adrian pointed at his son with a wine glass like it was a commanding wand or warning weapon.

"Okay, what about Roman then? He's been sleeping all day!"

"Leave him alone," Adrian stressed.

"Oh, so what? He has sex all night, and now he doesn't have to help?"

Adrian sighed and rubbed the back of his head. Not wanting to argue, he settled sarcastically on "Yes."

"Wolf-God, by that standard, Rixen should be on rest for a month," Ryan muttered.

"What?" Adrian asked, only half listening as he dug for fancy presentation trays.

"Nothing," Ryan replied. He finished the elegant table with silver cloth, silver napkins, and white accents. The shining silverware was a nice touch. "There. Done."

"Wait. Sorry. You're short one," Adrian observed.

"What do you mean?" Ryan questioned. "You said there were three of them, and there's five of us. That's eight."

"Right, but Rixen is bringing over a friend. He's looked so depressed lately, I thought it would cheer him up." Adrian noticed the candle centerpiece missing and went to grab it, not seeing Ryan's visual response.

Ryan's stomach dropped. He didn't want to ask his dad who exactly it was, but he hoped against hope the answer wasn't the one person he couldn't handle right now. "Who?" his voiced cracked.

"A friend from his volleyball team. I hate to say it, but I don't remember his name."

Ryan braced himself, already knowing the answer. "Garrace?"

"Yes, that's it. Glad you know him," Adrian replied, still not fully committed to the conversation.

"I didn't say I did." Ryan spoke harshly, louder than he wanted to be heard.

"Is something wrong? Kind of grouchy, if I do say so myself."

"I'm good. I'm just tired," Ryan dismissed.

"Well hold out tonight the best you can. Everyone will be here in an hour. This is very important to your father. He wants this to go as smooth as possible. I can't believe he's worked with this man for five years, and we've never had him over here."

"Why is that?"

"Your father and I have been to several dinners with them. If I could guess, it was just so much easier to go out. Now that we're doing all this, I can see why. Oh hey, before I forget...I know you and your brother said you don't know Mikaél, but if you could make him feel welcome and keep him entertained, your father and I would be forever grateful. My fear is Rixen might leave him out of the loop with his friend Garrace here."

More than you know, Ryan thought.

With less than an hour to go, everyone forgot Roman was still asleep. Ryan was instructed to go down to wake him up. Roman grunted back at him which meant he'd be up in 20 minutes. Not really caring what his brother did, Ryan walked back upstairs to find Rixen coming in from taking out the trash. Anger flooding him, he grabbed Rixen by the arm and forcefully assisted him into the corner of the formal living room out of sight from the kitchen.

"What the hell?" Rixen said.

"Shhh! Keep your voice down," Ryan demanded.

"What the fuck is wrong with you?"

"No, that's my question." Ryan felt his body shake with anger. It was so hard for him to keep his voice down. Luckily, Veo in the kitchen was making quite the production noise while Sur helped him with the final touches.

"What do you mean?"

"You asked Veo if you could invite Garrace? Have you lost your mind?"

"You're serious? You're going to do this to me now?" Rixen's voice was frustrated.

"I'd have a lot better time getting used to your dumbass mistakes if you didn't choose to throw them right in my face!" Ryan condemned him, adding sharp and hasty hand gestures to fit his maddening position.

"Why are you making this such a big deal? I told you this before: this is my life and my decision. You need to let this go. I'm not your responsibility, and you don't have any control over me, so just get used to it!" Rixen declared.

Ryan bit his lip and tapped his foot. The words he wanted to say were difficult. He wanted to say anything to get Rixen back from the likes of Garrace. Ryan was the only one in his corner who could protect him and keep him safe. But nothing out of Ryan's mouth was helping his cause. Everything Ryan kept saying only pushed his brother further and further away, and it was killing him—more than Ryan ever wanted to admit.

"Look. I know I've been a horrible brother lately. And I wish I could express the right words on how I truly feel without hurting you as much as I have. I care about you, and I'm scared for you. I'm scared he's going to screw you over." Ryan paused. "I hope, by saying that, you can see I'm not trying to hurt you on purpose. I'm trying to protect you, and I'm failing at it. I'm sorry for what I did to you. You're my brother, and I love you. And if Garrace is here tonight because I hurt you, I can live with that. It's just one night."

Ryan sighed, knowing he did the best he could. He saw Rixen's anger and frustration melt from his face. He finally saw through the horrible words and actions to see the real Ryan underneath. Seeing

Rixen smile shortly thereafter made him feel so good—like he finally got somewhere with his brother for the first time in a long time.

Rixen nodded and took in the words. He barely remembered his brother being so kind, thoughtful, and emotional. It was the part he'd always desired from his brother. It was a beautiful moment, and he never wanted it to stop, but he had no choice but to respond.

"I don't know what to say other than 'thank you.' You saying this to me means a lot—it really does. When all the hate gets peeled away, I know how you feel about me and that it comes from a good place. Knowing you have my back is what I've always wanted. And you have no idea how happy I am to hear you say you want to protect me." Rixen saw his brother smile like it was the morning of Winter Solstice. The bona fide smile and soft expression warmed Rixen, and he reached out and gave his brother a deep hug, sighing into his shoulder. The apology was more than accepted. As he pulled away from his brother, he continued, "And I know you're always going to make protecting me your priority as long as we're here together. But that's not going to be for much longer."

Ryan's head tilted in confusion. "What do you mean 'not much longer'?"

Rixen braced himself, hoping the truce truly meant something. "I know you, Sur, and Veo think I invited Garrace because of how hard things have been for me since our fight, and yes, there is some truth to that. But that's not the full reason why I invited him, Ryan."

Ryan's voice became shallow. "Why did you then?"

"I wanted our parents to meet him because Garrace and I have talked about making a mating contract."

Ryan's brain went haywire, and he saw stars float in front of him. In a matter of seconds, his heart rate accelerated as if he'd run the mile in five minutes, and his breathing followed. "No," he said quietly. The distance between his brother not only grew physically, but emotional too as he backed away. "No, Rixen, you can't."

"Ryan, but I thought..."

Ryan's voice trembled on the verge of a breakdown. His mind warped and his heart shattered. His hands held his head, pretending to rewind his brain and play it all over again on mute so he didn't have to hear it. But he couldn't. "Please no, not that."

"Ryan, stop. You're scaring me." Rixen stepped forward in order to help calm his brother who was going into a panic attack.

Ryan felt Rixen's head against his as he attempted to call him down. There were words Rixen was speaking, but he wasn't sure what they were. The void moment was suddenly stopped in its tracks by a loud bell bouncing off all the walls in the house.

"Someone's here!" Jake yelled from the kitchen. "Rixen, that's for you. Can you get the door?"

A slender figure of a tall young man stood on the doorstep, peering in through the clear glass door. In a goldenrod button down, it made his fair skin pop. He had a full head of dark brown hair, thick eyebrows, long eyelashes with amber eyes, and soft pink lips. His baby face highlighted a bright outgoing personality.

Rixen watched his brother in the formal living room freeze like a deer in headlights. He stared at Ryan for a second, knowing they both had to pull themselves together—like yesterday. He stroked his shoulder a few times, then headed toward the door. Upon opening, Rixen smiled with glee as Garrace returned the expression.

"Good evening!" Garrace walked in with confidence and went straight to Rixen's arms. He hugged him gingerly as he balanced a small arrangement of seasonal flowers. Garrace leaned forward and gave him a soft kiss to show his elation, a gesture Rixen was more than wanting to return, although it sent nerves through him knowing Ryan was behind them watching in agony.

"I brought these; I hope your parents won't think it too weird of me." Garrace attempted a nervous smile, hoping he did the right thing.

"Veo will love it. I promise." He gave a kiss of approval and led him in into the kitchen. "Veo, Sur, this is Garrace."

Both parents looked up for the moment. Jake stepped forward with his posture held high to show Garrace he was the Alpha in the house. "Very nice to meet you," he said with a firm handshake.

Adrian walked up warmly with a hug and marveled at the bouquet Garrace presented. "Why, thank you! They're beautiful." He turned to the right to see a very full table. "I'm afraid our dining table is full, but I think they'd go great over by the window."

"Absolutely," Garrace beamed.

Rixen reached out with his left hand and stroked the center of Garrace's back while watching his reaction ever so carefully. He returned a cautious smile. Looking back at his Veo, Rixen saw his father give a gentle smile which read he understood the gesture.

"I hope you don't mind I'm early; I didn't know how long it would take for me to get out here."

Jake looked up from his deep inspection of the large dining room, kitchen, and living room seamlessly put together in the over-sized room. "No problem whatsoever. I respect early; it's late I can't stand. Would you like a drink?"

"Sure, if you're offering."

"Of course. Are you a wine drinker?"

"Thank you, Mr. Erricson."

Jake grabbed two glasses, knowing all too well Rixen would join him in the offering. "Here you are. Rixen, where's your brother?"

"Here." Ryan stood a few feet behind Rixen near the open entry way to the kitchen. His inner strength held his outward appearance together.

"Ryan, you want one?" his Sur offered.

"Yes, please," he remarked. Ryan ignored Rixen's stoic face studying him, giving Garrace a full look like he was an Alpha instead of a Beta.

For Garrace, seeing Ryan was a tense, awkward situation. He sensed the frustrated pheromones coming from him but kept his face civil and welcoming. "I don't think we've properly met."

Ryan accepted Garrace's outstretched hand with his noticeably warmer palm and shook confidently. Walking up to the island, he lifted the glass his Veo left on the bar adjacent to the back of the high-quality cabinetry of the kitchen.

"Dad, I hope you carded Garrace. I'd hate for him to chance an underage violation on the way home." He took his first drink, proud of his comment.

Rixen glared. "He's 18." He pivoted topics. "The Cavenbelles should be here shortly. Apparently, their son Mikaél is the same Level as us. I don't know him. Do you?"

Garrace's stomach fluttered, and he choked slightly on his present swallow of wine. Of all the nights to show his integrity for a goal of a mating contract, now he was going to be face-to-face with his ex-lover.

"Yeah, I know him," he said skittishly.

"You must be the gentleman who convinced Rixen to join the volleyball team," Adrian spoke with pep.

"I am." Garrace's joy returned as the conversation shifted to the topic of Rixen. He saw his current lover gesture to the far side of the granite countertop and two bar stools with metal backing.

"I think it's great Rixen's found a sport he's passionate about. We were always worried about him staying active." Adrian began putting delectable hors d'ouevres onto a tray, handing the leftovers to Rixen and Garrace for sampling. He sighed happily when they both complimented the well-thought-out combination.

Ryan made a bold move to the opposite side of the countertop, across from the two boys, forcing him to stand. "I have to ask, how were able to convince him? I could never get Rixen to feel passionate about any sport." A deliberate grin crossed his lips.

Garrace returned the expression as Rixen swallowed hard.

"We knew each other from a book talk over the summer and were excited to have our Wolf Mythology class together this year. We clicked so much it was an easy conversation to approach. It didn't take a lot of convincing at all." Garrace's hand went on Rixen's leg which was met with a joyous response.

Garrace was fortunate Ryan possessed self-control at the moment. He wanted to rush in and punch Garrace right in the face. His stomach sickened as he now realized how his brother was able to make this all work. Although Rixen did have a visible build, Ryan's was more defined due to his higher dedication to staying fit. While he did swim and jog, Rixen went to the library and participated in a book club. From there, they must have planned a schedule which included a course Ryan had zero interest in. Ryan chose a finance class instead—the only class the twins didn't have together. In front of him, Ryan saw two confident men who weren't afraid to show their obsession with each other with subtle affection. It made his heart hurt more than anything. "I think I'm going to find Roman," he grumbled.

"No need to." Roman stood in the entry in a white button down and black pants. His short hair was straight up, and it appeared as if he was going on another date, a look his father certainly appreciated.

"He lives!" his Sur gasped.

"Sorry. I didn't mean to be so behind. Still recovering from last night," Roman shared.

"I bet you are," Ryan teased.

All the family subtly reacted in their own way with Garrace missing the inside joke.

Roman chose to eye Ryan specifically with his classic "shut your face" look. He noticed the bar setup nicely in the traditional fashion of a party or a celebration. It called to him, and he poured himself a glass of red.

"When do they get here?" Roman asked.

"They should be here any minute," Adrian replied, finishing his masterpieces with a drying of his hands and a satisfied expression.

Ryan took a few steps to sit on the opposite side of the oversized granite island, getting a far view of Rixen staring at Garrace in quiet conversation.

"Oh, Roman," Rixen began, "this is Garrace. He's the one from the volleyball team." He threw his hand around to Garrace's far shoulder and squeezed him nearer. He saw Ryan turn and face him with a grimace.

"Nice to meet you." Roman lifted his glass in acknowledgement but as his glass came back toward him, the momentum sloshed back and landed scarlet pools on his clean shirt. "Damn it!" He stood up in immediate reaction.

Jake sighed. "Go change."

***

"Dustin and Alec. Welcome," Jake greeted with a smile. He gave hugs as if he met distant relatives or classmates from high school. "Mikaél, glad to you see you again." A gentle smile returned to Jake as he grinned at his co-worker. "Dustin, you have a mighty fine specimen of a boy there."

Dustin snorted. "Wolf-God, Jake, are you going to dissect him later?"

"Depends, are you charging or donating?" he returned sarcastically. He eyed Mikaél, who appeared a bit offput. "Ah, just kidding. Come on in! We have drinks ready and some pre-dinner appetizers."

Alec smiled. "Sounds wonderful." He followed his mate and his son through a formal living and dining room and into a large open kitchen space with a beautiful gray granite countertop and matching cabinets. Beyond it was a welcoming living space with high ceilings, large inset mantle, fireplace, couches, TV, and large open windows overlooking a beautiful well-kept green yard and brick patio. "Adrian, your home is absolutely gorgeous."

"Thank you. We've done so much to it over the years," he replied, admiring his own work.

"Wow. Any other projects planned?"

"If the ambition hits me, I'll start putting in a covered patio with a walkway to the water feature we have back there before winter comes. Damn thing gets covered in leaves and is a pain to clean out." Adrian sealed his words with a sip of a cool and crisp white wine.

Alec shook his head in disbelief. "I still can't believe you do all these handy jobs yourself. I can put nails in a wall and a file cabinet together with a 50-page instruction manual. Although I have the talent to visualize what I want, I could never construct an entire backyard. Guess that's why Wolf-God made me a photographer." Alec's focus turned to the two boys sitting near the sliding glass door. His mind snapped back. "Oh, Mikaél, this is Jake's son... um... Rixen?"

"You got it," Rixen confirmed with a smile. "Nice to meet you, Mikaél." He waved.

Alec continued, "And then that must be Ryan over there, but I don't know who you are. You don't look like an Erricson."

"I'm Garrace. Nice to meet you." Garrace stood up and greeted Alec with a frozen face keeping up appearances.

"Garrace," Alec mused, "now why does that name sound familiar?"

Mikaél interjected, "Oh, you know, just a guy from school. I've talked about him before. Nice to see you, again." Mikaél's enthusiasm was muted.

"Same," Garrace replied, eyeing the room to see who could read in between the lines.

"I've been told you're a Level 2, right?" Ryan walked up to the island.

"I am," Mikaél replied.

"I'm sorry. I can't say I've seen you before," Ryan confessed.

"I don't think you'd know me from a crowd or anything. That being said, I have seen you, or well, both of you for that matter." Mikaél acknowledged Rixen in the comment and studied Garrace's face ever so cautiously.

"How about after we go back to classes on Tuesday, we all hang out? There's a burger place we like to go. We could go there," Ryan offered, looking at Adrian for praise of his efforts.

"Thank you. I'd like that a lot, actually." Mikaél replied.

Adrian cut in, "We have starters if you'd like. Plates and napkins and Jake can assist everyone with drinks." All nodded with delight and began to settle into the evening.

"Can I use your restroom to wash my hands quickly?" Mikaél asked.

"Of course. Go down to the end of the hall and take a left," Adrian replied.

"I know where it is," Garrace motioned. "I can take him down there."

"Smooth, Garrace. Really smooth," Mikaél critiqued Garrace's shoddy attempt at getting a moment alone. He ran the water from the tap and waited for warm water.

"You have to know I had no idea this was going to happen tonight," Garrace stated, holding the door open in case Mikaél felt like slamming it in his face.

"Oh, I know that. I've known you to do a lot of stupid things, Garrace. But intentionally putting yourself in the position to pay the piper? No, you'd never do that." Mikaél eyed him sternly. Upon the sensation of hot water, he pumped a couple squirts of soap and rubbed his hands like he was trying to take the top layer of his epidermis off.

Garrace shifted his weight and put his cocky entitled face back on. "Come on, Mik. Why you gotta be like that?" With the words came a smile which showed Garrace was entertained by Mikaél's frustration, not concerned by it.

"Is that him?" Mikaél asked, finishing the warm rinse on his hands.

"Who?" Garrace looked confused.

"Rixen. Is that who I lost to when I wouldn't put out?" Mikaél grabbed the hanging towel and began to dry off his hands, this time wanting to look Garrace straight in the eyes.

"See. This right here is where we fell apart. You just think everything was about sex."

"No. You think everything is about sex. Every single time we'd find ourselves alone, it was a touch here, a grope there. Then there were the questions you didn't feel like waiting to hear the answers to. You're a nympho, for Wolf-God's sake!"

"Most find that to be a compliment," Garrace boasted.

"Let me guess: he does?" Mikaél asked.

"Yes, he does," Garrace said with confidence.

"Wow." Mikaél checked his disgust in the reflection of the bathroom mirror. "You know, I may have my own reservations about sex—in fact, I know I do—but it became my second biggest concern with you."

Garrace paused. "Okay. I'll bite. What was the first?"

"Hypothetically, if I did end up sleeping with you, were you going to leave? Was I just your conquest because I wasn't going to give in so easy? Was I going to be yesterday's lay? Because, clearly, I know the drill when you don't get sex on your terms. You find it anyway, and I find out later."

"I think you'll find most guys leave the relationship when their lovers don't put out," Garrace defended.

"No, that's what pouty, insensitive, selfish pricks do. They put out a 'Want Ad' titled 'Begging for Ass,' and then pick their favorite sleaze to fulfill it."

"Are you really going characterize Rixen like that in his own home?"

"No," Mikaél stated firmly.

"Why not?"

"Because I'm hoping he's a good guy; I'm hoping maybe since you are finally having your cake and eating it too, maybe you'll stop to see how good you have it and quit throwing everyone away when the relationship gets tough."

"Is that what you think I do?" Garrace asked suspiciously.

"I know you do it. It's not hard to find a past lover of yours willing to tell all, Garrace. Rixen thinks he's got it 'good.' I can see it in the way he looks at you, but he doesn't know the side of you I do."

"Maybe it's because everyone else is minding their own damn business."

"Or maybe it's because no one knows you're an item yet?" Mikaél gazed at Garrace: no response. "Of course, that's what it is. I mean, I didn't even know. I can only imagine what's going to happen once people do."

"Are you going to be the one to tell all, now that you do know?"

Mikaél paused, looking down. "I don't know."

Garrace stood up, knowing they were on borrowed time before the scout was sent out to see where they were. "What about tonight?"

"I'm here for my Sur. I'm not going to do anything here. But this isn't over."

"Is that a threat?" Garrace narrowed his eyes.

"No, it's a fact. I got invited to hang out after school Tuesday. I'm sure I'll see you. Looking forward to it." Mikaél walked out, feeling the chill register in Garrace's haunted face.

CHAPTER 13:

A Dinner with Destiny

Roman began to unbutton his shirt as he descended the stairs. Walking down to the landing, he heard the doorbell and sighed. This was all happening so perfectly—not. He walked to the laundry room on the way to his room, threw the soiled shirt in the wash bin, and ran the water mixed with detergent. While letting it soak, he could hear the welcoming conversations continue. He walked back to his bedroom and choose a desert rose shirt and completed his look in the mirror.

As he walked out of his room toward the stairs, a headache rushed over him. The pain ran down to his extremities and threw off his balance. As it subsided to a dull memory, he reached the main floor. A couple of deep voices reached his ears followed by a lighter, younger one. The younger voice rang in his ears continuously, and he couldn't stop the sound. The sudden discomfort aggravated him. Peering into the kitchen, he eyed his wine glass on the table in hopes that it would provide immediate relief. After a generous swallow, he glanced to his left to see three new faces.

Both Cavenbelle fathers stood firmly and bore a twinkle in their eyes, feeling welcomed into the home by both his parents. Next to them, in front of the armrest of the large couch, stood a slender boy with a kind, innocent, and timid face. Roman felt his body temperature rise and senses heighten. In his nostrils, he inhaled a seductive clove and orange aroma and narrowed in on the boy, who was still focused on the discussion taking place.

Ryan, Rixen, and Garrace noticed the changes in Roman first. They observed for a few seconds, not registering the danger about to occur. Garrace turned his head slightly and began to trust his intuition as he smelled a strong dominating Alpha scent.

"Is he okay?" was all he could muster in a delicate, perplexing voice, hoping someone else noticed too.

Jake turned around as the comment reached his ear, missing Roman's scent completely. "Roman, there you are. I want you to meet Dustin and Alec Cavenbelle, and this is their son Mikaél."

Something about hearing the boy's name pushed Roman to a point of no return—ensuring no one would forget what happened next. The muscles in his hands flexed as his arms pushed out, completely sending his wine glass shooting off the kitchen island and crashing to the floor. He eyed Mikaél who stared back at him in an equally concerned expression shared around the room. Pushing himself off the granite, Roman thrust himself forward, straight into Mikaél, forcefully lifting and knocking him back onto the couch.

"What the hell!" Dustin exclaimed as he saw his son fall back.

"Roman, what are you doing?" Jake boomed, watching his son stand over Mikaél, shaking with adrenaline.

Mikaél stared back at Roman's commanding form watching him pant like a wild animal a couple feet away from his face. His eyes were wide and full of fright. He wanted to get up and escape, but as his head flooded with Roman's scent, he couldn't make himself move. He heard Roman grunt and crawl hastily over the arm of the couch to plant his body on top of him. Mikaél made an involuntary thrust forward with a gasp, but Roman quickly met it with two hands, pushing hard onto his chest.

"Roman, are you mad?! Get off of him!" Adrian yelled. As he stepped forward to intervene, he felt Jake stop him with an arm outstretched like a crossing gate.

All of Roman's human stability vanished. Internally, his brain morphed into a primitive wolf looking to take ownership of what was rightfully his. Nothing was going to stop him from his goal. Nothing. As he pushed his body tighter against Mikaél, his loins heated and throbbed like he never experienced before in his life. Feeling Mikaél struggle under him only made Roman want to control him more.

There was enough of a struggle for Roman to lose his balance and fall off the couch, bringing Mikaél right down on top of him. The position caused Roman to lie vulnerable on his back which angered him. He watched Mikaél catch his breath as he regained more freedom of his upper body. It wasn't what Roman wanted. He needed to control this Omega and make him submit to his demands.

Roman wrapped his muscled legs around him and in a swift motion forced Mikaél beneath him once more, flat against the floor. In this position, he felt Mikaél's hands reach up in order to force him off. Grabbing both of his hands in his, he pushed Mikaél's arms back flat against the floor and readjusted to hold his forearms down as he continued to try and get Mikaél to submit.

"Dustin, do something!" Alec demanded.

Jake once again warned. "No, you can't do that."

"Why?" Alec screamed.

"It will only make it worse!" Jake stressed. He looked at his twin sons who were now at their father's side in a state of shock.

Mikaél groaned in discomfort as his mind began to spin. He couldn't figure out why he wasn't being forthright in screaming at Roman to stop or demanding help. He felt Roman thrust his heavy hips against him which made him feel violated at first. Mikaél noticed his own body sweat, his manhood stiffening in his pants as his reproductive glands contracted without warning, producing slick which felt hot and moist on the outside of his pulsing hole. It confused and embarrassed him at the same time, but he didn't want it to stop.

Mikaél's strength was beginning to weaken, preventing him from making any movement of consequence. He saw Roman's eyes sparkle as if they were a kaleidoscope in motion. The longer he stared at them, the more he noticed Roman's pupils were throbbing, making the beautiful color disappear into an ominous black. Having a sudden moment of panic overtake him, Mikaél took the final piece of energy he had and kneed Roman in his rock-hard groin.

Roman grunted in pain. "Fuck! Just submit! Come on!" His voice was gruff and menacing. He readjusted his body weight which successfully controlled Mikaél's lower body again. Not getting what he wanted from Mikaél built his rage even more. He scented Mikaél's overpowering fear which hid the fragrance he desired to be bathed in. Attempting to get back the intoxicating smell he was now addicted to, he wanted to get closer to Mikaél's skin.

With Mikaél still thrashing and grunting, Roman grabbed the first thing he could get his hands on. In a quick motion, Roman released his left hand from Mikaél's forearm, snagged the fabric at the top of Mikaél's shirt in his fist, and tore the shirt completely down the center to his stomach.

Mikaél screamed and began to shudder, squeezing his eyes tight. "Why are you doing this to me!" Mikaél began to whimper beneath the Alpha. A sharp, hot pain blossomed on his chest as he could feel heavy scratch marks dig into his skin from his collarbone down across his chest. As his eyes began to tear up, he felt his body collapse to Roman's will. Surprisingly enough, Roman held still on top of him and didn't move to attack him any further. Focusing for the first time since the attack, Mikaél felt his own senses change. A magnetism grew and his heart warmed. He took note of his own voice trembling. His fear turned into intrigue as feelings began to surface. As Roman's dark fiery scent subsided, Mikaél felt his true scent of forest and fresh rain rush in. Finally, he realized what Roman wanted—what he needed.

Roman's torch of fury died to a smolder, and the true aura of this Omega below him came through. Mikaél's true scent calmed the beast inside him. But as his face began to soften, he felt an unwanted presence rush near him without warning and grab his shoulders.

It was Ryan, trying to apprehend his older brother.

"Wolf-God, Roman! Get off of him!"

Roman's weight became heavier on Mikaél as he used him for leverage in order to take a violent swing which knocked Ryan back into the armrest of the couch.

"Ryan, stop!" Jake shouted.

"How can you just stand there and let Roman tear him apart?!" Ryan yelled, hearing Mikaél's frustration return after his brother struck him.

"There's too many of us in the room! Roman feels threatened. If you attack him, it's going to cause a dangerous chain reaction which Mikaél is going to have to pay for!"

"Jake, we can't just do nothing!" Dustin fumed, wanting to tear Roman into pieces for what he was doing to his son.

"That's exactly what we need to do. We're getting out of this room. Now!" Jake demanded, pushing his own sons out of the room, with everyone else following.

***

Roman looked down at Mikaél who appeared somewhere between fear and relief. Feeling like Mikaél was finally understanding his needs, he relaxed his grip on his arms and began to hold his own upper body weight. As he did so, he felt Mikaél's hands instantly grab his muscled arms and squeeze. But this time, Roman didn't flinch, he didn't growl, and he didn't try to prove he was stronger than him. Mikaél must have noticed because his grip softened and melted away.

Roman took his hand and held the back of Mikaél's head and brought it to his. "I feel it. Don't pretend you don't," Roman whispered. He heard Mikaél resist for a moment, then felt his body shake ever so lightly beneath him. Looking into his eyes, Roman saw Mikaél's beautiful blue eyes pulse to black just like his. The connection sent a wave through both of them simultaneously. Roman felt Mikaél's pelvis thrust into him, eliciting a satisfied moan.

Mikaél watched as Roman's head fell to his chest while he listened to his racing heart, but any chance of relief from the ordeal was quickly tossed aside as Mikaél's neck became extremely sore. It caused an intense headache which made him wince. He grabbed at the side of his neck and felt his mating gland beneath his skin push up like a rock and throb, ready to burst.

"Wolf-God, fuck! It hurts!" he yelped.

Roman's head flew from Mikaél's chest and stared down at the cause of his pain. He forced the hand covering the gland away and stared at it—red and pulsing. Roman's instincts took over without even thinking about it. He put his mouth to it, licked it slightly, then bit down. Hard. He felt Mikaél's hands come around to the back of his shoulders and squeeze intensely. Soon, the sensation of slight puncture marks from fingernails radiated into Roman's skin as he heard harsh sounds of pain coming from the boy beneath him. The sensation only made Roman continue. A slight tear of the skin on Mikaél's neck sent a few drops onto Roman's tongue. It had a sweet and sour taste mixed with a trace of iron. Moaning into Mikaél's neck, he began to hear his cries of pain fade into moans of pleasure.

Mikaél couldn't believe what was happening to him. In a complete switch, the same beast who was inflicting so much pain on him was now relieving him of it. He couldn't comprehend the act until the pain subsided and the pleasure set in: Roman was imprinting on him, soaking his own scent into Mikaél's body, now becoming a part of him.

As euphoria grew, his Omega reproductive glands began to work in tandem with the powerful beats of his heart. Soon, he felt slick leak out of his body in a steady stream he'd never experienced before. Not caring anymore, he sank into the floor and let Roman continue his job as an Alpha. However, another change began to take place as he felt Roman tense his body. He felt Roman's teeth retract and heard him exhale in pain.

A second later, Roman's head arched back as his face turned red. In the exact same way, the natural response transferred. Roman's inhale of the highly concentrated scent from Mikaél caused the pheromone gland in his neck to beat in heavy pulses just below the surface of the skin. The once near-invincible Alpha was now crumbling and staring at Mikaél in unguarded misery.

Roman stretched his neck out as best as he could, hoping Mikaél would instinctively know, just as he did, what to do. But it didn't come fast enough. "Do it," Roman panted. "Mark me. Please," he repeated in agony.

Mikaél stared at him, feeling the empathy wash over him. But his head stopped him and forced him to think about what it meant when he did return the imprint. His life was going to change. Everything he knew was about to change. Forever. Choosing to accept this was the scariest decision he felt ever had to make.

The momentary reflection was broken by a panic-stricken yelp coming deep from within Roman. Mikaél's own primal instinct pushed him forward, and he felt the throbbing gland on his lips. His worry over whether he could do what was needed faded as the strongest, richest scent of Roman engulfed him. Instinctively, he licked the hard knot in Roman's neck, then opened his mouth over it. Unlike Roman, however, he did not bite down as hard but slowly pushed in and stopped.

Roman whimpered. "Not like that. Harder. Harder!" In an instant, the pulsing pain was replaced by miniature sharp knives stabbing his sore gland. Roman didn't know if he'd said the right thing because it hurt like hell. Not wanting to do anything which would cause Mikaél to stop, he lowered his head to the carpet below and let Mikaél do his job as Omega. He cried out in soft moans and tore at the carpet on both sides of Mikaél's body. The taut skin on his neck gave slightly, and he knew the Omega had successfully broken through. Not a moment too soon, he felt the pain subside which pushed a flood of pleasure throughout his body. Roman felt what he assumed was his prostate gland throb while the base of his cock pulsed. It didn't create a full-on ejaculation, but he could feel the pre-fluid produce generously. Mikaél's imprint was done.

After catching his breath, Roman lifted his head up and dislodged Mikaél's teeth. Everything was in such a warped haze. Roman had no idea where he was or how long he'd been there. All he knew was the beautiful Omega in front of him was his. He positioned his head right above Mikaél's face and stared into his eyes. They were blue once again, but not just blue, a brilliant blue which glowed.

"I'm yours. I'm your Alpha," he whispered.

Mikaél didn't think he could feel his heart beat harder, but it did. Staring back into Roman's full blinding jade eyes made everything around him disappear. The vulnerable look Roman possessed made him want to reach up and hold him forever. But his mind couldn't think at all. He wasn't even confident he could perform basic tasks, let alone perform intricate movements with the man who just declared ownership of him.

A lack of confidence consumed him, and his mouth went dry, but he attempted whatever he could with a shaky, quiet voice. "I.... I'm..."

"Shh," Roman whispered, "it's okay." His face was serious yet nurturing.

"I'm your Omega," Mikaél's voice trembled, but he was thankful he was able to say it. His arm was a brick glued to the floor, but he wanted nothing more than to reach out and touch his Alpha. Like a baby first learning to walk, Mikaél used the back of his hand to stroke Roman's quivering lips and cheek.

Roman slowly closed the gap between them and laid his forehead on top of Mikaél's, hoping to seal their connection with a passionate kiss. But in a flash, he heard Dustin roar, ripping him off of his son.

"Get him up!"

Roman didn't understand what was happening. He couldn't think clear enough to see Mikaél's father and his own manhandle him to the back patio.

"Rixen, Ryan, I need you two out there with him. Garrace, I need your help in here," Jake instructed.

And just like that, Roman was staring into a night sky quiet enough to allow him to hear the ringing in his head. His breaths were deep and rugged as if he'd been holding his breath underwater too long. On weak legs, he stumbled toward the wrought-iron fence on the perimeter of the property, his giant shadow following. While holding onto the fence, he rested his head against the cooler temperature of the metal and closed his eyes.

"Mikaél!"

He heard his Veo first. He looked up and saw Alec's face, even more scared and emotional than he was. His arms wrapped around him tight as he held him close to him. Something about feeling the safety of his father's arms let loose a faucet as tears and whimpers from within him.

"It's okay; you're okay," Alec said, trying to keep himself together. "Wolf-God, your chest!"

"What was that, Jake?!" Dustin's voice boomed. His Alpha pheromones were one step away from tearing his co-worker apart—an eye for an eye.

"Just give me a second!" Jake roared back. He looked at his mate first. "Babe, I want you to take Mikaél and Alec downstairs. Get him cleaned up and see if we have anything we can fit him into." Adrian complied, and Jake's eyes shifted to Garrace. "Garrace, my boy, I need you to take this and call the numbers until you reach someone. Leave a message saying it's from me, and it's urgent. Wait by the phone, and don't move unless it rings. You got that?"

Garrace took a business card which read: Dr. Paul Birowack S.M. S.C.P. – Lead D.H. Tauris Research Center. On the back were two printed telephone numbers and a third written in pen.

"Yes, sir." He followed Jake's finger in the direction of the long hallway. To the right were French doors opening to a generous office. Among other office supplies and tools sat a phone on the mahogany desk. He picked it up and did as he was told.

After Dustin heard the office door close, signaling he was alone with Jake, he continued again unfiltered. "What the hell, Jake! Your psycho son was about ready to kill my son!"

"Dustin, I know how this looks, but Roman would never do that," Jake attempted to calm his co-worker down.

"HE JUST DID!" Dustin roared, swearing he could hear his voice bounce off the walls. "Wolf-God, did you give him his rabies shot?"

"Okay, let's be serious now."

"I am serious! Did you see the way he looked at him? At us? At Ryan when he tried to save Mikaél's life? He could have killed your own kid, and you don't even look like you care!"

"Dustin, of course I care. But I will tell you once more, this was not a territorial attack."

"Then what the hell was it?"

Jake paused and swallowed. "I don't know." He swayed side to side a bit, rationalizing everything going through his head in the moment.

"Really? Because your face doesn't look like you 'don't know.'"

"Because I don't know what it means if I'm right."

"What, Jake. WHAT?!" Dustin demanded.

"Imprinting. Roman wanted to imprint on Mikaél."

"That was NOT imprinting, Jake."

"We both walked in on them in the end. That's exactly what it was, and you know it."

"So, what? Imprinting happens every day! Stupid, horny, uncontrollable Alphas go in secluded parks and dark corners of the streets and force unsuspecting victims to submit to them all the time."

"Roman is not one of those 'stupid, horny, uncontrollable Alphas'; he's my son, damn it!"

"Did you have him on suppressants?" Dustin interrogated.

"No."

"Then there's your answer! Your out-of-control adult son doesn't know how to civilly take care of his sexual needs, and my son was his next rape victim. Clearly! He did it all right in front of us."

"Did you put Mikaél on suppressants?" Jake returned.

"Yes," Dustin returned hastily. "I mean—no. We planned to."

"What does that mean?"

"It means," Dustin controlled his tone and voice, "Mikaél started giving off stronger pheromones lately. Alec and I talked to him about it this week. We were going to start him tomorrow, actually, since we were coming here. The side effects can be grueling, so we waited."

"But only Roman is the problem now?" Jake returned.

"It's not the Omega who needs to be controlled, Jake. It's the Alpha! Why can't you see that's what matters?!"

"Because none of it matters," Jake spoke somberly.

Dustin was exasperated. "How can you stand there and say that?"

"How can you ignore what we both saw as if we, as Alphas, don't know how to recognize it the most?"

"Recognize what?"

"Roman is contracted; he has a mate. He has no reason to go after Mikaél except for one—"

"Yeah, he's unhappy with the contract to Whitmore's son," Dustin surmised.

"No one who is unhappy with their contract puts on a stunt like that for everyone to see. Wolf-God, get your head out of your ass, Dustin. Roman imprinted Mikaél as his Fate."

Dustin's face twisted in disbelief. He began to rebuke the statement, but the more he played the terrifying moments in his head, the more he saw the connections he didn't want to see. Finding a Fated Mate was supposed to be a beautiful, serene dance between two willing people. What Dustin saw, what everyone saw, was nothing like anyone had seen, read, or heard before.

"This was not an imprinting to a Fated Mate. This was animalistic rage which Mikaél felt helpless to and had no other choice but to submit."

"When you look on the surface, yes. Had it not been deeper, I'd have contacted the authorities and put Roman in handcuffs myself. Mikaél didn't know how to react because Roman's pheromones were heated, brash, and threatening. But when he finally got it, he accepted. If you bring it down to its basic level, Roman and Mikaél are Fates."

"If I were to believe that for even one second, what happened to Roman not being able to find a Fated Mate because of his Type 6 Status? You're the one who told me he couldn't!"

"And that's what I was told. The research I've looked at, the research I've done, it all supports it. Paul wouldn't have me working in that lab, approving all of my findings, and publishing the work under his name if he thought I was an idiot playing 'doctor' to the entire science and medical community." A long hush fell over the empty room. "I'm sorry, Dustin. What happened to Mikaél was horrific. Please know we would never mean harm to him or your family."

"I know that," he finally accepted. Dustin stared out the large bay windows to the highlighted silhouettes of all three Erricson sons staring at one another. He saw Jake look out too with the same solemn expression. There was no denying Jake's sincerity in his apology or even his explanation. There was no blame nor distraction put into play. All were equally blindsided by tonight and needed a way to move forward. "What do we do now?"

"What do you mean?" Jake asked. Now he needed some clarity.

"Let's cut the science crap for a second. We're two fathers who just saw their sons imprint on each other. In any other scenario, we'd all get drunk and smoke cigars in celebration. But we're all shellshocked. And even that has to be second to the fact Roman is in a contract with the man whose father paid for the construction of our entire building. And if you believe they are Fated—which I don't— our sons are not going to settle for anything less than each other."

Jake held his head low. His family was going to be put into a situation no one wanted to go through. To admit defeat in a voluntary contract was like murder without the physical affliction. There were exceptions to the rule, of course, but this defeat wasn't on Roman, Adrian, Alec, Dustin, or Mikaél. This was on him. Jake rushed the course for what he thought was a medical and scientific certainty to regrettable consequences, and no one was going to be spared in its actions.

"You're right. I've never hated admitting fault more in my life than this."

"So," Dustin turned to him, "what do we do?"

"What the fuck, Roman!" Ryan screamed at his brother. He saw Roman hang his weight on the fence in the backyard like a lifeless scarecrow. No movement or noise came in response. "Hey, I'm talking to you!" Ryan grabbed Roman's shoulder and pulled it back. Usually, Roman's build could withstand Ryan's attack with minimal effort. But tonight, Roman's body was putty; he lost his balance and fell to the ground.

"Roman!" Rixen yelled with concern. He ran and attempted to help Roman up.

Roman spasmed in defiance. "Get off me!" he growled like a demon had possessed his body. His body ached and the throbbing pains all over him were enough to drive Wolf-God himself to madness. Roman felt as if he'd been tossed around a professional wrestling ring for practice, but even that would have been a blessing compared to this. In addition to the physical pain, he was facing emotional grievances and needs worse than he could ever imagine. Every emotion tugged on his brain and sent audible moans and groans out of his throat.

Slowly, Roman stood and hobbled over to the brick patio. The lights from inside the house shining through the windows as well as the outdoor patio lights were murder to his senses, so he faced out toward the backyard, staring into the darkness of the night. He held his head with both hands to help keep the sanity in, and he rocked back and forth slightly for a calming spell. Occasionally, his hand slid against his tender neck, still unable to fathom what happened.

Rixen walked next to his brother but did not dare enter his personal space. Among the continuous taps of his feet and the songs of the crickets, he could hear his eldest brother trying his hardest to hold back an emotional downpour.

"Roman," he said quietly, holding back his own tears, "what was that?"

"I don't know, I don't know, I don't know!" Roman's voice teetered on hysterics. He couldn't make sense nor focus on anything other than Mikaél. He focused on his dark hair, delicate skin, beautiful eyes, glossy lips, everything. Those thoughts kept him from completely going insane. But every time after he found momentary relief, he remembered the anger, the desire, and the hunt of doing whatever it took to make Mikaél his, even if it meant turning into a wild animal to do so. And that's exactly what he had done.

Ryan screamed, "You almost killed him, Roman! Was I going to be next? Huh? HUH!" Although the hatred for his brother was unhinged, Ryan knew what Roman was capable of. He had seen it, experienced it.

Occasionally, Ryan rubbed his tender side where he had fallen into the couch. It did hurt some; it made him think of when he pushed his own brother with a full concentrated force and that, most likely, he had done more damage to Rixen. With that in mind, Ryan considered himself lucky. For those reasons, he walked diagonally a fair distance away while keeping both of his brothers in view.

"I didn't mean to. I...I don't..." Roman looked up to find Ryan. It was hard to see him in the lights. "That wasn't me."

"Then what was happening?" Rixen asked in a calm voice, wiping away his own tear.

"I...I wanted him. But it was...it was deeper than that." The words came out hard and quavering as Roman tried to logically explain the horrible act he just committed. "I needed him. Once I saw him there, something just came over me, and I wanted him to know he was mine, and I wanted him to treat me like I was his... but... nothing was working right. I wanted to say the words to comfort him, I wanted to stand there and say 'I think we're connected,' give him a hug, and talk about it or something. But it... it didn't... I couldn't control..." Roman began breathing heavily.

"Shh," Rixen whispered. He knelt down and put his hand on Roman's head. "You're back now. You're not that person anymore."

"Let me get this straight," Ryan started pacing in the grass. "You're telling me you damn near murdered him because you think he's 'the one'?"

The clarity of the words struck Roman's soul. He looked up with confession and nodded like a helpless pup.

"Fuck!" Ryan kicked a rock to the back fence.

"Ryan, can you stop?" Rixen criticized. "He doesn't need this now."

"Don't you get it? Am I the only one who gets it?" Ryan held out his hands to the skies.

"What?" Rixen asked.

"Roman is telling us that Mikaél is his Fate!"

"So? What's the problem?" Rixen replied.

"Am I the only one here who remembers Roman is already mated and contracted to Peyton? He just spent a night in a hotel with Peyton orchestrated by his father. What the hell do you think Whitmore is going to say when he finds out Roman discovered the mate he's supposed to spend the rest of his life with and it's Mikaél—not Peyton!"

"Oh Wolf-God," Roman muttered. "I think I'm going to be sick." Roman pushed himself off the patio and flew a few feet away in a soft patch of grass as involuntary contractions and retching sounds came from his throat.

Rixen stood up and marched over to his twin brother. "You can be a real piece of shit, you know that?"

"Me?" Ryan replied, offended by the implication.

"Why do you feel the need to kick everyone in this family when they are down?"

"I'm the only one in this family who apparently has any reason left. This is not a good thing, Rix!"

Roman spit a couple of times and lay on his back to help keep the sky from spinning. He had no interest in participating in the banter of his feuding brothers. He hoped their voices would lull him to sleep.

Rixen replied, "This is not for us to decide. Roman needs to make his own call! And not just Roman, but Mikaél, too. This is their decision."

"Oh, right," Ryan replied sarcastically. "Did you see what Roman did to him? There's no way Mikaél is going to even want to see Roman again, let alone talk to him."

Rixen paused and turned to a new sight. "He just might." A flicker in the light of the sliding glass door shone on a new figure. "Look." Rixen pointed.

Roman dared to look at his dismal chances of seeing what he needed to make the night right again. As the light adjusted, Mikaél's face glowed back at him. Like the first breath of oxygen, seeing his face gave new life to Roman. With a couple of ravenous heaves, he hoisted himself up and made his way back to the brick patio. The initial rush must have scared Mikaél at first because his body jumped back a bit. Seeing his response, Roman slowed down and walked silently to the door.

Once there, Roman attempted to open the sliding glass. After his initial moves failed, he tried once more with force. With no physical or emotional change coming from the other side of the door, Roman knew it wasn't going to open. He had been locked out, and this was his goodbye to Mikaél. He tried to find his nearest way to connect, but all there was before them was the thin glass.

Roman saw Mikaél's eyes; they were emotionless. They studied Roman as they would any predator, waiting to see reactions to new stimuli. The only thing he could do was place his hand flat against the glass and attempt to absorb all he could.

To Roman, Mikaél's skin radiated like an angel. His dark hair was now wet, most likely from a shower. A few beads of water went down his neck to his shoulders. It took every bit of prudence Roman had to not turn the sight into a sexual fantasy, especially when he examined the deep purple bite marks and bruises he had imprinted onto his neck. Mikaél must have noticed him looking, for at the same time, his eyes went to Roman's mark as well. Below the shoulder, Roman noticed the new shirt Mikaél wore to replace the one he ripped to bits was oversized and ill-fitting.

An even closer look revealed the shirt to be a former adolescent school shirt of his, still with his initials and campus name embroidered into it. A smile slowly crept onto his heart and face as he enjoyed watching Mikaél accept something personal from him—from the man who ambushed him. Then, he saw it. Below the neckline and to Mikaél's left were the start of three heavy scratch marks which glistened in the direct kitchen light.

Seeing the wounds he inflicted on Mikaél sent shockwaves of memories—and all the wrong ones. He saw and heard Mikaél's terror all over again in his mind and could only imagine what a brute or feral being he must have appeared to be. For Roman, it was the pin prick he needed to let loose what he should have right when he came to his senses and Mikaél was underneath him. His tears began falling, and with it, his voice sobbed. Whatever worth he had as an Alpha was gone.

He was in an unhappy state of affairs with his contracted mate and now had physically and emotionally scarred his Fated Mate. The pain of it all was too much, and he felt his legs give out. Using both hands against the glass, they allowed his body to fall with some grace before he hit the patio beneath him. As he sat there, he kept one hand on the glass as if he could actually reach Mikaél. But it didn't matter. Mikaél didn't deserve the pain he already put him through. Roman couldn't even consider the idea of getting a chance to redeem himself.

Then, as he sat there, he saw Mikaél's form slowly come down to his level. With a gasp of elation, Roman readjusted himself and held his body weight against the glass. Continuing his mourning cries, he spoke gently,

"I'm sorry. I never wanted to hurt you. Please forgive me." Roman's eyes closed as he let his mind drift off to the sorrowful sound of his own voice.

Suddenly, a vibration from the glass came back at him, and he saw Mikaél staring back at him, then to his hand. Roman saw a gentle, warm hand reach out and press against the glass right where Roman's was. It was hard to conceive, but there it was: an olive branch. When Roman saw Mikaél's own tears stream down his face, his heart burst with emotion, not from sadness, but from relief that Mikaél was communicating to him in a way which comforted him. Tonight, that was what he needed. He needed his Fated Omega. Now, he was there, on the other side of the glass.

CHAPTER 14:

A NIGHT OF REVELATION

Being let back into his home was bittersweet. The prisoner had been granted access in, but there was no comfort waiting for Roman when he entered the kitchen. Mikaél was gone. Roman could still sense him and smell him in the house. Appearing on the far side of the room, he saw the area where he and his Omega imprinted each other.

"Rixen," Adrian's words broke the silence, staring at his son who was still comforting his brother, "why don't you say goodnight to Garrace, okay?" His body turned to reveal Garrace standing near him, looking as aimless as everyone else in the room.

Rixen acknowledged slowly and led Garrace to the front door. "I don't really know what to say right now. I'm so sorry." His embarrassment and disappointment were visible like the dry tear marks on his face.

"You don't have to apologize! I mean, I saw it. I get it. I don't know what I would have done or said in that situation either."

Rixen sighed, communicating he understood, but the words were weak in the moment. "I wanted this to be a good night for us, you know?"

Garrace opened the door and walked out. With Rixen following him, he gave him a deep kiss to cut through the chill air. "It was good for us; it just wasn't our time. That was a wild ride. I've never seen anything like it."

"It was scary as hell."

"I hope everything works out for your brother, and Mikaél, for that matter."

Rixen stood there, contemplating his emotions and intuition. "Is there something about you and Mikaél I don't know? I just got this feeling."

Garrace sighed. "Yeah. We were an item once."

"I figured." It was an uncomfortable revelation; however, it wasn't something he wanted to dwell on. Garrace's life before Rixen wasn't his prerogative, just like vice versa. "There's nothing I need to worry about, is there?"

"Wow. Do I detect some jealously?" Garrace chuckled.

"Is it that obvious?"

"Don't worry about it. This is for real. No need to worry," Garrace reassured.

Rixen wanted nothing more than to spend the entire night with Garrace in his bed. This night was unsettling to say the least. In addition, his brother Ryan did not make the night any smoother. To comfort him in the only presentable way, Rixen needed his tender connection again, and he went in for the kiss. It was natural yet so magnetized. After several complimentary exchanges, the two parted.

"I better go," Garrace said with a face forlorn.

"Yeah," Rixen returned reluctantly.

Garrace went to his car and turned the ignition. The bright lights cut the darkness and lit the current macabre aura of the house. After glancing back one final time, he vacated the driveway and drove off into the night.

"Sur, you have to know I didn't do that on purpose; that wasn't me! Or I mean," Roman struggled for words, "not the right me."

"I know," Jake replied flatly.

Roman and his Sur sat adjacent from one another on the now cleared dining room table. His Veo stood in the kitchen, leaning on the island and getting a direct view of his son. Ryan opted for the couch, laying back and watching the scene. Internally, he felt the furniture mentally stained. But he wasn't going to avoid the living room like a hurt pup. His pride hurt enough.

Roman continued, "All I know is the moment I saw him—no—the moment I scented him, there was something about him I needed, and I didn't want anyone to take that away from me."

"I know," Jake repeated in a similar fashion.

"I must be crazy." Roman silenced himself to gather the thoughts he hoped his parents could understand. "He's the one, Sur: my Fate. I feel it. It's the worst thing that could happen right now, I know. But it's also the best thing I've ever known in my life. I can't explain it in any other way."

"Let's not get ahead of ourselves," Jake cautioned.

Roman reflexed his upper body back in his chair, feeling verbally pushed. "What do you mean? Dad, this isn't a question; I know this for a fact. I've anticipated and waited half my life to find him; everyone says when it happens, they know it. There is no doubt."

"I get that; I understand the feeling. Your father and I went through the same experience." Jake pushed his eyes up to the ceiling and bounced his head side-to-side. "Well, not quite the same experience. Nowhere near it, actually." Jake shifted in his chair.

"I don't understand then why you are doubting my internal wolf instinct here."

Jake took in a deep breath and eyed his mate. Adrian shared the unfortunate look on his face. They both knew the conversation they were about to have was going to be devastating. They braced their bodies in preparation.

"Roman," Jake started, "there's something I've never told you about your Type 6 Status which I've realized now in hindsight was a grave mistake." Jake peered into the worry branded into his son's eyes. Roman held his breath, waiting for it. "Part of requesting your DNA samples your entire life since you were identified was to see your growth both physically and biologically. As you know, we humans aren't born with the ability to find a Fated Mate before puberty. After it strikes and we transition to adulthood, the ability only grows stronger."

"I don't see the problem," Roman rushed.

"Certain markers in your DNA, pheromone profiles, and hormone levels are completely off the charts, making you easily identifiable as exceptional. But you're not perfect, Roman; no one is. Everyone comes with an undesirable trait; it's the natural way of life."

Roman scanned both of his parents' faces, still completely lost on the issue at hand. "What's the undesirable trait I have?"

The door closed and Rixen found himself walking into a very serious and disagreeable conversation.

As much as Jake welcomed the interruption, there was no further delaying. "You don't have the ability to find your Fated Mate."

The sentence didn't register. Staring at both of his parents and even acknowledging his brothers in the room, he hoped for some answers in their faces and found none. It was a formal command Roman's mind couldn't process. He was a defunct device. Yet, there was no chance of continued silence.

"That's not possible. Everyone has that. Tonight was living proof I can."

Jake shook his head. "Science knows how this works, Roman. There is no mistaking the marker. There are natural chemicals responsible for growing the ability to do so, and yours never matured—not even close."

"Then the science is wrong, Dad." Roman's tone changed, his voice colder and straight forward.

"I'm sorry, Roman."

"This is… this is bullshit! In that living room, I attacked Mikaél. It was horrible! But after that, we had a beautiful moment, and I connected to him. We imprinted. I have the ability. You saw it!"

"What happened tonight was nothing more than a hormonal overload. Mates don't imprint like that Roman—nothing like it. You were having a pheromone carryover from last night. Which, by the way, tells me your night with Peyton didn't go right. When you knotted Peyton, it should have done a hormone release to satisfy you. That's one of the benefits for doing it. Cleary, it's something else we're going to have to look into at the lab."

Roman's muscles became so agitated, he felt his chair creak from the pressure he was now forcing upon it. "First of all, that is none of your damn business. But since I clearly have to make a point here, I'll tell you. I never knotted him. I never even fucked him."

All pleasantries and unspoken rules of how to address his parents went out the window. It was too hard not to look at everyone in the room post-reveal. His Veo was shocked the most—that was evident. Seeing it made Roman feel stronger. He wasn't going to let anyone try to tell him what he felt.

"There!" Jake responded, ignoring his son's disrespectful burst in favor of addressing evidence. "All you did was confirm my suspicion. Other than letting go of inhibitions during an Omega's heat, Alphas don't do what you did, Roman. And after talking with Mikaél's father, it was clear to see Mikaél hasn't even gone through his first cycle yet; he's 17. Plus, he wasn't on suppressants, and neither were you. This was a recipe for disaster waiting to happen."

Roman ejected out of his seat, slammed the chair against the table, and descended into the basement. Briskly charging into his room, he snatched his wallet and car keys and made his way back up, body temperature and blood boiling with every second. He heard his Veo say something to his Sur but didn't take time to note what.

"Where are you going?" Jake demanded.

"I'm leaving. I'm not staying in this fucking place tonight. No way," Roman declared.

"You're not going anywhere tonight!"

"What the fuck am I to do, Dad? Do you honestly expect me to just sit here while you continue to tell me how I'm delusional? Not to mention, you want me to believe you have been hoarding this ultimate betrayal for half of my life and think I'm just going to sit there, hug it out, and go on like this never happened? What the hell? What was your goal?" Roman's voice vibrated off the walls.

Rixen and Ryan froze, barely blinking.

Adrian closed his eyes, sensing every individual hurt phero-mone smashing through the air like continuous lightning strikes. "The goal was to find you a mate before you completely lost hope in companionship. Everyone deserves that happiness and yet even that didn't go as we imagined. This truly was an unforeseeable event no one could have thought to consider."

Roman turned to his Veo. "And you. You knew? This entire time, you knew this?"

"Babe, I'm so sorry," Veo squeaked out.

"How could you do this to me, Veo?" Roman pointed to both his parents. "You are both monsters!"

"Now you listen here!" Jake stood up in his dominating Alpha position. "We did what we thought was best."

"No, your best would have been to trust me enough to tell me the truth. What you did was allow me to constantly watch everyone around me find their mates while I foolishly waited for mine. What you did was give me a complex of feeling inadequate. What you did was convince me that I, a 24-year-old adult, still needed to live at home in the tradition of a Wolf pack so I could better my life before getting out there in the real world. What you did was make every-thing easier and more comfortable for you and left me in the gutter!" Once again, Roman found himself staring down his Veo. "This isn't you. How could you watch me go through this?"

"You have to believe me, Roman. This was completely a heart-breaking decision. Every year you didn't find your mate, I saw you slide deeper into a depression. Telling you was the most dangerous think we could have done. And yes, I did watch you go through it, and it hurt like hell. When your contract with Peyton finally came to fruition, it was a knife to my heart. That night in the restaurant, it killed me inside. Every ounce of my being hated it, and I felt myself on the verge of a mental breakdown worrying it was going to be a disaster, and you were going to be left with nothing."

"So, then that's why you were going spastic that night. You were worried your guilty conscience was at risk of being chronic if I didn't agree to Peyton."

"I was worried you wouldn't know how to pick up the pieces after going through that."

Roman fumed. "Does anyone in this family actually care about my opinion?"

Rixen wanted to step up and say he did; there was no doubt. But the conversation was so heated and so deep, it was impossible to penetrate. All he could do was look at Ryan who showed the same visual sentiments.

Veo defended, "I care about you. We care about you."

"You have a disturbing way of showing it."

Adrian's heart hurt. The pain he showed on the outside was tough to view. He tried to hold it together as best as he could. Being in misery was going to set off his mate who was programed to come to his defense—a benefit of being fated. But he didn't want Jake to lash out at Roman, not for this.

"We're going to make this right, Roman. I promise."

Roman stared hard at his Veo. He saw the regret on his face. His pheromones drowned out any irrational hate he had. It aided him in his restraint from going off on his Sur who must have been using his mate's pheromones for the same virtue.

"I gotta go," Roman said.

Hearing the front door slam, echoing through the hallway, was hard to follow. No one in the house knew what to say next. A couple looked at each other while others just stared at the ceiling or the floor. Jake cleared his throat as he stood up. He had the attention of his mate and twin sons but said nothing. He pushed in his chair and walked upstairs.

Adrian turned and watched him go. When he heard the bedroom door shut, he acknowledged the boys in the room. "Why don't you both head downstairs for awhile? I need to talk to your father. Come up later and get yourselves something to eat. It's all in the fridge." His sons didn't move at first. Ryan slowly moved his body to assess a reaction. After concluding it was safe, he rounded the couch and headed toward the landing door. "Hey, Rixen," Adrian spoke.

"Yeah, Dad?" he answered.

"This Garrace boy...is it serious?" Adrian observed his son, looking for a reaction which could reveal his truth more than his words.

Rixen thought about all the possible scenarios he could choose from. At this point, he didn't feel the need to hide. It was a strategy not welcomed to the family right now. "Yeah, it is. I like him. I like him a lot, Veo."

"Okay." Adrian nodded without judgement or praise. He hugged both of his sons individually and began his own ascent to his mate who needed several different wounds licked tonight. His Alpha's ego had been blown to bits, and he mentally prepared himself to be the soothing medication. "Goodnight, boys. I love you."

Ryan made his mood overtly known as he sharply opened the door and walked down the stairs, barely recognizing Rixen's existence. The trip to his room was swift and intentional down to the closed door. He lifted off his shirt and threw it on the floor. As he grabbed his phone, he heard his bedroom door open.

"Just say it," Rixen huffed.

"Say what?" Ryan griped.

"Whatever horrible thing you want to say. I know you're thinking it. You're going to say it eventually, so might as well be now."

Ryan tossed his phone on the bed. "I just...have these internal thoughts in my head, and they're just bothering me to no end."

Rixen dared to sit on the edge Ryan's bed. "Care to share?"

"It's sick and obsessive, I realize that, but I imagine you and Garrace doing what Roman and Mikaél did, and it infuriates me to no end."

"That's not a bad thing," Rixen assured. "If Garrace tried to kill me in the way Roman did, I'd want you to come to my rescue. I'm just sorry you weren't allowed to do more."

Ryan eyed his brother sternly. "That's not what I meant."

"Oh. Then what did you mean?" Rixen's stomach tightened.

Ryan shifted his body weight and squinted his eyes, looking out at the pitch-black night through the window. "Imagining Garrace imprinting you makes me want to punch his nose right up into his skull."

"Okay." Rixen's word came immediately. He shuffled himself to sit just a foot or two away from Ryan, demanding his full attention. "I have a theory, and I think it's time you just admit it."

Ryan's gaze shot through his brother. Instantly, he felt his pulse in his head and his hands twitched. "Admit what?" He tried to hide his nerves.

Rixen inhaled a large scent of his brother. Although muted due to his Beta's rank, Ryan's scent was a clean crisp cucumber with a touch of sweet melon. But the giveaway was the pronounced scent of nerves, which meant Rixen had cornered him into spilling his guts.

"I've thought about this a lot lately, and I've connected the dots. I don't know how it's going to affect our relationship, nor do I know how to move forward from it once it comes out, but I have to say it." Rixen paused, reading the fear in Ryan's face. "You have strong feelings for Garrace, don't you?"

"What?" Ryan's eyes grew wide. "No!" He brushed off the comment.

"You can admit it: I know you do. You've been wrapped up in this argument between us and have been very forward in divulging all the details of his life which I didn't know. Clearly, you've been taking notice of him long before I ever did."

"I..." Ryan began on shaky ground. "It was very refreshing he wasn't the asshole I made him out to be. Also, I can't deny he's very attractive and very confident."

"See? Was that so hard?" Rixen rubbed his brother's leg in comfort.

"Rixen, it's hard enough to see you go, and yes, it's hard to see you go with him but—"

"I've talked to him about it," Rixen admitted.

Ryan lost the oxygen in his lungs. He never wished a comment to be a lie more than this. "You did what?"

"He's not offended, Ryan. In addition, he said he understood the defensiveness. But I needed to be honest with him, and I needed to be honest with you."

Ryan flew himself off the bed in such a threatening way, Rixen followed his movement in reverse closer to the door with his hands slowly raised. "Get out." The words were clear and deliberate.

"Ryan—"

"Now!"

Rixen curled his lips in frustration and yet with understanding. He bowed his head slightly and left.

Ryan walked to the door and shut it. His head fell on the door as he rocked it back and forth, feeling the hard wood press against him like a massage. He replayed the moment over and over in his head, wishing it could have never happened. A hard fist to the door sealed his anger.

In the hours that passed, Roman couldn't remember how he got to the bar. Four shots later, Roman was frustrated at the alcohol's inability to soothe him. After the bartender cut him off, he studied glowing bottles of booze and occasional glances from onlookers. However, the smell of Mikaél was very noticeable. A few Omegas and Betas quickly backed off sensing the pungent smell, alerting them the imprint was recent. Two willing to take the challenge found themselves quickly dismissed by a cold shoulder.

He decided his family's betrayal was the hardest to move on from. He felt like a stranger to his own blood. The trust gone, the camaraderie gone, and his willingness to be an open son and brother gone. Several future expressions ran through his warped mind: a silent treatment, a temporary departure from the home, another lambasting condescension, and dare he envision it—a violent outburst. His anger grew. His scent alerted a few patrons and staff members which told him he needed to calm down.

Unable to drown out his misery with cognitive thoughts, he pulled out his phone. Swipes to move several apps eventually displayed a photograph of his date with Peyton. Immediately, he noticed Peyton's reserved personality replaced with an outgoing Omega persona. Also, in the picture was the distant memory of his own joyous expression. Opening the message thread, he sent a text which received an immediate response:

[Roman: Are you up by chance?]

[Peyton: Yeah. It's not that late. Lol, I almost got worried not hearing from you.]

[Roman: We need to talk... ☹]

[Peyton: Okay? Is something wrong?]

[Roman: Is there any way I can come over bypassing your parents?]

[Peyton: Uhm. Yes, I think I can make that happen. Roman... are you okay? Are you hurt?]

[Roman: I don't want to have this conversation through text. What needs to happen for me to avoid your parents?]

[Peyton: I'll tell security you are coming. Text me and I'll meet you at the entrance. We'll go around back and go to a secluded area in the house my parents never venture to.]

[Roman: I think I can get there in 20 min or so.]
[Peyton: Okay.]

Chugging of two glasses of water and taking a piss before exiting the bar gave him confidence to drive. He held steady and avoided any worry or fear of impaired driving. Unfortunately, that didn't mean he didn't have any dangerous distractions. Every mile closer to the Whitmore house elevated his nerves, which soon became unbearable. Several times, he contemplated pulling over and calling or texting instead, but Roman knew better than that.

Arriving there went just as smoothly as he could have hoped for. He parked just beyond the gate. It surprised him that he didn't initiate a suspicious inquiry from security, but his arrival was anticipated. At the door, he saw Peyton on the side appearing blurred from the distorted glass. Seeing his face was the hardest.

"Hi," Roman said in a deflated tone.

Peyton rushed up in a hug. It was hard not to smile while smelling the faint presence of his true scent, but he knew it wasn't the time. He felt Roman return it softly which indicated to him a serious circumstance; his scent also communicated distress.

"Come on. This way," Peyton whispered. Roman followed.

The rear of the home was lit by large pool lights. Both slipped inside, and Peyton cautiously led him from large lounge furniture within a game room and bar to a well-presented guest room. They entered in the dark, but Peyton quickly turned on a single lamp near the bed and returned to the entrance to shut the door.

"Okay. I've been near death this entire time. What's going on?" Peyton's eyes were sad and full of anxiety that Roman's expression did little to soothe. And there was something else coming through—another scent. It was strange and unknown but definitely new. The anxiety grew deep within him as he feared the worst.

"Peyton," Roman began. His direct focus was impossible to hold. He turned around, scratching his head, and walked to the pseudo comfort of the bed. "Tonight, the most amazing thing happened to me."

Peyton was taken aback. "Uh, okay. Wow, I've never anticipated such good fortune to be accompanied by such dread. Are you sure it's good news?" He snorted.

Roman's hands trembled and his expression fell further. "The problem, Peyton, is this will be the worst news for you." His following silence was deafening. "I found my Fated Mate at my father's dinner party tonight."

Shocked and dismayed, Peyton had no words at first. "What? No, no that can't be, Roman."

"It's crazy, I get it. I never thought this would happen—I never planned for this to happen. I mean, no one can anticipate it happening; they just hope and wait for it." Roman's mind struggled to sort out words. "This hurts so much to say to you. I honestly don't know what else to say."

"No, Roman, seriously. You know better; this can't happen. By the way, have you been drinking? And what is that other scent on you?" Peyton declared with doubt and confusion all over his face.

Roman couldn't comprehend this déjà vu. Although he knew the news was going to devastating, this wasn't the reaction he anticipated at all. Any reaction other than this made sense. Worse were the chaotic feelings from earlier in the night bubbling up again.

"I don't understand what you are saying to me. What do you mean by 'I know better'?"

"Just answer my other questions, please," Peyton demanded, raising his own voice to match Roman's.

"Yes, I've been drinking. Believe me, if you had the night I did, you'd drink too. The other scent is Mikaél, I mean, my Fate. We imprinted. Now, answer my question."

"I don't find this amusing. You've got be playing some sick joke on me." Peyton's voice showed his agitation. *How on Earth is Roman doing this?* It was hurtful, disgusting, and damn near psychotic.

"This is not a joke, Peyton! Now, what do you mean?!" Roman's voice forgot any of the caution he came here with.

"A Type 6 can't find their mate. You can't find your mate. You're spewing nothing but excuses for poor behavior."

"Who told you that?" Roman's breathing became heavy. The indignation moved front and center, and he removed himself from the bed and walked forward.

"What?"

"Who told you that I couldn't find a mate? I want to know!"

"Keep your voice down! If my Sur hears you spewing this nonsense, he's going to call the cops, for Wolf-God's sake."

"Peyton, I need to know this, and I need to know this now!"

"My Sur told me. I found it out the same night we first met. How could you not know this?"

He groaned. "My Sur kept it a secret. The asshole thought he was doing me a favor! All he's done is create a living hell by keeping what he deems confidential just because he thinks he's some hotshot researcher, convincing everyone he knows me better than even I do." Then, it hit him. "Wolf-God! He told your father, didn't he? There's no other explanation. He told your father before he even told me!"

Peyton seethed. "Maybe? I don't know who told him."

"DAMN IT!" Roman found the nearest wall and punched it with force, breaking the drywall.

"ROMAN! Are you out of your mind?" Peyton grabbed Roman's arm to center him.

"What the hell is happening! Everyone in my life has turned against me." The outrage overload caused his voice to begin to tremble. The panic began to set in. He felt a repeat breakdown was imminent.

"I haven't turned against you, Roman. I've been nothing but on your side. We just shared what I thought was a beautiful bond, and now you're dismissing it like it was nothing. How do I know you're not just using this as some excuse to get out of our contract?"

"I'm not, Peyton. I promise. Regardless, if no believes me about finding my Fated Mate, it happened."

Peyton shook his head in disgust. "You know, this cowardice doesn't surprise me one bit."

"What? 'Coward'? Why the fuck would you say that?"

"Your discomfort has been evident from the start. From the first night we met to greeting me at the contract appointment, our date, and even the sex. You've showed this vacant, regretful appearance before. And you know what? It fucking sucks!" Peyton couldn't believe the words coming out of his mouth. His reserved personality had been tossed completely out the window.

"The sex? Seriously?"

"Why didn't you go all the way? Why didn't you fuck me?" Peyton crossed his arms, shocked he could even say it out loud.

"Did you even want to?" Roman interrogated.

"Of course, I did!" Peyton blushed, but it was hard to tell from the heat already displayed on his face from the anger.

"Are you sure?" he stressed.

"Why would you question that? That was my question to you."

"Because you had every opportunity to do it. You sat on top of me and didn't do it. Was it because you didn't want it either?" Peyton stood there with no response. "Tell me!" Roman demanded.

"You're so easy to read, Roman. Even though you're being a piece of shit right now, the message has been loud and clear all along. Your face, your demeanor, your scent, everything. You don't want this, and now you're shoving it in my face. Message received loud and clear! I get this was an arranged mating contract, but you said 'Yes' right across from me at the table and signed the paper. It was just a sham." Peyton walked to the bedroom door. "So, go then. I can't be with you anyway when you don't want this. I'd be a fool to convince you. Even more foolish would be to spend the rest of my life knowing you'd want to be anywhere else but with me. Hell, you'd probably just end up cheating on me."

Roman grimaced. "I'm not like that!"

"The fuck you aren't. You imprinted the guy—what—hours ago?"

"Peyton, I didn't have control over it. No Alpha does in that situation," Roman defended.

"Do you even hear yourself?" Peyton waited for any sign of sanity in a response. The words never found Roman. "You sick bastard. Get out."

"You don't have to like this, but I need you to believe me. Please, I'm begging you."

"You need to leave, or I'll call security myself and have you thrown in a cell downtown for harassment. You need help, Roman, that's all I can say. I'll get my Sur to get this over with so you can be with your degenerate whore."

"Don't you dare call him that!"

"What part of 'Get out' didn't you hear?! Last chance, Roman, I swear!" Peyton's eyes became wet and blurry.

Roman swiftly walked past Peyton in a huff, looking for another wall to punch. He contained himself this time, but barely. He hurried himself out the same way he entered. The walk back to the car was brisk and couldn't come fast enough. His tires squealed out of the distant driveway to the darkness beyond.

Reaching the outskirts of the city, he pulled over on a side street and parked. A sickness came over him, and he heaved, thrusting his head against the steering wheel for concentration and prayer for an avoidance of another vomiting experience. Luckily, he was given a break and avoided such. *What can I do now?* Everywhere and everybody were enemies to him. No one was honest; no one was helpful. He was on an island of one. However, there was indeed one person he hoped didn't abandon him. He was the only person who could make this pain go away. The more he thought of him, the more the pull grew, and he couldn't hold back anymore.

CHAPTER 15:

A Chance of a Lifetime

Putting his life in the hands of complete strangers had to be his craziest idea yet. But Roman found himself standing at the front door of Dustin and Alec Cavenbelle's home. So much of him wanted to turn back; this had so much potential to go awry. Invoking one last ounce of courage, he pushed the doorbell. He couldn't believe how one simple act made his stomach feel like he was on a rollercoaster. Every second waiting was agony. Maybe no one would answer the door, making this destined venture a misfire.

Soon, footsteps neared the door, and when he opened the door, Alec's face was bleak. "Roman, what on Wolf-God's green Earth are you doing here?" The voice was harsh but controlled.

"I know this is not what you want, but I have to make this right with Mikaél. There's no other way I can survive without doing this. Please." Roman quivered as he made the emotional plea.

Alec shifted to a defensive stance, expression unchanged. "I have no intention of making you feel any better about what you did. You violated my son, not to mention the assault! Do you have any idea how fortunate you are we're not pressing charges?"

"I'm grateful for it. Absolutely." Roman paused. "Why aren't you?"

Alec sighed. "My mate seems to think there's some validity to why you attacked him. Why, I couldn't tell you. I have no idea what in Wolf-God's name he is thinking." He rolled his eyes.

"I don't know how many people I have to tell tonight, but I'll say it until the day I die: I am so sorry for what happened. The shameful way I couldn't control myself is killing me. And I know from everything I've learned and have been told that imprinting like that isn't normal, but I can't change that. If I could, I would give anything to do it." Roman gulped, closing his eyes in fear. "Mr. Cavenbelle, Mikaél is my Fated Mate." Roman observed Alec getting ready to contradict him. "I know—I've had so many people tonight tell me my Type 6 identity prevents me from doing it. I don't believe that; I can't."

"So my mate says. As such, I have no choice but to agree with him. No one knows more on the subject than him, other than your own Sur, of course. And based on what you've just told me, he's said the same to you."

Roman hung his head. "I personally can't take one more person telling me who I am as if I'm an invalid. That's why I need to see Mikaél."

Alec shook his head. "I don't understand."

"The point of Fated Mates is that the connection is equal. It doesn't work any other way. Now, I will drop this entire crusade and accept my broken instinct if I can hear Mikaél tell me he doesn't feel what I feel. But I need this chance more than anything. Please, I am begging you with every last part of my humanity."

"I..." Alec hesitated. The audacity of such a request was regrettable. However, Alec couldn't ignore the strength and virtue of Roman taking ownership of his wrongdoing—regardless of his warped interpretation of it all. "I can't imagine Mikaél is in any condition or mindset to have this conversation now, maybe not ever. You've scarred him both physically and mentally over this. That alone gives me all the validation I need to wipe you off the face of this Earth myself. I don't think I can live with myself as a parent otherwise. And if you think I'm being irrational, just wait until my mate finds out you showed up. You'll be dead where you stand."

"If you can stand there right now and tell me Mikaél has said I'm crazy and wants nothing to do with me, I will withdraw my plea and do whatever I can to apologize and make this right in a less obtrusive way. But if you can't, would you please consider asking him if he'd see me?"

Alec was sympathetic, and he knew this wasn't going away. With Dustin in a drunken sleep upstairs, this might be the only opportunity Roman was going to get. In addition, no conversation had occurred in which his son ever stated he didn't want to see the Alpha again. "Stay here."

A weight lifted off Roman's shoulders, and he felt light-headed. He stepped back, rubbing his hands over his face and thumbing his temples. Beyond the gift of this opportunity, Roman couldn't ignore the stipulations which made this possible. Did Mikaél truly not feel Roman was out of his mind? Did he dig below the surface and experience the same connection he did, sealed with his imprint? He hoped against every part of this misfortune Mikaél did.

And so, he waited. If he had to, he'd wait all night.

***

Mikaél laid on his bed with phone in hand. In the aftermath, he was still in disbelief. The night was a blur from the moment he walked in the door at Roman's home. Mikaél couldn't ignore the natural inability of his parents to comfort him in every way he needed. Luckily, that's what friends were for.

"Dude, what happened after that?" Laycin was keen to Mikaél's every word. He imagined every step like an action movie playing out. If it were food, he'd be uncontrollably salivating.

"That was the worst part. When he didn't get the response he wanted, he tore my shirt right off. It ripped the fabric like a weak old rag. I don't think he meant to, but he scratched the hell out of my chest. It's like a wolf attacked me. Actually, that's exactly how I'd describe him in that moment: a wolf out for blood."

"Holy fucking shit." Every word was enunciated with disbelief. It all soaked in slowly. "How on Earth did your parents not kill him?"

"My Sur told me later if he intervened Roman would have felt threatened and gone on a rampage worse than he already had. He might have even attacked his own family if it came down to it."

"Are your parents pressing charges? Sounds like he beat you up pretty bad."

"It's not that bad. I mean, I'm not trying to diminish what he did, but this wasn't a brawl or an intentional battery. At least, I don't think it was. Anyway, no, I begged them not to."

Laycin gasped. "You're not serious."

"Yes, I am." Mikaél's answer came with confidence. He only imagined what Laycin's face looked like right now.

"Are you insane? What on earth are you thinking this was exactly?"

"He imprinted me, Laycin."

No words came immediately from Laycin. It completely interrupted the natural flow of the conversation, making the phone call uncomfortable. "Imprinted? He wants to be blood bound? Like... sexually?"

"I don't think there's any other way to say it, but it's not just sexual. He wants me to be his. And he...thinks I'm his Fate." In all of the details he eloquently described so far, this was the hardest for him to say.

"No fucking way. This psychopath thinks all of that was to declare you as his Fated Mate?"

Mikaél swallowed. "Yes."

"And what do you think?"

A knock came at the door, and Mikaél's Veo entered with a solemn face. "Mik, we need to talk." The dreaded tone every parent naturally possesses for a serious conversation was unsettling.

"Can it wait tonight? I'm on the phone with Laycin."

"This can't wait. This has to happen now." Alec demanded the compliance immediately, yet his tone was gentle.

"May I ask what's so important?"

Alec heaved. "Roman is here. He's standing outside the house by the front door."

Laycin heard every word. "Wolf-God, is he serious? He's psycho! Call the police!"

"Laycin, I have to go."

"No, wait!" Laycin pleaded.

The words were already too late. Mikaél hung up and stared down his Veo like he'd just heard a car crash killed his Sur. "What does he want?"

"I suppose among other things, he wants to apologize. He wants to rectify what happened. If you want me to turn him away, you let me know, and I'll do it right now."

"What does Sur think?"

Alec's face fell. "He doesn't know."

"Are you serious? He's going to flip."

"Look, I'm giving you this opportunity. I may regret this, but I respect him for coming forward, and I don't think your father is going to give him a chance. I'll say it again: if this too much for you, I will completely forget this ever happened and get him out of here."

"How is he?" Mikaél was dissatisfied with his question. "Does he seem okay? I mean, you're really not afraid of him right now?"

"I think he's all right now. That being said, I don't know how he'll react when he sees you. So, what do you say? Do you really want to take this chance? I'll be here when he comes in with claws out if I have to."

A million thoughts rushed through Mikaél's mind. All of it was surreal; this whole day was a strange dream he wanted to wake up from. *Can I really risk my life like this?* An Omega's intuition was one of the most powerful natural abilities they possessed. Trusting his Veo was easy, but this situation was not. In all the fear which blanketed him, there was no denying he wanted the opportunity to see the Alpha again; Roman's pull was too strong. Mikaél remembered the moment he met Roman's hand on the opposite side of the glass. It also was hard not to acknowledge Veo's truth. This may be the only chance he'd get. With a heavy breath, he agreed.

Alec nodded his head cautiously. Following his son's wishes, he returned upstairs. Maybe Roman became impatient and left? A change of heart? An overcome sensation of trepidation, perhaps? Arriving at the door, Alec saw Roman still stood there, barely the Alpha he had witnessed earlier. It was helpful to his cause at least.

"Follow me," he instructed.

Roman entered the house. The home was nice. He admired the wood ceiling and stone fireplace. They descended to the walkout basement. It was very common for sons to have bedrooms on lower floors or basements. It showed the dominance of the parents over their pups, and the Cavenbelle family was no different. A long hallway to the left led to a closed wooden door on the right.

Alec halted, turning to Roman with a commanding face. "Listen here. He's a 17-year-old boy. He's our responsibility. If anything happens to him, you won't be answering to the authorities—you'll be answering to me. Any disgusting move on him, and you're going to wish you never met me." His eyes pierced Roman's soul, looking for any reason to call the situation off. But nothing came through which warranted it. "I must be insane for doing this. Don't make me regret it."

"You have my word." Roman's honesty was underscored by the control on his face. He wasn't going to let anything happen to Mikaél, not ever again.

After a slight knock, Mikaél watched both Alec and Roman enter the room. Like it was only a second ago, Roman's scent reminded him of every act which transpired between the two of them, some more pleasant than others. There was instant relief to see the Roman he last departed and not the Roman resembling some furious beast. In addition to his sad expression and apologies, he did scent an undeniable submissive pheromone.

Alec also noticed the tranquility between them. The former threatening spirit Roman once possessed had passed. There was little doubt that Roman couldn't control his urges.

"I think I'd be okay with leaving you two here in private, if you're okay with that, Mik?"

Mikaél nodded first. "Yeah. I'm okay with that."

With one final sentimental look, Alec turned to Roman with a clear intent to remind him of their conversation. But his face gentled as he left the room and shut the door out of courtesy.

"Hi," Roman spoke cautiously.

Mikaél swallowed hard, sitting up in his bed, holding his weight with both arms pushing down on his mattress. "Hi."

"I'd normally ask anyone how they are doing. But in this case, I think I know."

"I've had better nights," Mikaél answered timidly yet honestly.

"There really are no words I can think of to describe what happened to me. Something inside me took control, and I could do nothing but focus on you. Hurting you was never in the realm of anything I could imagine. I've never done that to anyone in my life. To do it to you of all people tears every bit of me apart."

Mikaél heard the sincerity in every word. Roman's apology pierced his soul. It was a moment he wanted to keep deep in his heart. It made everything else bearable.

"I don't know if I've ever been so scared in my life. I couldn't think; I could barely breathe. My mind couldn't comprehend what you were trying to do." He paused. "I didn't know if it was a trick or some sort of madness. But then…"

Roman didn't want him to stop talking. His voice alone was beautiful. If Roman was forced to choose what was the most beautiful about him, he couldn't have done it. "What?"

"Everything changed. It went from fearing for my life to feeling the safest I'd ever been in a matter of minutes. It's enough to make a person lose his sanity. I kept thinking it was a dream." The next thought burst nerves from his heart. "Roman, you imprinted me."

Roman nodded, feeling guilty and ashamed, but it also felt so right. "It was truly the only desire I had, Mikaél. Everything else was a nightmare for me too. I know it will never compare to what you went through." Roman took a few steps forward; he was thankful Mikaél didn't protest.

"Thank you," Mikaél responded quietly.

"You imprinted me back," Roman pointed out.

"Yes."

"Did you only do it because I forced you to do it?"

Here it was. This was the matter Mikaél struggled with most of all. He tried to clear his mind of any thoughts of Stockholm Syndrome. Unfortunately, it read textbook. Even so, this was one moment in time. Remorse was all over his face. This was a true testament of something greater, deeper, and purer.

"My mind scrambled to comprehend the moment. When your eyes darkened, there was something inside me which wanted it equally as much as I wanted everything to stop. And when my gland reacted—Wolf-God—it felt like a knife was bursting out of my neck. It was the worst pain I've ever experienced in my life. Having you there, knowing what to do, it was such a relief. When the pain subsided, the release was so serene and beautiful. I just still couldn't figure it all out fast enough. To answer your question: no, you didn't force me to. I wanted it just as much as you did."

Roman's legs shook and turned to melted butter. He took a few awkward steps forward. Carefully, he made it to Mikaél's soft bed.

All Mikaél did to respond was eye him closely. After watching him settle in, he lifted his back and found his new center of gravity sitting upright. Butterflies hit his stomach with Roman so close to him.

Seeing Mikaél's eyes up close again was a present on the morning of Winter Solstice. He loved examining all his facial features again to help cement them in his mind, especially if this was the last time he ever saw him. He prayed the fortune cards wouldn't fall that way.

"Is it true you are contracted?" Mikaél asked.

Roman's stared at Mikaél's black plush comforter. "Yes, it is. Though it's gone now."

"Seriously? Why?" He gasped.

"I imprinted you, Mikaél. To go back to my contracted mate is impossible for me. I never even imprinted on him."

"Why not?"

"I reluctantly agreed to settle into a contract because my family insisted all hopes of my Fate coming along were long gone. I wanted a mate, but this wasn't the way I wanted it. In addition, I couldn't shake the feeling it was wrong. Inside myself, I couldn't give up finding the one who was meant to be mine. My family and, well, everyone around me crushed me when they said they knew all along what I never did. I guess according to my genes, I have no instinct to detect a Fate."

"My Sur works with your Sur. He says their main job is to research about Type 6. You're one of them?"

Roman nodded. The pride in it all was the smallest it had ever been. "I never hated it so much as I do now."

"Don't say that." Automatically, without thinking, Mikaél's hand went to Roman's shoulder. He was warm; his colorful shirt warm. Touching him lit a spark inside of him.

Roman's heart skipped a beat as his gaze went to Mikaél's hand. It was soft and full of care. He pleaded for it to last forever.

Mikaél continued, "You're special, one of the most extraordinary wolf-descendants out there. I'm sorry you were never told about your inability; it's so wrong you weren't told. I can't imagine what that must have been like."

"You're more special than I am." Roman's own moment was upon him. "Mikaél, other than apologizing from the depths of my heart, I came here to ask you a question, and I have to know the answer. I need you to be the most honest you could imagine yourself to be. Can you do that for me? Even if you know the answer hurts me?"

The pressure weighed on Mikaél. The numerous possibilities stressed him out a bit. Somewhere, deep inside, he felt he knew the question. His Omega instinct kicked into full force. He gently nodded his head in acknowledgement and agreement.

"I don't care what scientists have to say about me, even if one of them is my father. I am a wolf with wolf instincts—all of them. I know it. Everything within me is telling me tonight with you wasn't a miscalculation or weakness from a hypersexual degenerate. I found you for a reason. But the only way to know for sure is to know what you know. Every being on Earth is capable of knowing who their Fate is. No one needs their parent to tell them what's right or wrong. So, with that, I need you to answer me this: do you feel I just committed some sort of desperate act, or do you feel like I do? Am I truly your Fated Mate?"

Whether Mikaél knew it or not, the rest of Roman's life rested on this moment.

Mikaél's lungs tightened. His mind went to the moment the imprint happened. There was one final moment which never received the attention it deserved. After it all, their eyes locked, and they declared themselves to each other. Now, staring into Roman's eyes, it was time to say exactly what he knew.

"I'm yours, Roman. I know it in my heart and in my soul. It's real." Saying it out loud made it permanent in the deepest part of his being. The room blurred in his vision.

Roman's face barely changed. Inside, fireworks were exploding by the hundreds. Finally, the world made sense. Roman's terrible journey resulted in the most rewarding moment he'd ever experienced. No more doubt, no more second guessing, no more arguments. They didn't matter. All that mattered was this.

In an instant, a hunger grew within him. It wasn't violent; it was passionate. He needed what was robbed from him the moment he was forced away. He searched Mikaél's face, studying every bit of it. His eyes watered; he wanted to make a quick movement before losing emotional control.

Suddenly, his body pushed forward and easily found Mikaél's soft full lips. The pheromone surge clouded the room. It was the sweetest scent he'd ever sensed, and he wanted it more and more.

The kiss blinded Mikaél in the best way. Roman's tender expression was hypnotic, and he wanted it so badly, more than anything. He didn't hesitate for a moment to return the passionate move. The exchange was subtle and sweet and difficult to end. Roman was the first to pull away as apprehension settled in his pheromone pattern.

"I'm so sorry. I shouldn't have—" His words were quickly interrupted with Mikaél now chasing him. If the kiss alone wasn't enough to demonstrate his desire, the hand on the back of Roman's head pulling him close removed all doubt.

Hearing Mikaél's whimpers and strained moans drove him wild. It was too much. The urge to take him right then and there amplified as he began to smell Mikaél's slick. The smell was sweet and potent. He knew there was need for control, but it wasn't going to happen until after he laid Mikaél down on his bed and felt his body beneath him.

It was natural for Mikaél to slowly let his body drift back. When his head hit the pillow, it was the moment he wanted so long ago.

Feeling his insides pulse warmed his body inside and out. His own primal urge began to take over as his anal glands thumped to the beat of his heart. He always imagined this moment, but nothing prepared him for what it really was. To show his undying desire, he opened his mouth and licked Roman's lips. When Roman pressed his tongue into Mikaél's mouth, his body twitched.

This time, Roman moaned with a low growl, and he pushed his hips deep against him. It was intentional for the expression of affection and adoration. When his own pre-cum began to spill out, he pulled himself back and stared at Mikaél. The emotion he intended to hold back flooded in again, and his breath became harsh.

"I can't believe I found you. I'm never going to let you go. You're my Fate, baby."

Mikaél's face and heart warmed. "And you're mine." He slid his hand across his cheek and felt Roman's inhalations.

Roman chuckled in disbelief. "This is incredible. I'm so glad this isn't a dream." Roman took the time to study his Omega again. As his eyes trailed to his chest, he noticed he still wore the shirt he left his house in. "You know, this is mine. It's one of my old school shirts."

"I know," Mikaél said, delighted.

"How?"

"After you...left, I showered in the basement and was presented with a pile of clothes to see what fit. Nothing really did. Your family's build doesn't match mine," he mused. "Anyway, when I looked at this shirt, I scented you in it. I brought it close to me, and it comforted me. I knew I wanted it instantly. My Veo didn't notice it, but I think yours did. I swear he smiled at me. On the drive home, your smell was the only thing that kept me from breaking down."

"That's so amazing," Roman whispered. He stroked his hand down to the embroidered emblem and rubbed it with his index finger. Feeling adventurous, he began to explore the fabric covering the rest of his chest. He heard Mikaél's painful wince. Seeing his face like that scared him. It took a moment, but then he realized what it was. The oversized shirt made it easy to push down the front, revealing the start of the distinguished, irritated scratch marks. The cuts horrified him and forced him to pull down his shirt as much as could. "Oh, Wolf-God!" he cried.

"No, don't worry about it. Really. You don't have to—" Mikaél tried to soothe him, holding his shirt as best as he could.

"I have to; I can't pretend this didn't happen." Roman's face was heartbroken.

Mikaél hands reluctantly relaxed at his sides. It was a defeated act more than anything. He felt Roman's hands sneak under the bottom of his shirt, slowly pulling the fabric up to reveal his skin. Knowing Roman wasn't going to stop there, he put his arms up, allowing the shirt to completely come off.

A rock hit Roman's own chest as he saw his despicable work. In sharp thin marks, bright red lines exposed themselves, a few even weeping. To make it even worse, these weren't going to go away tomorrow, in a week, or perhaps even a month. Unable to comprehend most of what happened in the altercation, there was no question of what happened here. The memory became vivid with the proof right in front of his eyes. The person he was Fated to spend the rest of his life with was bloodied by his own hands, a betrayal in the simplest of terms.

"I'm a monster, pure evil. I'm just fucked up," he lamented.

"Roman, no. Every part of me believes what you have said this entire time. That wasn't you. They're flesh wounds. I'm not in pain, I promise. And I forgive you. The man in front of me is who you really are and is the man I want to be with." His hand cupped Roman's cheek. As he felt Roman's hand compliment his, he saw a tear escape his mate's eye.

"How do I begin to make this right?" Roman's hopelessness bled through.

Mikaél eased in close and gave him another lip-locking embrace. "This is a good start," he whispered.

Not wanting to argue or disagree, Roman obliged. The natural burden of all Alphas was their programming to please their Omegas. A severed tie triggered a heart-wrenching response requiring immediate rectification, one of the few advantages Omegas had in order to level the social inequality. And so, a beautiful movement took place between the two: heavy breaths, hungry lip sounds, and moans. Mikaél's hands began to rhythmically stroke Roman's back before coming around to his chest.

Roman's chest felt hard. As best as he could in the hot moment, Mikaél began to tackle the top buttons on the shirt. Part of him considered ripping the shirt right off in a familiar fashion, but he decided against it, saving the tactic for later. Soon, Roman's chest was fully exposed. Roman assisted in removing the shirt from his shoulders and arms. Finally, he was equally naked from the waist up.

Mikaél began an act Roman was not going to be able to reciprocate for the time being. Starting at his neck while engaging in another passionate kiss, his hands slowly slid down his tight pecs. Roman's chest hair was delicate and not overpowering. It was a natural tease and satisfying to explore. Mikaél couldn't tell if this was truly Roman's representation of his chest hair or if he trimmed. Either way, it was turning him on. It was easy to immediately focus attention on his nipples. The touch resulted in a body jerk and gasp from Roman who had to break the kiss to do so. Forcing his mouth back on him, Mikaél massaged and occasionally tweaked them, trying to discover what his mate's tolerance was. His shapes were larger than a generous coin but not by much. His nipples did extend, however, making the erogenous zone all too easy to exploit. Not quite achieving all the reaction he wanted, Mikaél broke away and attached his mouth to the right first.

Roman moaned harder now. "Ah, fuck!" Looking down at his Omega pleasing him was euphoria on top of euphoria. He combed his fingers through Mikaél's dark hair. It was soft and had a natural flow. Hearing and feeling an extra-long exhale on his chest demonstrated to Roman he had approval and perhaps even a compliment. But the pleasure thrust upon him was stronger. When the sensitivity became almost too much, Mikaél found a way to compliment strong sucking with gentle bites. Then, he switched and went to the other one. The apparent build-up of pleasure made the second engagement even more effective than the first. Roman began a pattern of moans for what seemed like a full minute.

The agony of not giving Mikaél attention was obvious; for soon, he felt Roman's big arms push him off and direct him down on his back into the soft bed. Laying down in a steady pattern of inhales and exhales, he saw Roman's body lay on top of him again. But this time, it wasn't to connect to his mouth.

Angling his head, Roman spotted another example of his strong ownership. In a couple of decent-sized splotches, dark bruises were visible on the left side of Mikaél's neck. "Man, there's just one injury after another on you."

"Hmph," Mikaél smiled, "this one I wear with pride."

"Let's see what else I can do to help that then." In a quick dive, Roman attached himself to Mikaél's neck again with the same goal he had before—to begin another cycle of a sexual pheromone release.

Thrusting licks started first, right over the previous wounds. Mikaél's whimpers were strong, painful. To show the agony, Mikaél dug his nails into Roman's back, earning an animalistic growl that vibrated on his neck—turning the discomfort to pleasure. Still, the mix of pleasure and pain on an already sensitive spot was undeniably frustrating and gratifying. Feeling Roman's mouth close and lock down on his neck thrusted his body upward. It didn't take too long before both hard throbbing cocks rubbed each other through soaked fabric.

The outside of Mikaél's hole began to get very slippery. Perspiration settled on his taint below his heavy agonizing package. In the minutes that followed, he felt a bead of sweat mix with his wet slick. The sensation triggered a new sensitivity from his chest up to his shoulder. Once again, he felt an almost unbearable pain come up into an already beat-up pheromone gland.

"Roman! Oh, Wolf-God, it's coming. It's coming." It was a shout of pleasure but also a plea of pain. This time, Roman was on top of it. As he felt the gland spasm, he was certain Roman felt it with his tongue. Instantly, he felt teeth bite into him. Not knowing what to do with the extreme feeling, he whimpered into Roman's neck which was beginning to show its own signs of a sexual reaction.

Also, for the first time, Mikaél wrapped his legs around Roman's waist. It caused Roman's hips to thrust up against his virgin ass which started to vibrate. Finally, the burst of pleasure went through him. Slick felt like it was almost shooting out of him. The soft fabric of his sweatpants saturated. It was impossible for Roman not to notice. The smell was pungent and filled the room.

Roman wanted nothing more than to taste the Omega, but it would lead to things he promised Mikaél's Veo he wouldn't do. Hearing Mikaél's voice did exactly what he hoped for. Soon, a pressure glided up Roman's neck just the same and caused his pheromone gland to throb. He was forced to stop as his gasps and moans came out from his throat. Roman wanted it more than anything. Mikaél claiming him brought satisfaction to a whole new level.

Hearing Roman moan uncontrollably was music to Mikaél's ears. Turning Roman's neck slightly, Mikaél saw his own imprint again, barely noticing it before. Carefully examining himself after the incident, he was very aware Roman's was not as big nor pronounced. But now, he was going to change that. As if he was kissing Roman, he entered a solo make out session on the Alpha's gland. He didn't mind letting Roman suffer a second longer before finally taking what he wanted. This time, no hesitation, no gentle start, no quick end.

Mikaél's teeth were sharp and felt even more so than before. But Roman manned up like the Alpha he was and grunted like the animal he knew he could be. The strong male response challenged

Mikaél. Roman felt his neck being pulled down harder. Should Mikaél's teeth sink in any deeper, Roman was going to yelp in new pain. Luckily, it wasn't too much longer before the release came, and he moaned in ecstasy instead. The signal allowed Mikaél to disengage. Tight up against Mikaél, Roman's cock spasmed. Like before, it wasn't a full-on orgasm. Doing so would have completely soaked the front of his pants equal to Mikaél's. And this time, he wasn't in any position to get new clothes.

He pressed his forehead against Mikaél's as they both panted and occasionally moaned into each other's mouths. The sight and smell of gland secretion still lingered on their tongues. Roman's head fell to the side onto a pillow. He turned his head to Mikaél, carefully observing every expression. He was overjoyed, knowing he had given his Omega so much pleasure. His heart flooded with a powerful emotion he never wanted to diminish. He softly pressed his hand against Mikaél's cheek and gave him one final kiss.

"Please don't let this be the last time I see you," Roman pleaded.

"There's no way I'm going to let that happen. We belong to each other. No one can stop that," Mikaél reassured him.

A staring contest ensued between them both. Neither wanted to look away or even blink, if possible. Each second was too precious. A heavy sense of exhaustion fell upon them both like a blanket. Seeing Mikaél's shining face fall first triggered a spell over Roman. Soon, he fell into his own deep sleep next to his Omega, where he always wanted to be.

CHAPTER 16:

A Disproportion of Power

Without the boys' knowledge, Alec snuck down to his son's bedroom just before dawn. It was easy to know Roman still lingered considering his car was still in the driveway. Against his own principles, he woke up earlier than his mate, already an early riser, to resolve the situation. An uneasy feeling took over him as the absence of noise in the room could have indicated terrible actions he'd never forgive himself for.

His ear went right up to Mikaél's bedroom door first—still no noise. Turning the handle ever so slightly, like a burglar would, he cracked the door. In the faint light of sunrise, he saw Mikaél's face first, peaceful and free of the trauma plastered on his face the night before. His body faced him, his arm slightly hanging off the bed. Opening the door a bit more displayed a large figure of man holding his petite son with an arm wrapped around his chest. The man's face was equally serene and nonthreatening.

Immediately, Alec's focus fell to the two shirts thrown about the floor. Two nude chests were partially visible on the bed. He contained his discontent however when a shine bounced off Roman's belt which was snug around the waist of his pants. Mikaél had pants on as well, he saw, since no blanket covered either of them. Right now, there was no point in building a catastrophe in his mind. To better himself and the situation, he chose ignorance and assumed Roman didn't make a move worth regretting. He cleared his throat which sparked a twitch from Roman who became an alert guard dog.

"I hate to break this up," he spoke sternly, "but it's time for you to go."

Roman realized it was too much to ask for him to walk out this morning without being detected. However, he assumed being discovered by Alec was a blessing by comparison. Taking one more look at his Omega sleeping like an angel was heaven. Leaning down, he sealed his rendezvous with a gentle peck on his mate's cheek. From there, he sat up from the bed, confident there was no way for his exit to be not embarrassing—especially since he was shirtless. He grabbed his shirt from the floor, slipped it on, and approached Alec without buttoning it.

To see Mikaél's Veo roll his eyes was tough, but Roman was thankful that was all as he stealthily climbed the stairs.

"Thank you," Roman said before he walked out. Alec nodded as he held the door.

Roman didn't hesitate to start the car and leave. Seeing Mikaél was a once in a lifetime opportunity, and he didn't want to press his luck. Getting out of sight of the house allowed him to relax for the first time in almost 48 hours. In that time frame, he'd been on a first date, had first sex with his contracted mate, found and assaulted his Fated Mate, broke it off with his contracted mate, and bonded with his Fated Mate. No part of this seems real—it can't be. But Roman knew the worst was yet to come—his problems had only just started.

Entering his home, Roman didn't walk into the familiar greeting. For the most part, it was quiet.

Both of Roman's parents sat at the kitchen table, silent and hollow. His Veo wore flannel pants and white shirt while his Sur was perfectly put together for work. Neither Ryan nor Rixen were present. With no classes scheduled on the holiday, they wouldn't be up for hours.

They exchanged gazes, but no one spoke. Finally, Jake gestured to an open chair; Roman complied slowly. "How was your night?" Jake began. The tone was inquisitive, laced with a hint of condescension.

Roman shrugged. "I don't know. Words couldn't describe it accurately."

"Where did you go?" Jake inquired. The question came earlier than Roman expected. He looked at his Veo, whose concerned expression was remorseful. Roman chose to stare at the table instead, focusing on the lines of the leaf insert—the table now much smaller than it was last night. He knew this wasn't to act like an adolescent. He was a man capable of handling his life.

"With Mikaél, where I belong."

"You can't be serious!" Jake lamented.

"I am."

"Wolf-God! Roman, did you break into the home?"

"Why the hell would you ask that?" Roman snarled.

"Don't be so ignorant. That family has every right to destroy your record and reputation for the rest of your life." Jake's voice strained barely above a whisper. "Mikaél is a minor. No cop or judge needs to hear anything else." Jake couldn't believe it; his Alpha son had somehow snaked his way into his colleague's home and spent the night with the traumatized Omega. Jake swore he heard police sirens go off in the distance while gazing into the rising sun, but it was nothing more than his mind warping from Roman's nonchalant confession. But Jake refused to accept the casual statement. The dark pheromones going through the air confirmed it. His fingernails reached into fabric of pants as he tried to comprehend it all. He stared at his mate, hoping for some sort of comfort.

Adrian's reaction didn't please his mate. The initial disbelief faded as the Omega's instincts added up the clues. Remembering his own Alpha mate's courtship years ago, it all made sense on why Roman went there. Mikaél belonged to him now.

Roman sat there unchanged from his position. "For your information, I had their blessing to be there. In addition, my life is my decision. Mikaél, to me, is worth fighting for. The consequences are mine to deal with—not yours!"

"Damn it, Roman!" Jake hit his fist against the table.

"Jake, that's enough! You can't be hypocritical about this now," Adrian interjected.

Roman's head snapped as he saw his Alpha father lower his head. "What are you talking about?"

Adrian's face faltered. It occurred to him that it never was a topic of discussion before. Regardless, the evidence was there out in the open the entire time. "Oh, come on, Roman. Do basic math. I'm 41 and you're 24. Your father and I conceived and had you when I was 17. Your father is so passionate about this because he's lived it—we lived it."

Roman's frustration grew. "So, it's the exact same situation!"

"No, it's not!" Jake insisted, hitting his fist again. His family waited for the explanation, but he couldn't come up with a reason.

Adrian nodded his head. "It will be okay, Roman."

Jake gritted his teeth. "No, Adrian. You're not going to charm your way through this to help him." His attention turned back to Roman. "This is what I hate most about education these days. There's no course which takes you through all the procedures of law when contracting. They just expect everything to go perfectly unless an Omega attempts to overthrow the power of an Alpha. Those laws they'll teach you in Level 1. They'll also point out it's illegal for an adult to mate with a minor without the consent of the minor's parents. Plus, they can tell you to your face they're fine with it one second, then show up with the authorities at the contract signing to cuff you and take you away."

"There's a gray zone with those who are seventeen. It's not a slam dunk prosecution," Roman defended.

Jake threw his hands up. "I can't believe I'm having this conversation with my own son. I never anticipated one of my kids to fail at common sense."

"What's your point, Dad?!" Roman huffed.

"Once a contract is signed, there's no recourse anyone can take, including the Omega, even if they're a minor. It's signing away most of their Wolf-God given rights. After that, it's up to a judge to determine any sympathy. With seven out of every ten judges being Alphas, good luck to them. But before a contract, it'd be the kiss of death to any judge's career to not award compensation in a civil case not to mention the legal consequences."

"Okay, I'll admit being on the losing side of that would suck, but it's not like they'd take much. I don't have a house. I have a car and an amount of cash they wouldn't be satisfied with."

"This is exactly the problem, Roman. Mating laws have their own rules which don't apply elsewhere. Your attack last night, with, let's see, seven witnesses, including Dustin and Alec, will be prosecuted as the result of a successful sexual assault criminal case. You haven't finished school, you have no job, no independent insurance, and you live with your parents. The court will deem you as a dependent under the Pack Act, and they'll come after us."

"There's no way that's possible." Roman's face turned skeptical. "If that were true, no doubt there'd be stories all over the news of this happening all the time."

"Another flaw in today's system."

"Then why isn't this common?"

"Lower-Types are often left to fend for themselves. They hit the minimum requirement for school, take on their adult status, and run. They struggle or thrive on their own and the law views them as independent."

"That doesn't explain why you don't hear of these crimes."

"That's because Lower-Type Alphas typically mate with Lower-Type Omegas. They're viewed as lesser people, less trustworthy, and doubt that both parties weren't complicit. Even if an Alpha is convicted, it's a slap on the wrist, and no one pursues civilly."

"Why?"

Jake boomed, "Because they don't have money!" His voice made his mate wince. "No judge is going to award money which renders an Alpha homeless—it doesn't happen. But us? They'll consider a ridiculous amount, especially from a crime against an Omega 5. We'll be made an example for the justice system. I'll lose my credibility; your Veo will lose his with his construction work. It will follow Ryan and Rixen. Oh, and wait until Matthew Whitmore finds out. Talk about a lawsuit."

"I want to dissolve the contract with Peyton," Roman declared.

"Damn it! Ugh!" A pain flooded Jake's head.

"I can't do this, Dad. I can't go forward with Peyton. Peyton will understand; I think he will part amicably."

Jake snorted. "What makes you so sure?"

Roman halted. "I went there and told Peyton before I went to Mikaél's."

Another lashing was about to rush out of Jake's lips, but Adrian berated him first. "Roman, are you serious? How could you do that?"

"Son, what is wrong with you? Do you care about your life at all?" Jake added.

"I had to be honest with him and tell him where this was going to go," Roman answered. "Granted, I didn't know I was going to see Mikaél last night at that moment, but I knew I was going to put all my effort into seeing him before I saw Peyton if I didn't get it out of the way first. That's just the way I'm wired, and I can't help it. I wanted to do it the right way."

Jake shook his head. "You didn't do any of it right! You confessed to his face you imprinted someone else, then told him you were forcing a severance to be with Mikaél?"

"Yes."

"Oh, good. Let's add alimony for infidelity," Jake scorned.

"Why?" Roman asked.

"Because it's Matthew Whitmore's son, plain and simple. You shit on the most powerful man on the city. That doesn't come without consequences."

Suddenly, Roman had a flashback to an earlier conversation with Siro spewing his ominous warning. The thought made his stomach turn.

"There won't be any," Adrian inserted.

"What?" The words came simultaneously from both Roman and Jake.

"I asked for the no-fault clause right before they signed the contract. They have no recourse."

Adrian's statement melted the hatred off Roman's face. Roman's voice was barely above a whisper. "Veo, why did you do that?"

"I knew, Roman. I always knew. From the moment Peyton tried to connect with you at the restaurant and was failing miserably, I sensed your heart was not into this. Did I know this contract would fail? No, of course not. But I wanted to protect you in some way. That's what an Omega does for their son. The whole time knowing you were waiting for your Fate—I had to do something. I guess, in a sense, it was my way of rectifying what we didn't tell you about it."

Jake's eyes softened as he looked upon his own mate. "Babe, I love you. And I can't say I was naïve, but a 'No-fault clause' doesn't waive a committed crime."

"What crime?" Adrian asked.

"Infidelity. He confessed it. Peyton has clout. There isn't a judge who won't believe him."

"Except if there ever was an exception, finding a Fate would be it."

"One can only hope." Jake's shoulders fell with exhaustion, realizing the day had just started and work was imminent. "People don't go around asking to find people who have been through this stuff.

I don't know what's about to happen." He massaged the bridge of his nose. "I have to go to work." He turned to his son. "Roman, I am sorry for all of this. Veo and I are going to be by your side every step of the way. We love you."

Roman's eyes softened for his father. He needed support more than anything. He needed his family. "I love you, too."

A subtle smile and head nod came from Jake. Adrian clasped his hand over his son's and appeared misty-eyed. A much-needed repair was in progress.

"Dustin," Jake acknowledged, walking into the lab.

"Morning," Dustin replied neutrally as he yawned. He began printing daily reports and organizing them into vertical trays.

"Did you get any sleep last night?"

"Mental exhaustion, rum, and a sleeping pill helps." Dustin eyed Jake, partially kidding.

"Heh. I don't blame you."

"And yourself?" Dustin asked.

Jake found his computer and logged in with his credentials. "No," he paused, "not really. Honestly, I'm surprised I'm even functioning this morning. This is not going to be a good day."

"Ah. You must have already talked to Matthew Whitmore then?"

Jake groaned. "That's the problem: I haven't yet."

"You never called him?" Dustin looked up from his paperwork.

"That's the beauty of it. Roman got brave, no doubt from liquid courage, and told Peyton himself it was off."

Dustin swallowed. "Really?" He tapped his pencil thoughtfully. *How much of what I'm working on will fade away to nothing in an instant? What will be my punishment by association? Demotion? Laid Off? Fired? What exactly will appease a Whitmore out for blood?*

"I guess it will happen anytime now. Still can't believe you didn't call him this morning."

"I was dealing with Roman—who didn't come home until dawn—thank you very much." Jake's eyes looked at Dustin like he'd been inconvenienced.

Dustin's head turned. "What do you mean by that?"

"If you just would have sent him back home or at least called me, I could have slept a little better. That's all." Jake gave one final judgmental look at Dustin like he was teaching him how to be courteous to other people.

"What are you talking about, Jake?" Dustin walked to Jake's lab desk.

"Look, I'm happy you entertained Roman last night. As a father of an Omega myself, I'm not sure I'd have the same virtue of giving him the benefit of a doubt. It's just I didn't know where he was, and he didn't answer phone calls or texts."

Dustin dropped his pen and rubbed his forehead, lost in a haze of information which didn't add up. "You're actually serious."

Jake examined the shock which flooded Dustin's face. "You did know that Roman was with Mikaél last night, right?"

"Are you honestly suggesting I'd have let him into my home after what he did?"

Jake's stomach turned. "You didn't know then."

Dustin clenched his fist and his teeth. "No! How on earth did you think I'd be okay with that?"

"Roman said this morning he had your blessing and that everything was okay," Jake defended.

"Your deranged son probably broke into my home and went in for a second ambush!" Dustin's voice carried throughout the lab. An audience was forming, staring at the two men volleying their dispute.

"Roman isn't deranged. We talked about this last night and you agreed!"

Dustin's Alpha pheromones triggered, and he rushed into his colleague's space. "That was before I found out you couldn't keep a leash on your ravager of a son!"

"He's an adult, Dustin. I'm not going to imprison him in the house. He's capable of making his own decisions."

"I can't believe you are defending him on this!" Dustin roared. "You just said you couldn't see yourself doing this—why is my response suddenly wrong?"

"It's not!"

"Gentlemen!" A voice interrupted, cutting through the rising volume. The hushed silence of the room carried across the entire audience.

"Paul, I'm sorry," Jake responded.

"Sorry, sir," Dustin followed.

"All right, everyone. Back to work." Dr. Birowack made a straight path to his office door and continued his words without even looking at his constituents. "Follow me." His demand was oddly without vexation; as a matter of fact, it was almost bubbly. Upon entering, he added, "Please close the door."

Dustin closed the door, and they both turned to observe Dr. Birowack sitting in his large extravagant chair like a principal getting ready to scold his pupils. "Gentlemen," he paused, "I'm beginning to think these spats are the result of a much deeper inability to be an effective team for our cause here. What say you?"

Dustin pleaded, "Paul, I beg of you not to view us that way,"

Dr. Birowack rubbed his chin. "And how should it be viewed, then?"

Jake peered next to him to see Dustin's disapproval. His shame kept his gaze on the floor. "There was a development last night which has left us both shaken up a bit."

"Some more than others," Dustin added.

"Yes," Jake continued. "If you recall, earlier I extended the offer for Dustin's family to join my family for dinner as we 'buried the hatchet' as you might say." He paused; Dr. Birowack was unchanged and unmoved. "My son Roman, upon seeing Dustin's son, attacked him. It was a scary scene—frightening actually."

Dr. Birowack' furrowed his brow. "That's quite a concern. What was the reason for such savagery?"

"We didn't know at first. It all happened so quickly; no one knew what to do or even think of it." Jake once again looked at Dustin, silently signaling what his next reveal was. "It is my son's belief that Mikaél is his Fate."

All of Dr. Birowack's attention went to Dustin. He analyzed him and scented a profile revealing his dissent. "I'm afraid I'm hearing two separate actions: an assault and an imprint. Which happened exactly?"

Dustin replied, "Both." His tone was flat.

"So, you are in agreement of what took place then?" Dr. Birowack asked for clarification. A sigh and reluctant nod came from Dustin. "I'm a bit disappointed I wasn't informed about this earlier."

"I tried. Well, let me rephrase that, I had a guest of Rixen's held up in my office trying to call you. It conveniently doubled as a distancing tool; having him see the fray was quite embarrassing enough. I had to utilize my twin boys to keep Roman occupied as we made sure Mikaél was okay and sorted this out."

Dr. Birowack nodded. "It is unfortunate to hear. I could only imagine what that was like to observe. My apologies about not receiving such messages. There must have been an error somewhere. I am, however, intrigued about this missing transition between the first and second event that look place."

Jake answered, "Without being Roman, or Mikaél for that matter, I'm afraid I can't speak to how it all specifically happened. But Roman insists the entire incident was due to Fate pheromones. Essentially, it is his belief that the desire to imprint Mikaél caused him to ambush. My other son even tried to intervene and was struck by him too. At that point, I used my judgement to force everyone to back off. It was successful; Roman didn't appear to hurt Mikaél anymore and didn't choose to lash out on anyone else."

Dr. Birowack shifted his gaze. "And you, Dustin. What do you think?"

"I, for one," Dustin scoffed, "think the theory is a sham. And look, I'll give Jake a lot of credit here: he didn't sugarcoat anything. Albeit, he didn't say the specifics on how his son clawed mine with his bare hands like a savage beast." Dustin curled his lips as he glanced at Jake. "But otherwise, I have to say, the rest is accurate. As far as what I think, I believe this was nothing more than a horrific incident caused by a repressed hypersexual man and a coming-of-age boy, my son."

"I think that's a bit far," Jake dissented.

"Really? Because I don't remember you picking up my emotionally traumatized son off the floor," Dustin spat.

"Now, now, we're all scientists here." Dr. Birowack attempted to refocus the young professionals who seemed hell bent on outdoing each other. "This is what we do. So, let's talk. Obviously, the skepticism comes from our research. The science is laid out and has been for years. A Type 6 Alpha never develops the ability to find a Fate. It's a dysfunction of puberty."

"What if it's wrong?" Jake inquired.

"Let's switch gears," Dr. Birowack continued. "A hypersexual who is deemed uncontrollable and violent typically does not initiate mating without clear warning signs well in advance that the urge is upon him. It's an Alpha's version of an Omega heat. Was Roman showing any signs over the past few days?"

"No. None," Jake stated.

"All right. When did he last copulate?"

Jake winced. He couldn't believe he actually knew so much about his son's sex life. "Uh. The previous night actually. He was with Peyton, his contracted mate." Jake decided to table any judgement on how he was able to answer such detail so quickly. He shouldn't know any of it.

"Ah, indeed. That's a conundrum in itself. One that I'm confident concerns you too, Dustin."

"Why?" Dustin asked.

"Regardless of if this Fated Mate Theory comes to fruition, an imprint is scannable from yards away. Roman's contracted mate will know it instantly the next time he sees him. As for Mikaél, he will be attracted to Roman, no doubt."

"It seems Roman has talked to Peyton already. I sense quite the battle coming up between Whitmore's family and my own."

Dr. Birowack nodded in dismay.

"I'm sorry," Dustin inserted. "I don't buy the arguments that since no one could read Roman's heat signs combined with Mikaél's attraction to him must mean they're Fated Mates. Let's not forget: I don't know any history which has recorded an assault as courting a Fate. Fating is supposed to be one of the most beautiful moments two individuals go through: a mutual scent, a glimmer in the eyes, a soft embrace, and some even start crying."

"Well, let's not forget the other part," Jake insisted.

"A dilation and hormonal gland response doesn't happen until an Omega hits their heat. And I told you already, Mikaél hasn't even had his first one."

"You could be wrong."

"Any idiot can tell you whether or not an Omega has had their first heat. Don't condescend to me, Jake."

"Jake, what do you think about all this?" Dr. Birowack asked.

"I'm a scientist, Paul. I try to remain impartial as best as I can. But what I saw in person and heard from my son gives me doubts that all our research is as superior as we hoped."

"That's the entire reason science exists. That's why we're here. But I'm confident Roman appreciates the support you've given him."

Jake winced. "I wish I could say that."

"Pardon?" Dr. Birowack asked.

"I haven't told Roman I believe he's right."

Dustin turned. "You're kidding." He examined Jake's expression, knowing this was true. "You berated me last night! You tore me down to convince me of this, and you didn't even tell Roman?"

"If I had told him 'Yes,' and you had done everything in your power to make sure Mikaél never saw him again, what good was it going to do? You'd break his heart!"

"I'd break his fingers if I found out he really spent the night with Mikaél." Dustin crossed his arms.

"He told me he had permission," Jake reiterated. "Roman doesn't break into a home and stalk a person. He would have scared the shit out of Mikaél. It would have been a stupid move."

"Then who on earth do you really believe gave him—" Dustin stopped himself the moment he realized how it was all possible. "Alec." Alec's surprise early bird morning with his stoic face matched his suspicion something was up. Although when asked, Alec had said the stress remained from the dinner-that-wasn't, he now knew the real story. His face dimmed. "Alec did it; he let him in. Roman was there, and Alec made sure he left before I got up. Let me guess: Roman came home around sunup?"

"Yeah, not much later than that actually. Adrian and I didn't get a lot of sleep, and we both watched him walk in."

Dustin swallowed his pride. "I apologize, Jake. I didn't know. Apparently, I'm last to know again, even when it involves my own family."

"No one deserves that, Dustin. Truly." Jake attempted to comfort his partner. "But this is important to Roman; he's trying to make this right for who he believes Mikaél is supposed to be."

Dr. Birowack cut in, "Clearly we know how Roman feels. What has Mikaél said about all this?"

All eyes fell upon Dustin. "He has expressed the same sentiment. He believes Roman is his Fate, too."

"Then that's where we'll continue our work."

"Wait, huh?" Dustin asked, thrown off by Dr. Birowack's comment.

"Let us use this remarkable scenario in the best way we know how. On one hand, we have two individuals who may just be caught up with infatuation pheromones, and on the other, we have the belief a Type 6 Alpha has defied years of recorded science which says a Fated Mate isn't possible. Our goal has always been to unlock secrets of the Type 6 Alpha. And even if this all adds up to nothing, at least we know what we can rule out. Hmm?"

Dustin contemplated. "I suppose this is what we're all needing in this situation. But I won't overstep my son's consent. If he doesn't want this scrutiny, I won't subject him to it."

Jake twitched. "Does this mean you are going to entertain a contract?"

"What choice do I have? If Roman stayed the night with Mikaél, then that's the answer right there. This isn't a phase, and it's not going away. That being said, you're going to have your own battle with Whitmore. So, we'll see if this is even possible."

A knock on the door startled all as a lab technician opened the door. "I'm sorry for interrupting. Dr. Erricson, you have a call from Matthew Whitmore. He's called three times now, and I don't think he's going to take a 'He's in a meeting' for an answer again."

"That man knows just how to move all the chess pieces he wants." Dustin shook his head. "As I said before, deal with him, then we'll talk. And hopefully tomorrow all of us will still have jobs." Dustin headed for the door.

"It will all work out, Dustin!" Jake assured him.

"Glad you're optimistic!" Dustin yelled back, a few steps out the door.

"I'll answer it in a minute. Just put him on hold, please," Jake told the tech, who acknowledged him and left. Jake moved closer to Dr. Birowack's desk. His boss was sorting emails as if nothing had transpired. "Paul?"

The doctor looked up. "Jake. I thought you left. Was there something else?"

"I need to ask something of you which I hope doesn't end all the respect you have for me. But I don't know what we're going to do if you don't."

Dr. Birowack leaned in as if he'd been tasked with a novel challenge. "And what exactly are you asking me to do?"

For the entire Erricson family, returning to the lawyer's office was a nightmare. As they reached the clear glass doors, Jake turned around and faced his son, reaching for the highest focus he'd ever required.

He grabbed his son's shoulders. "Roman, I need you to listen to me more than you ever have in your entire life. Whatever happens in that conference room, I need you to trust me. You cannot question anything I say in that room. If you do, it will destroy anything you want with Mikaél, okay? Do you understand me?"

Roman huffed in frustration. This wasn't a time for his father to demand anything from him. But the thought of possibly losing his Fated Mate brought back all his years of feeling subservient to his father. "Yes, Sur," he stated stoically.

Jake felt comforted by Roman's conviction, nodded slightly, then looked at his mate behind him, extending the same nod to him. "Okay, let's go."

The secretary acknowledged the family as a ball of nerves. "Mr. Erricson, Mr. Whitmore is waiting for you in the—"

Matthew boomed out of the conference room, flinging the double doors wide open. "Look who the dog dragged in!" After a searing stare, he turned and walked back into the room.

"He's, um, in the conference room," the secretary finished, a bit startled himself.

Jake and his family walked into the viper's pit and found the same seats they had the first time. It was as if they never left. But this time, the room appeared smaller, almost claustrophobic.

Roman noticed Peyton right away. His expression was distantly scornful. Seeing it was bad enough, but scenting Peyton was worse. His beautiful vanilla and citrus fragrance had dulled to nothing. A harsh burning smell replaced it; the scent was vaguely familiar. The drive to search in the recesses of his mind stopped when he examined Peyton's pale, sick-looking face. He looked like death warmed up.

"Peyton, what's wrong? Are you feeling okay?"

Terrence blurted. "Oh, now you care?" His expression was icy, and his words had teeth ready to rip Roman apart.

"Yes, I care!" Roman insisted.

"I don't think it's any of your business to know anymore, Roman," Terrence snapped back.

"Veo, please!" Peyton spoke up.

"Oh, yes," Matthew piggybacked, "let's tell Roman exactly what he's doing to our son. Give him every last detail."

"Is this necessary, Terrence?" Adrian pleaded.

"Peyton is starting suppressants," Terrence continued. "In normal cases, these are taken right after a cycle. They drop hormone and pheromone production as you know. The heats themselves greatly reduce—not painful or incessant. But Peyton is too close to a heat. So, he's on an elevated dose. Do you have any idea what those medications do when they are taken so close to a heat, Roman? Do you?"

"We should move on," Jake suggested. Terrence ignored the comment.

"It's poison! That's what is going through my son right now. It's cutting off his natural cycle. It's like being on a rollercoaster and slamming the brake mid-descent. Mentally, physically, emotionally, he is hitting a wall. That's what you are doing to him. It's the worst thing I think an Alpha can do to an Omega next to abandoning them during their heat. And what's worse is this might be all for naught which means he'll have to be subjected to a medical professional again. How on earth are you living with yourself?"

Roman held his mouth open in awe, barely remembering to breathe, let alone knowing the words to say. "Like I've already told Peyton, in any other life with him, I would have never done this. I didn't anticipate going through a severance ever in my life. This is not something I'm jumping up and down for. The number of apologies I've been giving over the last few days could be its own book. I've told Peyton to his face what happened and hope he can find it in himself to understand this is the rarest exception any human could go through. I'm not asking him to like it; I'm asking him to understand." Regret went through Roman's head as he realized he was talking about Peyton as if he wasn't there staring right back at him.

"You mean finding another mate?" Terrence scoffed. "It's not an original idea. It's the oldest, not to mention, the ugliest betrayal any person can do."

"I—" Roman began.

"This isn't helping anyone. Let's get this going." Adrian sat upright, staring down Terrence. Like Alpha-to-Alpha, Omegas themselves became very territorial for their offspring—no matter how old they were. He glanced at his mate, then at their lawyer who began the proceedings.

"Okay," he breathed, "we are here for a dissolution of the Partnership and Copulation Agreement or P&C of #1 Alpha—Roman Edward Erricson—and #2 Omega—Peyton Reginald Whitmore. Do all parties agree including their legal representation this is why we are here?" All agreed, trying not to show any immaturity during the open proceeding. A paper was handed to Jake who centered it front of his family. "Do you, Roman, under the advisement of your parents, Jacob Tyler Erricson and Adrian Asher (Omarro) Erricson, acknowledge and find legally accurate your wish to terminate your P&C agreement?"

The paper in front of him read like a death sentence. Roman never looked up, but he knew all eyes were lasered in on him. It was natural for him to hesitate. He held no ill will against Peyton. How could he? He'd been nothing but supportive of their contract since day one. When he went to his house to break the news, Peyton's words stung, but they revealed just how much he had emotionally invested. Could he really end it all in just a matter of minutes? Clearing his throat, Roman thought of every little bit of detail in how to respond: voice, posture, eye contact, tone, volume, everything. After a quick adjustment in his chair, he nodded, adding a verbal "Yes."

The lawyer acknowledged the word and handed Roman a pen. The sounds of the pen scratching the paper were harsh on his ears. After Roman signed his name, both his parents signed below as witnesses and endorsers.

The attention moved to Whitmore's lawyer who read aloud the same legal prompt. The words spun in Peyton's head faster than the room itself. He couldn't figure out which hurt more: the side effects of the poisonous suppressants or hearing the ever-binding words which destroyed every chance he felt he had in having a mate to call his own. The ability to drown out everything in the room dissipated as he anticipated the lawyer's words ending which forced his response. All he could do his nod his head as his throat felt like cotton.

"I'm sorry, Mr. Whitmore. I have to hear a verbal response," the lawyer instructed.

"Yes," his groggy voice uttered. In that moment, Peyton's control ceased, and he felt his eyes water. His strong exhale was heard throughout the room.

Roman wanted to get up and run to him. Peyton didn't deserve this—he alone deserved all the pain. Even though he caused it, he wanted to be the one to take it all away. Yet, he couldn't—not anymore. Peyton was no longer his to soothe. The guilt was, however, his to eternally bear.

"Now," the lawyer continued, "we are by law required to report the reason for the dissolution."

"Infidelity," Matthew rushed in.

"Preposterous!" Jake exclaimed.

"That's not fair," Roman chimed in.

Matthew tilted his head. "But it is fair, Roman. It is! My son told me he had a very interesting conversation with you, in my home no less, about quite the lewd act you committed well before today. Is this not true?"

Roman lost his wind. "Yes, it's true."

Matthew's head jolted back to Jake. "Now, mating contracts aren't my expertise, but I do believe infidelity carries with it a very steep monetary penalty should the aggrieved wish it. After having to hear and see my son's own heartbreak for not only what was committed but also for what is to come, we think it's the least your family can do."

Jake smirked. "You can't seriously be forgetting the 'no-fault' clause in this contract. What recourse do you think you have in this?"

"Well, now, that's where you need to do your homework. In this territory and state, the 'no-fault' clause says neither party has to declare an outstanding reason nor any reason for that matter for it be recognized. It doesn't remove liability of a crime, however. His accountability will still be judged in court and be punishable to the full extent of the law. The beauty of it all is Roman just admitted in front of seven witnesses today his infidelity, so Peyton has no burden of proof. Your son doesn't know how to be inconspicuous at all. After all, I hear he found his new trick at your dinner party?" Matthew grinned as he turned to face Roman. "Tell me, boy, did you give the show to everyone for free, or did you become a wise businessman and charge the audience a fee?"

Roman jumped up from his chair and scowled with a grunt.

"Roman!" Jake stood and puffed his chest, sending a wave of pheromones to warn him to stand down. Adrian grabbed Roman's arm and squeezed gently, his eyes pleading.

Matthew laughed. "Now, Roman, don't make this so easy. Give us a little challenge." His eyes sparkled as he looked at his mate who returned the look. He could not, however, get the same facial expression out of Peyton. He toned down his enthusiasm out of respect.

"This constant ridicule isn't amusing, Matthew!" Jake barked.

"That, sir, is up for interpretation. I don't know what you expect to do. There is no choice but to accept responsibility. That is why we are requesting 100K in compensation."

"There's no way that's happening," Adrian stressed.

"It's the full extent of the law, and we plan to use it as our right," Terrence replied.

"No one is going to look at that request without laughing their ass off. Everyone knows your financial capability. They'll view it as a pitiful cash grab."

"Me, perhaps. Not Peyton," Matthew corrected.

"Peyton? He's under the Pack Act. He has no self-sufficiency."

"Once again, not true. You see, after the contract was signed, I moved assets into Peyton's name. He has a car, a home, his own insurance, and a job."

"A job?" Roman asked.

"Of course," Matthew's voice became dramatic, loving every minute of it.

"What job?"

Matthew paused, holding the moment for effect. "He's the owner and CEO of a non-profit organization to help underprivileged Omegas and Betas get off the streets and help them become productive citizens. Peyton, being of the proper background, knows the value of being independent once mated. It's virtuous to want to contribute to his household—commendable even. Now, we apologize for not saying anything right away. It wasn't a stress we wanted to burden you with. Our son's health and his impending heat was the priority. We felt it was appropriate to leave this matter for a later time."

Jake seethed. "You put your Omega son as the owner and CEO of a business? This was nothing more than a tactic to be used later."

"Really? Because my family didn't ask for a 'No-fault' clause—yours did. And as a parent, I'm allowed to give any assets to my son's business without cause or explanation."

"A house, car, insurance, and the financial means all to run a business?"

"Especially to run a business, and I'll gladly fight in court any man who says I did anything wrong by helping my family; it's just unfortunate that family doesn't include Roman. Well, fortunate now." Matthew smirked, satisfied with himself. "So, I think you know how this is going to play out, Erricson."

Adrian chimed in, "What about the fact the boy who Roman found is his Fated Mate?"

Matthew jerked his head in disgust. "You can't really be throwing that out now. Seriously? How desperate can you get?"

"I told Peyton that night he was," Roman clarified.

"Oh, I heard," Matthew replied. "I also heard you were drunk out of your mind that night. In regard to your claim, I'm not surprised you'd try anything to get mercy out of all of this."

"Then why doesn't it matter?" Roman asked.

Matthew sighed. "Number one: I don't care. Number two: Your father is the one who tattooed across his forehead, 'My Alpha Type 6 son can't find a Fated Mate.' The conversation was cemented even before we talked to you and Peyton about the contract. And contrary to what you may believe now, Roman, I really did feel bad for you. No one wants to be told that, and no one wants to believe it about themselves. But when one of the top medical professionals, whose research is the standard on the Type 6 Alpha, tells me it can't happen, you better believe I'm going to listen to what he has to say."

Roman hummed. "I should be grateful you view my Sur in such high regard."

"Don't be ridiculous! I'm not talking about your father. Dr. Birowack! The man has the respect of the world. The opportunity to have that man here in Tauris City on the front lines of research to help our kind survive is invaluable. Assuming your Sur is taking the same defensive approach as you and your Veo, then I am to assume he's lost his mind and has gone against his own employer's work."

"Regardless," Jake chimed in, "you would agree that if Roman had indeed found his Fate, then today's conversation would be very different."

"Sure." Matthew spoke with an enthusiasm while also entertained at such notion. "But that's not going to happen unless you can prove it. Roman's sexual prowess isn't going to sway anyone in district court."

"No," Jake stressed, "but this will." On cue, Jake's lawyer retrieved a sealed folder from his belongings and placed it in front of Matthew. He folded his hands and studied all of Matthew's movements, his breathing and subtle changes in his pheromone patterns indicating a slip in confidence.

The envelope was blank other than medical tape with a stamp below which bore the name of the research facility and address. He saw Jake's cheeky grin, and he wanted to strike it off his face. His attention drifted to everyone else in the room whose expressions matched his own. The lawyers, his mate, Jake's mate, and even Roman and Peyton—all were perplexed at this mysterious envelope. Flushing the awkward expression away, Matthew refocused with his usual stature and opened the envelope.

The letterhead was formalized and written on thick paper. The language was professional all the way down to the medical terminology. No commoner was ever going to be able understand the jargon. However, it didn't take a genius to understand the overall message. While reading most of it, Matthew's skin flushed red, and his hands shook with adrenaline. He impulsively pushed the paper back toward Jake, fearing he'd rip it to shreds otherwise.

"What the hell you trying to pull, Erricson?" Matthew roared.

"Matthew!" Terrence shouted, shocked at his mate's inability to control himself.

"Your entire family is nothing but two-faced backstabbers!" Matthew screamed.

Adrian gasped. "I beg your pardon!"

"Adrian, let me handle this," Jake cut in.

"Sur, what's going on?" Roman asked, a calm voice in the storm.

"Roman, I mean it! Just let me handle this," Jake demanded.

Matthew muttered more things to himself he wished he could say without damaging his professional integrity. "There is no way you honestly expect me to believe that sham of a paper."

Jake paused. "Actually, yes. I expect you to believe what is now law on that paper."

"What?" Matthew asked in disbelief.

Whitmore's lawyer lifted the paper. In a similar way, his expression went from intrigued to dismayed. After reading each new paragraph, he shot looks at Jake and then to Matthew, who seemed to be communicating back telepathically.

"For Wolf-God's sake, Matthew! What does it say?" Terrence asked impatiently.

Matthew cleared his throat in an attempt to begin but was swiftly cut off and deferred to his lawyer. "According to this, Roman's Alpha Type 6 Status was placed in error. Although a few biological marker percentiles are top rated, it has been determined he does not qualify for the indication and has been recategorized from Alpha Type 5 Accelerate to Alpha Type 5."

"Roman's identity is being replaced?" Adrian queried.

Roman sulked. "Wait. Am I being demoted?"

Jake corrected, "No, Roman, don't look at it like that. Ever since you were born, your levels have always made professional heads turn.

And today it's no different. But the Alpha Type 6 is a very, very elusive subject which constantly proves science wrong. After what happened with Mikaél, I was forced to look at all your data again. It's the only explanation, Roman." Jake watched his son's pride take a hit. He furrowed his brows. "Look, it's okay. Your 'Exceptional' identity still tells everyone you possess abilities almost no others do. I know right now this looks like it's taking everything away from you. But this also reinstates things you were told didn't exist for you like—"

"Like finding a Fated Mate," Peyton said. Most seemed to forget he was in the room with his hunched posture and non-existent presence. All eyes zoomed to him, and the room waited on his every breath. He shook his head in amusement. "Here it is. You did whatever you could to make sure everyone believed you. Now, everyone has to believe you—legally anyway."

"Peyton, none of this is making me feel better. This doesn't allow me to get off scot-free," Roman lamented.

"Hm. We'll see about that," Peyton replied.

"This is an abuse of power." Matthew shook his finger at Jake. "You've used your position to rewrite the playbook. So, you did what? Tweak numbers? Change the rules? Do whatever you had to make this look legit? I mean: printed, signed, notarized, and embossed in one day? It's a disgrace! Then, to have the audacity to write and approve your own letter. This is precisely why you aren't fit to be in your position. When this gets out, you'll have no integrity at all. You'll be stripped of everything: your position, your title, and your name. I, personally, cannot wait until Dr. Birowack, in all of his wisdom, gets ahold of all this and sees you for the rat you really are."

Jake nodded, in complete control. "I completely agree. That is exactly what would happen," he paused, "if that is how it happened."

"Of course, that's what happened. How else would—" Matthew was cut off by his lawyer clearing his throat while handing the document back to him. In reverse, Matthew's face now drained of all color.

Jake's voice sauntered in, "As a businessman, I fully expected you to read the full document before continuing proceedings. If you had, you could have saved your breath."

Terrence breathed. "What's he blabbering about now?"

Jake smiled. "To put it plainly, that 'invaluable doctor of wisdom' is the one who orchestrated this, not me."

Terrence's expression fell. "Matthew, what's he saying?"

Matthew grimaced. "This letter is from Dr. Birowack himself. He wrote it and had the magistrate finish it off. Hot off the press, I'm sure."

"Now," Jake began, "I do believe Roman's new classification entitles him to the protections of every Alpha on this Earth. We can't prepare for this; no one can really. But the law is clear on how this works, am I right?" Jake turned to his lawyer.

The lawyer nodded. "Yes, this event falls under the protection of the Fate Act. Although Roman was already in contract, finding a Fate allows him, or anyone for that matter, to voluntarily leave the existing one without penalty. Essentially, in this scenario, the 'no-fault' clause is rendered noneffective. Roman's imprint will be viewed as an instinctual act and a necessary one in order to move toward his viable future."

"Fraud 101. The case can, and will, be made to show Roman's displeasure caused him to arrange a fictional Fate to usurp his promise to Peyton." Matthew sat back, trying to show himself at ease.

"I can't stop you from doing so," Jake returned.

"Damn right you can't!"

"But only a week into the contract makes this seem very odd. We're not the ones asking for alimony, even though Roman is the one leaving, while acknowledging Roman is financially disproportionate to Peyton."

"That's weak at best, Erricson," Matthew dismissed.

"Perhaps. But like you said, my son doesn't seem to know how to 'commit a crime' as you put it. He also has seven witnesses from the dinner who will corroborate his story, not to mention the Omega he imprinted."

"Oh, what? Seven people who saw the two go up, sniff each other, and hug? Wow, how avant-garde." Matthew shook his head in his own amusement.

Jake looked at Roman. His son's eyes were heavy with the memory of the encounter. "I'm not going to discuss the details on what happened between the two, but I can assure you it wasn't conventional. There's some compelling details which will prove more convincing than a standard courting ritual."

Matthew thrust his hand on the table. "I'm not going to stand for this, Erricson! You can sit there with a smug face and think you've bested me, but you have no idea the trouble you've created for yourself and your family. If you think I'm the only one you're going to answer to for this, you're severely mistaken."

Jake tilted his head. "Is that a threat, Mr. Whitmore?"

"You know," Whitmore's lawyer interjected, "I think my client is done here. We just need to fill out the cause for dissolution and then make copies including the letter from Dr. Birowack."

"Make sure you write 'Fated Mate' as the reason. Not 'infidelity,'" Jake pointed out.

Matthew huffed and stood up, everyone else followed. He grinned as he buttoned the lower part of his suit coat. "I'm telling you right now—this isn't over."

"Yes, it is, and you know it," Jake replied. Pheromones from both Surs permeated the room.

Matthew's face turned stoic and went to his family. "Come on. We've had enough of this. And by the way, expect to see a hefty bill coming your way from your son punching a hole in my wall."

Looks of unease were shared by all parents in the room. Roman's focus moved from Peyton's face down to the table, searching for anything to say or do. The coarse atmosphere from last time reared its ugly head. Only this time, it wasn't going to be replaced by a subtle sense of joy and accomplishment.

Peyton used strength he didn't have to stand up. His head and body hurt. No one's description of the suppressant's side effects accurately described what he was experiencing. He hoped against everything having this short yet agonizing chapter in his life closed would provide some, no, *any* relief. A trembling lip was replaced with a push of steadiness.

"I hope this works out for you, Roman," Peyton commented.

All Roman managed was a nod as he watched Peyton follow Matthew and Terrence, who shifted from aggravated wolves to concerned parents. After the Whitmores left, Roman and his family stood in the privacy of the conference room. What he compartmentalized into the back of his head rushed forward.

"Sur, what's going on?" Roman demanded.

"Not now, Roman. Wait until the car."

"But this—"

"I said, wait until the car, Roman," Jake repeated.

Adrian looked at his mate with anxiety and then to his son with empathy. He threw his arm around his son's shoulder and led them both out of the building behind Jake.

***

The car doors barely shut before Roman continued his crusade. "Dad, what is this?"

"The contract ended, Roman. It's over. You can move on with your life now," Jake assured him.

"No, no. You don't get to skirt this. How could you do this behind my back? I'm a Type 5? Are you serious right now?"

"Roman, I—"

"No!" Roman interrupted. "Who the hell are you? You're acting like some sort of secret agent or something. This is just one more covert operation at my expense."

"More than you know."

Roman's head jerked back. "What?"

Jake leaned in with a heavy stare. "I want you to listen because I'm not going to say this again. I had to do what I had to in order to rectify the wrong I committed and to protect you from Matthew. This was the only way to do it."

The look on both Roman's and Adrian's faces was shock.

"Dad, are you seriously telling me this was all a set up?"

"Your Type was changed to protect you and give you the best chance at a life you deserved. You're not a Type 5, Roman. You never will be." Jake's eyes scanned everywhere, like a spy wanting to avoid any exposure.

"How on earth was this possible?"

"I took a shot in the dark and prayed I could get what I needed to secure a way out of this in which Whitmore couldn't come after you. Matthew was right: I had explicitly told him about you, and he could have subpoenaed your records and all the research—my research—to prove you didn't have any natural ability to Fate anyone. I knew if I could get you reclassified, you'd be subjected to standard law. Getting Dr. Birowack on board was the only way to do it. In a sense, he singlehandedly did what I could not: he saved you from a fate which could've destroyed you. The burden on you to keep this a secret and go with it is the most unfair thing to ask of you, but it's the only way you can avoid Whitmore's wrath. And to tell you the truth, I don't even know if it's enough. All I know is this is the best chance we have. Do you understand?"

Roman's blood chilled in his body. The words crashed in like icicles. He couldn't say anything—the words escaped him. Silently, he nodded his head.

Seeing it gave Jake the promise of a brighter future. Unfortunately, his mate couldn't have been more opposite. His heart was crushed and riled at the same time. The urge to comfort Adrian in that moment was strong, but he needed to get as far away from that office as he could. He started the car and began the trek home. Getting onto the highway allowed him to breathe.

While driving down a long, endless road, it didn't take long for Adrian to fall asleep.

Roman was lost in a haze, staring out the back passenger window.

All Jake could do was recall the conversation with his superior earlier in the day:

Jake stammered. "Paul, in addition to mine, I'm about to ask you to consider compromising your position."

Dr. Birowack devoted his entire attention to his subordinate. "Such a request has never been asked of me. I fear your position has already been compromised by asking it." His expression neutralized to curiosity. "Well, let's have it."

"I've hurt my son in a way that might not ever get repaired. And I know that's not your problem."

"You are correct in that."

"If I had known there was any chance of Roman finding a Fated Mate, I would have done everything differently for the past twenty years. But I want to believe him. I want to believe him so badly."

Dr. Birowack agreed. "It would be quite the revelation in everything we have done; it also would set back your life's work. So, other than family matters, what could you ask of me which is worthy of compromising my integrity?"

"If we want to know what Roman is capable of, we have to get him out of the contract with Whitmore's son. He needs to play this out with Mikaél. This isn't an experiment to Roman; this is his life and the way he wants it. From what I know, Mikaél is the same. If Roman stays with Peyton, everything stops there. Roman becomes obsolete—if not logistically, then viscerally. Roman will refuse to work with us."

"Break the contract then. Simple as that."

"Paul, please. You know it's not that simple. Whitmore will blow up the court system and undeniably win and rake us over the coals. I'm not even convinced going the right way won't destroy my career. The only thing I know is, after looking into it myself, if Roman has the Fate Act to protect him, Whitmore's recourse essentially disappears."

"The Fate Act?" Dr. Birowack paused as the connection set in. "Ah I see," he nodded. "You wish for me to reclassify him—lower his Status."

"I can't do it myself. I don't have the clout, and that doesn't even address the severe conflict of interest. I respect Dustin, but it won't go anywhere with him. Thrusting him into this is more than I could ask of him. It already has affected his life more than any man should have to go through."

Dr. Birowack leaned back in his chair, reaction unreadable. The seconds ticked by like hours. "Consider it done."

Jake's head exploded. His comprehension failed him. "What? That's it? That's all you're going to say?"

He chuckled. "A man of few words, I am not. Unfortunately, my empathy is skewed in all of this; it's my own downfall of being Beta. However, this request is of little consequence to me, and as you know, I value the opportunity of science just as much as any medical researcher."

"You don't think anyone is going to question all of the validity our research has once Whitmore shouts at the top of his lungs he feels he's been had? What about all criteria we use to define a Type 6 Alpha?"

"Jake, I wrote the criteria for identifying a Type 6 Alpha. I, and only two other scientists in the whole world, determine the entire existence of Type 6 Alphas. All I have to do is make my colleagues aware that I am experimenting with changing the criteria and seeing how it affects the existing population. I'll get instant approval, and no one else in the medical community will question it—they have no expertise nor clout to do so."

"What about Roman's classification? He's grown up with this his entire life. Right now, that life is chipping away piece by piece. To take that away from him now, I don't know what it would do to him."

"Six months," Dr. Birowack stated. "In six months, Roman's status will be reinstated. After all, I refuse to let him lose his qualifications over a petty failure to contract."

Jake took another look at his boss, his superior, his teacher, in disbelief. "Paul, do you really think Whitmore isn't going to come back on us and destroy everything we've worked for?"

"He's not going to get anywhere near our research, Jake. That I can promise you. Unfortunately, I have no control on what he does to you personally. Do keep me abreast of the situation." Dr. Birowack sat up in his chair and resumed his work, appearing to forget the conversation. Jake turned around to leave, not knowing anything else to say. "Don't leave work. I'll have the paperwork done for you promptly. It seems you'll be needing it."

"Thank you," Jake replied softly.

"No need for that," Dr. Birowack affirmed. He picked up the phone and began making arrangements.

Walking out the office was surreal. It made his stomach hurt. Dustin casually walked by, clearly preoccupied, but even then, Jake couldn't look him in the eye.

By the time the event finished replaying in his head, the car had made it home, seemingly on autopilot. Pulling up to the house was false security, but Jake made his mind believe it anyway. He rubbed Adrian's arm to wake him up. He smiled at his mate; Adrian gave a reluctantly cautious smile back. The attempt to connect to his mate was shook by the door slam from the back seat. Both he and

Adrian watched as Roman avoided any eye contact as he hurried into the house.

CHAPTER 17:

A Chance to Get
to Know Fate

A doorbell rang throughout the Cavenbelle home. Knowing whose arrival was planned, Dustin answered the door himself. There in front of him stood a tall, statuesque Alpha in a forest green button-down shirt and black slacks. In his hand, he held a red rose.

"Roman," Dustin spoke in a military tone.

"Mr. Cavenbelle," he replied. Roman hoped his nerves weren't perfuming his scent. He held out his hand in show of good faith; he even lowered his head slightly to show Dustin he honored him as the top Alpha in the home.

Dustin returned the gesture, really looking Roman over for the first time. He held back the urge to verbally assault Roman, to return one-tenth of what Roman had done to his son. But the fact was, not even Dustin could deny what fate had planned. Doing so would surely destroy any compromise which allowed Roman and Mikaél to have their first date in exchange for the two of them to be on their best behavior.

"Mik will be up in a minute or two, I'm sure. Wait here in the kitchen."

"Yes, sir." Roman had no intention of challenging Mikaél's Sur in anyway. Walking into the kitchen, he saw Mikaél's Veo once again, an unexpected ally Roman was very grateful to have.

Alec greeted him with a smile much brighter than Dustin. "Roman, nice to see you again." He decided to skip the handshake and go for the hug, an expression he knew neither man in the room expected. "How are you?"

Roman proceeded with caution. He wasn't sure if he heard Dustin grunt in displeasure or if it was in his head. "Grateful to be here. Thank you." Roman criticized his own redundancy.

"Come have a seat," Alec insisted. "Can I get you something to drink?"

"A water?" Anything would help to get rid of the cotton mouth feeling lingering on his tongue.

"A water it is."

As Alec fetched a cold bottle of water from the fridge, Roman took a chair at the table only to be quickly followed by Dustin across from him. His stern expression had Roman wondering if he was going to get the proverbial "talking to." Roman's eyes irrationally searched around the room for a hunter's rifle. But the thought was nothing more than a fleeting joke. Mostly.

"Now if I may..." As Dustin began, Alec handed Roman the bottle of water, which he took advantage of right away. Then Alec sat down, countering the brooding vibe he wanted to instill. "It has come to my attention you and Mikaél have already...mended the transgression," Dustin shot his mate a look, "but that doesn't mean you have mended things with me."

Alec gave Roman an uncomfortable smile. He wasn't going to deny his mate his right to be a parent, a parent who was forced to watch his son scream in agony.

"Mr. Cavenbelle, I don't think there are enough words I can say to you to show my remorse. Please accept my words that I hated every moment of it, and it won't ever happen again."

"I want you to know if Mikaél comes to me with even just a frown on his face in regard to how you treat him, I'll turn you into a Beta myself." Dustin studied Roman's posture and pheromone palette. He was satisfied with Roman's concession of his Alpha status. It demonstrated the correct response he needed to show respect. "Back at your place, your Sur and I discussed whether or not you were on a prescription of—"

"Mik!" Alec acknowledged, seeing his son enter the room.

Roman's attention turned to his future mate standing there in a white dress shirt and black pants. He wasn't as formal as Roman, not that he cared. All he needed was to see Mikaél's shining face and smell his hypnotic scent. Touching him was also high on the list, but he wasn't about to make a sensual move in front of his Sur. But he was going to attempt a hug.

Embracing Mikaél, knowing he was smiling back at him, was everything he needed. All else in his mind faded with the embrace.

"Glad to see you again," Mikaél whispered into Roman's ear.

"You too." Roman inhaled Mikaél. To bottle it up was a dream. He handed over the red rose and watched his face light up.

Dustin tried to get the focus back. "As I was saying—"

"Oh, now, come on, babe. Let them have their night," Alec urged.

Dustin furrowed his brows. "Where are you two going? It can't be a bar or a club; he isn't old enough yet." He felt the impact of a love tap from his mate on his chest. "What?"

Roman cleared his throat. "I was hoping to treat Mikaél to a nice dinner and then tour Tauris Square to see the night parade."

Mikaél beamed with anticipation. He knew the area like the back of his hand.

"What a great idea," Alec delighted. "I've done several photo-shoots down there. It's fantastic at night."

"Be back by 9:00 then," Dustin instructed.

"Really?" Mikaél's face dimmed.

"10:00," Alec corrected. He saw the not-so-subtle disapproval from his mate. He mouthed a barely audible "You're good" back in his direction.

Roman held Mikaél's hand in an attempt to take him out the door far away from here. But his feet felt glued to the floor.

Luckily, Mikaél had the same mindset. They left with him taking the lead.

"Have a good time!" Alec yelled from the kitchen.

"Keep your cell phone on!" Dustin added.

Alec shook his head and rolled his eyes, avoiding the gaze of his mate.

Knowing Mikaél's heritage, Roman hoped he chose a quality restaurant when it came to pasta and specialty sauces. The ambiance was off to a good start: the welcome warmth contrasted with the cool air of the beginning fall season. A hum of cultural jazz surrounded the restaurant with its lighted bulbs on strings and marbled floors. Sconces and occasional greenery decorated the archways throughout and classic advertisements in their native language from yesteryear were immortalized on the walls. All were worthy of a good first impression.

After they were seated, a few patrons of the restaurant stole glances at their table every now and then. Mate ownership, even in dating, was hardly ever challenged in a restaurant. However, in a bar or club, some consider carrying a small bat. Lower-Types loved the thrill of challenging the loyalty of a mate, and with a rush of alcohol, Higher-Types weren't above the practice either. That was one benefit of being in an upscale restaurant. One could enjoy and experience a night with ease and take the eyes of strangers as a safe compliment.

After ordering, Roman felt enough time had passed to start figuring out who Mikaél really was—but not without asking the most important question first. "How is the," Roman gestured to his chest, "healing?"

Mikaél was glad to hear Roman cared but was a little embarrassed to discuss it in public. "It's going well. Itches now and then but good."

Roman nodded, accepting Mikaél's words as sincere. "I'm glad this is happening. I was worried we were going to be exiled away from each other."

"You and me both. Sur wasn't particularly happy when he found out you came over."

"I'm guessing he's over it now?"

Mikaél shrugged. "We're here, so I guess."

A thought went through Roman's mind which saddened him; time was precious tonight. "What do you think of all this?"

Mikaél pondered the question a bit. "I don't know. It's so new. I feel like so little has happened, and yet so much has changed. Does that make sense?"

"Yeah, I agree." Roman decided to test the waters. "But I do like it."

"Me too." Mikaél smiled back.

"So," Roman began as he changed the subject, "I want to get to know you, but I don't want to just start asking random questions like I'm checking off a list. Normally, I'm not so lost for words." A quiet nervous laughter hit him.

"I get that. You've met my parents before. Did I hear that right?"

"Our dads used to go out occasionally after work. I was normally stuck at home watching my brothers, so I never got to go with when I wanted to. By the time Rixen and Ryan could be trusted alone, my parents had to convince me to go. My Sur wanted yours to meet me."

"I never went. My older brother had to stay home with me. The night at your house was the first time I'd met any of you," Mikaél paused, "and the rest is history."

Roman laughed. "Ha. That's true. So, your Veo is a ..."

"Photographer," Mikaél finished. "He just got a new studio. He's hoping to have the place open before Winter Solstice. He wants to throw a party there opening night."

"Are you looking for a date to accompany you?" Roman bit his lip.

Mikaél stared back at Roman's coy vulnerability. This must have been what courting was supposed to be like. "Absolutely."

An appetizer of breads and fresh tomatoes with herbs were placed in front of them. After trying the complimentary combination, Mikaél continued, "I'm not sure if I have this right, but is your dad a builder?"

"Of sorts. He's a custom builder and designer for hire. His passion is woodwork: tables, chairs, built-ins, décor. But every now and then, he gets ambitious and decides to construct large patios and decks." Roman took a bite of artisan bread complete with beautiful garlic, tomato, and basil.

"Wow. Impressive. I wouldn't have guessed," Mikaél replied.

"I know. You look at him, and you'd never know that's his profession. He gets stressed over the big projects a lot. Every single time he finishes he says, 'Never again' and then a few months later, he does it again."

"Wow, that's crazy." Mikaél paused. "So, what is it you do?"

"I'm currently in clinicals to be a doctor."

For Mikaél, there was some irony to the statement. "Which specialty?"

"Sports Medicine and Physical Therapy. I've been active in sports during the winter and spring all my life. Felt like a natural transition. And of course, I had my Sur's blessing, him being a doctor also."

Mikaél smiled as he remembered now who Roman was. "That's right. You're Ashershire's star basketball player! I've seen you on the team posters throughout the school."

Roman's expression fell. "You've never been to a game?"

"That's obvious, isn't it?"

After a few moments, Roman realized it made perfect sense his Omega never made an appearance. "Oh. I suppose we would have met earlier then." The details on how that encounter would have went down if they met at a basketball game was something he didn't want to fixate on. He chose to steer the conversation elsewhere. "What about you? What are your career goals?"

"I know it's going to be something in the arts. Like your Sur, my Veo is very passionate about his career, and he's encouraged me to express myself—a lot."

"Hm. So, he really wants you to be an artist or something?" Roman asked.

"Yes and no," Mikaél admitted. "He'd be ecstatic if I became a photographer, but that's not really what it's ever been about."

"Oh? What is it then?" Roman asked naturally.

The food flavors danced on Mikaél's tongue as he searched for the words. "My brother and I are two very different people. He's the outgoing one, the popular one, the accomplished one, and the one everyone notices. And I'm just 'Mik.'"

Roman's face softly disagreed. "You're not just 'Mik' to me."

"Thank you." There was a release of pheromones which had to have been noticeable, a compliment back if Roman sensed them. "So," Mikaél continued, "I've told you about my entire family, but I don't know anything about your brothers, even though we're the same age I guess?"

"Mhm. They're identical twins: Rixen and Ryan."

"Cool. What are they like?"

"Uh," Roman chuckled, "they are two peas in a pod: goofy, adventurous, easy-going most of the time. Sometimes they're so similar, people can't tell them apart. I mean, I can tell them apart pretty easy. Once you meet them and get to know them a bit, you'll even see the visual differences."

"You think I'm going to get the chance?"

Roman paused, a bit taken aback. "Well, yeah. They're going to be your family, too."

Mikaél's heart skipped a beat. So many things were going right to make his heart float, but this comment certainly made his heart flutter. The personal connections Roman was making by accepting him as family were everything; he wanted this from him the moment they connected. If the battle had to be fought in order to get to this moment, it was worth it.

Plates of golden pasta were laid before them. The smell of marinara and alfredo filled the surrounding tables. Roman enjoyed a smoked sausage in a red sauce while Mikaél enjoyed a white sauce with mushroom. Out of respect for Mikaél's age, Roman chose not to pair it with an appropriate wine.

Roman wiped his lips with a dark cloth napkin. "Okay, then. Fate has brought us together, so I suppose we ought to get to know one another," he stated with playful sarcasm. "Favorite food, favorite book, favorite movie, favorite color, and favorite sport. Go!"

That surprised Mikaél. Roman was going through the checklist after all. "You're looking at my favorite food hands down. The book is *Diving* by Manny LuRoux, and favorite movie is the *Forever Night* series, color is teal, and favorite sport is probably track. I would pick basketball, but passionate Alphas don't really want an Omega on their team, so I sit that one out. Plus, I don't have your gift of height. And you?"

Roman tried to remember what he asked of Mikaél. "Food easily has to be steak or any variation of it. My Sur wishes I was more of a chicken person when it comes to him paying the bill at a restaurant. The last book I read was pretty good: *Wildfire* by Duncan Rowe. I'm an action movie guy, so it's going to be *Gunfire: Round One* and *Round Three,* but the second was horrible so not that one. Color is black, and I myself do basketball and lacrosse."

"See? Now we know each other." Mikaél bounced in his chair.

The rest of meal was a comfortable experience. Light conversation about other interests came about: video games, various hobbies, and seasonal favorites. Roman divulged the crazy dynamic of his family, including his brothers, while Mikaél shared his brotherly love for Laycin. The final conversation during the meal was Roman introducing Siro and Nico.

"What are they like?" Mikaél asked, digging in his spoon into the flaky crust and warm insides of an apple dessert.

"Nico is a good guy to hang around. He's thoughtful and considerate. He's kind of shy and not particularly fond of large groups, but to get him one-on-one or with Siro and me, he's cool and a really good listener."

"I'd like to meet him sometime," Mikaél insisted.

"Absolutely." Roman glided his spoon over the now soft cream dripping down into the cervices of his dessert.

"And Siro?"

Roman reflected. "Siro is very different than Nico. Siro's your center of attention social butterfly. He's high energy, fun, opinionated, and a little dangerous every now and then. It's always a good time hanging around him when he's not going too crazy. He always seems to know what's going on with people's lives. He's like a social newspaper complete with a gossip column."

"That sounds a bit unnerving," Mikaél surmised.

"I know it wasn't the most complimentary description about him. The good thing about Siro is that he's a protector. He'd give the shirt off his back to a friend in need. I mean, he gives Nico and I shit sometimes, but if anyone came after either of us, he'd be on it in heartbeat."

"I can appreciate the importance of someone always having your back; it's nice to know someone cares." Mikaél took his last bite and put his fork down next to his plate. He attempted to pay his fair share, but Roman wouldn't hear of it. This was indeed an official date, the first he'd ever had.

The dinner ended with enough time to take a leisurely stroll around Tauris Square before the bi-weekly Parade of Lights show. Other than a few modern updates, Tauris Square was an untouched area of the city which harkened back hundreds of years to the Pre-Wolf Era. The nostalgia was a beautiful, romantic village sure to spark love in those wanting an almost fairytale experience. Buildings of different shapes and sizes, made with bricks and natural woods, lined both sides of the cobblestone streets. Indeed, this was a tourist attraction, a welcome one at that. Merchant tents scattered around the middle, creating a natural two-lane traffic flow. For the night of the parade, the attendance was heavier than usual.

The flute, mandolin, violin, and bell musicians on the corner were spotlighted by canister lights and flame torches. In the shops, every specialty gift or practical item was available for purchase. For the thrill of it, the couple shared in toasting a crêpe over an open flame. They topped the treat with a fresh strawberry and a drizzle of chocolate.

Standing near any open flame was a pleasure. When not under such warmth, it was easy to notice the colder temperature of the night. Mikaél shivered.

"Cold?" Roman asked, a bit concerned.

"Just a bit." Mikaél wrapped his arms around his chest.

"We can leave. We don't have to stay."

"Oh, I wouldn't dream of leaving. It's been a long time since I've seen this," Mikaél insisted.

"When was the last time?" Roman asked out of curiosity.

"Believe it or not, it was the night Drew met Will. It was here. Somewhere." He looked around as if he could even remember where it was.

"Will is his mate?"

"Fated Mate," Mikaél specified.

"Wow, what a place to find someone."

"Yeah." Mikaél's face dimmed.

Roman evaluated the expression. "Was that the reason you haven't been here since?"

Mikaél winced. "It was just too perfect. Like everything else in his life." He caught Roman's eyes looking down at him. "I need to stop talking about him. You're going to think I care about nothing other than obsessing over him and self-pity."

"I don't think that at all." A horn off in the distance blared. "Ah, I think it's getting ready to start."

The crowds abandoned the streets, gathering at the edges. Since no motorized vehicle was allowed on these timeless, decorated streets, there weren't designated sidewalks. Like any parade, the crowds tucked themselves in tight like a can of sardines. This pushed Roman behind Mikaél as they both waited in anticipation.

A couple blocks away, instruments and cheers were heard, indicating the lineup was near. When the footfalls of large horses came into view, Mikaél shivered once again.

Sensing his mate's discomfort, Roman pulled him back up against his warm body. It caused Mikaél to tense up before finally melting back into him as he felt both of Roman's arms wrapped around him.

The horses were outlined with leather reins and jingling bells. Behind them, wooden carts carried actors in attire worn centuries before now. Acknowledging the Pre-Wolf Era had female counterparts, some men dressed up to imitate such. The sentiment was entertaining; crowds whooped, shrieked, and applauded their commitment.

Several different acts followed: jugglers, flame artists, lords and "ladies," clowns, hecklers, more musicians, and several vendors advertising with banners written in celestial fonts. In the rear, a large carriage came forth with a king and queen of the festival. In mere moments, it seemed, the parade faded into the distance.

By the end, Roman had placed his chin on top of Mikaél's head. Acknowledging this moment too had to fade, he planted a quick peck on the side of his neck. Getting a breath of Mikaél's scent made it difficult to not want to passionately take him right then and there in a shadowy alleyway behind them. But tonight, Roman played the part of a gentleman.

When Mikaél turned to face Roman, he found his lips and returned the soft kiss. Roman decided he wanted to push further and made his mouth more aggressive. He felt Mikaél adjust himself and breathe deep into the kiss. Taking it as his approval, Roman pushed in his tongue slightly and it glided along Mikaél's lips. Before long, Mikaél relaxed his mouth. As he did, Roman pushed his tongue in farther and felt Mikaél's soft, wet muscle and massaged it with his own. Doing it sent a shiver down his own spine, hoping it did the same for his mate. When Mikaél gave a deep, calming sigh in response to his gesture, Roman was satisfied.

As they began to walk out of the square, they passed one final merchant in a brightly lit tent soliciting professional memorabilia photographs. In any other visit to the Square, Roman would have passed, pretending not to see the vendor at all. But the night already had him like soft butter, so he see-sawed his head and finally gave in.

The photographer, an older jovial man in a bard outfit, placed them in front of a green screen. Based upon the display pictures, the "real" background was going to be them standing on a castle balcony. Sensing the two were a couple, the photographer placed them in a similar embrace they were in just moments ago. The first shot caught them both looking at the camera. For the second, they were instructed to look at one another: Roman down to Mikaél and Mikaél up to him. In the final, the bard dared to request they do something more romantic. An easy attraction pushed them both together for one more kiss which resulted in a few "aww" sounds from the bard and a couple patrons who were passing by.

After paying an overpriced amount, Roman was given a code to find the photographs online. Slowly walking out of the tent, he located and downloaded them to his phone. Examining the captured moments made his heart happy, especially when Mikaél showed his obvious elation.

They made it back to Mikaél's house with generous time to spare. Although Mikaél had the impression the two would part in the car, Roman told him he had every intention of walking him up to the door. If he could have walked backward to make time reverse itself for the sake of never having to leave, he would have. But he didn't possess that kind of power.

Touching the door handle, Mikaél took one final glance at his mate.

"I hope you enjoyed yourself." Roman tensed.

Mikaél hummed. "It was magical." His last word was met with a deep kiss, sealing the night on the best note he could think of. He sighed. "Yeah, it was magical."

"You have a great night, Mik."

"You too, Roman." Mikaél found it very difficult to watch Roman drive away. Walking into the house, he found both of his parents sitting in the formal living room by lamplight. His Sur concentrated on a book while his Veo looked up immediately.

"Honey, you're back a bit early. Did everything go okay?"

"Oh yeah," Mikaél assured them. "Roman thought it a good idea to get back earlier just in case of any trouble."

Dustin looked up from his book. "Smart."

"And? How was it?" Alec pried.

Without doing cartwheels or jumping for joy, a content look fell across his face. It didn't matter; his pheromones gave it away. "It was great."

Veo smiled; Sur acknowledged him.

Not wanting to stay in his parents' presence longer than he had to, he excused himself to the basement to find his room.

After shutting his door, he ran to his bed and body slammed into it. Turning around, he stared at the ceiling, trying to remember every detail of the night. The journey of spacing out ended quickly when he felt several vibrations from his pocket. Pulling out his phone, he saw a few different texts from Roman:

[ROMAN: Hope you had a great night. I know I did. Can't wait to do this again. Here...]

Below the text, Roman forwarded the pictures from Tauris Square. Seeing them were a dream come true. He wanted to permanently photograph them in his mind until the day he saw Roman again. But he also wanted to call Laycin.

"What's up?" Laycin answered.

"I just got back," Mikaél began.

"From....?" Laycin asked.

"A date with Roman," he said.

"Ohhhh. Wait a second." A few rumbling noises came through the phone, and then Laycin's voice came again. "Had to get comfortable. You may proceed."

CHAPTER 18:

A Breakdown of
Walls & Emotion

"Did anyone get extra sauce?" Ryan asked while staring down at his masterpiece of a burger.

"Here." Mikaél passed a small throwaway container full of Prowler Burger's secret sauce, the crack cocaine of condiments as far as casual restaurants went. "Sorry I wasn't able to join you guys last week."

"Don't worry about it," Rixen assured him. "You're here now."

Prowler Burger had hit the area by storm. In a ten-year span, the once lone restaurant expanded to six locations, not bad for a city with a population of almost 200,000. Coming here to the campus location right after classes on a Tuesday made life so much easier for hunger-stricken souls.

In essence, the place gave off a steakhouse vibe, very cabin in the woods. Every restaurant had its signature layout: a dark mood-lit area for a deeper dining experience, and then a brightly lit second area where the younger crowds gathered. At 4pm, the restaurant was half full already. The five boys were able to snag one of the last open tables. Smells perfumed the space: well-seasoned grills firing quality meats, deep fried starches, breading full of flavor, and fresh bakery buns for their signature burgers. To any virgin, it was the first taste of sex. To a virtuoso, it was a satisfying complimentary experience.

Laycin moaned into his first bite of juicy warm meat surrounded by smoked cheese, peppered bacon, and brioche bun. "Mmmm, I can't believe it's been so long since I've been here."

"Who was stopping you?" Garrace wondered.

"Hmph. Mikaél is more of a sandwich and salad connoisseur. I guess he just bats those eyes, and we end up at one of those whenever we do go out."

"Ah yes, that's right. I remember." Garrace nodded.

"Hey," Mikaél gulped down a generous portion of his drink, "we don't always end up at those."

"Most then," Laycin replied.

"Sure," Mikaél relented.

"Like 99 out of 100." Laycin stuck his tongue out as he heard approval from his entertained audience at the table.

"Okay! We get it." Mikaél rolled his eyes.

Ryan's eyes widened in amusement. "Damn, you two fight like a mated couple."

"Wouldn't be the first time we've heard that, isn't that right, babe?" Laycin pushed out his lips toward Mikaél. As Mikaél smiled back, he kicked Laycin under the table. "Ow!"

Ryan laughed and shook his finger. "Better be careful, Laycin. My brother isn't going to tolerate someone else smoochin' on his man."

All eyes turned to Mikaél.

"So, I've heard," Laycin replied. As if he had x-ray vision, he zeroed in on Mikaél's shirt and imagined seeing the claw scars from Roman's attack.

Ryan took his opportunity and looked at Garrace. "Speaking of, I heard you and Mikaél were a couple once?"

The entire table couldn't figure out who to give their attention to. Rixen's eyes daggered his brother's, Laycin tensed as he saw

Mikaél's eyes show frustration to Garrace, and Garrace cautiously looked back at Rixen's discontent.

"That is true, yes." Mikaél took a cloth napkin and spread it across his lap in order to find something else to look at.

"Why didn't it work out?" Ryan asked casually, as if it was no big deal.

"Shit, Ryan! Really?" Rixen gasped under his breath, shouldering his brother.

Garrace looked at Mikaél cautiously. He waited to see if Mikaél would say something. He didn't. In the silence, Garrace began, "We wanted different things from the relationship. Our ideas on what a relationship looked like didn't match up."

"Mm, yes. How pageant of you," Ryan sneered.

"Wolf-God, are you done?" Rixen protested.

"No, it's okay." Garrace grinned. "After all, you only rile up the ones you care about." He winked at Ryan. Ryan's face froze, unmoved.

Rixen shook his head. "He's just being a dirt bag. Ignore him." Ryan turned to his brother, seeing him upset but composed.

"Mik!" A voice came from a few feet away. Roman walked up, eyeing his prize as it came nearer in his view.

Mikaél lit up like a Winter Solstice tree, got out of his seat, and gave his mate the biggest hug as if his life depended on it. He inhaled Roman's scent as if it gave him life. It was difficult for him to decide whether to memorize Roman's scent or his appearance. He was quite the romantic sailor today in his tight tan pants and equally tight blue and white striped sweater that accentuated his natural chest curves. The hug was short but followed up by a beautiful, sensual kiss like Roman had just returned from battle.

"Dudes, you're in the restaurant!" Siro criticized.

"What? Jealous?" Nico followed behind them.

This time Ryan got up. "Hi guys, it's been too long! You guys never come over anymore!" He bro-hugged Siro first, then went to Nico.

"Ha!" Siro burst. "With all the drama happening in your house, I'm staying away until the plague blows over."

"Got room for one more? I don't want to be there either," Rixen joked, following the same embraces his brother gave.

"No!" Siro remarked. "All of you are contagious."

"I do miss you guys," Nico added. "I barely get to see Roman anymore."

"We thought he was dead!" Siro howled.

Roman let go of Mikaél to confront Siro with an annoyed expression. "Bro, you gotta stop."

"What?" Siro spoke, half-heartedly offended. "I'm telling you—Whitmore is going to come after you. I'm going to be at the cemetery smoking a cigarette and pourin' booze on your gravesite."

Roman laughed. "Make it Mountain Sound whiskey, and I'll be good with that."

"Top shelf? Fuck no. Iced tea with rubbing alcohol. I'm drinkin' the Mountain Sound. Not going to waste that on your rotting corpse."

Mikaél blinked. "That's quite the way to look at this."

"Ah, and here he is: the prodigy." Siro sized him up. "Okay, bring it in." Siro opened his arms, giving Mikaél the gesture to embrace him. Mikaél cautiously accepted, not wanting to cause a scene in the restaurant or worse, an awkward rift. A deep conspicuous inhale and exhale was heard from Siro. "Ooo. Damn, Roman. You gotta nice one here. Is... is that cinnamon?"

"That is disgusting, Siro. And you're wrong anyway." Roman grabbed Mikaél's hand, releasing him from Siro's grasp.

"Smooth," Nico added.

"What? I have to know the scent of who I need to protect." Siro's gaze went to Mikaél. "It's okay. I got your back."

"Why? Do you expect something to happen to him?" Roman interrogated.

"Man, when are you going to wake up?" Siro shook his head. "In a week, your mate is going to be the talk of this entire city. Mikaél is going to be labeled as the rival who beat out the Whitmore Empire. That doesn't go without consequences."

Roman looked down at his Omega, who was beginning to show signs of concerned curiosity. Not wanting to expose Mikaél to such problems, he bear-hugged him tight to his chest while sternly looking back at Siro. "Look, can you keep your apocalyptic premonitions to yourself?" It wasn't a question; it was a warning.

"Okay," Siro stressed, holding his hands up in defense.

"Way to kill the mood; you're going to spoil the surprise," Nico commented.

"What surprise?" Mikaél looked up.

"That's what I'm here for," Roman began. "My Sur called me earlier today. He was able to talk to your Sur about his thoughts about our contract."

A grin crossed Mikaél's face. This could only be good news. He did say "surprise" after all. "And...?" Mikaél held out.

"It's happening, Mik. We're going into contract on Friday." Roman's face showed the most excitement it ever had. Whether it was the words he said or Mikaél's own expression which gave him never-ending joy, he didn't know. He was just happy it was there. He nuzzled Mikaél's neck one more time before giving him one more deep kiss. With every breath, it was getting harder to control his sexual urges. So, he forced himself away and settled on staring into his blue eyes instead which appeared glossy with moisture of elation. "My baby," he whispered.

Mikaél giggled into his ear and then sighed deeply. "Are you going to stay?"

"Unfortunately, no," Roman frowned. "For the last two weeks, my head's been in a fog. I haven't paid attention to school at all, so I'll be spending the evenings with these knuckleheads studying for exams."

Rixen spoke up. "You think you're going to get any studying done at Siro's place?"

"No, my place," Nico corrected. "I don't have any nude posters, incense, or porn soundtracks at my place. We'll concentrate better there." Nico felt a hard backhand to his chest—a firm acknowledgement from Siro that he heard his comments. Mikaél's expression fell.

Seeing it, Roman felt that pull, the one he knew would be there for the rest of his life: the duty to please his Omega. "Hey, it's okay. I'll call you," Roman assured him.

"Okay." Mikaél approved with one more kiss, then watched Roman and his friends leave the restaurant.

"Damn," Laycin said a few moments later. "You two got it bad."

Mikaél looked up at his best friend and smiled. "Yeah. I guess we do."

"I think it's beautiful," Rixen asserted. He stared at the campus gardens across the street from the restaurant through its tinted windows. "I hope to be that happy one day." He noticed Garrace trying to grab his attention with a soft smile. He broke his concentration to return the expression, ignoring the dark pheromones coming off his brother Ryan.

⁂

"I just don't see why we had to bring him back to the house," Ryan whispered exhaustedly.

"Because I want him here." Rixen had no qualms about saying his words louder.

"Just because we carpooled with him today doesn't mean we had to invite him in the house."

"Did you not hear me the first time? I said I want him to be here." Rixen pulled the bottom freezer out and filled a metal chest with ice.

"Why today? Why not—" He broke off, solving the riddle. "You told him Sur and Veo would be gone all night for Sur's fundraiser, didn't you?" Ryan crossed his arms.

Rixen paused, unfazed. "Yes."

"So, the goal is to get him all liquored up and then send him home?" Ryan glared.

"I guess you could say that." Rixen gave a grin which acknowledged more mischievous thoughts in mind.

"Unbelievable."

Rixen's patience began to run out. "Knock it off. I'm not in the mood for this crap."

"Was this the plan all along? The carpool, our dads being gone, Roman studying at Nico's?"

"No." Rixen tried to hide his guilt. "I found out Roman was studying at Nico's tonight at the same time you did."

Ryan moaned. "This can't be happening."

Rixen pointed at his brother with an ice pick. "Okay, you know what? I'm not listening to your eternal whining anymore. You're my brother, and I love you, but you are going to have to lay off."

"I can't shake this feeling if you go through with this, and you know exactly what I'm talking about, it's going to end badly."

"Look," Rixen put the drinking glasses down on the island and held his brother's shoulders, "tonight is going to be the best opportunity to clear the air and all those feelings you have for him. If after tonight, this doesn't go well, I promise I will talk to you more about what's bothering you, okay?" It took a few moments, but eventually Ryan nodded in agreement. Rixen sighed. "Good. Now, can you bring those bottles down? My hands are full, and they are heavy. Oh, Garrace likes the vodka. I'll bring these."

Ryan gave a half smile and a hum of a reply. Grabbing the chilled bottles from the bar fridge, he followed his brother down the stairs to the finished basement as if Rixen wore a target. At the bottom of the stairs, another lion waited in the den, both figuratively and literally.

Several conversations helped give the alcohol time to absorb and lacquer their systems. They covered the typical topics: criticizing teachers, venting about parents, complaining about homework, discussing hobbies, and reviewing different points of knowing each other. By the time the topics died, drinks had been refilled a few times.

Garrace set his drink on the side table, then stretched his long length out on the couch. His bright red shirt lifted to expose the lower part of his stomach, giving a hint of a treasure trail of hair hidden by the black band of his tight underwear. Upon releasing the stretch, he ran a hand through his chestnut brown hair and patted the other on his chest. He gleamed at Rixen who was sitting on the little part of the couch not occupied, half-drunk and half-pleased to see such a beautiful sight.

"All right. My turn for a question," Garrace began. Rixen smiled and Ryan winced. "Where do you see yourselves in ten years?" Both brothers stared aimlessly. The answers weren't coming to either of them right away. Not wanting to give the momentum up, he started, "Okay, I'll go first. I...hm...okay, I'll be 28. I'll have completely finished school for two years already at that point. I'm going to be a Senior Media Planner and live somewhere on the coast."

Ryan squinted. "A Senior Media Planner? What's that?"

Garrace turned his head on the pillow of the couch, not moving his body. "I'd make the decisions on how companies should brand themselves with the ever-changing fads and trends. I would get to go and meet people to convince them I could capture and keep an audience for their business. It's a job for people who are forward thinkers."

"And you think you're one of those people?" Ryan asked with a touch of attitude. Rixen scowled at him.

"Yes, I do," Garrace replied confidently.

"I feel like deciding on the job is the easy part." Rixen in turn set his own glass on the side table opposite Garrace. "Tell me about the other stuff." He jumped slightly on the seat cushion and adjusted himself to give Garrace his full attention.

"The other stuff, huh?" Garrace laughed, seeing right through Rixen's question. He put both hands behind his head and painted a picture. "My home would be a solid two-story white house with black lantern light accents. Two large open doors would reveal a massive open staircase to the second level. Behind it, an extra-large 5-star kitchen, not that I cook. I want a beautiful patio which overlooks the turquoise waves hitting the black boulders below. The house would have one of those rainfall pools which makes it look you could just fall off the edge down into the ocean below. When I walk up the staircase, I'm going to hear classical music seamlessly played throughout the floor. It's going to get interrupted by the sounds of my pups playing in their room. After I play cars and build tall buildings out of blocks with them for a little bit, I'll walk to my bedroom to find the French doors over the balcony open, the sounds and scents of the crashing saltwater filling my room, and find my mate laying on the bed reading a book or enjoying a show." Garrace's head turned back toward Ryan. "Whoever that may be."

Ryan's throat closed and he gulped hard. Grabbing his drink, he took a cold swallow of liquor and caramel soda. "Cool."

Rixen squealed. "You are so dreamy sometimes. I love that about you." He lay his body on top of Garrace's and massaged his head into his chest, his face toward the generous cushions of the back of the couch. "Now, me." Rixen's voice was muffled in Garrace's shirt. He lifted himself awkwardly, enough to balance and speak. "I am going to travel the world."

"Really?" Ryan asked uncomfortably.

"Mhm. I have to get out of here. This place is too small for me."

"Tauris is one of the biggest metropolitan cities around. Is Gray City too small for you, too?"

"There's too much out there I want to see. I'm going to be a blogger and take pictures of everywhere I go and have my own travel agency one day."

Ryan analyzed his words. "How are you going to have an agency if you're going to travel around the world all the time?"

"I won't travel all the time, Ryan. Duh!" He looked at Garrace and sighed impatiently. "I'll have a place to call home. The love of my life will be there, and so will my pups someday."

"Okay… where's the home then?" Ryan asked.

Rixen peered through the patio door to the setting sun behind the high hills. "I'm not sure. Haven't decided yet." He laid his head back down on Garrace's chest, once again facing the couch.

"That's weird at best, Rix." Ryan downed the last sip from his glass, got up from the floor, and began to make himself another drink at the bar.

"I think that's a beautiful vision." Garrace spoke enthusiastically as he began to stroke Rixen's hair. Ryan coughed disapprovingly as he faced away, thrusting ice cubes into his empty glass. "And you, Ryan?" Garrace asked.

"Me?"

"Yes, you. You haven't answered yet, silly."

"I think I'm good without answering," Ryan replied.

Rixen spoke gingerly, "Be nice, Ryan. Speak to the man."

Ryan sighed. "Fine." Ryan finished making his drink and returned to his spot on the floor. He swirled the glass slowly and took his first drink from his new concoction. "I don't know."

Garrace raspberried. "Oh, come on. You can't get out of this that easy."

"No, I'm serious. I mean I don't know." Ryan collapsed his shoulders in defeat. "I've thought about this for a long time, and all I see is the same thing: nothing. I have flashes on what I think it could be and then, as fast as it appears to me, it goes away."

"What about your career?" Rixen prompted. "I thought you were talking about accounting or something. Isn't that why you took that class? Because you liked it so much?"

"I like that as much as any other career: law enforcement, medicine, public works, business, you name it." Falling into a trance, Ryan wrapped his arms around his legs and pulled them into his chest.

"What about a family?" Garrace questioned. "Do you want one?"

Ryan rocked back and forth slightly. "I don't want to talk about this anymore."

The three boys sat there, quiet. No noises were heard, even from outside. The world had been put on pause.

Garrace looked at Rixen who seemed equally lost for words. Not wanting to give this evening up, he offered, "How about we play some video games?"

Ryan jumped up. "I'm all for that. My room has the best setup."

Rixen moaned. "Are you really going to make me get up?"

"Yes," Garrace crooned, patting Rixen on the back.

Rixen sighed. He sat atop Garrace and looked down at his soft sly face. He bent down and meshed his mouth against Garrace's lips begging to be used. After a few vocal vibrations of approval, he got up off the couch to observe Garrace lost in a spell.

The game luckily had the option for all three to play at the same time. For Garrace, this was a game which had him strolling down memory lane. He and Ryan became very enthusiastic, which lowered the tension; more liquid courage helped.

Although Rixen participated, he was more relieved watching his brother and lover get along. He hoped this would lighten the ultimatum of a future chat he had promised earlier.

"Wow! Bomb much?" Ryan said after Garrace made a foolish mistake in the game.

"What? There was a fireball in the way! How did you expect me to dodge that?" Garrace defended.

"It's called the 'jump' button." Ryan laughed.

"I pressed it; nothing happened!"

"Uh huh. I think the booze is making your fingers numb."

"I'm almost there."

Rixen clicked his tongue. "Tsk tsk. Excuses, excuses."

Garrace gasped. "Are you seriously taking his side?" He smiled.

"Maybe?" Rixen claimed innocently.

"Ohhh, that's it. You are so gonna get it!" Garrace turned on the bed and went after him, pinning him down by sitting on his waist, going straight for the sides of his stomach, and dug his fingers in, tickling him unrelentingly.

"Oh, Wolf-God, stop!" Rixen began with a chuckle before going into full out hysterics.

In the struggle, Garrace found Rixen stronger than he anticipated. He cried out for help when he felt Rixen successfully grab his hands and prevent him from continuing his onslaught. "Ryan, come on!"

Ryan walked around the bed and sat on his pillows, back against the headboard. Grabbing Rixen's arms and holding them back was way too easy. Rixen's fate was sealed.

Garrace crooned, "Hmm. You don't know how to really encourage someone to stop, do you?"

"Oh, you two are so dead when I get up from this," Rixen panted. His words were doubly muffled from his patterned cries as well as a strong, loud ringtone. Coming to the focus of it made him realize it had been ringing for not just one interval but a few. "Okay, I think I need to get that!"

"I don't think so," Garrace stressed and sang each word.

"Oh, I think I do." Rixen used his muscular strength to give a massive pull which ejected his arms down.

The fast momentum sent Ryan unexpectedly forward. Leading with his head, he pushed into Garrace's chest and neck but not without hitting his chin. It made Garrace howl in a moment of pain.

The focus on the collision allowed Rixen to slip out as he thrust himself to the left and onto the floor.

"Told ya!" Rixen touted.

"Fuck, Rixen!" Ryan whined, touching his head lightly. "Dude, are you okay?" he asked Garrace.

"Yeah, I'm super. That's bruising tomorrow." Garrace laughed in agony.

The phone continued to wail on the floor where Rixen had placed it. He got up and saw it was Veo calling, along with two other missed calls from him.

"Hello?" he began. "No, we're just playing video games." Turning his head back to Ryan, he covered the phone with his hand and whispered, "Veo's pissed we didn't answer. Sounds like a lecture coming. I'm going to take this upstairs." Without getting acknowledgement from either party in the room, he continued the conversation as he left toward the stairs. "Uh-huh. No, I just didn't hear it right away..."

"Uhhhh, that hurt," Garrace groaned and pointed out again.

"You want ice?" Ryan offered.

"Nah, I'm good." He decided to tough it out.

Ryan sat his bed, slowing down his own breathing, and trailing his eyes across the room. Rixen's voice was barely audible with the basement door open, but he recognized the tone just the same. He chuckled.

Garrace laughed. "Oops." He sighed as he noticed Ryan's own smile fade back to a level right below contentment. "Can I ask you something?"

"Yeah." Even before the question came, Ryan felt himself sober up a little.

"Are you and Rixen fighting...because of me?"

A deep breath left Ryan's mouth as his eyes lifted in thought. "I guess it's dumb to try and deny it at this point. Clearly, you wouldn't have asked unless you heard something."

"I've heard a couple things, yes." Garrace took a moment and tilted his head. "Actually, I heard a couple of interesting things."

"So, I've been told."

"Are they true?"

Ryan slid his hands down the comforter and let his head fall. His body lay sideways on the bed, feet still on the floor. With both hands, he rubbed his face. "Look, what I can say about this is I'm running through a lot of different emotions. I feel horrible that I've been lashing out at him so much. I need to get over all these unresolved issues."

Garrace sat on the bed. "So, what are they? Can they get resolved now?"

Heat rushed over Ryan's body, nerves taking over him. "Ever since you've been in the picture, I've just felt this hurt. And it hasn't been easy living with." Here it was. "Being a Beta is difficult from the standpoint that hardly any guys out there have interest in me. They just judge me because I don't have any reproduction capability and completely forget what I have to offer in a relationship. In my head, there's just a lot of unrequited feelings which get pushed away until I'm forced to deal with them. Having you front and center destroyed any composure I had." His eyes closed, and he concentrated on his own heart trying to tear out of his chest.

Garrace stared Ryan down, observing every movement and every emotion pouring out of pheromones. It was beautiful to feel Ryan let go of such weariness in front of him. "And?" he pushed.

"I was unfair to you about things I said in anger to Rix. I did hear things about your former relationships, but I had no problem embellishing them a little."

"I imagine my version of the relationships are very different from my exes."

Another hurt breath expelled from Ryan. "This is so fucking hard to say. I...was just so hurt by the fact he chose you. I always thought I had courage to do anything in life but dealing with this has proven otherwise. Watching you from afar though, it was easy to see the attraction. You're good-looking, smart, have confidence—well, too much maybe."

Garrace snorted. "Yeah. I suppose I can come off a bit cocky. I have no problem expressing who I am and what I want, and that puts others in a defensive position when they feel turned off by it or feel out of place by it. But thank you. I have it on good authority you're all of those too, especially the good-looking."

Ryan smirked. "Hmm. Thanks. You think I'm cocky too, eh?"

"Ohhh, it's not like I haven't observed you too. You're not as shy as your brother. Let's just say that."

"He's such a gentle soul; it'd break my heart to see him get hurt."

Garrace nodded. "I get that, really I do. I think it's awesome you care about him so much. Maybe I'm even a bit jealous."

"Oh? Of what?" Ryan turned to face Garrace, intrigued by the moment of vulnerability.

"First off, I don't have any siblings. Second, you already said it: I'm a bit cocky. When you're like that, even your friends don't bother to check in on you much. They just assume you're always fine, even when it's obvious things are not. I think that's what really hurts; people who you want to understand you the most sometimes are the people who don't understand you at all."

Ryan nodded. "I know what you mean. Sometimes, when I'm upset with Rix, the things I'm screaming at him have nothing to do with what I'm really trying to say. It's infuriating and yet there seems to be nothing changing it, no matter how hard I try." Ryan's voice weakened.

Garrace reached out and touched Ryan's arm. "It's okay," he whispered. In a gentle cautious motion, he started to rub the soft fabric covering up his firm muscle.

Ryan froze. He couldn't move; he could barely breathe. His heart thumped in his chest and in his throat. His eyes locked onto Garrace who was slowly bringing his body closer. By the time Garrace came within range to feel his breath, he became light-headed.

With eyes wide open, Garrace and Ryan's lips pressed together. It was slow, it was firm, and it was complete. The kiss held for long seconds. As the natural pull broke them apart, they came together again, this time closing their eyes.

A thunderbolt within Ryan's head went off, and he pulled himself up and off the bed. "No! I can't do this; I can't do this to Rix!" He began pacing back and forth, focusing on the floor.

"Ryan, it's okay," Garrace said calmly.

"How can you say that?" Ryan fretted.

"Because I've talked to Rixen, and he understands you have feelings for me which have tormented you. I really didn't think there was any other way to solve this without you getting it out of your system."

"Wolf-God! Everything is about you all the time, isn't it?" Ryan threw up his hands.

Garrace furrowed his eyebrows. "What do you mean? I thought that's what this was all about. And from what you've said, I haven't heard otherwise."

"You just don't understand. You never will. I constantly hear 'Garrace is kind, Garrace is attentive, Garrace is sensual, Garrace should be my contracted mate,' but the worst part about it all is the nerve you have to come into this house and act like you're the best thing in his life!" Ryan scoffed. "Like you're better than me. You don't even know what love is."

Garrace's head turned with a perplexed expression. "I have no idea what you are talking about. This is textbook jealousy if I ever saw it. All I know is, if I had a brother who wanted to care for me as much as you want to care for Rixen, I'd—" The thoughts which ran through Garrace's mind were swift and illogical. He wanted to push them away so he could talk with common sense, but the interpretation refused to go away. All of the looks, all of the self-doubts, all of the pain, all of the impatience, and all of them were unacceptance. It wasn't adding up any other way. "Ryan, are you jealous of Rixen? Or are you jealous of me?"

The drop in Ryan's stomach muscles cleared the anger on his face quickly. The notion was outrageous and yet the words to deny such allegation refused to come out. "I..." Ryan's body became heavy. He walked over to the windowsill to steady himself. All he could do was breathe and stare into nothing.

"You're in love with your brother." Garrace slowly walked closer. "Aren't you?"

Every word stung. It didn't just focus on one place; it was everywhere. Ryan's head, shoulders, chest, back, arms, and legs: everything hurt with a sharp pain as if he'd been electrocuted. "Garrace, please," he wept. "I can't do this."

"Do what? Admit it? Tell him?"

"Fuck, I can't tell him." His words stammered. "He couldn't handle something like that. It would destroy him. He'd cast me out of his life forever."

"Rixen isn't like that. He's empathetic; he's understanding. He'd never judge you to oblivion like that."

"He'd kill me, Garrace!" he maintained.

As the bedroom door slowly opened, a whisper came in. "No, Ryan, I won't." Rixen spoke with a somber face.

Foolishly forgetting Rixen wasn't going to be upstairs forever, both Ryan and Garrace were horrified when they realized he must have been standing there for some time.

Ryan, of course, took it the hardest. He gasped and pushed his hands off the windowsill in misery. He then turned to his bedroom wall and pushed his head against it with his fists repeatedly hitting it. "Damn it! No, no, no!" Slowly Ryan came to a stop. In the end, he couldn't get the words out anymore. He started sobbing as he wished he had the power to erase his confession.

Garrace spoke up. "How long were you standing there?"

"Long enough." A few tears dripped down Rixen's face, and he sniffed a pressured nose. He walked up behind his brother and gently put his hand on the center of his back. It was hot and trembling. Not feeling any objection or sudden moves, he slowly wrapped his arms around his brother's chest in a deep hug and laid his head where his hand was.

"I'm a fucking screw up," Ryan squeaked out.

"Shhh. Don't do that." Rixen exhaled as his arms around Ryan's chest felt a tremendous heart beating for dear life. "Why didn't you say something? You can tell me anything. You're my brother; I love you."

"You don't tell a brother that ever," Ryan whispered back. "It's pathetic, it's psychotic, it's...disgusting."

"You are none of those things to me."

"Maybe. But I am a jerk, asshole, and a liar." Ryan trembled.

"No." Rixen shook his head. "That's what you act like when you're struggling. But that's not who you are. You have the biggest heart of any person I know. You're my confidante, my protector, and my best friend."

"Just let me go, please," Ryan begged with painful emotion.

"No," Rixen spoke confidently. "Not now. Not ever. Come on."

With emotions still strong and alive, Ryan walked over to his bed, unable to look at Rixen or Garrace. He managed to set his body on the bed and crawled himself as far from Rixen as he could.

Rixen wasn't bothered by his brother's distance; it didn't matter. He laid down right alongside his brother, returning his arm around his chest and his head right behind Ryan's.

"You shouldn't be here; I should be alone," Ryan lamented.

"I'm never going to go away. I am here for you." Rixen looked behind him to see Garrace standing there with sadness. "We're here for you." He gestured to Garrace and patted the bed.

Garrace moved, taking up the remaining space on the large bed. He stroked Rixen's hair and wrapped his arm around him in the same fashion Rixen was holding his brother. After a few minutes of patterned breathing, he started to rub his lover's chest. Inhaling Rixen's scent calmed and excited him at the same time. The flavor was a rich iced apple, and he never got enough of it. Feeling Garrace's breath must have pleased Rixen as he sensed the tiny hairs on his neck stand up. Unable to resist, he planted a soft wet kiss on his neck. As he felt Rixen's neck tense up, he used it as permission to do it again...and then again.

Rixen's breathing began to accelerate, unwilling to stop Garrace's advancement. It became much harder to maintain his composure, especially after his lover began to add his tongue to the open-mouthed embraces on his neck. It caused him to involuntarily stiffen his body up against his brother and exhale hot air onto his neck. As it continued, he grabbed his brother's arm and squeezed it. That's when his slick began to moisten the outside of his body. The pheromone scent began to seep out.

Ryan didn't know what to think at first. Only minutes ago, he was being lulled into a state of tranquility. Now, he was witnessing and experiencing a lustful encounter between two individuals he had taboo feelings toward. He didn't dare move.

For Ryan, as if the sensation of his brother's heavy breathing wasn't enough, things became even more difficult when he felt Rixen's hand squeezing his arm like a blood pressure cuff over and over again. Moving his own arm felt like moving concrete; however, he managed to adjust enough to find Rixen's hand with his own. Instead of any objection, he felt his brother's hand continue its previous actions, now squeezing his hand. Unable to refuse further, he returned the pressure back which caused his brother to clasp back even harder. It was hard to fathom what was happening, but he liked it. He liked it more than he was willing to say out loud. Still convinced this was going to be a disaster at any moment, he continued to stay still as water on a windless night.

Incapable of resisting Garrace's constant persistence, Rixen found himself involuntarily turning to face him. In doing so, he barely got a look at his face before he felt Garrace descend on him. The continuous embracing of lips was not soft. They were deep, fast, and hungry. He pulled Garrace's neck into him, forcing his body to remove any distance. Hearing him moan into his mouth elicited the same from the depths of his own lungs. The wolf inside him took over, telling him to keep going.

Garrace himself was taken aback a bit as he continued his progress. His left hand started to massage Rixen's shirt. The touch gradually became firmer which drove Rixen's chest up and down. Wanting to explore him more, his hand glided up underneath and lifted it so the only part which remained covered with fabric was his upper chest. Rubbing his smooth skin thrilled Garrace. It was at this time when they felt the bed move a bit as Ryan turned his body to face them both.

Ryan was transfixed. The sight of seeing Rixen and Garrace together was fascinating. Mixed emotions danced around his head. There was a weight being lifted as he saw Rixen's current ease while also remembering the unconditional love and support he pledged. Then, there was Garrace who hadn't been the ogre he envisioned him to be. With the ravaged emotions finally draining, he accepted his fondness of Garrace before he found out he was with his brother. But he couldn't ignore right there, before his very eyes, was Garrace taking Rixen. The steamy transaction was inspiring; however, a slight gnawing feeling overcame him as he watched his brother getting owned.

Garrace noticed Ryan's face deep in thought and pulled his hand toward him. Having Ryan now touching him felt new and electrifying. *What a crazy experience to be sensual with two very attractive brothers—twins no less. Is this some dreamy illusion I'll wake up from seconds from now? Or is this truly real?* Frustrated by his shirt deadening Ryan's touch, Garrace sat up and removed it entirely. Not seeing any point in toying with Rixen's shirt, he pulled it off.

Rixen continued to be lost in a haze of ardor. Garrace had a power over him, and he enjoyed it every single time. He heard Garrace's voice go deeper and longer in his approval once Ryan accepted him.

For the first time in a long time, Rixen's Omega intuition told him things were going to be better between his brother and his lover. But there was still the question of what was to become of the relationship with his own blood. As the seconds became minutes in this continuous physical expression, the answer to the question was uncertain at best. Fate played its own hand in the form of Garrace.

Out of the corner of Rixen's eye, he saw Garrace grab Ryan's arm and slowly redirect it to him. And suddenly, there it was. Ryan's large, warm hand sat flat in the middle of Rixen's chest. By reflex, he parted the passionate exchange from Garrace and turned his attention to the new sensation on him.

As Rixen paused, it wasn't Ryan he specifically thought about. It was the final crossroad he knew he couldn't come back from. Slowly, he began to move his eyes to his brother's. Ryan appeared petrified; it wasn't any different than his own expression. But he remembered so many times his brother Ryan consumed by hatred, it made this situation alluring. Deciding the future for both of them in that moment was the most pivotal decision Rixen ever made. As if being affected by only a gentle breeze, he allowed the distance between them to dissipate.

The slight act caused Ryan to focus on his brother. It was a confirmation of what Ryan wanted and now, in this moment, Rixen prepared to give himself to him.

CHAPTER 19:

A Touch of
Transcendence

For Rixen, the first kiss with his brother was a rush of virginal expression he couldn't digest fast enough. Knowing he'd practiced exchanging fervid and vulnerable emotions with his other sexual partners, he was taken aback at just how intense the pheromone connection was between him and Ryan. The kiss was complimented with an exhale which released every stress of the last week. The energy from the wounding words, physical aggression, and mental anguish became a catalyst for something even stronger and unbreakable.

Words couldn't describe what Ryan felt in that moment. He'd hate for it to be interpreted as a dream come true, but at the same time, it couldn't have been anything else. The blow of passion stopped his heart. Any harder and Rixen's lips were going to have to be used for resuscitation instead. A small caress of his brother's chest was followed by a grasp of Rixen's neck. If Ryan was going to embark on the most dangerous journey of his life, he wasn't going to hold anything back. Ryan hoped the noises of painful emotion seeping out his own lips weren't too audible. They weren't to cause alarm but instead showed an act he needed but could never express before.

Garrace's point of view was completely different. There was no way for him to understand the powerful connection Rixen and Ryan shared. They'd been a part of each other's lives since conception—Garrace couldn't relate to that. What he did know was Rixen was a passionate and sensitive person who was changing his entire life before Garrace's very eyes. As much as he knew the consequences of the exchange taking place, there was no denying the power it was creating. Although Ryan was an enigma to him in the beginning, the eros he demonstrated peeled back the harsh layers, revealing a purer representation of not only himself but also what true feelings he had for his brother. Not wanting to forget he was Rixen's lover, Garrace attached himself to Rixen's neck and pushed the boundary of pleasure and pain. Rixen slightly threw his head back in a small gasp but went back to his own agenda with Ryan. It was an unbelievable sight to watch.

"Fuck," Garrace whispered into Rixen's ear with a hot, wet breath. There was no way he was going to let this night rest. He thrust himself up and paused. After a quick glance from both brothers, he continued his journey between Rixen's legs. The act of getting Rixen's pants unbuttoned and unzipped was quick, but the air in the room froze to a halt.

Rixen looked down with an expression as if a foreign animal had come upon him. Garrace had done this action so many times before, but this time it was the most nerve-wracking experience. When he felt Garrace's fingers dig into the underwear's elastic band, it was damn near embarrassing watching his own firm cock spring to life. Semi-erect, it couldn't figure out its natural resting place immediately. Once it had, the support was short lived as he continually felt his pulse firm up his expanding organ. When Garrace wrapped his lips around his cockhead with purpose, Rixen moaned. After opening his eyes from the initial rush of pleasure, he once again took time to assess his brother.

For Ryan, seeing Rixen's cock wasn't anything new. Neither of them was prudish; there was no reason for it. Both were comfortable with their bodies, but Ryan had never seen him like this: body red, breath heaving, cock raging, and pheromones wild. Watching Garrace continue to claim Rixen was becoming more comfortable from the standpoint of knowing he'd hold, comfort, and claim him as well. The idea of sharing Rixen became less and less traumatic— even if it was with someone he had complicated feelings for.

Ryan wondered if his brother thought about things getting complicated too. To show his brother he had nothing to fear, Ryan began stroking his cheek with the back of his fingertips. The gesture didn't produce an equally tranquil response. Instead, he felt Rixen's own hand clawing at his shirt, clearly communicating to Ryan he had too many clothes on. The persistence from Rixen shocked him, but he assisted in helping him remove it anyway. Now, for the first time, Ryan felt Rixen's hand upon his body out of admiration. He closed his eyes to focus on the physical attention Rixen bestowed upon him.

With his hands, Rixen massaged Ryan's taut chest. The muscles from his shoulders all the way down to his belly button contracted periodically as Rixen's fingers explored every part of him. Ryan was a strong focus, of course, but his focus was splitting in two. Garrace's talents between his legs had his cock's length at full mast and balls regularly flexing in their low perspiring sack. Finally, when he felt Garrace begin his attempts at deep throating, Rixen found himself needing to moan without reservation. He nuzzled into his brother's neck and locked his mouth on it. Hearing Ryan moan for the first time in pleasure drove Rixen insane. Wanting to hear more, Rixen began experimenting with his tongue pressed hard on his neck. After a few intervals, he led his tongue down to Ryan's chest and began to lick the muscular definition. He felt Ryan's hand massage the back of head as he did so. When he got to his nipples, he licked shyly at first.

The small taste of ecstasy was a tease for Ryan. It sent his breath in and out of a clenched jaw. Inhibitions began to fade as he dared to explore Rixen's back. He wasn't able to get access to much below it; Garrace's head still preoccupied the prize he cherished so much. Ryan watched the show of Garrace licking down Rixen's shaft to his underneath.

Abruptly, Rixen began moaning louder, vibrating off of Ryan's chest. It turned into grunting as his soft touch began to switch to pressured pushes into Ryan's skin. Then, he decided it was time to relieve Ryan of the rest of his clothes, especially since he noticed Garrace at some point had done the same for himself. Observing Ryan's own appendage revealed some minor differences compared to his own. Ryan's was thicker and had a slight curve up. He couldn't immediately tell if it was longer, not that it mattered. With Ryan being born a different rank, a Beta, it was natural for him to possess a larger cock. He squeezed Ryan's balls, causing a deep growl like a siren's call. Its effect was a shiny string of pre-cum falling onto his lower stomach. Rixen used his finger to use what remained on Ryan's slit to massage the sensitive area.

Seeing both Ryan and Rixen now fully exposed drove Garrace mad. His own hard length pulsed, occasionally leaving evidence soaked into Ryan's top sheet. Lifting Rixen's legs to expose the entrance to his insides allowed Garrace to probe him—prepare him. After repeated thrusts with his tongue, Rixen's hole was throbbing in anticipation. "Ryan, do you have any lube?"

Both brothers' heavenly sounds stopped. Ryan looked at Rixen's blank face, and then to Garrace's full of lust. Cautiously, he lifted himself off the bed. While walking to the computer desk, he wondered if both boys were gawking at his meaty backside, if not at that moment, then when he bent over to the bottom drawer and pulled out a small lube bottle from the back.

When Garrace stood up to intercept the bottle, Ryan went in for a deep, open mouth exchange. Garrace's initial audible response wasn't enough for Ryan, so he grabbed hold of his cock and began to stroke it. As an Alpha, it was expected that Garrace would have the largest, and he didn't disappoint. It wasn't as thick as Ryan's, but the longer length was considerable. Soon, he felt Garrace's hand grab hold of him, and both began regular strokes on each other.

With hands behind his head, Rixen watched the two share their moment. It was not only hot; it was beautiful. Unintentionally, his deep sigh broke their concentration. That's when he felt Garrace's eyes target him. The look was all too familiar. Garrace was about to go to the strongest act of copulation there was. While Ryan watched, Garrace situated himself between his legs. After lifting them, he felt a strong, wet cock push against him. A few drops of slick glided down the outside of Rixen's body. The pressure from Garrace's cock was uncomfortable at first; he softened his efforts. After another attempt, Rixen relaxed and allowed him to enter. Large, strong breaths escaped him as he felt the hard length go deeper and deeper into him. When he felt Garrace's ball sack tight up against him, he let go of his breath in pleasure.

Garrace pushed forward and grabbed Rixen's lips with his own. Gently rocking back and forth allowed Rixen to adjust to such a large member inside him just as it was countless times before.

Ryan's face was open wide as he saw the most amazing sight. Wanting his presence known, he went behind Garrace and began kissing the back of his neck. Garrace seemed to have no problem pushing his body forward, giving Ryan a full view of the small globes of his ass. Right down the middle, Ryan observed a sweaty opening, slowly bouncing up and down as Garrace built up a regular rhythm. Unable to resist, he bit the firm skin and then began to use his mouth on his tight pucker. Garrace moaned words of approval, but it wasn't going to stop there. Using the same lube, Ryan lathered himself up and balanced himself on the remaining space of the end of the bed. As Garrace's body fell forward, Ryan's thick cockhead kept getting massaged by Garrace's opening. He held firm, not knowing what

Garrace's reaction was going to be. Incredibly, he appeared to be enjoying it. With slower thrusts, more and more time was spent with Garrace getting used to Ryan. Slow to a pause, there was a slight give in pressure which meant all three of them were connected to each other. The physical, emotional, and mental synapses were flashing like intense strobe lights. Being inside an Alpha was a rarity; at least, it wasn't spoken about. Yet, here Ryan was, owning Garrace in the moment.

Garrace knew the social condemnation of allowing himself to be penetrated. To be fair, he only had a short time to decide whether or not to approve. In those moments, he decided there wasn't anyone else he'd even consider penetrating him. But this situation changed so much more than just the rules. What did this step mean? What was supposed to happen after? How were the three going to move forward? Philosophy was replaced with the necessity of dealing with the intense pain.

Without being an Omega, Garrace's slick gland ability paled by comparison which meant his body gave no natural forgiveness to Ryan's massive cock. But the discomfort was blown away as the sensitivity overload proved to be too much. Feeling the extreme gratification from both sides of his body boiled the liquids held inside him. A few more thrusts from Ryan deep inside him opened a flood gate.

Garrace arched himself. "Wolf-God, I'm cumming, I'm cumming!" Almost as he spoke the words, he felt his orgasm push deep inside Rixen who began to pant just as much as he was. Even though it was ecstasy, he needed Ryan to stop his efforts before it hurt. A flat palm against his chest successfully communicated the need. He deeply kissed Ryan in order to prevent fears he might have done something wrong. Then, he did the same to Rixen, who appeared lost in his own world.

Ryan watched as Garrace moved forward and removed Ryan's rock-hard length from inside him. Next, he observed Garrace pull out of his brother. Although Ryan's cock had a thin coat of lubricant remaining on him, Garrace presented his own semi-hard cock lacquered in Rixen's perfumed slick still dripping a generous amount of cum from its tip.

"Here, use this," Garrace offered. Taking a few fingers, he entered Rixen once again and coated them with the juices built up inside his lover, then wrapped his other hand around Ryan's cock. Ryan gasped at first, then enjoyed every moment which followed. A trade of tongue presses ensued between the two before Garrace guided Ryan's body up to his brother's, removing himself from the bed. Not seeing Ryan fully grasping the concept, he pulled Ryan's hand down to Rixen's swollen and open entrance.

"Finish him off," he instructed while licking his lips.

Staring down at his brother's vulnerable face gave Ryan the courage to place three fingers up against him. Rixen nodded once to show his approval. The insides of his brother were warm and unbelievably wet. It didn't take long for him to find the source of Rixen's release. His slick glands were swollen and quite firm. Upon reaching them, Rixen yelped out his brother's name and squirmed his body. As both stroked their own cocks, Ryan quickened the pace, knowing the moment was nearing.

The slick glands insides Rixen vibrated. It was time. He felt a wave overcome him and then powerful contractions came from deep inside him.

"Oh fuck," Rixen moaned, "don't stop, please don't stop!" In the little crevices of Ryan's fingers which exposed tiny exits from Rixen's body, hot slick began to shoot out onto the bed. The pulsing made it difficult for Ryan to keep his fingers inside him. When they crept out, a small flood of slick and cum drained out. Feeling the lengthy orgasm inside triggered another one from his own cock. Suddenly, spurts flew up to his neck and all over his lower stomach.

The sight was too much for Ryan. He always imagined what it would be like to know Rixen was having an orgasm caused by him, but it didn't prepare him enough. The emotional overload is what triggered his physical one. Ryan didn't vocalize words, but the escalated pitch in moans gave his impending end away. Combined with the sight of Rixen's exhilaration, Ryan's own cock shot out load after load onto his brother below. His balls tucked up tight against his body; they even hurt. The shallow breathing made him lightheaded, and he fell forward, catching himself with his hand on the bed next to Rixen's body. He stared into his brother's eyes still in disbelief this all happened. The afterglow of the orgasm threw his face down to his brother's. The two exchanged their lips, tongues, and pheromones to a soft ending.

"That was amazing," Garrace spoke quietly. He knelt at the side of the bed, resting his head on his arms, also enjoying a stuck satisfied look on his face. Both brothers gave a short laugh as they stared at Garrace and each other. Garrace leaned over Rixen's face and kissed him deeply, holding his face in place to make sure every act was perfect. After letting go, he smiled. "Damn, I love you." Rixen returned the words. Then, he turned to Ryan. "And you, mister..." he grabbed him for the repeated transaction, "are an unbelievable, sexy human being."

"Yeah. I have to say, so are you." Ryan smoldered, giving him one last kiss and deep embrace.

"So," Garrace stood, "anyone up for a shower?"

"Uh, yeah." Rixen laughed. "There's no way I'm staying like this."

"I don't know," Ryan joked. "I think I like you cream-covered in our spunk."

"Cute," Rixen replied. "It's going to be hard enough getting both of your scents off me, let alone the smell out of this room. It smells like sex in here so bad."

"I'll throw the sheets in the laundry now and join you two in a second," Ryan assured him.

Ryan backed off the bed and offered his brother his hand. Rixen accepted and led Garrace down the hall to the bathroom as Ryan began to strip the bed.

"So, what did you think of that?" Garrace asked.

Rixen waited until the bathroom door was shut. "Wolf-God, I don't know what just happened." He threw his hands down on the granite sink, barely able to hold himself up.

"Are you okay?" Garrace asked, full of concern.

"I just had sex with you and my brother; I'm not sure what 'okay' means."

"What are you worried about?"

"Seriously? Are you kidding me? What am I going to do? What are we going to do? What happens if people find out? Wolf-God, Garrace, please don't tell anyone about this!"

Garrace grimaced with disappointment. "Rixen, I would never say anything. You know me better than that." He put his hand on Rixen's shoulder. The hot spell wore off from the sex, and he felt Rixen's skin begin to form cold bumps.

"What is Ryan going to think about all this?"

"Do you really think he's going to flip out? He was the one who confessed all this."

Rixen sighed. "Well, pardon me," he voiced sarcastically. "I don't know too many brothers who confess they have the hots for their sibling."

"The hots?" Garrace paused. "Rixen, Ryan confessed a lot more than that. He loves you."

"Of course, he loves me. I'm his brother."

Garrace's shoulders dropped. "Are you really going to be in denial right now?"

"What?" Rixen tried innocently.

"He's in love with you, babe."

Rixen's stomach knotted upon hearing the words. He knew it. But now he had to face it—in front of his lover of all people. "Garrace, if he really is, what do I do?"

"That depends. Can you answer this question?" Rixen waited for it with breath held. "Are you in love with Ryan?"

The bathroom door opened with an equally nude Ryan walking in. A gentle smile set on his face. "Are you two done showering or are we all doing this together?" he half-joked.

Rixen's previous expression floated away. He lifted his eyebrows. "How about together?"

Garrace joined Rixen's poker face and displayed a sly smile. "Ooo, I'm game."

Ryan was a bit stunned at Rixen's reaction. But in a moment's time, he led all three to the generous-sized shower. The encounter gave way to a lot of exploration: touching, caressing, massaging. All in all, this was an apparition Ryan didn't want to end. Every second was a new experience and each one he cherished, right down to his first three-way kiss as the hot water rained down on all of them.

CHAPTER 20:

A Shattering of
Hearts and Law

Both Mikaél and Roman agreed the next few days took forever. It was "suggested" they stay apart physically until after the signing of the contract. Since it was revealed neither Roman nor Mikaél were on any suppressants, their last escapade, according to Dustin, was labeled as an inappropriate affair.

But Friday was here; today was the start of a brighter future. After classes, both families met in a hotel's conference room of Mikaél's Sur's choosing. Considering the delicate nature of Mikaél's age, there weren't too many requests the Erricsons were going to make before even attending the appointment.

Upon seeing Mikaél in the hotel on this particular day, Roman embraced him in seconds while standing in the lobby of the grand location. All four parents gave some sort of sound or look which obviously was interpreted as the old condescending quip "Kids," even though Roman was well into adulthood.

Roman looked at Mikaél's parents. Dustin displayed a neutral face while Alec found it a bit more difficult to look him in the eye. No doubt, there were tensions in the household concerning the secretly approved rendezvous they had in Mikaél's room earlier.

An attendant from the hotel led them and the lawyers to a reserved room down an impressive, gigantic hallway complete with intricate carpet, archways, large windows with curtains, and subtle music pumped in from speakers easily 20-feet high from the vaulted ceilings. The conference room itself was impressive too, much more inviting than the Whitmores' location. The table and leatherback chairs were similar, but the room was gently lit with mahogany accents and a large saltwater fish tank. A glass-front mini-fridge revealed any upscale snack a patron in a luxurious hotel could want. After the attendant assured them the room was theirs for an over-generous amount of time and offered any comforts in the room, he left and shut the door quietly.

"Well, are we ready?" Erricson's lawyer spoke. A consensus was felt around the room. "I'm Duane, and I do believe your lawyer's name is Benjamin?"

"Yes, that's right," Cavenbelle's lawyer confirmed.

"You know, I don't think we even properly introduced you last time we did a contract," Jake noted.

Duane nodded. "It wasn't really the atmosphere to do so. I don't think the other client cared much."

"I think you're right there," Jake tittered.

Like before, the parents sat across from each other: Alpha to Alpha and Omega to Omega. The lawyers sat to their rights and Roman and Mikaél sat to their lefts.

If there was anything Roman could comment on regarding the difference between this contract and the last, it was the fact the energy and aura in the room was alive and cheerful. Roman grinned from ear to ear; Mikaél joined him in his expression. As they began, Roman reached out and held Mikaél's hand as if they were getting ready to exchange vows.

"Out of curiosity, how much of this has to go like last time?" It was an awkward question to ask in present company, but Roman's excitement caught the better of him.

"I'm afraid, Mr. Erricson, this will be exactly as before word-for-word. The only difference will be the final negotiations if there are any."

Roman curled his lips and nodded; it wasn't the response he was hoping for, but nonetheless, this was worth waiting for.

As before, paperwork and identification started with Roman and his family. The process was familiar and swift. In identifying Mikaél, Roman learned Mikaél's middle name was Alexander, named after his father.

"Okay," Duane continued, "are we ready for the Blood-Type paperwork?"

All approved.

"I had to get my blood drawn this morning before heading to classes," Mikaél commented.

"Same here," Roman added. "Though, I don't know why they just couldn't use my previous test results. Was that really necessary?"

"Legal precautions, that's all Mr. Erricson," Duane assured. "Roman Erricson is ranked as an Alpha and Blood-Type 5 Exceptionality. Bloodline purity at 79%."

Dustin furrowed his brows. "Wait. Type 5? Your son is Type 6."

"Dr. Birowack is experimenting with the Blood-Type numbers for population purposes. That's all. All is otherwise the same." Jake spoke nonchalantly as if he was discussing simple math problems.

It took a second for Dustin to accept the words. When discussing a P&C agreement, the words on a legal document held more water than what was said out loud. But Roman was an exception to everything, and Dustin had worked on his file for years. There was no reason to not believe Jake; he knew the data. "Oh, okay."

The Erricson family all exchanged a neutral look, communicating to each other about what they really knew. They were, however, satisfied at this point they'd dodged a bullet concerning the issue.

The paper was handed to Dustin who passed it down to Alec who passed it down to Mikaél. For legal purposes, all had to acknowledge seeing it. After their approval, Mikaél's results were also opened from a sealed envelope from Benjamin, Cavenbelle's lawyer.

"Okay. Mikaél has been ranked as an Omega. He—" Benjamin paused and looked over the blood test results.

Dustin voiced concern first. "What? What's wrong?"

"These results don't seem right."

Jake firmed up. "Is there something wrong with the Blood-Type? Is Mikaél not a Type 5?"

Dustin gave Jake a dirty look. "Really? Was that necessary?"

"What? I'm just asking," Jake pleaded innocently.

"No, not that," Benjamin continued. "There are just a bunch of big number values printed all over it."

"What?" Dustin pulled the paper out of his lawyer's hand and studied it for himself.

"That's what it says," Benjamin reaffirmed, "and at the bottom it says Error Code 31. I imagine something went wrong with the system. If you want, we can tentatively approve the contract today and make it official once Mikaél gets retested."

Jake's eyes stared at Dustin like he saw a murder take place in front of him. "Dustin, does it really say, 'Error Code 31' on it?"

Dustin swallowed hard and handed the paper to his co-worker. "It's right there on the bottom."

Alec interjected. "Babe, what's wrong? Did Mikaél get a faulty test?" Everyone in the room stared at both Alphas.

All were perplexed and a bit scared for the reactions they observed.

"I, uh… I think we need to go," Dustin claimed softly.

Mikaél sat up straight as nerves began to flow over him. "Go? What do you mean 'Go'? What about the contract?"

"We can't do this, Mikaél. We need to stop, now," Dustin reaffirmed, his voice rising.

"No, wait." Roman stood up, not believing his ears. "The lawyer said we can tentatively agree now and just finish it off after the second blood test comes in. I mean, honestly, I don't care about the blood test anyway."

"Roman, you don't understand," Jake protested and stood by the table. "We're not just stopping it to put it on hold. We're stopping for good."

Adrian stood there flabbergasted. "Jake, you can't be serious."

"I don't understand." Roman's heart sank. He didn't know what was going on. This had to be a mistake.

"I'm sorry, Roman. This can't happen," Jake said solemnly.

"What? That's it?" Roman held his arms up. "Does anyone care to explain to me why I can't be with my Fated Mate? Has anyone come up with a good reason for that yet?"

"Sur, please," Mikaél joined in, "what is going on? Why is this happening?"

"Son, I have been open to you about everything in this process. But this one, you just have to let it be for now," Dustin demanded.

"There's no way. This is the moment everyone waits for their entire life. Roman is meant for me, and I'm meant for him. You can't take this away." Mikaél's hurt beat out the commanding tone he hoped for in this voice. He saw Roman stare at him, embracing the emotional pheromones floating in the air.

"Mik, you are 17 years old, and I have every authority over you on this. When I say it's over, that means it's over!"

Alec came to his son's defense. "Dustin, let's be rational about this. There's gotta be some way—"

"I said it's over!" Dustin's voice shook the room.

No one spoke another word of dissent.

It was when both lawyers rose and packed up in silence that Mikaél began to cry.

Like a mate instinctually does, Roman rushed around the long table and held Mikaél tight against his body, brushed his back, and repeated hushing sounds to keep Mikaél from having a breakdown right there and then.

"I don't understand," Mikaél squeaked out in pain.

"Don't worry," Roman spoke quietly. "I'm not giving up on you; this isn't the end. I'm going to make this right. I promise."

"Mikaél, it's time." Dustin's voice was calm but still dictatorial. He glanced at Jake. "Are you calling him?"

"Right after this. Are you going to be available?"

"Anytime, anyplace."

Alec walked up to his son and rubbed his shoulder. He gave Roman a look which told him he needed to let go. Roman complied, and Alec began the procession out of the conference room followed by both lawyers.

Roman stood there, trying to hold back the sharp knife pains in his heart. He closed his eyes and held his breath, waiting for the door to shut again. When it did, he finally exhaled, feeling his blood boil.

"Jake, you better start talking now," Adrian ordered.

"Babe, I'm sorry. I can't." Jake frowned.

"Don't you see what this is doing to him?"

"I know and I wish I could make this go all away." Jake paced the room as he lamented.

Roman turned around with his own daggers in his eyes. "Seriously? I don't believe the audacity you have."

"I—" Jake began.

"You have been an integral part of my misery this entire time. You promised me this would get better. You promised you wouldn't treat me like an invalid, and here you are, controlling all the pieces again and keeping another secret from me. I ought to punch you into tomorrow." Roman began to walk toward his father, fists clenched and arms tightening. His attack mode set in, and he could think of nothing else.

"Roman!" Adrian yelled. With all the might he could muster, he held Roman back. Roman's skin was hot to the touch.

Roman stared at his father with extreme disdain. Although Jake exhibited his own Alpha instincts, it was Roman's Veo who deterred him. He relaxed his body but held onto his piercing stare. He held a finger a mere space from his father's eyes.

"I will never forgive you for this." Roman threw open the door and slammed it shut, placing him back into the extravagant hallway. Hustling to the main lobby, he got a quick glance at Mikaél entering their car right before it drove away.

Wanting to remember any other emotion on Mikaél's face, Roman pulled out his phone and swiped through the pictures from their date at Tauris Square. The current ordeal brought dark clouds upon his face. It was even worse when he swiped too far, revealing the pictures of his date with Peyton. Before his eyes, two pinnacle souls in his life faded away like ghosts, leaving him alone. Roman hung his head and cried to himself, ignoring every person and action going on around him.

***

"Gentleman." Dr. Birowack welcomed Jake and Dustin back into his office as sunset fell upon the city. "Your urgency on the phone has me concerned." He observed the macabre and agitated dispositions. "And your demeanors as well."

"Please tell me you didn't know about this." Dustin sighed.

"I'm sorry. What are you speaking of?" Dr. Birowack pushed himself forward in his chair.

"My son's blood test results. You had to have seen them."

Dr. Birowack smirked. "Yes, you're right. I have nothing better to do with my time other than anticipating your son's blood test results for his P&C contract. Which, by the way, congratulations to you both." Dr. Birowack shook his head.

Jake assisted, "Paul, that's the problem. We stopped the contract."

The doctor's face dimmed. "How troubling. Why so?"

Dustin crossed his arms. "Mikaél's blood results errored out."

"Have him retested then. Several tests error out daily for one reason or another."

Jake chimed in, "It's not an error code that's going to get fixed on a retest."

"That's not really possible. Which error code came up?"

"Check for yourself." Dustin's voice carried a hint of attitude.

Dr. Birowack scanned the men in his room. Holding his composure was a challenge. He felt criticized for something he apparently wasn't showing the right response to. Finding test results on the computer database wasn't difficult. He knew the family last name, and this morning's test date brought up the file quickly. After scanning, he found himself pleased with the results, but his face remained neutral. He turned back to his audience and waited.

"What? No comment?" Dustin asked in disbelief.

"Please tell me what you want to hear," Dr. Birowack replied.

"Paul, you know what this is." Jake walked forward. "Error 31 is same result we get when we get Alphas out of percentile ranges."

"I do believe so. Yes."

"This doesn't happen with Omegas; it's never happened with an Omega. I mean, am I wrong?" Jake asked, feeling a bit juvenile.

"Your assessment is correct. Error 31 has never come from an Omega blood test before. And as I look at his array, he's quite remarkable for an Omega."

Jake looked at Dustin. "How could you not know this?"

"Know what? That his levels were so high?" Dustin clarified.

"That Mikaél is... he's..." Jake couldn't believe the words coming out of his mouth. "He's a Type 6 Omega," he said, still in shock.

Dustin himself found the words hard to comprehend. "I...I didn't. Sure, I knew his levels were rather high compared to his peers, but as parents we were thrilled. My mate and I are Type 4 ourselves. Not even my son Drew is a Type 5 Alpha. We celebrated who Mikaél was and left it at that. I mean, no one told us he was a

Type 6. If they had, believe me, I would have said something. Hell, I could have been running my own research lab on this discovery."

"Indeed," Dr. Birowack confirmed.

"Then why are we just finding this out now?" Jake pressed. "How come a test result didn't come back from when he was born?"

"As you can imagine, science and technology has changed drastically in just the last ten years, even more since your son was born. Beyond that, Omegas aren't rated to such scrutiny as Alphas. Only now has there been such social advocacy for reform to include such detailed rankings." Dr. Birowack sat back and observed his colleagues. They were stunned, dumbfounded, and beyond logical processing. He, however, waited for the questions to continue.

Jake's eyes narrowed. "You weren't surprised at all, were you?"

Dr. Birowack folded his arms. "Why should I be?"

Dustin commented, "You can't be serious."

Dr. Birowack smiled. "Gentlemen, we only recently discussed a revolutionary theory of how a Type 6 Alpha was able to find a Fated Mate when we seemingly provided enough evidence to the world of medicine to prove they couldn't. In entertaining the theory, did neither of you consider the reason Roman could find his Fated Mate was because Mikaél was a Type 6 himself?"

After catching a long, disheartened look at Jake, Dustin replied, "That's quite the long shot."

"Maybe not as much as you think."

"Oh, why's that?"

Getting up from his chair and opening a file cabinet, Dr. Birowack continued, "While you two were working this week, I found time to examine some of my own hunches. It's amazing what a person can't see right in front of them when they're not looking for it." He opened a thick file folder and turned to a page he'd already bookmarked for the occasion. "Tell me, what do you see here?"

Jake leaned over and examined the detailed image and the research notes below it. "It's a picture of an amygdala. Glancing at the notes, I have to agree, this is a rather large amygdala. But it's not unheard of for an adult to have it."

"I implore you to look a bit further."

Jake squinted his eye and pulled his head back quickly. "Is this patient really 13 years old?"

"Was," Dr. Birowack corrected. "Now, I do believe he is 24."

The number in Jake's head connected the pieces. "This is Roman? 11 years ago?"

"Mm. Indeed. As you know the amygdala is responsible for our emotional control center and assists with our memory bank. But you will also remember it is the origin of our wolf instincts as well."

"Of course. I understand this enlargement is now perhaps significant to look into further. But I'm not seeing the connection yet."

"Dustin, my good man. A quick biology lesson if you will. Describe the scientific process of finding a Fated Mate."

Dustin looked cautiously at Jake and then began. "78 chromosomes make up a wolf. As we evolved, we copied primate-descendants all the way down to their 46 chromosomes. However, we wolf-descendants have an extra pair. It is believed chromosomes 47 and 48 are responsible for the extra enhancement of tracking— including finding a Fated Mate. Our reproductive system is possible because of this too. A hormonal adolescent or pup with a thyroid problem could theoretically track a Fate quite early, or in the case of Omegas, give off the pheromones in order to be tracked."

"Right. And in regard to your son?" Dr. Birowack gestured.

Jake cleared his throat and adjusted his stance. "When looking at Roman's case, he does possess chromosomes 47 and 48, but the integrity is low. His chromosome makeup refuses to advance the chemicals in his body to the state where he can track a Fated Mate. Or so we thought."

"Beautiful. Well done," Dr. Birowack celebrated.

"Paul, that's the classic introduction to our entire work. What on earth is this all about?"

"That enlarged amygdala is not typical. Roman himself his not typical—hence his Type 6 Status."

"Hey, why was Roman listed as a Type 5 in the contract?" Dustin interjected.

Dr. Birowack glanced at Jake and then back to Dustin. "I'm observing thresholds for cases. As cases continue to rise of the existence of Type 6 candidates, I want to make sure we're not diluting the sampling."

"So, he's a weak Type 6?"

"Oh, no, of course not. Every Type 6 is low in one or more of their indicators. It was an intentional choice to start with Roman's insufficiencies. He is, after all, our foremost volunteer. Anyway," Dr. Birowack switched topics, "every living thing on this planet at its core has one goal: to survive. When there are inadequacies which threaten this goal, the lifeform adapts. Plants will change the way they grow based on whether or not they want full exposure to the sun, insects change their colors to help camouflage themselves from enemies, and humans change their skin, eye, and hair tone to adapt to their climate surroundings. These, of course, take years, thousands perhaps. But what if, gentlemen, we are experiencing the first ever recorded account of how a modern wolf-descendant adapts to their threatened ability to find that Fated Mate?"

"Wait a second." Jake held up his hand. "Are you suggesting Roman's amygdala is enlarged to compensate for his inability to track someone?"

Dr. Birowack nodded. "Now, let's be scientists. We already know the reasons why we claim this a dead theory. But let's reflect and make suggestions on why this could be true."

"Both Roman and Mikaél are adamant they were meant for each other. Even today, it was as if they were never apart."

Dustin added to the conversation, "Plus, both recognize the imprint they made on each other was a Fated imprint, no matter how violent that was." He grimaced, still annoyed at such foolish notion.

"That's it," Jake connected. "That's the theory, isn't it?"

Dr. Birowack nodded.

"Uh, someone want to fill me in here?" Dustin requested.

"Sorry, Dustin. Uh, let's see. I'm not sure on how the specifics of it works, but I'm guessing in some ways Roman's chemical responses are working but just not in a conventional way. Hormones are free-flowing and always changing their levels. I could suggest that Roman's tracking hormones are being stored in his amygdala."

"So, then that's what is supposed to explain why Roman's courtship was so flawed? His hormones were attached to his emotional center which caused him to lash out instead of present himself?" Dustin offered.

"That's my thought on it. It's what I said when it happened. Roman was feeling threatened. He didn't like us there because Mikaél wasn't claimed yet. He didn't want anyone near Mikaél until he imprinted him."

Dustin tapped his foot. "Okay. I'm not saying you're wrong. But that doesn't explain anything about my son. Other than high levels, what are we suggesting makes him a Type 6?"

"We need to consider there is most likely no research here in the territory much less our state. Our research center would be under-taking this for the first time. Our efforts stop if Mikaél chooses not to cooperate with us."

"I told you before—I have no intention of guilting or coercing him into such invasive process," Dustin reminded. "If he says no at any time, even for a second, it's over."

"Of course," Dr. Birowack assured him. "Now, let us not forget, this idea is not new. Theorists have conjectured the idea of a Type 6 Omega for years, ever since the confirmation of the existence of a Type 6 Alpha."

Jake scoffed. "Yeah, but they also went outlandish trying to prove a Type 7 Alpha. Every time a scientist makes a proud discovery, conspiracists take it one step too far and think there's always something else."

Dr. Birowack agreed. "Yes. However, it is that population which drives curiosity and keeps us willing to accept the challenge. You were barely walking I suppose when the term Type 6 Alpha was even being considered. Those who were willing to believe in their existence had a great sect of people who were certain scientists were creating these beings in laboratories or that their discovery was the sign of the Wolf-Devil to bring about another apocalypse similar to what wiped out the primate-descendants. And yet, here we are, gentlemen. Here we are."

"This is crazy." Dustin exhaled. "I hate to say it, but all the theories, including the insane ones, make me question logic entirely. I know I'm a scientist, a good one at that, but at the same time, all the discoveries which excite me also scare me to death."

Dr. Birowack concurred, "The burden to stay centered and professional is a great one. Bias for your own families is expected; you are human. These theories are what made you knee-jerk on the rescission of the P&C agreement?"

Dustin looked at Jake with a somber face. "I'm almost certain Jake and I thought of the same theory. Scared us both, I think."

A slow nod ensued from Jake. "Yeah, it scared me. I know it hurts Roman and us, but to put Mikaél in that position...I couldn't imagine."

"The time to act is fleeting, gentlemen." Dr. Birowack spoke with undeterred wisdom. "It seems your sons have already done whatever it takes to keep themselves as Fated Mates. I'm not a parent, so I'll never have the balancing act you both subject yourselves to. But it is my professional opinion some compromise may have to be made. If not, I fear your sons' decisions will be made without either of your considerations."

"Dustin, Mikaél is still under your authority. What do you say to this?"

A labyrinth lay in Dustin's mind. All possible outcomes in the maze ran through his head. There was no doubt in his mind he clearly knew the answer to some of the questions. Others were enigmas. Both Mikaél and Roman did their part well in surprising him with their devotion since they met. And finally, he imagined scenarios which came naturally to every parent. Perhaps, it was these that scared him so much. Identifying his own son as a Type 6 Omega meant the security blanket of his entire career had fallen through the floor. He no longer had science to rely on. The only thing left was the human condition. That was the most frightening realization of all.

CHAPTER 21:

A Shoulder to Cry On

Mikaél sat in the cafeteria. Normally, he sat in the crowded space with several of his friends. But today was the day he chose to sit alone up against the floor-to-ceiling windows. Rainy days were tough to deal with. Rainy days in the fall were even tougher. The sky was a cloudy mess. He had to wipe his hand against the glass to see out better. Leaves were starting to change on the trees, not that he could see them clearly. A few fell in a random rush of wind. They floated down to the concrete sidewalks and in the overflow ditches.

Jordan, Matt, and Victor weren't going to press the issue. Laycin had filled them in, whether or not Mikaél wanted him to. The group sat huddled at the table.

"We're not seriously going to just leave him there, are we?" Jordan asked.

Matt grimaced. "No way. I'm not going to get in the middle of a doomed love story. Victor made me deal with his last time. Not doing it again."

"Well, fuck you, too," Victor replied.

"Come on, guys," Laycin centered the group. He peered over at his friend on the far side of the room. Mikaél just sat there, staring into nothing. "He looks so miserable."

"Jordan, you go," Matt offered.

"Shouldn't we all go?" Jordan questioned.

"Laycin, you go," Victor suggested.

"Me? Why me?"

Matt added, "Because you're the only one who's good at this."

Victor nodded. "And you're the only one who can reach him. We send Matt over there, and he's going to make him commit suicide." That was payback. It was short lived. Matt returned the comment with a swift punch in the arm. "Ugh! Damn it!"

"Fine," Laycin conceded. He took his tray and went through the table maze to find his friend. He knew Mikaél sensed his presence, but he didn't acknowledge or flinch. "Hey." Laycin put his hand on Mikaél's shoulder. From the back, his shoulder felt warm, but in the front, the cool air from outside permeated the window. It was easy to focus on the sensation since Mikaél said nothing in return.

"Are you gonna eat that?" Laycin pointed to a lukewarm chicken sandwich, completely untouched. Without a response, he helped himself to it. He had no intention of eating it; it was just for a reaction. Unsuccessful. "Look, I get it—"

"No, you don't get it. A Beta will never know what this is like." Mikaél's words had teeth. They were the wrong ones to say. He softened his voice. "Sorry, I didn't mean that."

This time it was Laycin's turn to remain silent. The last thing to ever tell a Beta was a reminder of their "disability" as some characterized it. But that word was also one not said in front of a Beta— not unless you wanted a mouth with a few less teeth.

"I just didn't think it was going to be this hard." Mikaél pretended the raindrops on the large windows were tears. That way, he didn't have to make any of his own.

"Have you talked to Roman yet?" Laycin asked.

Mikaél shook his head. "No. He called me a couple times, left a couple texts. But I haven't answered him yet. I don't think I'd be anything more than a pathetic mess."

"Maybe that's what he needs to hear?" Laycin challenged.

Mikaél exhaled. "Heh. I think there's a 50/50 shot that would end terribly. A part of me still worries about whether or not he'd blow up a building or something."

"I thought you said his freak out was just a one-time thing. You convinced me a hundred times of that."

"I know," Mikaél whined. "Don't listen to me. I'm just saying whatever comes to my head."

Laycin looked back at all their friends who were eyeing the scene like adolescents who had snuck into an NC-17 movie. They gave him looks and gestures to signal the "What's going on?" question. Laycin's nonverbal response didn't do much to satisfy them. "I think this is the part where I say, 'Everything is going to work out and love will find a way,' but that's just bullshit."

That comment made Mikaél move his head back over his shoulder and glare at his friend. "You should try therapy."

"My dad says I'd make a good therapist."

"No, I mean, you should be in therapy. You have a messed-up idea on what to say to help someone. Just leave me alone."

Laycin sighed. "Look, I care about you. You know that. I'm here when you want me. But having the title of being your best friend also means you get me when you don't. Because that's what friends do."

Hearing Laycin's words from the heart, no matter how rough around the edges they were, cut down a few walls. Mikaél turned to give his friend his full attention. "You know, if Roman and I had different parents, we'd already be living together by now."

"Yikes, tiger! You work fast." Laycin cracked up.

Mikaél evaluated his statement and reluctantly agreed. "I must be compensating for the fact everything is moving backward in the wrong direction. It's like forcing the sun back, so it can't rise or stuffing a flower back into its seed. It shouldn't work that way. It can't."

"Ah, there he is, our poet is back at last! Say Shakespeare, you should jot this stuff down. You know, write yourself out of this funk. But then again, most of Shakespeare's stuff ended in tragedy. Have you thought about painting instead?"

"Thanks, Laycin. I think I'll try this one on my own." Mikaél laid his head on arms.

"Wait. You're coming to class, right?" Mikaél shook his head no. "You're not seriously going to bail on Dr. Birowack's class, are you? Your Sur's gonna kill you." Suffering through another silence, Laycin decided to save himself from the wrath of his own parents finding out he skipped a class.

Mikaél kept an ear open for any conversation once Laycin returned to the crew at the other table. A few words from Laycin were audible, but that was it. Moments later, the bell tone sounded, and a rush of people scattered in all directions. He was unfazed. His mind was trained to get up and head to class, but his body was having none of it. Soon, the voices and noises faded to silence. He sat among the cafeteria workers cleaning up the whirlwind left behind.

A voice cut the silence, "You make it a thrill of an adventure to find you."

Just hearing the voice wiped away all the sadness within Mikaél with one brushstroke. Looking up, it was too good to be true. There standing in jeans and a jacket was Roman staring back with the same sober expression. The boulder Mikaél felt on his body lifted, and he ran into his arms, smashing their bodies together.

"How did you find me up here? Did Laycin tell you?" Mikaél wondered.

"You're my Fate. I can scent you from the parking lot. You should be able to do the same for me."

"I guess my wolf senses are broken at the moment."

Roman's hand touched his face. There was a healing power to it. "You're avoiding me?" Roman asked.

"No," Mikaél sighed. "Avoiding myself." He returned to his own little corner and sat back down again. The space was beginning to feel like home.

"What do you mean?" Roman followed his every step. As soon as he sat next to him, he pulled Mikaél's limp head and placed it on his shoulder.

"My wall. Veo says it's what stops me from reaching my full potential. Keeps me from having to deal with disappointment. It leads me to my self-sabotage."

"You were avoiding me so you wouldn't have to deal with the disappointment of the contract falling apart?"

"Wouldn't be the first time I did that to you," Mikaél admitted.

Perplexed, Roman pushed. "When?"

"Before you imprinted me," Mikaél stated. "You don't honestly think I didn't know who you were, did you?" The look on Roman's face said otherwise. "I may not have understood what was physically happening to me, but I knew you were meant to be mine."

Roman jerked his head back in amazement. "Why were you trying to avoid me then?"

"I feared you wouldn't like me. What if after you came to your senses, you decided I wasn't worthy of who you are? I'm not ignorant. Every Omega in this city would die for the opportunity to be with you."

Roman rolled his eyes. "I don't care about anyone else. And I think you know by now, I do want you, and I do think you're good enough."

"Yeah, not that any of that matters now. That's my point. We had our chance, and now that's over."

"If you really think I'm going to let some stupid legal document determine whether or not I'm going to be with you, then you don't know me very well." He softly stroked Mikaél's hair.

"Did your Sur even tell you why yet?" Mikaél wanted to know.

"No. Not that I care. Unless he says our union is going to bring about the End of Days, I don't give a shit. Even if it does, I don't care. How about yours?"

"No," Mikaél groaned. "He's keeping his lips sealed on this one. It sucks because my dad doesn't do this. He's not a secretive person. He can't even keep my birthday gifts a secret."

"I'd trade with you in a second. That's all my Sur's been all of my life. His philosophy has always been about a 'need to know' basis. And most of it always has to do with me." Mikaél's expression was unmoved. "Listen, we're going to make it. I promise." Unable to change his expression or pheromone pattern, Roman decided to switch to more primitive tactics. His hand innocently slid down the side of Mikaél's chest. Slowly, he began to massage his fingertips into his side.

"Don't," Mikaél voiced in monotone. His body involuntarily squirmed a bit and rested again once Roman slowed the moment to a stop. But as quickly as the relief came, the hand came in harder. "Ah!" he screamed with laughter. In trying to compensate for his defense, Mikaél left his other side vulnerable. Now, Roman had both hands on either side of him, rapidly digging his hands in to force synthetic happiness. "Stop!"

Roman stopped but only for a second. "Hmmm, nope." He instantly went back to terrorizing his mate. Seeing Mikaél change instantaneously to a lively being was fresh air. This was the only way he wanted his mate to be. When his agonized screams began smelling of annoyance, he knew it was time to stop. In the final heavy breaths, he watched Mikaél's smile fade as he cleared his wet eyes.

"Ugh! You're horrible, you know that?" Mikaél tried to return to his former attitude, but it was to no avail. The laughter injected into him had staying power. Although the contract was gone, Roman was sitting right there in front of him. "Thank you."

"That's what I'm here for. Always." Roman leaned in and gave Mikaél a much-needed embrace with his arms and his lips.

Mikaél picked up his phone off his bed as best as he could while sitting in his floor rocker. "Hello?" He turned down the volume on his flat screen.

"Hello?" the voice on the other side stressed. "Why are you sounding like you didn't know it was me?"

"Because the delete button is a wondrous thing," Mikaél said flatly.

"You deleted me out of your phone?" the voice replied, very offended.

"Garrace, what do you want?"

"Fuck, Mik. I just wanted to say I'm sorry about your contract falling apart."

"Thanks," Mikaél replied sarcastically.

"Hey, I thought my words meant a lot to you."

Mikaél scoffed. "Why on earth would you think that?"

"Uh, did you forget? I was there the night that all went down."

"Forgive me. You weren't high on my list all things considered. But thanks. You're right. I do appreciate it."

Garrace sighed. "Good. There's also something else I wanted to talk to you about."

"Shocking," Mikaél answered. If only Garrace could see his face. "Sheesh!"

"I told you I knew you." He walked to his bed and stretched on it, waiting.

Garrace paused. "Can I tell you something in confidence?"

The request took Mikaél by surprise. "Okay?"

"I'm serious!"

"Okay! Okay! Yes!" Mikaél's voice was concrete.

"I got myself into a situation."

"What kind of situation?"

Garrace sighed. "With Ryan and Rixen Erricson."

"Roman's brothers?"

"Yes." Garrace's voice hesitated more with every response.

"Yikes. Did you piss them off or something?"

"No. Quite the opposite, actually."

"So, you excited them?" Mikaél laughed.

"You could say that." No further details followed.

Something hit in the pit of Mikaél's stomach. "My thoughts are going south quickly here. Did you...did you—"

"Mik, you CANNOT say anything."

"Holy shit! It really is what I'm thinking. Right?"

"I don't know. What are you thinking?"

"Did you...sleep with them?" The pause was not reassuring.

"Yes."

Mikaél's mouth went dry. "At the same time?" No answer. "Wolf-God. I...I don't know how to respond to that."

"I have to admit, there's a part of me that resents you came to that conclusion so easily."

"That's because I know you, Garrace. More than I want to. And that includes knowing you only think about one thing."

"How many times do I have to tell you that's not what I'm all about?"

Mikaél shrugged. "How about once more?"

Garrace grunted. "That's not what I'm about."

Mikaél massaged his eyes. "What possessed you to tell me this?"

"Because I don't know anyone else I can tell."

"Hm. How about Hayden?" Mikaél spat back.

"Ouch. And no. That flame has a mouth bigger than his hole."

"That. Is. Disgusting."

"Anyway, I called you because...because it's deeper than that."

"What? Hayden's hole?" Mikaél snickered, pleased with himself.

"You really are a heartless human being, you know that? No, Rixen and Ryan."

"Hm. Takes one to know one. Anyway, what?"

"We're not just sleeping with each other. We're wanting to start a relationship." An involuntary cough came from Mikaél's lungs. "That's telling."

"All three of you? Garrace, have you lost your mind?"

"I've considered it. But I like it. I really do."

Mikaél snorted. "Wow."

"What?" Garrace replied, offended.

"You really are a slime."

"Where did that come from?"

Mikaél sat up. "We all sat in Prowler, and you downplayed our breakup, and I let you do it. I let you escape without any responsibility for what you did to me. And now, here you are, proudly boasting to me that you're in a committed relationship. And the cherry on top is you're not just in a relationship with one guy but two."

"I realize this isn't the most conventional, not to mention widely accepted, but there must be something else I'm not seeing."

"You. Left. Me," replied Mikaél. "You broke my heart, Garrace. You made me feel special. You made me feel loved. You made me feel like I mattered. I realize I have my own self-confidence issues already. But you made me feel like I could accept myself because you accepted me. And yet, you threw it all away when we had our first big fight over not getting into my pants?"

"Look, I knew I made a mistake. I even tried to get you back!"

"You really think you deserved it?"

"You didn't even let me apologize! I had to play the telephone game just to get a message to you."

"Doesn't matter. You've got a pretty active sex life now."

"Oh, what? You're telling me you don't have one with your Fated Mate yet?"

"Not any of your damn business, but no. I don't."

"Really? Because Fates can't wait to fuck. Some don't even wait for the contract."

Mikaél had enough of this nonsense. "I have to go."

A plea set in Garrace's voice. "Mik—"

"I wish you nothing but luck for your...whatever it is you call it. But just leave me alone. I have someone who really does care for me. So, you don't need to worry about me. I'm not your concern anymore. And it gives me the strength to tell you 'Goodbye,' Garrace."

Garrace swallowed hard. "Then goodbye it is."

Hearing the dial tone was bittersweet. Mikaél fell back onto the bed, throwing the phone down on the floor in defeat.

CHAPTER 22:

A PERFECTION OF OPPORTUNITY

"Wolf-God, is it Tuesday yet?" Jake sighed, walking in uncharacteristically late to work.

"Hm. Just Tuesday?" Dustin looked up. "Man! You look like death."

"Makes sense. People are acting like someone died at home," Jake croaked.

"It's not any better at my house. I can barely get Mikaél to talk to me."

"Did you tell him yet?"

"No." Dustin tapped his pen. "I don't want to until we go over the test results with Paul."

"So, he was able to still use Mikaél's sample then?"

"He had the night shift take care of it. We'll get a look at it in an hour or so." Jake stared down the long lab, station after station. It was only a few weeks ago that he walked into the place an eager scientist excited to see all of his employees being productive, actively collaborating, and even having fun and making mischief from time to time. Now this place was beginning to resemble an aseptic office. Waiting with nerves for a doctor to come back with pending lab results was agonizing. *Can Wolf-God give me a break? Or is this the eternal punishment of bearing a Type 6 child?*

As it turned out, Wolf-God was willing to throw him a bone as Dr. Birowack entered the lab a short while later. Jake watched him make a steady stride to his office, readying his face the entire time for any sort of hint or acknowledgement he and Dustin had permission to follow. When the doctor reached his office and shut the door, the sound vibrated through his heart.

Dustin equally wore a look of disappointment on his face and turned to Jake for a response. Jake shrugged his shoulders at him, and they both sighed almost in unison. The door opened again.

"Doctors, come on in." Dr. Birowack spoke like a father inviting his children to the floor in front of his big chair, prepping to tell them a good life lesson.

Like trained dogs excited to see their master, both men stood and strode to his office. Jake had no problem shutting the door this time, even without Dr. Birowack's instruction to do so.

Dustin spoke, "Surprised it came back so fast." He cracked a smile, hoping to set a positive tone for the conversation.

Dr. Birowack nodded. "Considering the circumstances, I decided it was important to put a priority on the matter."

"I thank you for that," Dustin acknowledged. "Were we able to get the results we're looking for?"

Dr. Birowack reviewed the paperwork again and looked up at Dustin. "Yes." The answer was simple and yet troublesome. "With your son's DNA, as early as it may be, there is enough reason to believe our suspicions are valid. The news is dismal, I'm afraid."

Dustin held his head up toward the ceiling, trying to keep himself focused on the logistics rather than the emotions. "In this theory, are we to believe the conception of a Type 6 is an anomaly allocated only to Blood-Types 1 through 5?"

Jake answered. "It very much explains why there are so few. The conditions are so specific, it makes it nearly impossible. One can liken it to finding a red or white wolf in the wild."

"Not a bad comparison," Dr. Birowack confirmed. "However, it's not so much probability as it is viability of the pregnancy. And of course, with that comes severe implications for the carrier."

Dustin tensed. "How bad are we talking?"

Dr. Birowack exhaled. "By my calculations, though I'd never publish such statistics at this point, I find the viability of the pregnancy to be at 20%."

Dustin was stunned. "20%?!" Dr. Birowack nodded. "And what of the Omega?"

"If your son's results are indicative of all Omega Type 6, if there are any, the damage of anything going wrong during the pregnancy or birth are quite dire. I'd say that's 20% as well."

From the back of his throat, Dustin grunted in frustration. "How are you getting these numbers with basically no research? This is the most ridiculous thing yet!"

Jake tensed. "Dustin!"

"It's okay, Jake," Dr. Birowack replied and then turned his attention back towards Dustin. "It's not difficult to assess these things now that we have DNA. The basics are clear enough: negative traits and carriers result in consequences when they can't be suppressed. We've known for years different Blood-Types are predisposed with desirable probabilities and those which are undesirable. Type 6 at this point in time has already demonstrated complications. There's no reason to believe the viability is equal to High-Types or even better considering their scarcity."

Dustin tilted his head. "That's a pretty bold statement to make considering all our information is new."

"The research is new. Wolf-descendant existence is thousands of years old. Our dominance and advocacy for research on our existence is indeed in its infancy by comparison—no thanks to the primate-descendants."

A white flag showed on Jake's face. "I'll never fully understand the plight of a Type 6. I'll be reminded of that for the rest of my life until the day I die as I watch my boy battle everything: his safety, his acceptance, his life, and now, his legacy. Since evolution and civilization, we've been taught this hierarchy of Ranks and Blood-Types. I realize now it's come full circle. When you're on top, the only place for you to go is down. And the higher they are, the harder they'll fall."

The door handle turned, and a face peered into the office. "Dr. Erricson, you have a Matthew Whitmore calling for you. He says it's urgent."

"Thanks, Daniel. I'll take it out there." He excused himself from present company and went to the phone in near his station. "Dr. Erricson."

A sly voice spoke back to him. Even the first audible sound of Matthew's voice wrenched his stomach and burned his ears.

"You want to do what?"

"You can't be serious?"

"Well, I...."

"Fine. We'll be there."

Looking upon Whitmore's building once again felt like walking into a death trap in a horror movie. Roman couldn't believe his father forced him back into this nightmare. No one knew why Whitmore called another meeting with the lawyers. What they did know was they were told it was easier to show up here rather than the courtroom.

This time the secretary didn't have to acknowledge or announce the arrival of the Erricsons. Matthew stood there at the door of the conference room waiting for them.

"Jake, glad to see you again. And Roman."

A tepid handshake ensued between the Alpha parents, Roman shortly after.

Once inside, they observed Terrence's satisfied expression while his hands were folded and placed properly on the table.

Peyton sat next to his Veo, shoulders slouched. He watched Roman walk in and take the seat directly across from him.

Jake began with an agitated tone, "I assume this meeting has quite the critical information, considering you threatened us into attendance."

"Threaten?" Whitmore raspberried. "I did no such thing. I merely said we have one of two options in taking care of this meeting. Since you are here this afternoon, I can only imagine you found it advantageous to pick option number one."

"Which brings me to the obvious question you refuse to announce. I think we're done watching you enjoy this. So, what is it?"

"We are seeking financial support granted to us by law." Matthew spoke confidently.

Everyone who was not part of the Whitmore bloodline, including his own lawyer, traded looks like Matthew was trying to convince them all the sky was falling.

"That's funny." Jake laughed.

"We've been through this," Adrian added. "You have no recourse; if you did, it would have been taken care of at this point."

Roman contributed, hitting an uninterrupted focus on Matthew, "So what is it you think you've earned the right to get compensated for?"

"Roman!" Matthew gasped dramatically like a bad actor. "I think compensation is a deplorable interpretation of financial support when it comes to your heir."

A bomb dropped in the room. Roman's face turned white. He looked at Peyton who sat there motionless once again, refusing to acknowledge him. With him being a dead end, he had no choice but to entertain Matthew once more. "What? What are you saying?"

"Congratulations, Roman. You are going to be a father," Terrence announced.

"No," Roman huffed, "that's not possible."

"Ouch," Matthew tsked. "I must say, Roman, I'm disappointed in you. A father's response should be of joy, not panic. After all, this is what you wanted."

"Where are you getting that from?"

"You accepted the proposal for an evening with Peyton at the hotel. I have respected my son's privacy regarding the matter unless you would like to tell me now relations never took place?"

Roman flushed red. "No, I can't deny that..."

"Then I do believe this is a fine catalyst for a new contract."

"Contract?!" Jake exploded. "You never said anything about a contract!"

Terrence shook his head while condescending the resistance. "This is so disgusting. At least now I realize I can't blame you personally Roman for the dissolving the first contract. I see where this all stems from." His gaze locked to Adrian. "Your parents have clearly raised you to dodge responsibility and commitment."

"That is so out of line!" Adrian defended.

Matthew interjected, "Then why is everyone here shocked about this being the natural conclusion? It's shameful and an embarrassment to consider the other option."

"What other option?" Roman asked.

"As I said before: we can either go to a courtroom and have Roman file a motion he wants nothing to do with a contract to support a home with his mate and his pup in which a judge will certainly throw the book at him and grant significant financial support, or we can settle on a P&C Contract right here, out of the public eye, just as we have before, with a few minor changes."

"What changes?" Jake demanded.

"I don't think we need to get into the specific details, but let's just say I think it's appropriate to put the financial support back on the table: $2500 a month"

"You're talking crazy!"

"Hey, it's a lot cheaper than what it would be if Peyton is forced to parent alone. You're going to have to add another $1000 in that scenario, easily."

Roman tensed his fists. "How can this be happening? I remember getting reamed for leaving Peyton to take care of his upcoming heat on his own. What the fuck happened with that?"

Matthew gritted his teeth. "You will use proper language in front of my family, young man!"

"Oh, I suppose, Matthew, he does deserve to know how this came about." Terrence looked at Peyton. He refused to look back, even at his own Veo. "You are correct. We all thought, and had no reason to think otherwise, Peyton was getting ready to hit his heat. My doctor thoroughly explained the dangers of taking the suppressants so close to it, but I insisted we try everything to make the process even a tiny bit less painful for him. With emotional distress, which you did well to cause, a heat is even worse than it usually is." He cleared his throat. "So, the night before our last mediation, Peyton began showing symptoms of what the doctor told us to anticipate: headaches, nausea, vomiting, weak spells. The heat came two days later, and the nurse showed up to begin the painstaking task. When he medically punctured Peyton's womb, it began to bleed. Thus, a fertile implantation had already taken place."

"Luckily, to start, the instrument they use to infiltrate is quite small. Too much and the hemorrhage could have caused a miscarriage," Matthew finished.

Roman hit his hand against the table to emphasize every word. "This. Is. Not. Possible. I didn't penetrate him." All eyes looked back on him, including Peyton's, as if he'd let the clue out which confessed a murder he committed. Like watching a bouncing ball ricochet off the walls, Roman stared at an audience who didn't believe him. He ended on Peyton. "Peyton, tell them!"

Jake turned his chair. "Roman, can I see you outside for a moment?"

"Dad, I—"

"Now!" he commanded.

Roman grunted and stormed out of the conference room, pushing the doors open with all his might, allowing his father to walk seamlessly without touching them. "Dad, this is bullshit!" Roman whispered in the hallway, very aware of the secretary in the lobby.

Jake returned the same reduced volume, "Roman, listen to me. If there ever was a time to come clean about a situation in life, this would be it."

"I have nothing to confess." Roman paced a few steps back and forth, scratching the back of his head. "I can't believe I'm having this conversation."

"Think hard, son. Something clearly happened. Are you certain you're remembering it right? I know this whole ordeal from the beginning has been hard to absorb."

"Yeah, no shit."

"Then, is it so hard to believe perhaps you're not remembering the night accurately? I mean, let's face it, you both were drinking at the restaurant—that I remember. If you continued into the night, maybe the experience became fuzzy?"

"I know exactly what happened that night."

"Care to share?"

Roman's eyes shot wide. "Are you out of your mind?"

"I'm trying to help, Roman," Jake tried desperately.

"I am NOT telling you the details of my sex life!"

At some point, Roman's voice must have become louder. He and his father turned at the same time to observe the secretary carrying an expression of seeing a ghost. Acknowledging now the sensitive subject of the conversation, he politely excused himself from his large desk and went to the back room.

Jake slid both hands from his forehead to his chin and continued once he heard the backdoor close, "Peyton is pregnant." He let the words sink in. "I don't think Whitmore let his son find an Alpha in a matter of days to satisfy his heat. Therefore, there's little reason to assume this was done by someone else."

"Not true. Peyton could have rebelled and found someone in a one-night stand," Roman fumbled while quickly coming up with an alternative.

Jake narrowed in. "I highly doubt that."

"Okay. Maybe the nurse committed foul play and used himself versus the instruments to relieve Peyton's heat. It's not unheard of. Now that he's pregnant, they decide they want me in the picture to erase the public embarrassment and disgrace."

"That's...that's dark."

"I know, I know." Roman moaned. "And I'd hate to think that happened or have someone think I hoped that happened." Another possibility set in. "Okay, okay. How about this? What if Peyton has a donor or has elected to be a surrogate?"

Jake tilted his head side-to-side, pondering the thought. "Using a donor isn't that far-fetched. But a surrogate? Peyton would be in contract with the intended parents; there's no legal nor ethical way to bring you into the matter."

"I wouldn't put it past Whitmore to somehow slime into stripping their rights away or threatening some sort of blackmail or ultimatum to get what he wants. I mean, look at what he's doing here."

Jake nodded and breathed out heavily of his mouth. "Then, there's only one recourse we have left. We need a DNA test. It's early, but I think we can get it."

For a moment, both shared a moment of empathy. The feeling was unfamiliar and yet welcomed. With their bond, they agreed it was time to return to the lion's den. Both men reentered the room in a much calmer state than when they left. They sat down, all eyes waiting on them.

"So, Matthew. Roman and I chatted and as far he's concerned, there's doubt he's responsible for this. And that's even if you've verified the pregnancy."

"We have the verification right here." Matthew gestured to his lawyer who gave a sealed envelope to Jake.

After a few moments of looking it over, the paperwork did confirm the pregnancy. "Now all we have to do is get Roman to… which clinic?"

"It's on there," Matthew pointed out. "Lunar Medical Center."

Jake gave a stoic acknowledgement. "Are you willing to give us the courtesy of putting these negotiations on hold? Say 48 hours?"

"I'm certain my family will find that sufficient. After all, we're not going anywhere," Matthew reassured.

Terrence smiled. "We look forward to hearing from you soon."

Roman glared. "Yes. It would be a shame if something happened which forced you to wait longer, you prick."

A sneer came across Matthew's face. "I'm sorry. Do you have something to say?"

Roman mulled it over. "No."

Like a hawk, Matthew watched Roman's every move, waiting for anything to surface.

Jake stood first and everyone else at the table followed. Formal handshakes with neutral faces were exchanged.

Roman took one last look at Peyton before leaving the room. Even though he was very skeptical of the entire situation, he had no ill will to his former mate. *How could I? None of this is his fault in the least.* He offered his hand, and Peyton politely returned. Peyton's gentle side reappeared, and it was if, even for just a second, all the drama never happened, and they were still an item.

"You know, when I agreed to this study buddy group, I didn't know I was signing up for a regular night class." Siro grimaced as he made himself another drink. At this point in time, he really didn't care what he mixed with the cola as long as it burned a little on the way down.

"Come on. It's not that bad," Roman defended. He opted for the floor in the living room instead of the kitchen table where Siro and Nico had their own stuff sprawled out. The space soothed him more with the floor lamp and cushioned comforts rather than the bright dining room light and wooden chairs.

"I don't know how you're so upbeat about all of this," Siro commented as he single-handedly decided to make Roman a drink. "Do you know how many guys on your basketball team have come up to me wondering if you've died?"

Roman kept his focus on his notebook appearing unphased by the comment. "I've been dealing with other things, Siro."

"Yeah? No shit." Siro loomed over Roman with a tumbler extended out. Roman glanced and ignored the offer at first. But Siro wasn't going to take no for an answer. Finally, he saw Roman give in and chug the drink in seconds. "There ya go!" Siro grinned.

Roman coughed. "Damn, Siro! Was there anything mixed in this one?"

"Of course, there was! Just a splash." Siro rocked back on his heels, proud of himself. "The boys are worried you won't show up for pre-season training."

Roman snorted. "Considering I can do laps around most of them in my sleep, I'm not the one they should be worried about."

"You still thinking about going pro?" Nico piped up.

Roman tapped his pen onto his notebook. "I don't think so." He looked up in solemn face.

An uncomfortable silence followed. "It's been a long time since we've all hung out like this," Nico added, copying down terms in his notebook.

"Ha!" Siro laughed. "That's not a bad thing."

Nico eyes furrowed as he tried his best to ignore Siro's comment. The advantage of having these study sessions at his place was beginning to wear down with each negative remark Siro had over the past week.

"We should be at a club or down at the boardwalk scoping out our next lays." Neither Nico nor Roman answered. Siro's patience shrank. "Why are we doing these again?" Siro asked while lighting a cigarette. Although he had permission to smoke, he knew Nico hated every time he lit up.

"Because Roman needed help during his whole mating fiasco," Nico replied.

"And," Roman stressed, "because it doesn't hurt to improve test scores. The medical simulations test was a nail biter. And we've got another one coming up."

"How did that go, by the way?" Nico asked.

"I got an 89. I was so pissed." Roman growled.

Siro coughed. "You got an 89? I got a 69!"

Nico's eyes narrowed in skepticism. "Really? You legit got 69?"

"Yeah, seriously! Normally, I'd welcome that number any day of the week. But believe me, I'd rather not have that number tied to my test score. It doesn't satisfy in the same way." Siro smiled as he heard Roman snort in the other room.

Nico shook his head and sighed as he glanced at Roman. "That's not what I meant. I meant your mate. What's going on with that?"

"I was trying to figure out a way to talk to you both about it. I couldn't seem to figure out the way to bring it up. But since we're upon it, I need another drink...or six."

Siro jumped out of his chair like a springboard. He prepped a glass and stood behind the small island, waiting on Roman like a bartender.

Roman pointed to a shot glass and then to a favorite caramel-colored delight he found comfort in many times before. After slamming down one, he gestured for Siro to make another. He happily obliged. After the second, Siro held his breath, waiting for his next instruction. Roman tapped his hand twice near the shot glass and took one more down.

"Roman, are you okay?" Nico asked, his voice filled with concern.

Siro jumped. "Hey, how about we just set up a game? Nico, do you have plastic cups?"

Nico grunted. "Not the time, Siro."

Roman gave Siro a sincere look. "I just want to drink and vent. That's all I can handle right now." There wasn't any compromise to be had.

"Oh. Okay." Siro made himself and Nico a drink. Both sat next to each other as they stared at Roman with undivided attention.

Roman tapped his foot and fingered the rim of the glass in his hand. "You guys remember when I talked about the night I was with Peyton at the hotel?"

"You mean Whitmore's son?" Siro asked.

"Yes," Roman confirmed.

"Sounded like a snooze-fest to me."

Nico cracked, "It didn't sound that bad. I thought it was kind of hot actually." He bit his lip.

"Boy, you have low standards." Siro laughed at Nico.

"Guys, come on!" Roman growled with frustration. Considering his previous tone, it was quite the contrast and stood the other two at attention.

"Sorry. Just trying to make a joke," Siro defended.

Roman tensed. "I can't believe I'm going there." The words were meant for him more than his friends. "Okay, so I told you guys I never...penetrated him, right?"

Nico and Siro looked at each other as if it was the first time they were hearing the sex talk.

Luckily, Nico was the only one who chose to say anything in return. "Um...yeah." His eyes went back to Siro, trying to figure out where this was going.

Roman continued, "It's still true. Well, kind of. I..." he grunted, "why is this so hard?"

"It needs to be in order to do it." It rolled off Siro's tongue. So did Nico's slap to the back of his head. "Seriously, punk!" he spat back.

"Damn it, Siro! Peyton's pregnant!" Roman roared.

Both Nico and Siro stopped dead in their tracks like they were caught shoplifting.

"Are you serious?" Nico began. Roman confirmed it, laying with head on his fist. "Are you sure? How?"

"We found out earlier today. We showed up at Peyton's Sur's office, and Matthew just dropped it on me and my parents. You could tell by the look in his face, he was enjoying every second of it." Roman's eyes burned with fire as he dared to envision the face Matthew Whitmore carried throughout the meeting. "He had his paperwork ready, and now all I'm doing is waiting for a phone call I'm expecting to get at any minute now."

"What phone call?" Nico asked, looking again at Siro to see how he was taking the news. Both looked more like parents than friends at this point.

"The phone to prove whether or not I'm the father. I'm scared shitless right now." His hands began shaking.

Siro connected the dots. "So, this is why you're discussing the whole 'penetration' thing? If you didn't do it, then there's no need to worry about it. So, what's the problem?"

Roman took a deep breath. "This is the part that's difficult. If you can just bear with me, this would be a great time to take me seriously and not joke. I couldn't even tell my father this." Roman waited until he felt he had enough acknowledgement from both. "I didn't penetrate him with my dick, but when I came, I used my cum as lube and fingered him to orgasm."

Siro choked. "Sorry," he croaked, "and now you're thinking that got him pregnant?" Roman nodded. "That's insane!"

"You see, that's what I think." Roman took a seat, convinced he hit a logical understanding. "I mean, even on the outside chance it is a thing, Peyton wasn't in heat. He can't get pregnant."

Nico lifted his finger. "Uh, that's not true. Just because an Omega's not in full heat doesn't mean he becomes his own birth control. He can still get pregnant."

Siro pushed his hand into Nico's arm with a grimace. "You're not helping, Dr. Hallen."

"Look, I'm just giving him the facts since both of you seem to have forgotten about the sex talk we had in school at the age of 12. All you need is sperm and a fertile candidate. There were no discussions specifically on the methods to get it there. So, yes, if that's how it happened with Peyton, it is possible."

"So, then bigger question is, why are you so unsure about it all?" Siro knocked back the rest of his drink. It gave Roman the permission he needed to do the same.

"I just have this gut feeling, guys. Something is not right about this. The last time I saw Peyton, he was on the verge of a heat and on suppressants. He looked miserable as fuck, but he didn't give off that... you know... that essence of being pregnant."

"You mean the scent change?" Nico clarified.

"Yeah, his scent. It was the same today. No change. At least, there wasn't to me." He paused and pondered. "Maybe it was there, and I just didn't want it to be."

The room was quiet for a few moments. For once, Siro didn't have another smart remark to end the conversation with.

"Have you talked to Mikaél yet?" Nico wondered.

"Wolf-God, no!" Roman pushed his chair back and walked over to the carpeted living room. A small bay window looked out over the street. The sidewalks were empty, and the streetlights revealed no movements nor item out of place. The view of serenity was very different than the storm brewing inside the house. "I was actually supposed to meet him tonight. But after all this went down, I couldn't bear to even look at him, not before knowing how this was going to end."

"When you said you thought something wasn't right, you think this was a set-up?" Siro asked, tapping his fingers on the table as his gears turned.

"I have to say, your conspiracy theories on Peyton's father definitely have—" A vibration in Roman's pocket stopped his words instantly. He rushed to his phone like it was his heart monitor. There on the screen was a call waiting from his Sur. He pressed the answer button and stood up and faced back out to the stillness outside. He could feel both Siro and Nico staring their laser eyes against his back. "Did we get the results back?" A pause. "And?" A longer pause. Nico swore he could hear someone talking to Roman, but Roman wasn't answering. "Okay."

The phone slid down Roman's hand and into the chair. A person could hear a pin drop in the quiet. After what seemed like forever, Nico spoke up. "So, who was that?"

"That was my dad. The clinic's results came in." Roman heaved himself forward and began to breathe harder. "It's mine. He's pregnant, and it's mine." His first thought went to Mikaél when he broke down after he Fated him. Similarly, now, he began to break down and become frantic. "Wolf-God, what is happening to me?"

Nico looked at Siro with heavy eyes. Neither of them knew what to say.

Roman stood up and began to talk. The alcohol's soothing relief stopped in its tracks, but its side effects became more apparent as it was difficult to walk in a straight line. A stinging sensation came over his eyes as he struggled to speak. "You know...I wished for this. My entire life, I always wished I'd find a Fate and become a father, and now, it happened." Somewhere in his teary eyes, he was able to sneak out a smile in the cruelness of his own joke. "And I've never been so miserable in my entire life. I can't do this, guys."

Roman's introduction to vocal sorrows were cut short when Siro stood up. "You won't have to."

Roman turned around to Siro, completely confused. "What do you mean?" Nico gave the same expression.

"You said it yourself, Roman. Whitmore is a fiend; he's behind this."

"I never said that, Siro. I said—"

"I know what you meant and so do you," Siro huffed. "I told you this would happen."

"That what would happen?" Roman played off.

"You denied Whitmore's son his contract. I'm surprised he didn't just blow your head off, especially when he found out it was because Mikaél was in the picture. He's good. But damn, I didn't know he was that good."

Nico stepped in. "What do you mean?"

"Whitmore wanted Roman to pay for the insult. He orchestrated some scheme to get Roman back. Let me guess, he gave you some sort of penalty in the contract this time around?" Roman looked down, refusing to acknowledge the comment. "Yeah, that's what I thought."

"That's not what's going on," Roman rebuked.

"Oh, that's exactly what's going on!"

Roman's face snarled as he pointed his finger. "You know, there are a lot of annoying things about you Siro, but this has to be the most unbearable of them all."

Unable to comprehend Roman's claim, Siro held his arms out in confusion. "What the fuck are you talking about?"

"You assume the worst in everybody. You're so goddamn paranoid, and no one has ever called you out on your bullshit, so you think you're right all the time."

Siro tensed and walked toward Roman. "Hey! Just because you don't like what I have to say doesn't mean it's wrong. And while you stand there tucking your tail between your legs, Whitmore is sitting somewhere getting a blowjob and sipping champagne at your expense."

"You are such a childish prick sometimes. Wolf-God!" Roman shook his head. "I'm sorry Whitmore got the best of your family, but that's not what this is. If the pup is mine, this is my fault."

"Wow, you are just playing right into their hands, Roman. This is exactly what they want you think. All those people are the same. If they have position, entitlement, and power, they want the rest of us to just roll over and not have us question anything they do. And here's Roman, Wolf-God's gift to mankind, Type 6 and all, being the poster child for a pushover all because Whitmore's got you by the balls." Siro shook his head. "I can only think of what your pretty boy Fate would think of you now."

Roman's anger raced through veins and into his biceps. Leaping forward, he grabbed Siro's leather jacket, turned him around, and threw him into the armchair. "You shut your mouth, or I'll shut it for you! Leave him out of this!"

Siro's eyes were shocked, but only for a second. Then they narrowed with disgust. He gripped the arms of the chair and stood up, Alpha-to-Alpha. "Do you remember what primate-descendants used to call our kind? That stupid word 'Gay,' but that was the nice way of saying it? They used 'Faggot' when they wanted people like us to know we were less than them. They hated us, beat us, killed us, took our rights away just for being us. Then, their fragile world fell apart when the disease began wiping them out, and then we wolf-descendants came out of shadows. Suddenly, we were gods because we were the only ones surviving. They worshipped us because they finally found out that we were useful, then they adored us. But for thousands of years, my ancestors, our ancestors, were tucked away in those shadows waiting to be slaughtered. I didn't get put in this lifetime with my Type 5 Alpha Status to have anyone tell me how to live. And when I see ASSHOLES like Whitmore walk around telling my family we're an obstruction to progress and that he'll only play nice if we hand over everything we have, then you better believe I'm going to raise hell and fight to the end. And the fact that I see you groveling at his feet makes me sick! You're pushing us back years, Roman, exposing your underbelly to a fiend like Whitmore who is fighting to make sure we repeat history by manipulating everyone else into thinking they're inferior just because he flaunts his family's purity bloodline."

Roman stood there in disbelief. "You have serious problems you need to get help for." He stepped away for a moment but came back again harder. "I hate the situation I'm in more than anything, but I'm not going to let your endless anger send me on some assassination mission just because you have issues!"

Siro nodded. "I guess I know where I stand with you then. First one to tap out when it gets tough." Siro flapped his jacket and made his way to the staircase to begin his exit out of Nico's house. "You know, I'd have done anything for you, Roman. I consider you the brother I never had. If anyone hurt you, I'd be the first one there to have your back."

"Thanks, but I don't need you to fight my battles for me. You need to figure out how you're going to make peace with yourself, Siro."

"Yeah, we'll see about that." Siro headed down the stairs and opened the door.

Nico stood up, unable to see Siro from the main floor back in the dining room. "Where are you going?" No reply came, just a slam of the door. Through the windows, both heard Siro's tires scream out of the driveway and off into the night. "What the fuck was that?"

"I don't know," Roman whined as he found a resting place on the nearby couch. With his eyes closed, he could hear Nico back in the kitchen clanking glasses. Moments later, he returned with a shot each. Roman didn't speak any hesitation, but there was a pause before he took the drink and swallowed it down just like the others. "Thanks."

"So," Nico began, "what are you doing to do?"

"I don't know." Roman reflected on the whole situation. As much as he didn't want to admit it, Siro did have some good points. "I always wanted to be a father but...this was the last way I wanted it to happen."

"What do you think about Siro's claim on the whole Whitmore domination thing?"

"Siro's got a chip on his shoulder. And I'm not so sure that I don't too. But Siro is definitely a crusader. He wasn't the first; he won't be the last." Roman balanced his elbows on his knees and held his head in his hands while his eyes gently closed. The room was getting hazy. In a fleeting thought, he worried about Siro driving down the road in a drunken rage. Then, he pondered what his own attempt to drive home would be. But in those seconds came a warm hand on his back stroking up and down. "Hmph." Roman smiled. "Thanks."

"Come on now. Siro isn't the only friend who has your back, you know."

Roman nodded. "Yeah, you're right. I'm sorry, but sometimes I forget you're always there."

"Apology accepted," Nico replied. "I mean, let's face it: anyone constantly standing one step behind Siro all the time is easily forgettable."

"You got a point there. But still, I'm glad I have you too."

Nico stared into Roman's glassy eyes and wavering expression. "That means a lot to me."

The hand he held steady on Roman's back slowly crept up to his neck. A slight tickle grew into a pressured massage. He saw Roman's expression fade to a serious, steady stare. Nico slowed his grip ever so slightly but still kept his pattern deliberate. Soon, neither of them was blinking anymore. After licking his own lips, he leaned in until his lips were all but touching Roman's. No signals came, for or against. Finally, Nico gathered the final drops of his courage and kissed him ever so gently.

What came over Roman was the realization Nico represented a clean slate, untarnished from everything going on around him. Any benefits or consequences in the moment eluded him. Soon, like a puppeteer controlling him, he found himself returning the technique complete with the slight brush of his mouth and hand on the back of Nico's neck.

It was the only green light Nico needed. He pressed against Roman in the way he needed to express physically how he really felt about him. The following exchanges were breathy and deep. To his elation, Roman moved from his lips, to his cheek, to his ear, and then to his neck. A gasp escaped his throat in pleasure. "Wolf-God, I've wanted this for so long."

Clouds rolled into the minds of both men as movements and decisions continued. The mist surrounded them as the silver moon in the sky faded to black.

"People don't typically buy those prescriptions back-to-back. Is everything okay, Mr. Whitmore?" The pharmacist counted and reviewed several different prescriptions before putting them in a large bag.

"Please, Derrick, call me Terrence. I've only been coming here for 15 years," he insisted.

"Yes, sir. Terrence."

"You're right, though. Believe it or not, we've had a one-eighty turn of fortune. Oh, and I almost forgot." Terrence set a new bottle on the counter.

"Hmm. Prenatal? Am I to assume...?" Derrick smiled.

"Oh please, did you really need the vitamins to know that?"

Derrick laughed. "No, the other prescriptions were pretty obvious. But I have to get my kicks in somehow. Congratulations to your family!"

An unnerved chuckle slipped out of Terrence's mouth. "Thank you."

"Didn't recognize the doctor who called. A new one?" Derrick asked.

"Mhm," was all Terrence replied.

"I think that's everything. Charge to the usual account?"

"Yes, please. Thank you, Derrick."

"Have a good night! It's chilly out there."

The bright lights of the supermarket faded as Terrence stepped onto the cold, damp asphalt of the parking lot. A steady breath reflected in the streetlight from a shape hidden in the shadows underneath it. Ignoring the man completely, Terrence removed his keys from his pocket and began to unlock the door. After setting the shopping bag in the backseat, he heard quickened feet come up from behind him. Before getting a good look at who approached, Terrence felt a harsh pain accompanied by a muffled thud as the front of his head slammed against the car frame. Another sound of pain came after the back of his head hit squarely on the unforgiving pavement. A roar and a cough came from Terrence's diaphragm as the singular streetlamp's light became many in his eyes.

"This is the end of you!" a voice roared out.

Terrence attempted to speak, but lightning bolts screamed from his head as he felt his body being lifted from his hair being pulled from a tight fist. Another hard thud filled his ears as his head once again hit the rock-hard surface. This time the pain invoked a higher pitched cry. As he attempted to get his bearings and crawl to the parking lot, searching for any signs of help, he heard the voice again.

"Oh, no you don't." Once again, Terrence felt his head being pulled up from his hair. Up against his now red-hot ears, the voice whispered, "I should have done this a long time ago."

Now on his stomach, Terrence gave all his energy to stand on wobbly legs. The storefront zig-zagged in his vision but even so, he convinced himself if he could make a few steps, somewhere someone would see him.

As much as Terrence wanted to see his attacker, his fear didn't risk looking back. A blow to his back from a heavy shoe knocked the wind out of him. All noises and all oxygen ceased as he could focus on nothing but the pain. Some involuntary movement forced him onto his back again.

At this point, Terrence begged to see his attacker. Should he survive this nightmare, he needed to know what animal on this earth could do such a thing. But the monster evaded his vision. He sensed the once bright streetlamp shining down must have burnt out; he was certain of it. He couldn't explain it in any other way. But the concentration was short lived as he felt blows to his sides from the impossibly strong foot demanding his insides be torn apart. Eventually, closing his eyes became effortless, and the pain didn't hurt anymore.

CHAPTER 23:

A Plea for Understanding

Waking up to a bright light searing at him was not what Roman had in mind as a good start. It was even worse to know it wasn't daylight shining in; it was a bathroom light cutting into the dark, blackened bedroom.

As he turned his head, his body followed in a sluggish way. Attempting to find his nightstand with his eyes closed failed miserably, and he hit the floor. Feeling the carpet catch his fall was a blessing and a curse. He was thankful for the soft landing, but the feeling of dread came over him as the texture and smell of the carpet was not that of his own room. His mind cleared once he realized the bathroom was not in his own home. The sound of an on-going shower ceased, and he heard its glass door slide open.

For a moment, he expected this all to be a dream. All he had to do was turn on a light, and all of it would disappear. But before he got the chance to, a clicking sound led to a wave of rays shining down from the bedroom ceiling. It felt like the rising sun to a were-wolf or a vampire. As his eyes adjusted, he saw a figure of man. His silhouette was smooth, lightly muscled, and angelic. Hopes his own Fated Mate was at the doorframe were dashed quickly. Soon, he saw Nico's soft face with beads of water gliding down his five-o'clock shadow and falling off the tips of his shaggy hair. His eyes sparkled back at him, but not as a friend. This was more.

Nico gasped. "Sorry. Didn't mean to wake you." The towel in Nico's hand sat perfectly below his belly button. All the right lines of definition one could ask for were clearly visible from his waist, hips, and lower stomach.

For Roman, it wasn't seeing Nico's naked body which hurt the most, it was sensing the pheromones falling off his newly showered body. The soap scents and perfumes from the shower didn't cover enough. What was coming off of Nico was desire. "Nico... what were... what..?"

"You didn't expect me to sleep in all that sweat, did you?" Nico giggled, proud of himself as he stared down Roman's taut body.

Looking down, Roman realized his natural state. A wince and grunt led him back to the bed, searching for his boxers.

"They're over there," Nico pointed out.

"What time is it?" Roman winced.

"It's not quite midnight yet."

"Listen, Nico." Roman grabbed his boxers and slipped them on. "I'm not exactly certain what happened. I mean... what did happen?" He braced himself for the answer.

Nico paused as the tone began to set in. "I wouldn't give the details to my grandfather, I'll say that. Not that I have to worry about that. He's in his grave."

Roman grunted. "Mine is too, but you know who isn't? Mikaél." Roman found his pants and fitted them on. "Fuck! What is wrong with me?"

Nico's shoulders fell. The writing was on the wall. He shook his head and went back in the bathroom. He returned shortly after with a shirt and high-cut bikini underwear. Whatever pheromone expression he was showing, the change now was distinct.

"Nico, I'm sorry. I didn't mean for this to happen. This was a mistake." With lips curled and side-eye setting in, Nico gave a sarcastic hum in return. "Please say something," Roman pleaded.

"Why? You seem to be doing all right. A greeting card company should hire you for your sheer poetry in apologies."

Roman sighed. "Okay, I deserve that. But where did you really expect this to go?"

"I guess it was too much to ask for it to go anywhere but here. Selfish of me."

Roman searched for his memories of what transpired mere hours before. As much as he tried, he came up blank. The only thing he remembered was Nico's last words, and now they plastered every image in his mind. "Did you mean what you said?"

"What?" Nico crossed his arms and stared at the floor.

"Have you really been holding feelings in for me all this time?" Why the question needed to be asked, he didn't know. The answer at this point wasn't going to help anything.

Likewise, Nico thought the same. Confessing such feelings to someone who already said it was over before it began was nothing more than having egg on your face—twice in fact. "You've been right there in front of me for years, and yet you just stared right through me like glass. How can you have been friends with me for so long and completely not have read any of the signs?"

"I guess... I don't know." It became apparent Roman was due for reflections on more than one topic. *Could I have connected the dots? Maybe.* "All I know is, right now, I desperately need a friend. My life is coming apart at the seams. I don't know how to stop this. Please, I beg of you, don't be the next thing which disappears." Nico looked up but didn't answer him. "I don't deserve it. But maybe you'll consider it?"

"Are you going to answer that?" Nico said in a completely different tone.

"Huh?" Roman listened. He keened in on a continuous vibration coming from the floor. There, radiating on the carpet, was his phone. In missing the call, he realized he had several calls, not just from his parents, from Peyton and Mikaél too. He only had seconds to glance at partial text messages coming through as notifications when another call from his Sur came in.

"Hello?" Roman began.

"For Wolf-God's sake, Roman!" Jake yelled into the phone.

"What? What's going on?"

"Your Veo and I have been trying to get ahold of you for over an hour!"

"Sorry. I," he paused, "fell asleep at Nico's." He looked up at Nico who rolled his eyes and returned to the bathroom.

"So, you've been at Nico's this entire time?" Jake asked, a bit hopeful.

"Uh, yeah?" A confused expression fell over Roman.

"Is he willing to confirm that?"

"Dad, what the hell is going on?"

Nico returned with flannel pants on. His judgement flipped to concern as the call appeared serious and a bit ominous.

Roman leapt from the bed after hearing his father's response. "Are you serious?!"

Nico's eyes flared. "What's wrong?"

"Okay! Okay! I'm going to go there," he answered into the phone.

"No, Roman, you need to come home!" Jake insisted.

"I'll call you later."

"Roman, NO!" Jake pleaded. His demands fell upon a dial tone.

Roman looked up. "Nico, I have to leave."

"Where? What's wrong?"

"The hospital." Roman's face was grim.

"Why? What happened?"

"I'll explain later. I'm sorry. I gotta go."

If there was one thing Roman's self-pitied drink sessions helped with, it was the fact his tolerance of alcohol built up in his system for ten years. Regardless, nothing sobered a person up more than hearing about a brutality on someone they knew. Death was the only rivalry. And from the brief exchange he had with his father, it was a dark possibility.

Arriving at the bright red cross of Mountain Ridge Hospital felt more like walking up the steps of the Underworld. Being at a hospital couldn't have felt worse than this. Not knowing what he was walking into was scarier than Hell itself. But his body didn't burn as he stepped into the lobby.

He walked up to the service desk where a young nurse sat at his station. "Excuse me, I'm looking for—" A glimpse of a familiar face hit him from the long hallway behind the entry. "Peyton!" Ignoring the orderly completely, he ran up to his former mate and hugged him.

Peyton's cold expression matched the cold temperature of his body. No embrace was returned. Instead, his eyes widened out of fear upon releasing the connection. They were puffy and exhausted.

Peyton's words were strained. "Are you insane, Roman? Do you have a death wish?"

Roman's heart sank at his callous greeting. "What? Why would you say that?"

"If my father saw you here, he wouldn't hesitate to kill you on sight. And for Wolf-God's sake, Roman, I'm not exaggerating right now."

Roman's head snapped back. The words were unbelievable. "Peyton, you can't seriously think I did this?"

"It doesn't matter what I think. My Sur thinks you threatened my Veo during the last contract negotiations."

"How?" Roman replied, flabbergasted.

"I guess you said some comment to my Veo on how it would be nice if we couldn't get the contract reinstated because of something happening to him."

"Oh, hell! You can't be serious?" Roman was beside himself. Peyton stood there and shrugged. Roman saw Peyton's eyes dart to an empty waiting room to his left. Once again, silence. "You have to believe me. I could never do this. I wouldn't! You know me better than that!"

"Do I?" Peyton's words were louder, sharper.

"How can you say that?" The words hurt Roman like a gun to the forehead.

"All I know is, for the past month, you have been the most unpredictable and inconsiderate person I have ever known in my life!"

"Peyton, please!"

"Knowing you has been nothing but a sickness. It's permeated everything in my life! You act like a child in an adult's body. You care nothing about the consequences of your actions. I know I'm a bit inept myself, but you take it to a whole new level."

"What do you mean?" Roman's expression showed his vexation.

"I could have handled your apathy, and your hesitation, and your discontent, and even your betrayal, but my Veo is in that room down on the hall on life support barely holding on." Peyton's bottom lip quivered. "How in the world do you expect me to move past this?"

A whirlwind of emotion showed in Roman's eyes. "Listen to me!" He grabbed Peyton's shoulders and held him still. Observing Peyton's expression showed him perhaps it wasn't the best move. But Peyton froze and didn't panic. "I. Didn't. Do. This." An exhale of exhaustion came from Peyton, but no comfort showed. "Look at me." Peyton refused. "Look at me!" On the final try, Peyton's eyes smoothly glided to his. "You are one of the strongest, most powerful Omegas I have ever met in my life. And right now, I need you to use every Wolf-God given power you have to use on me and find the truth. Stare into me and tell me what you already know. I know you do. I didn't do this. Please."

With his breath held, Peyton reached deep inside Roman and took in every slight change in his eyes, facial expression, presence, and finally, his pheromone pallet. Tears ran first, followed by involuntary guttural whimpers. Needing support physically, mentally, and emotionally, he collapsed into Roman's arms and let every piece of fear and anger he harbored since his father claimed it was Roman who was responsible for the heinous act dissolved in thin air.

He didn't express much vocal relief, but Roman squeezed Peyton as if his life depended on it. And in an essence, it did. Getting Peyton on his side was a much-needed relief, but he was fully aware it wasn't his wrath he had to fear most. But he was going to enjoy this moment now for as long as he could.

"Thank you," Roman breathed. It came out in desperation. Time stopped. There was a gentle sway in their bodies as they clung to one another. Two broken hearts comforted each other in this disgusting hand of Fate. Somewhere in his imagination, there was a melodic lullaby hushing the emotional cries. As a gesture of security, he kissed Peyton on the forehead and felt his body tense and relax at the gesture.

There wasn't ever going to be a good time to part ways, but Roman needed to know the gravity of what was upon him. Slowly drifting, he made a cautious attempt. "Can I see him?" The answer didn't come right away, but Peyton eventually agreed.

Peyton grabbed Roman's hand and led him down the quiet corridor. It was stealthy and slow. "My dad has security around somewhere. He's protecting my Veo's every breath. I'm surprised he doesn't have your face on a 'Wanted' poster around here." His steps stopped and turned to face Roman. "Wait here," he whispered.

As Peyton disappeared around the corner, Roman observed men in green scrubs, black scrubs, and white coats bustling around the circular floor. No one paid him any attention. Without knowing how much paranoia he should have been carrying, he wasn't sure if it was a good thing or not. Either Matthew hadn't conferenced with every staff member, and they didn't recognize him, or he was just lucky no one zeroed in on him like a deer in the wilderness.

Suddenly, an officer exited a room, out of Roman's line of sight. Remembering Peyton's warning, his heart bounced at the chances of being seen. But the officer never turned in his direction. Instead, he walked farther in the opposite direction down another hallway to a secure double door exit. Seconds later, Peyton came around again and gestured Roman to follow.

"Okay. I think we're good for the time being. I sent him on an errand to the rear parking lot. I said I had a gut feeling."

Roman tilted his head. "What? That I was stalking the place?" They came upon a closed door, no doubt Terrence's room.

"Like you said, I have Omega instincts. No one is going to dispute me right now. I guess that's one perk of being a Whitmore."

"Where is your Sur?" Roman peered around the room, swallowing hard.

"He went home to gather some things. I offered to go in his stead, but he insisted I stay." Peyton's eyes scoped once more, then returned to Roman with a somber look. "You ready?"

Silently, Roman nodded, and they both entered. Roman's body felt weak at the sight before him; a slight gasp escaped. Peyton looked away upon hearing it. A soft light revealed a mannequin wrapped in bandages from the head all the way to the torso. Blood stains soaked through various white wraps around the body. A breathing apparatus was attached to the center of what was once a face—not that one was particularly visible. The sounds of machines working their hardest filled the room.

Seeing Peyton's despair again drew Roman near him to embrace him once more. "I'm so sorry."

The hug was brief this time. Coming out of it, Peyton began, "Doctors said they're not sure what's going to happen. The next 24 hours are critical; they just want him stable during that time. After that, they hope to maybe get a read on what exactly they're dealing with as far as head trauma." He began to choke up again. "But he has a slight skull fracture, broken ribs, and some internal bleeding." He couldn't say anything more.

"Wolf-God, Peyton, what happened?"

"As far as authorities know, he was jumped in a parking lot of a pharmacy while running some late-night errands. They don't know exactly how long he'd been laying there, but any longer and they said it would have been too late."

"No one saw this? No one knows who did it?" The concern was laced with a growing anger.

"The cameras apparently don't go back that far in the parking lot. They have the time he walked out of the store, but an ambulance didn't show up until about 20-30 minutes later. Someone found him on the ground up against the car, so they assumed it was hard for anyone else to see him lying there." Staring at his father never got easier. Every time was the first time. A cry escaped his lips, "This is all my fault!"

Roman looked down at him. "What? No. No, how can you say that?"

"He was getting my medication for the pregnancy. If I had just... if we hadn't... if you hadn't... No. Sorry. I didn't mean that," Peyton corrected.

Roman hung his head. "I know. It's okay. This whole situation is fucked up. But don't you ever blame yourself."

Another stare at his father's lifeless body made Peyton grit his teeth. "Damn it, Roman! What kind of savage does this?"

"I don't know. There are some sick people out there in the world."

"Yeah, no kidding. I suppose some people think this is karma." Peyton rolled his eyes.

"Karma?"

Peyton carried on, "We're not exactly everyone's favorite family, Roman. You may not have known me before, but everyone knows my parents. On the highest executive floors of every business in town, my Sur is the Wolf-God of Prosperity, and my Veo is his loyal mate attached to his arm. But on the street level where the real people are, we are feral dogs ripping apart the fabric of this city."

"That's not true."

"Oh, yes, it is. I'm not naïve, and I'm not stupid. Give me a little credit." He paused. "With that sentiment, I'm just going to have live with the fact this could have been anybody. They're never going to find out who did this. I guess the only comfort I have in this is whatever fiend did this is going to have to live with this forever. One day, this is going to haunt them in some way for the rest of their life, and they're going to pray to the Great Gray Wolf in the sky and beg for death. Hm. Maybe I'll get lucky, and they won't ever be able to make peace with that."

Roman's stomach dropped. "Wait. What did you just say?"

"Oh, don't listen to me. I'm just rambling."

Like a puzzle in a murder mystery, it all came together at once. An intensity built up like a volcano. Without a word, he turned, and headed to the door, never looking back.

"Roman?" Peyton's attempt was futile. "Roman!"

As if he was an underground racecar driver, Roman whipped past every stoplight, stop sign, and turn he could. He only had one mission in his mind: locate who he knew was responsible. He had no doubt. It was record time arriving at the lavish farmhouse. It couldn't have been more convenient to find Siro on the wraparound porch, sitting on a wooden chair drinking straight out of a paper bag. A part of Roman wanted to bypass the driveway and stop right over Siro's body. He reconsidered, knowing he was going to get his satisfaction one way or another.

The glaring headlights forced Siro to turn his head away and block the burn. Siro heard the stomps of feet on the ground coming toward him and then on the porch itself. He could smell Roman even before he made it to him. "Hmm. Not a social call, I take it?"

A hard hand swiped the comment right off his face. He dropped the open bottle to the porch as piercing pain radiated off his skin. "Fuck, Roman! What the hell?!" He grabbed his nose and felt the blood begin to gush out. Without any time to react, Siro's whole body rose and turned as Roman grabbed him by the jacket.

With a loud roar from Roman, Siro's body was thrown a substantial distance into the air off the porch and onto the ground below. Siro coughed and groaned like an adolescent in a cycling accident.

In any other situation, Roman knew Siro was a worthy opponent. Knowing Roman possessed a natural strength always had Siro doing what he could to try and compete with him. But tonight, Siro had no bite, and no bark. He was a pathetic drunken worm wiggling in the grass.

Siro lifted his head, spit out blood, and groaned in pain. "Are you trying to kill me?!"

"I can make peace with that. Get my drift?" Roman walked down the stairs, not caring if any family member in the home noticed his savage rage.

"Wha...what are you talking about?" He used his shaky arms to sit up. Roman's body was a demonic presence standing over him with fists dangling. Like a bullet, another punch slammed down into his face. "Ahh!" he screamed.

"Did you think it was funny? Did you think I gave you some sort of invitation?"

"I...I didn't mean to," Siro confessed. "I went there just to talk to him."

Roman balled up Siro's shirt and lifted him with one arm, conjuring strength he didn't know he had. The wolf inside was out. "Liar!"

Siro could barely feel his feet touch the ground. "No, I'm telling the truth. Please!"

Roman dropped him. His body hit with a thud. Siro heaved on the ground, thankful Roman chose not to charge him again. "I wanted to let him know I was done with their family's shit. Ugh!" His stomach felt rotten. "When I heard Matthew made your life miserable too, I wanted to try and get them off your back. I wanted to help you out!"

"YOU MADE IT WORSE!" He charged forward, a tick away from slugging Siro again. "Peyton's Sur wants my head because he thinks I did this!"

"There's no way they're going to be able to prove that. It's a taste of their own medicine." Siro found the courage to stand up. "Besides, he'll get through it. A few painkillers and an ice pack—he'll live." Quicker than Siro could register, Roman hooked his leg behind Siro and shoved him back. Once again, he became one with the earth. "Damn it, stop!"

"You idiot, you nearly killed him!" Roman shook his head. "You honestly have no idea what you did, do you?"

"Look. I'll say it again. I didn't go there with the intention to rough him up."

"Yeah, and?" Roman's patience wore thin again.

"Something came over me. When I saw him, I wanted him to feel pain. After tonight, I couldn't take it anymore. Their voices, their faces, they're everywhere: T.V., radio, social media. It's sickening. I figured one night of pain was mercy compared to the years I've had to deal with watching that family walk over my family as if they were kings."

"Mercy? That's what you thought that was? You're a coward!"

"A coward? How?" Siro's vision blurred. He wanted to throw up.

"You went after Terrence, you asshole!"

"So?" Siro barked.

"He's an Omega, Siro. You knew better. The odds were against him. You went after him because it was easy. You snuck up on him, ambushed him, and didn't even give him a fair fight." Gravel from the driveway rocked Roman's feet. As a final touch to the onslaught, he kicked a few in Siro's direction.

Siro tried again to stand, hoping over to overcome the nausea. "Would it help—"

Roman's Alpha Wolf did not like the move. "Stay down!"

Returning to the ground, Siro tried again. "Would it help you to know I tried getting to Matthew? He locks himself up in that fortress of his."

Roman paused. "You waited for him?"

"I almost left the place. Right before I considered giving up, I saw Terrence drive out. I followed him to the store."

"Unbelievable." Roman had enough of Siro's excuses. He turned and headed back to his car which was still running.

Seeing Roman walk off gave him the confidence to return to a firm stand. "So, what are you going to do now? Turn me in?" he yelled.

Roman reached his car door and opened. He turned around. "Why don't you do me a favor and turn yourself in, so I don't have to?"

Slamming the car door shut, he checked his phone. Several messages, including voicemails, were listed all over. Feeling brave, he began to listen to each one as his voicemail inbox was full.

Starting in order were a couple of concerned, then angry phone calls from his Sur trying to get ahold of him. No doubt to tell him what happened. Ryan and Rixen were next, obviously under direction of his father. There was even a phone call from Peyton. In the rush from seeing Roman at the hospital, Peyton must have forgotten to tell him he contacted him. And finally, two messages from his mate:

[MIKAÉL: Hey, I know you said you were studying, but we were getting together, right? I hope I didn't miss a message from you, but you're not answering any texts. Just let me know either way. I miss you.]

And later...

[MIKAÉL: Roman, are you there? * Sigh * Listen, I'm hearing some horrible things of what your Sur says you might have done. Please call me. Call someone. No one can get ahold of you. I'm scared, Roman. Please call and tell me you're safe.]

Roman closed his eyes and centered his thoughts. No matter how he heard his Fated Mate's voice, even in distress, it comforted him in some way. Of course, he never wanted Mikaél to feel any drop of hurt or fear. He peeled out of Siro's driveway and began the journey across the city again.

As expected, the phone call between Roman and his Sur did not go well. Roman couldn't have claimed his innocence enough, but it was like talking to a brick wall. His Sur nearly had a heart attack when he heard Roman visited Terrence and Peyton in the hospital. Had Roman called earlier, he was going to be told he was a wanted man for assault and battery and attempted murder. But since the initial calls, Peyton caught his father in a weak moment and convinced him to call off the manhunt as long as Roman agreed to turn himself in for questioning the next day. Owning the city came with quite the power.

Both Jake and Adrian tried in vain to get Roman to return home. There was no surprise however, when he expressed his next move. He had to see Mikaél; it was his only comfort.

Upon calling Mikaél, it only took one ring for him to answer the phone. "Roman?" he gasped.

"Hi, Mik." His tone was flat. The situation was bleak all around. He may not have known everything, but he knew enough. The exhale of emotion he heard Mikaél produce was haunting. And it hurt.

"Roman, Wolf-God! What is going on? Are you okay? Are you hurt?"

"No, I'm fine." Relatively speaking, he thought. "Something terrible happened."

"Mr. Whitmore? Peyton's Veo?"

"Yes."

"Roman, were you, I mean...this wasn't you, was it?"

The question was inevitable, but it didn't hurt any less. Before Roman could answer, all he envisioned was Mikaél's face in horror as he ripped his chest open in his own home. Then, the next scene played out as he tossed Siro around like defenseless prey. "I don't know what this means to you hearing me say this but no, it wasn't me." The silence on other side made his stomach knot.

"It means everything as long as it's true."

"It is," Roman replied.

"Oh, thank you." Mikaél sighed.

"Mik," he paused, "is there any chance I can still see you tonight? We definitely have things to talk about."

<hr>

With Mikaél answering the door, Roman didn't have to worry about what type of reaction he'd get from his parents. No doubt it was Dustin who told Mikaél the news about Terrence.

It was nice to dodge any parental contact. Perhaps Mikaél's parents wanted to play ignorant. He had their specific permission, supposedly, to be in the home. It wasn't unheard of for parents to stay out of relationship drama. Otherwise, his own Veo would have to quit his job to deal with his knuckleheaded brothers. Something was going on there, but he didn't have the desire to figure out what. Not now.

Upon entering Mikaél's bedroom again, he already felt at ease. Without trying to become overly obsessive, he thought of the room like it was his home. In reflection, it was the happiest place he'd been in for the past month. But he feared the conversation he was about to have was going to taint this sacred space just like everywhere else.

What made it even more difficult was seeing the sparkle in Mikaél's eyes. Whatever distress he was about to cause was going to be put on hold for time being. He had to taste his mate again. As he touched Mikaél's lips with his own, the kiss generated its own power. The energy from it could keep a small town luminous for days. As they held each other's head in their hands, the bond they shared filled the emptiness created when they left the conference room separately in despair. But now, it was time.

Mikaél sat patiently with eyes transfixed on Roman's every word. Telling him about Siro and Terrence was difficult but also the easiest by comparison. He didn't want his Fate to have another incident filed away in his memory of him being a violent person, so he skirted some of the specifics on why Siro might tap out of clinicals tomorrow for a broken nose. Seeing Mikaél's horrified reaction on the details of Terrence's condition and Peyton's emotional state told him it was a good move.

"Mik, there's something else I need to tell you." The rising level of distress became obvious.

"What, what's wrong?" He rubbed Roman's leg as a calming technique.

Roman choked up. "After our contract failed, and before Peyton's Veo was attacked," Roman inhaled, "we were brought back to the negotiating table to put Peyton and me back into a P&C Agreement." Roman's eyes fell to the bed.

The shock hit Mikaél hard. "What?" The word was more of concern versus a question. "Why?"

Roman's eyes flared up. "Because Peyton is pregnant. And the pup is mine." His heart shattered the moment he could see in the pain in Mikaél's eyes.

To Mikaél, hitting a wall at the speed of 100 could have been easier than hearing this. His breath quickened and his eyes clouded. "I don't understand."

"After we were contracted, we spent a night together. What I thought was a clear dodge of a possible pregnancy resulted in my ignorance and poor judgement." Mikaél couldn't come up with any words to say. The silence scared Roman more than anything he could say. "I'm sorry." No reply. "I had no idea; it blindsided me."

"Yeah. That makes two of us." Mikaél's voice turned cold.

"I want this to get better. I need this to get better. Wolf-God, Mikaél, you are the only thing going right in my life." His words passed through. "We're meant to be together. And I'm not giving up on us."

A tear grazed Mikaél's cheek. "Maybe you should."

Roman realized he was wrong. Silence wasn't the scariest thing Mikaél could say. "What?"

"Roman, look at this." Mikaél shook his head. "I only just found out last week who it was you were in contract with—a detail you conveniently left out."

"I regret that."

"And you have some Omega's scent all over you, so I assume this realization came up with a make-up session?"

Roman froze. With rushing out of Nico's house, he didn't have any time to think of how his encounter left lasting effects. How could he have been so stupid? "Mikaél, I—"

"Just go." Mikaél's voice cracked.

Sliding off the bed, Roman felt the Omega pheromones throw him back. "I didn't mean to. This isn't what it looks like," Roman defended with pleading sorrow.

"Go!"

"Mikaél, please! I lov—"

"GO!" Mikaél yelled.

A thud came from upstairs. Several footsteps followed. Roman's world crashed in on him, and he couldn't bear the pain he inflicted on his true mate. As Roman opened the door and swiftly exited, Alec's body slid past him and into Mikaél's room.

"What's wrong?" Alec asked. After a few doubletakes between seeing Roman continue upstairs and hearing Mikaél's agonizing cries, he scented terrible pheromones all around him. "What is this?" he asked full of concern. Mikaél crumbled on the bed. His Veo's arm rubbing his back did little to soothe him. "It's okay! Just breathe. Just breathe." The hurt radiated off his son. It didn't take a genius to know what event transpired. He feared the worst.

CHAPTER 24:

A Dinner for the Devil

Coming home, Roman knew there was a snowball's chance in Hell that his parents would be asleep. The thought was nice, but the reality was disappointing. As Roman shut off the car, a backlit figure stood up from the large formal windows facing the driveway. No doubt his Veo was waiting there, buzzed on every caffeinated drink that existed, not to mention the booze. But between his two fathers, he'd take an inebriated Veo any day. The walk up to the door was slow. *Why should I hurry? The battle is going to happen either way.*

"Oh, Roman!" Adrian gasped, locking his arms around his son. "Are you okay?"

Roman didn't want to say anything. But even moving his head to answer carried consequences. "I don't know if I'm ever going to be able to say 'Yes' to that statement ever again, honestly."

Adrian's face showed his sense of helplessness.

The sound of his Sur's footsteps at the door meant the quiet moment was going to be short-lived. "Son."

The word was quick and emotionless. *Maybe he is exhausted like me?* Roman couldn't think of any other reason for why his father didn't put a gun to his forehead and pull the trigger. Instead, Jake gestured everyone into the home. Roman opted for the living room instead of the kitchen. Like with all of his childhood antics, not that there were too many, his parents sat next to each other while Roman sat opposite. Nothing made him feel like a rebellious adolescent more than this.

"So," Jake continued, "let's get the hard question out of the way first." He inhaled, bracing himself, "Did you do this?"

"No!" Roman's answer came fierce and fast.

Adrian's head fell into his tightly clasped hands as if he'd been praying to the Great Gray Wolf. "Thank Wolf-God!"

"Babe!" Jake's word was condescending.

"Jake, come on. This is what we were waiting for. You can believe Roman on this," Adrian pleaded.

Jake adjusted himself. "As far as I'm concerned, my trust came into question when Roman decided to claim immaculate conception."

Adrian air-batted his wrist, folded his arms, and leaned back into the couch. His head turned in the opposite direction as he crossed his legs. The effects of his liquor comforted him.

"Dad, I was telling you the truth back then, and I'm telling you the truth now," Roman defended.

"Yeah, half-truths, maybe," Jake spat back.

"Oh, come on, Dad! Let's not throw stones from a glass house."

Jake's scrunched his face as he looked to his mate for support. All he received was a non-verbal "Well, what are you going to say to that?" look. "Quite frankly, Roman, you should count your lucky stars you are even sitting here having this conversation. I'm about deaf from having Matthew Whitmore screaming through the phone with every other expletive in my ear with how he was going to have the entire police force take you down like a wild animal."

"Peyton claimed his Sur said as long as I show up at the police station tomorrow morning for a statement, he'd call off the search," Roman shared.

"I know. It was the last of the dozen phone conversations we had. How that happened, I have no idea."

"Peyton told him to do it."

"And why was he so willing to do that?"

"Because I told him I didn't do it!" Roman growled.

Adrian sat up on the edge of the cushion. "Roman, from what we heard, the police are claiming this as a random incident. Apparently, the perpetrator stole his wallet, and they don't have much else to go on."

Roman grimaced. Had he known that, he would have given Siro one more hit for good measure.

His Veo's face softened. "Do you know who did this?"

It was the question he dreaded most of all. Once he knew for sure it was Siro, he struggled with what his next move was. He wanted every satisfaction of seeing Siro being scrutinized and then locked away; Peyton deserved that. But at the same time, Matthew Whitmore caused suffering Roman wanted him to burn for. And Terrence may not have been enemy number one, but he was more than willing to be his mate's little minion. Not that he wished this on Terrence—of course not. However, Roman was on a roll of making decisions which hurt his ability to stand on the pedestal of justice. Finally, in this moment, Roman was getting his chance to make the next move in Matthew's sick game of chess. "No."

The word stuck in Jake's throat as he stared into the carpet. Eventually, he gave an acknowledgement. "Okay." The comment was apathetic at best. There was no need to press anything further tonight. He turned to his mate who displayed the same expression. "Why don't you try to get some rest? I imagine Matthew is going to count every second you're not downtown, so you better get there bright and early."

"Yes, sir." Roman decided to be grateful for what could have been the endless topics of conversation. He stood and stretched out, now realizing just how exhausted he really was. "Where are Rixen and Ryan?" he wondered out loud.

"I told them to go to bed an hour ago. They didn't need to be a part of this," Jake declared.

Roman softly nodded and made his way downstairs. He had all the intentions of going straight to bed but was delighted when he realized a bright glow emanated from the outer trim of Ryan's closed door. Knowing he was never going to fall to sleep tonight and that he was going to be forced to talk his brothers anyway, he decided he'd seek their comfort. As he stepped closer, he heard a strong steady rhythm of Ryan's music blaring at an annoying volume. Assuming Ryan was lost in a late-night gaming session, he opened the door to reveal what he never could have imagined in the deepest recesses of his mind.

There on Ryan's bed, both brothers were sitting up on their knees in nothing but their underwear facing each other with their naked chests pressed together. Their lips were deeply locked like only lovers do. But like two same poles of a magnet, upon seeing Roman, both brothers flew to the opposite sides of the room, trying to repel any thought of what must have been going through Roman's mind.

Roman's eyes widened. "What. The. Fuck?!"

"Oh, Wolf-God!" Rixen blurted, shaking like a young tree in a blackened storm.

"What the fuck is this?!" Roman's mind couldn't get the image out of his head. As he heard Rixen heaving in the left corner, he now eyed Ryan to his right. "What the hell is going on?!" His voice was furious.

It was a rare occurrence, but here Ryan was, tucking his tail so to speak. "Roman, this isn't what it looks like!" Nothing more came to mind. Hoping Roman blocked it all out, he went for the "playing dumb" route.

"Fuckin' A, Ryan. I'm pretty sure I know what this looks like." Roman rubbed the back of his head. "Have you two lost your minds?"

"Roman, please don't say anything about this!" Rixen pleaded.

Whether Rixen planned to or not, he had just confessed everything Roman needed to know. There was no mistaking anything. "No way!" Roman turned and headed straight for his bedroom. Perhaps the vision would erase. Maybe he was hallucinating it all. He definitely had enough trauma tonight to warrant it.

"Roman!" Ryan called out. Looking at his petrified brother, he threw Rixen's shirt at him to tell Rixen to get dressed. Both boys never put their clothes on so fast in their life. Ryan called out to his brother again as he and Rixen followed behind. They were greeted with a slammed door. It didn't deter Ryan from opening it.

Roman grimaced. "You two need to get out of my room!"

"Can we talk about this?" Rixen reached out.

"What?" Roman's sarcasm came through. "You want to give me some highlights? Get the fuck out of here!"

Ryan began to find his center. How, he didn't know. "This isn't something we can just hide and pretend didn't happen."

"Ohhhh, let me try!" Roman stressed.

"That's not fair! We've been there for you when you've needed us. Now we need you," Ryan protested.

"If what you need is anywhere near what you two were doing in there, forget it. You two can take a cyanide pill for all I care." Roman propped himself up on his bed. Realizing they weren't going away anytime soon, he didn't mind throwing the insults at any opportunity. He couldn't fathom what was happening. All his memories of his brothers were tainted to the point where it made him ill.

"That's not what I meant, and you know it!"

"Should I? Because from what I 'knew,' brothers don't screw each other!"

"That wasn't going to happen," Rixen dismissed.

"Really?" Roman squinted his eyes. "You two were definitely 'Up for it' if you know what I mean. Oh, my Wolf-God, I can't believe I'm talking about this!" The comment immediately made him sick.

Rixen's shoulders sank, and his head tilted in exhaustion. "Roman, can we please have a serious conversation about this? It's important."

"I can't believe I'm asking: Is this the first time you've done this?" The twins looked at each other. No answer was an answer. Roman shook his head. "You two are disgusting."

Rixen walked past Ryan and sat on the corner of Roman's bed. Doing so made Roman's legs fold up instantaneously, an expected response. "Roman, there's nothing we can say that's going to make you feel better, but you have to know, we didn't plan for this to happen."

Roman stayed silent. It was hard to deny an emotional connection to Rixen, but he didn't know what to say. Nothing was the best option for not hurting his feelings.

Rixen continued, "Ryan and I found ourselves at a moment neither of us thought would ever happen. We didn't know it was going to turn into this, but it did."

Roman mocked, "Yeah, but you can't take it back."

Ryan interjected, "And we don't want to."

Roman saw a sincerity in his brothers which damn near frightened him. "You two are serious?" Both of them nodded. "So, you two actually plan on continuing this?"

Ryan continued, "The feelings we have for each other—they're not going to go away."

The words fused the connections. "Are you two trying to tell me you're in love with each other?" Once again, a nonverbal acknowledgment affirmed the answer. "No, don't tell me that," Roman whined.

"But we are, Roman." Ryan stared at his brother. Rixen nodded his head slowly. "We're in love, and there's nothing that's going to change it. You don't have to like it. But it's there. And that's all we can say about it."

Roman tilted his head. "Wait. Aren't you seeing Garrace? I realize I haven't discussed it with you since the dinner party."

"I noticed," Rixen replied with attitude.

"I was little busy dealing with my own shit, okay? Give me a break!" Roman shook his head and waited. "So?"

"Well, we..." Rixen struggled.

"All three of us are a thing," Ryan finished.

Roman's eyes couldn't have been bigger. "Whoa." He threw his head back. "I didn't see that one coming." It took a minute for him to process the concept. It wasn't that he hadn't heard of polyamorous relationships, he just didn't anticipate he'd personally know anyone to do it. That being said, Siro had plenty of conversations on how he'd fantasized such things. Should he ever see him again, maybe he'd press to see how serious he was. "And that's working?" Curiosity hit him.

"It's fairly new," Rixen answered.

"I see."

The lull in conversation wasn't going to address what Ryan really wanted to know. "Now that you know, can we trust you?"

Roman was a bit taken aback. It wasn't the first time. "You want me to keep this a secret? You're keeping this a secret?"

"Well, yeah!" The conviction in Ryan's voice made the question sound stupid.

The practicality was a joke to Roman. "How far do you guys expect to get?"

Rixen replied, "We're taking it day by day. Right now, we think it has a lot of potential."

Dwelling on the conversation at this point was useless. Roman couldn't have been further away from accepting his brothers' decision. But the realization he was still dealing with his own problems snuffed out the need to continue his barrage of discontent.

Feeling a bit safer than he did a while ago, Ryan pivoted. "So? Is it true you killed Peyton's Veo?"

Roman glared at his brother. Considering he blasted him out of the water, Roman decided he'd give Ryan one free pass. But now, it was time for him to tell his story.

For the time being, the cops were satisfied Roman didn't have any direct involvement with Terrence's attack. Nico was more than willing to backup Roman's claim on his whereabouts, and there still wasn't any evidence to speak of. What the police weren't satisfied with was Roman's innocence on not knowing who could have been responsible. Although Omegas weren't typically used in active patrol duty, they were routinely used in tactics like these to properly assess witnesses. They were considered one step up from a polygraph test, especially since anyone could refuse to cooperate in a polygraph test.

At one point, Roman almost thought the Omega interrogator reached inside and pulled the four letters of Siro's name out of his soul. But Omegas had an impossible task when it came to pressing on an Alpha. Alphas didn't offer an intuitive wavelength like themselves, and being a Type 6 seemed to benefit Roman even more.

On the other hand, Alphas in the interrogation room were much harder to deal with. Roman was convinced somewhere in a back alley, professional cops gathered in order to question suspects in the way they really wanted. That's why there was always at least one Beta in the hot room. Otherwise, an Alpha interrogation was nothing more than a primal Rank battle. And that's where being a Type 6 didn't help Roman. The Type 5 Alpha cop did *not* like finding out Roman was Ranked above him. If Roman had any intuition like an Omega at all, he suspected the Alpha interrogator must also be working for Matthew Whitmore.

The biggest problem for Roman was the delusion that crime shows, even documentaries, painted interrogation rooms like they were soundproof chambers with one-way mirrors. The truth was interrogation rooms were stuffy confined spaces which arguably amplified noise versus muffled. Fortunately, although Matthew Whitmore was present at the police station, he wasn't allowed anywhere near Roman. Regardless of what view the authority had of Roman, he was protected from any wrath Peyton's father had, barring an insider hitman. But unfortunately for Roman, his own Sur waited right outside the interrogation room, taking in every word.

That night at dinner was rough. Every member of the Erricson household was on edge. Jake had daggers for Roman like he never had before in his life. As best as Roman could, he avoided his view, but he could still feel his father's eyes searing into him.

Adrian had been fully informed of what happened at the precinct. Without knowing enough, he found it difficult to interject himself into any more peacekeeping battles. So, when the conversations dropped completely, he decided to look at it with cautious optimism and a glass of wine.

Ryan and Rixen at least had the benefit of going to school that day without walking around feeling like they were being judged as criminals. Though, that didn't stop them from getting all the same questions Roman did.

"How was school, Rixen?" Adrian's gaze fell upon his son. He knew better than to direct the question at Roman.

Rixen shrugged off the question, not really wanting to divulge all the chatter and disgusting rumors going around. Not even Garrace was immune that morning from asking an outlandish question about whether or not Roman raped Terrence and killed Peyton in the process, since he was noticeably vacant at school that day.

After failing with Rixen, Adrian focused elsewhere. "Ryan? How was your day?"

Ryan decided to be less tactful. "Me? Are you sure just don't want to hear about Roman?"

Adrian sighed at his son's lack of sensitivity. "No, I'm asking about you."

"No, you're not. You don't care. All you care about is wanting to know is if people talked about Roman. That's what you're asking."

Adrian refused to entertain the thought, but at the same time, it was difficult for him to ignore. Part of him wanted to know the answer. In the absence of words, silverware gently tapped plates, and glasses were lifted and set down on the table a few times before Ryan decided to answer the question without provocation.

"Tyler and Grant made the rounds. From what I've been told, most people are convinced Roman has only 24 hours left to live. But most of those people also say Roman is a hero, interestingly enough." No one spared Ryan the look of death, including Rixen. "What?" Ryan asked innocently.

Jake pointed his fork at his son. "This is not a situation to be proud of."

"Oh, come on. We all know Roman didn't do it," Ryan defended.

"Well, thanks to Roman's 'convincing' testimony," Jake eyed his Alpha son with disdain, "when it hit the news, they made a point to say no suspects were considered yet."

"But that's my point. Roman should be basking in the glory of this before they catch the guy who really did this."

Roman stepped in. "Yeah, that's not happening. So, you can tell Tyler and Grant to dispel any rumors back to the captivated crowds, and then tell them to fuck off."

"Roman," Adrian disapproved.

Ryan tilted his head, amused. "I don't know why you feel the need to be so hostile to my friends who had nothing to do with you being a suspect for attempted murder."

"I am not a murder suspect." Roman's agitation began to climb the ladder.

"I'm not so sure Mikaél views it like that."

Roman's body may have stayed motionless, but his pheromones slapped everyone at the table in the face. While Ryan and Jake stared at Roman waiting for his next move, Rixen and Adrian stared at Ryan. Now, it was personal. His words were clear and steady. "What did he say?"

Ryan pretended to search his brain. "Something to the effect of being repulsed and not being able to trust you again."

Roman's eyes shifted to his Sur. For the first time during the night, his father looked back with some sort of empathy versus animosity. "I spoke with him last night, Ryan. I cleared all this up with him. I don't suppose you did anything to defend me in the process?"

"Oh, I didn't speak with him personally. This is coming from Laycin."

"And what did you say back to him?"

"Just that you're sitting on the issue because you're too afraid of who really did it." Ryan didn't realize how much power the sentence had until he said it out loud. He instantly regretted it.

Adrian gasped. "Roman? You do know who did this?"

Jake roared, "Damn it, Roman!"

"Damn it, Ryan!" Roman was about ready to strangle his brother.

"I didn't say that you knew! I didn't say that!" Ryan tried.

Rixen groaned. "Nice going, bro."

"Roman, I knew you weren't telling me everything. No one even at the precinct believed you." Jake began his ultimatum, "You have ten seconds to tell me what you know, or so help me, I will put you in that jail cell myself!"

The seconds ticked by. Roman swallowed hard as lasers were shooting back at him. The time for a response was yesterday. At this point, he had to come clean, regardless of the loyalty he had left to his ill-fated friend.

Ryan beat him to the punch. "It was Siro."

"Ryan! Seriously!" Roman cried.

"I'm trying to save your ass here! You clearly don't seem to be able to read the signs very well."

Roman pointed at Ryan with his steak knife. "Okay, some advice to you. Next time you feel like you're trying to save someone? Assume you're not. Just butt out and mind your own damn business!"

Adrian sat horrified as he looked at his mate who was about ready to explode. "Siro LaCroix? You have to be kidding!"

Jake showed an aversion to the name. "Why on earth would you be willing to protect that degenerate?"

"He's not a degenerate. He's my friend," Roman defended.

"He almost killed somebody, Roman! How you still consider him a friend is beyond me. What kind of friend asks you to keep that a secret?"

The fork in Roman's hand played with the little bit of salad left on his plate he didn't plan on eating. "He didn't ask me to. I just did."

Jake chuckled in disbelief. "And why would you do that?"

"I guess I had the foolish idea Siro would turn himself in."

"And you see where that went. But I'll tell you right now, you're going to be making a phone call to Siro and tell him to turn himself in now or you're going to." Roman attempted to respond. "End of discussion."

"And there's another dinner dedicated to the Roman Show," Ryan muttered.

Roman sighed and focused all his attention on his brother. Ryan must have thought he was in the clear. Not by a long shot. "You just don't know when to ever stop running your mouth, do you?"

Adrian stood up with his plate and walked toward the sink. "I think I'll get that dessert out now."

"What are you babbling about?" Ryan continued eating almost as if he had no role in tonight's conversation.

"You could have just kept your nose out of my business and kept your mouth shut!"

"You are the one who told me," Ryan pointed out.

"You're not six anymore, Ryan! I thought I could tell my brother something in confidence. You couldn't even last 24 hours, not to mention you decided to hit me below the belt."

"I'm sorry. I'm not interested in playing your accessory to breaking the law, Roman." Ryan shrugged with sarcasm. "I didn't know when you were telling me what happened last night, it came with the uncomfortable position of concealing a crime. And I'm not the only one who thinks so. Right, Rix?" Rixen sat there petrified. The brief second of attention on him was stolen away from Ryan in his continuous defense. "And what do you mean about hitting you below the belt?" Ryan still sat there on his perch of doing no wrong.

"I told you I talked to Mikaél last night. His name alone is a very sore subject for me, and you know that. And the fact you appear like this whole conversation was entertainment for you is beyond words."

Ryan shook his head. "You should be thankful, if anything. I did nothing more than ask the important questions and tell you the answers."

Roman pulled his head back in surprise. "Oh really? Because I didn't hear you ask me any questions on how I was doing today. Just because we're not on the same campus doesn't mean the phones are broken: a call, a text, a message. No, nothing. And you didn't ask who I talked to today. You didn't ask if I heard from Nico; hell, you didn't even ask if I heard from Siro."

"Okay. Did you hear from Siro today?" The question was mockery more than anything else.

"No, I didn't. He didn't come to clinicals, nor did he answer the phone when I called him."

Ryan snorted. "So, then what's your point?"

"My point is you chose Mikaél because you wanted to see what my reaction was going to be. And you got it. It's a low way to get it, but you got it. It'd be no different than me asking you if Garrace was able to sleep last night since he was alone!"

Ryan stopped in his tracks and didn't know how to proceed. Seeing Rixen's fear across his face was enough for him to go back to walking on a tight rope.

Adrian paused putting cream desserts on a dish only for a second as he chose to respond to the comment. "Why would you ask Ryan that? Rixen's dating Garrace—not Ryan."

Roman finally saw the sweat glisten on Ryan's forehead. Putting Mikaél into the conversation to make him squirm was a grave mistake. And he intended to make Ryan pay for it. "How do you want this to go, Ryan?"

"You wouldn't," Ryan muttered.

Rixen whispered, "Roman, please."

Jake lost his patience. "What the hell is going on now?"

"Apparently," Roman adjusted himself, "Rix and Ryan are fighting over the same guy. They couldn't declare a winner so now they're sharing him."

Adrian laughed at the thought. But as soon as he did, he noticed his entire family looking back at him doing anything but laugh. And it wasn't so much Jake, Roman, or even Ryan who changed his train of thought. It was Rixen, whose arms were shaking on the table. Then, the seriousness set in. "I, uh, I think I'll just save the dessert for later." Leaving the tray on the kitchen island, he began to put container toppings and coffee cups away.

"Boys, this is some sort of joke, right?" Jake scanned the room.

Ryan felt a spark ignite inside him. The toll of everything came to fruition. He didn't know any better, but he decided now was the time to tell Roman what he really felt. "You know, living in your shadow is hard enough."

"Oh, what are you going on about now? Spare me," Roman whined.

Jake attempted to insert himself, "Can we get back to the other conversation, please?"

Ryan ignored his Sur's request, "Everything is about you, and it always has been. 'Roman is a Type 6, Roman needs to be treated like he's special, Roman needs to be studied, Roman needs a mate. Oh, Roman needs two mates—'"

"Oh, you're gonna go there? Two mates? You should talk."

"It's pathetic and I'm sick of it. Thank Wolf-God, Rixen is an Omega. Otherwise, he'd be invisible just as much as I am in this house."

Roman howled in amusement., "And here it is."

Ryan groaned. "Ugh! See? That right there! That pisses me off the most!"

Roman wiped his eyes. "What does?"

"That attitude you have! The one where you act so bothered that anyone has a negative opinion of you. You come across like this is normal, as if every family deals with this. Are you really that ignorant for what it's like for the rest of us here?" It made Ryan feel so good to say it, but at the same time it only fueled him further.

"I think we've had enough for one night. This needs to stop." Adrian's voice became stern.

Roman dismissed the notion. "You're really being overdramatic about this."

"Overdramatic?!" Ryan yelled, pointing at their Sur. "Our Dad's job is nothing more than exploiting the wonder that you are. We eat, sleep, and breathe on the coattails of hoping you have another phenomenon waiting to be discovered so we don't go on food stamps when you become second rate news to a newly discovered bug!"

"Boys! That's enough!" Jake's voice rang out. But as quick as it came, the harrowing wind blew it away.

Rixen covered his mouth in disbelief. He wanted to calm the treacherous seas before him. He wanted to save the ship before it was too late. But he didn't know if he had the power to do so. And if he did, he didn't know where to start. All he did know was his Omega intuition was going off like an intense storm. He knew his Veo must have felt it, too. But Adrian didn't know what to do or say to this either. He stood there at the island still, giving pleading eyes to his mate.

Roman replied, "You have something wrong with you, you know that? Why don't you go to a doctor and get something for that fucked up head of yours?"

"Why don't you go to the doctor and figure out why your crippled wolf instincts can't find a mate properly? If you could have figured it out, you wouldn't be in this mess. You wouldn't be fucking up Peyton's life, you wouldn't be fucking up Mikaél's life, and, oh yeah, you wouldn't have fucked up Peyton's dad's life, too."

"Stop this now!" Adrian picked up the large tray and steadied it to the fridge.

To Roman, Ryan was already dead where he sat. This was one lesson Ryan wasn't going to forget. "At least I'm not in a dead-end relationship! Let me know how you feel when Rixen and Garrace leave you behind since you can't produce an heir!"

Ryan accepted the challenge with gritted teeth and tightened arm muscles. "At least I won't be standing on the sidelines watching my Fated Mate give another Alpha his pup while you open a Winter Solstice card every year with the message 'Wish you were here'!"

"At least I'm not fucking my own brother!"

The moment was met with a loud crash. Adrian's hand had jerked back upon hearing the shocking news, taking the entire tray down the front of the fridge. Ignoring every liquid splatter and glass shard on the floor, once again he found himself assessing for any hint of truth in the deranged comment. When no comfort came, he could barely contain the sounds from his lips with his hand around his mouth.

Rixen was devastated. The betrayal of Ryan refusing to come to his senses in the madness was hard enough. But the betrayal from Roman hit even harder. The brother he looked up to and felt safe with tore down every proud tower which was their relationship with one statement.

Ryan heard the thunder and felt the lightning inside him become louder and stronger. Hearing the cries of his Veo and the whimpers of Rixen destroyed any and all restraint he had. The time for talking was over. Before Roman had time to react, Ryan pounced on Roman like a wolf attacking its prey. Roman's chair fell backward with an eventual crack as he laid on top of him.

Not anticipating Ryan's move was a grave mistake. Roman's head hit the wood floor with force which created a momentarily fuzzy picture from his eyes. But Roman wasn't about to let his own brother get the best of him. Regardless of his exceptional Blood-Type, the power he possessed over his younger brother made Ryan a bigger fool than he thought. Still, for the one moment Ryan had the upper hand, he had to applaud his brother for the Alpha-like Status. After fully recognizing his brother's face full of wrath and his voice with a fierce growl, he was done playing games.

Roman grabbed onto Ryan's fists which had balled up his sweater. Ryan had less and less impact with his repeated attempts to slam Roman's upper body against the wood floor beneath him. With his body now tensed, Roman pushed Ryan upward and used all of his strength to throw his brother's body off like a rocket.

Ryan's body flew right up against the wall of the kitchen island. His entire being struck the wood hard, including his head. His face reacted with a severe pain, but his voice barely cracked. As he touched the back of his head with trembling fingers, he felt the heat of a moist sensation beginning to bubble. Unable to call a truce in the time needed, Roman came down upon him again and hit him in the face with an open palm. The resulting injury could have been worse with a loaded fist but with the side impact of his face hitting the floor, it was enough to cause a slight bleed from his nose and lip.

It was only then that Roman heard both of his parents' audible commands to stop his assault. His Sur grabbed him and pushed him back a foot or two with a strong Alpha fervor.

His Veo with somber eyes assessed Ryan and gingerly helped him up.

Rixen was standing against the sliding glass door in a complete state of shock. How he didn't collapse unconscious was a surprise to everyone.

"You!" Jake pointed to Roman. "Downstairs, now!" His next aim was at Ryan whose face was beet red with streaks of blood from various places. "You, to the upstairs bathroom." Then he targeted Rixen. "And you," he paused, "I don't even know what to do with you. Just get out of here!"

Adrian took one look at Rixen who was broken into pieces. "Jake, please!"

"Adrian, I want you upstairs with Ryan." Adrian attempted to respond. "Not another word out of you. I am the Alpha of this household, and you will do what I say!"

The words to Adrian were slices of an axe cutting into his legs. His own mate emasculated him in front of the entire family. He swallowed his pride and quietly assisted Ryan upstairs.

Roman stood there, staring into nothingness. His father's raging scent allowed him to be spared from the stare of his ruling pack leader. There was no escaping the house tonight as he did on many former occasions. His father had an ace up his sleeve about Roman's unofficial perjury, and he wasn't about to call his father's bluff on what he would do with it. After a slight sway of his legs, Roman carefully walked past his Alpha father and made his descent to his room.

While Rixen shook and whimpered, he considered his Sur's words. Ironically, with his Sur's indifferent command on what he should do, it in a way validated Ryan's claim describing his father's apathetic views on him. But that was a thought he was going to keep to himself.

In the most difficult way, Rixen surmised the only reason Ryan was relegated to upstairs was because his father didn't trust him—an obvious conclusion. With tiny steps, he tested his permission to join his brother downstairs. His father's eyes of death followed him all the way until he was out of sight. The last thing he heard was his own father slamming the landing door shut with a force which shook the entire house.

The last thing Rixen wanted was Roman standing in front of his bedroom door, yet he had the audacity to be there. As he wiped his tears away, it was his turn to give an off-putting scent and scowl on his face. Both stared at each other, barely blinking.

Roman began, "Rixen, I don't know what came over me."

"It doesn't matter anymore, Roman." Rixen's voice was barely above a whisper.

"It does to me. My life is in shambles, and I'm spending every other moment apologizing. And I don't know when it's going to stop."

"The way it sounds, you're going to be apologizing your entire life. And maybe you need to." Rixen opened his bedroom door.

Roman's eyes were heavy with tears. As his life crumbled, the salty drops were beginning to become the closest family members he had. "I can't do this anymore. At this point, I think killing myself is the only option."

"Hmph. I have my own problems now, no thanks to you. So, if you end up doing it, I'll say goodbye now."

Those words were the last Roman expected to hear from Rixen—Ryan, perhaps—but never Rixen. A sadness hit his face.

"If I could ask one final courtesy from you: stay out of my life. I'd be happy for the rest of my life if I never spoke to you again." He only stayed a moment longer to make sure the words stuck to Roman. They did, of course. He wanted them to hurt just as much if not more than what Roman perpetrated upstairs. The message was clear. Soon, Rixen entered his room and slammed the door behind him.

It had been a few hours now since Adrian tended to Ryan's wounds. They were mostly superficial, but the scene traumatized him so much, he had his son on concussion watch in the upstairs bedroom right next to theirs. It was fair to say the monitoring was more for him than Ryan. Most of it was guilt for not shielding him from Roman's wrath. But the entire dinner paralyzed him. From start to finish, it was a nightmare. By the end of the night, he didn't know what was left of his family.

He walked into the master bedroom, coming in from another check on Ryan, who was sleeping peacefully, to see his mate sitting in the bay window, staring into blue-night sky. The silent treatment couldn't last until morning, so he quietly shut the double doors.

"How is he?" Jake asked.

"He's sleeping. What are you staring at?" Adrian spoke softly.

Jake's chest rose and fell again. "The stars. At least, I think they're stars. Maybe they're just asteroids and meteors looking to end my life as I know it."

Adrian sat on the bed and looked at his mate from a distance. "You're too hard on yourself."

"No," Jake replied quickly. "I deserve every agonizing end Wolf-God can think of. I betrayed Roman, I betrayed Rixen, I betrayed Ryan, and I even betrayed you tonight." A shallow breath escaped him. "And for that, I am truly sorry."

Not that Jake bothered to look, but Adrian did nod his head. "I know you are."

"You're my mate. And I can't do this without you."

"I guess one thing I am wondering about in that whole mess is how does Garrace fit into that picture?"

Adrian shook his head. "I have no idea. I've wondered the same thing. The night we met him at the dinner party, I had the feeling Rixen was about ready to make a commitment to him."

Jake pushed his head back. "Seriously?"

"Rixen was laying it on thick that night. He wanted us to see it."

"Great. Another moment in my son's life I'm completely ignorant on."

"Ryan, on the other hand, was about ready to kill Rixen. So, this new triad happened fast."

"Ugh." Jake hated having to hear words which indicated such things. "Apparently."

"So," Adrian paused, "what are you going to do?"

"Do? I just said what I'm going to do."

"You know what I mean. Are you going to support your kids or are you going to ignore them in the way they claim you already ignore them?"

"Support? Adrian, are you out of your mind?" He sat up in bed and hit the bedside lamp on. He searched his mate's face to evaluate his sincerity. "I don't know what's going on with this family. But there's a room in the nuthouse reserved especially for each and every one of us. Support? No way in hell will I ever support this. If those two continue to go down this path, they are on their own. They can get an apartment, get jobs like everyone else, and finish school on their own. When they see how real life works when they're not living in the land of entitlement, which apparently has gone to their heads to the point to where they think this is okay, then maybe they'll come to their senses. Then, maybe—MAYBE, I'll consider inviting them back for Winter Solstice."

Jake hit the button again to turn the lamp off, then thrust his body to the side and left a cold shoulder to his mate. The absence of sound left the room in a harsh silence. He felt Adrian lift off the bed and walk out and assumed he'd gone back to check on Ryan once more. Or perhaps he was just using it as an excuse to leave the room. Either way, Jake Erricson zoned his mind to think of work the next day. It was the only thing he had left to look forward to.

CHAPTER 25:

A SCIENTIFIC SHAM

"He's doing better," Peyton replied cautiously. Hearing Roman's concerned voice over the phone was a comfort every single time he called. It was a regular occurrence every day for a week now. "They moved him out of ICU this morning. The doctor said they could have done it a couple days ago, but Sur wouldn't allow it. I guess he's become a doctor now since being here."

"Doesn't surprise me," Roman replied as he sat outside looking at the start of a beautiful sunset. The fall breeze brought down several leaves of a nearby tree and scattered them on the patio. "Is your Veo still talking up a storm?"

"Oh, yes. I don't know who he is going to kill first: the doctors or my Sur."

Roman laughed. "I have to admit, I'd enjoy seeing that."

A pause set into the conversation.

"I'm sorry about your friend," Peyton finally said.

As if Peyton was right there in front of him, Roman looked down and studied the pattern of the bricks in the patio. In the distance, a dog barked as his owner threw a frisbee. "I can't say I'm happy about it. But Siro has to reap what he sowed." He sighed. "We all do."

Peyton sat up in his chair in the hospital's atrium. The space was mostly cleared out for the evening. Only a middle-aged man remained in a chair a few rows down, focused heavily in on a book. "Can I ask your advice on something?"

"Sure," Roman affirmed.

"What would you do in a situation to where you knew the truth about something horrible, but in doing so, it'd destroy everything you have in front of you?"

Roman was taken aback at such scenario. A chill went down his spine, and it wasn't from the cool breeze. "Wow, Peyton. Are you okay? Are you in some sort of trouble?"

"I just...I need your opinion. I have no one else in my life to ask. You are the only one I have trust in to tell me the truth."

"I think you just answered your own question, really. If there's one thing I've learned from my life this past month, it's that the truth is the most important information you can give. Sometimes the pain from it hurts so bad, you feel the only way to make yourself feel better is to not be on this broken earth anymore." Roman set in motion all the events which changed his life as he knew it: the contract between him and Peyton, Matthew Whitmore's manipulations, his own Sur's secrets which weren't his to keep, hidden feelings and regrets toward Peyton, and even his own inabilities to be transparent with everything he should have. "I'm not even immune to all this. I've made so many mistakes. As much as I hate the people around me who have lied and manipulated me, there were so many times I created my own misery."

Roman's words were righteous in Peyton's mind. But they did little to calm his anxiety. In fact, they exacerbated it. "When you did it—confronted the truth—where did you find the strength?"

A smile crept onto Roman's face. "I don't even know. I guess I was just tired of all the bullshit."

Peyton was too. "I understand that." The view out the atrium was getting harder and harder to see. Many tall buildings surrounded the little courtyard outside, it was difficult to judge the evening sky. "So, are you ready for tomorrow?" Peyton dared to ask.

"As ready as I'll ever be." Roman glanced to the mountains swallowing the sun. He wished he was there, right where the giant fireball disappeared. "Are you sure you're alright?"

"It's going to be okay, Roman. Everything will be okay. I promise," Peyton assured.

"I guess you have more confidence than I do." Roman bit his lip. "How's the baby?"

The moment was here. Peyton knew what he had to do. "I have to go."

Roman couldn't comprehend the abrupt statement. "Wait. What was all that about?" The call disconnected.

When Peyton returned to the hospital room, his Sur was sitting by his Veo's side with his hands on the bed. Both looked exhausted while lost in T.V. reruns.

"Who was that?" Terrence asked. His bruises were still quite visible—would be for another week or so. But his head wounds were down to a single head wrap. His right wrist was in a brace, but otherwise his arms were free. The ribs were the hardest to deal with: two were broken. Still, he was in good spirits.

"That was Roman." Peyton studied his parents for their reaction. Veo was neutral, but Sur's reaction appeared agitated. Matthew barely looked up from the newspaper in his hands.

Terrence pressed his mate's hand which snapped out of his aggravated response whenever anyone from that family was mentioned. "What did he want?" Terrence's question was light and curious. No animosity was behind it.

"He just wanted an update on you. He calls me every day and asks."

Terrence looked at his mate and shook his wrist a bit to get his focused attention.

Matthew grunted behind the sports section. "That was nice of him." The words were forced. Getting a look from both of his family members, he felt obligated to continue, "And how is he?"

Peyton smiled at the gesture. "He's alright, I guess. I think he's still dealing with all of this. I'm not sure what he thinks about Siro. But I know he's completely standing behind getting justice."

Veo nodded, then looked to Matthew.

Matthew cleared his throat and continued to practice his positive commentary while pretending to read the headlines for the third time. "Good man. At least he has a sane head on his shoulders. It's a good quality. It will be important for when he's your mate and a father."

A feeling fell into the pit of Peyton's stomach. He had to hold his hands behind his back in order to not show the terror he possessed in his trembling. To even broach the idea of confronting his parents was like jumping off the side of a cliff and into a shallow ravine headfirst while praying for the Great Gray Wolf's mercy. But Roman's words held steady inside him. He embraced them as if Roman was standing right there protecting him. He sighed. "Sur, Veo, we need to talk."

"About what?" Matthew asked.

"I know what you're doing." Peyton's face became somber and serious. His mouth was dry and his throat damn near closed up.

"'Doing'? About what?" Matthew inquired.

"Can you give me a little credit on the fact that I'm an Omega and I know myself?"

With his back now straight, Matthew projected himself in the same attitude. "I'm afraid I don't know what you are talking about. What is it you want to say?"

If there was one thing Peyton had learned over the years, it was his father knew to never divulge any information he didn't have to.

With a deep breath, he gave the quiet command. "You are going to go to the mediation tomorrow and release Roman from the contract. If not, I'll fight it until it stops." His heart nearly burst from his chest. He felt like a panic attack could rise at any moment.

Matthew didn't show the grand reaction his mate had. He didn't even blink. He stayed there in the same position and expression like he still had all the power in his hand. "You want to end a contract with the best Blood-Type in the world with a family who are decently wealthy? After all I've done? Why on earth would I or you even want to consider that?"

"Because last I heard 'MSBP' was still a crime in every territory." Peyton crossed his arms, looking at both of his parents now.

Terrence showed immense confusion. "MS... what?"

"Munchausen Syndrome by Proxy," Peyton stated. "You're intentionally keeping me sick. Or more specifically, you're intentionally keeping me pregnant. Trying to anyway."

Matthew chortled at the accusation. "What on earth?" He turned to Terrence who didn't share his same humorous sentiment. "I don't know what books you are reading before you go to bed at night, Peyton, but I think the fiction is crawling into your subconscious."

Peyton furrowed his brows. "You really think so?"

"Peyton," Terrence began, "your mind is exhausted. It's only natural to have thoughts like this now. With me being in the hospital here for a week, it's expected you'd be going through some trauma right now."

"Actually, Veo, it's because you were in the hospital that I was able to figure it all out."

"Figure out what?" Matthew's disposition showed annoyance.

"How far back was this idea conceived?" Peyton pivoted.

"What idea?"

Peyton clarified, "Roman and me."

Terrence answered, "It wasn't too much after your Sur and I talked about it with you. We had this talk before."

"And it's a lie!" Peyton swore he heard a whisper of Roman's support in his ear.

"What makes you say that? And please, don't shout," Terrence asked. "It's embarrassing and beneath you."

Peyton knew he had no choice. Neither of them moved on their position. "You two are going to make me go through all of this, aren't you?" Both of his parents exchanged glances, but neither of them moved a muscle or said a word. "I know now how it was all done so easily. Being your sheltered 20-year-old 'child' has its advantages when you want it."

"Want what?" Terrence jumped in.

"To take care of me when I'm sick or going through a solo heat."

"I don't think there's one good parent out there who doesn't do that for their child, Peyton."

Peyton nodded. "True. But I know how to take a fever reducer or cough medicine. However, going through a heat without a mate is terrifying. So, when my Veo wants to take care of me through a time which frightens me to the core, I let him. And I did for four times now."

Terrence sighed. "Look. I'm sorry. But I can only do so much as your nursemaid. We hired a professional to take care of you which is expected. And as far as I know, you didn't complain about his work. So, if this is about how I, and a medically trained professional, pale in comparison to a real mate, I'm sorry. Nothing will compare to that. Not that Roman did a good job anyway."

Peyton tilted his head. "How do you know if he did a good job or not?"

Terrence paused. "You told me."

Another affirmation came to Peyton's mind. "No, I didn't. Dad even made a point in the mediation to tell Roman and his parents he 'respected my privacy' regarding the night we spent together."

Matthew piped up. "Then how is your Veo so sure the conversation did happen?"

"Because he looked at my diary, that's why. I've recorded every single time I've been with Roman. And yes, that included some pretty graphic details no less. You were right, Sur, when you said you respected my privacy. You never were one to carry out your own agendas. That's why Veo did it and told you."

Matthew snickered. "A peek at a diary doesn't prove this wild accusation you have of us."

"No, you're right. The medications tell a better story."

"What medications?" Terrence asked.

"All the ones which were supposed to help me with a pregnancy. And then, all the ones which were to stop my heat. That's what you told me, anyway." Peyton noticed both of their facades were cracking. "So, whenever you handed me an unmarked pill or helped me out with an injection, I took it like any trusting Omega would of their parent." Peyton's gaze fell to his Veo's broken body. "But then when you were attacked, you weren't there to help me with any of it."

Terrence heaved. "Peyton, I—"

"Just stop!" Peyton commanded. Terrence held silent. "Sur was too distracted by your attack to even notice. I suppose if there's ever a chance he'd slip up, it would be when he thought he was on the verge of losing you while also fighting against whoever did this to you."

"Peyton, I am so sorry I wasn't there for you when your Veo was attacked. But I didn't mean any harm by leaving you behind in that process," Matthew admitted.

"That's what you're going to apologize for?" Peyton scoffed. "As I was saying, Sur left my medications bag on the foyer table when he picked up stuff from home for you at the hospital. So, when I came early the next morning by myself, I saw them there. Thinking as anyone should, I brought them to my bathroom to prep as needed. The only problem was Veo always had my meds laid out and ready for me to take. So, as I was combing through them to make sure I was doing everything right, I noticed first off, the two different prescription types. Half of the meds' commentary said: 'to prevent a heat' and the other half said: 'fertility aid/induce heat.'"

"That makes sense, Peyton," Terrence interrupted. "We couldn't stop your heat, so we used the meds to at least minimize the pain. Once we found out you were pregnant, we put you back on the fertility aid to help reverse any damaging effects from the heat suppressants for the pregnancy."

Peyton hummed. "But I recognized every single pill and injection you were having me take up to the night of the attack. You didn't switch me over. You were having me take both at the same time! Naturally, I thought this was some mistake. Luckily, Derrick at the pharmacy helped me."

"Derrick?" Terrence inquired.

"Before I went to school the next day, I went to the pharmacy to drop off the drugs I swore were a mistake," Peyton continued. "After he congratulated me on the pregnancy, he took back the sealed medications I didn't need. Unfortunately, I was stuck with the ones I opened to verify I wasn't going crazy on my assumptions."

"Hopefully, he was able to get you back to your senses," Matthew commented.

Peyton ignored the comment. "My curiosity is what led me to the truth. I asked Derrick why a doctor would prescribe a heat suppressant and a fertility drug at the same time. He said doctors do it for patients who are struggling to get pregnant. Apparently, it gives Omegas a longer opportunity to get pregnant while also dulling the painful side effects of a heat. But Derrick mentioned it's a very risky combination, and it's only used as a last resort for couples who can't afford in vitro."

Terrence sighed. "Peyton, this is really going nowhere."

"My final question to him was if there was any good reason why a doctor would have a pregnant patient take both. He was very adamant that a doctor wouldn't prescribe it at all. After pregnancy, the drugs combined could rupture the womb and cause a miscarriage. Doctors could even get sued for malpractice with their names attached to that and lose their license. He said they even perform a pregnancy test in the office before prescribing the two. So, I did what any sensible person would do."

"What?" Terrence inquired.

"Take a pregnancy test. Six to be exact." Peyton's voice began to get cocky. Now Matthew and Terrence were scanning each other's reaction a lot more. Every time, their expressions became less and less confident. "Can you imagine my shock when six pee sticks continuously tell me I'm not pregnant?" Now, Peyton was finding his center. On the surface, he was scathing mad, but on the inside, he was terrified.

"Those things can't be trusted; the pregnancy is still early. When we were pregnant with you, your Veo and I tried the same thing three weeks later, and it didn't show," Matthew explained, his frustration stronger and his composure weakened.

"It's true, Peyton," Terrence added. "I was so scared at the false negatives, I ran to the doctor to get another blood test just to make sure."

Peyton gestured with his finger. "Which precisely brings me to my next point. I was equally devastated as well. So, I went to Lunar Medical Clinic and asked to look at my medical record. The man at the nursing station didn't suspect anything. Come to find out, my file had no record of me being there since my last physical two years ago. And yet, I sat in that doctor's office last week and had the blood draw ordered by a doctor I'd never seen before in my life."

Matthew exhaled, shaking his head. "The clinic misplaced the paperwork or didn't put it in yet, and doctors change all the time. Dr. Rowe wasn't available."

Now Peyton was losing his patience. He could smell their insecure pheromones grow and yet they wouldn't break. "Ugh! You just have an answer for everything! Stop lying! All your words, they mean nothing! Everything that should be there isn't! It's excuse after excuse!"

The outlandish position and poor composure from his son pushed Matthew to his limit. It was time to shut down his son once in for all. "Fine! You want to play this game, I'll play."

"Matthew, don't!" Terrence exclaimed.

"No," he spoke to his mate and then turned to his son. "You think you have this all figured out. Let's go! Answer this question then. How did we get an approval letter?" Matthew pushed his head forward with a sarcastic tone.

"You paid the doctor off. It wouldn't be the first time you made a shady deal. I'm sure of that."

Matthew sighed. "Why would your father and I risk all of this if Roman decided he wasn't going to contract with you? What then? How does that work with your theory? You would have found out pretty quick this was all a sham."

Peyton didn't miss a beat. "Based upon what happened at the last mediation, I don't think Roman had any plans on abandoning me while I carried his pup. Not unheard of with a Lower-Type, but it's rare for a High-Type to do it. So, the only reason I can think of is because you thought Roman and I would have sex soon after the contract became official. After Roman and I became official mates, I read in a textbook most Omegas are known to have a much higher sex drive which only increases as the pregnancy advances. Plus, having his Fated Mate still looming, I could see myself wanting it all the time to help calm my insecurities. With me on the power combo of meds, there was an understanding a pregnancy would happen instantly, assuming I truly didn't suffer from infertility."

Matthew laughed. "Um. You have an expected due date. Too much longer and it'd be suspicious."

"There'd be a week or two grace period, I admit. But it's a minimal risk at best."

For a parent confident with their conviction, Peyton's Sur didn't deny with the passion Peyton expected. "Hmph. It's a beautiful story, Peyton. You created an almost plausible story, except for one thing."

"What's that?" Peyton eyed his father.

"I said it!" Matthew shouted. "What if Roman chose not to contract with you?! And furthermore, what if Roman did abstain from you? What then?"

"Matthew, this has gone too far. You need to take a walk or something. Calm your emotions," Terrence insisted.

"Come on, Peyton! You're almost home! Let's see what you got!" Matthew dared.

This time, Peyton stopped in his tracks. This was indeed what he couldn't answer. *Does it even matter?* He knew he was right. *Why do I need this?* But at the same time, he was this close to owning his father, one of the strongest Alphas he'd ever known. His eyes closed in defeat. "I don't know. I guess pray for symptoms of a miscarriage. That's all I can think of."

To Matthew, the victory was there. Having to show his Alpha strength to his own son was never something he fathomed he'd have to do. There were many adversaries in his life, but he never anticipated his son trying to be one of them. "What a pitiful sight you are. Everything we've done for you, and this is how you repay us?" Staring at his son, for the first time in his life, repulsed him. "You WILL go to mediation tomorrow, and you will submit just as you have every time. You are a Whitmore, and I am your Sur. Even when you are out of my house and living with that weak bastard Roman, I will own you until the day I die! I always get what I want, Peyton: work contracts, land, political victories, submission, all of it. And if you have to be my next victim to my wrath, then so be it."

In that moment, Peyton hated his father more than he ever had in his entire life. A strength he never knew he had surrounded him, and he inhaled the power deep into him. "I don't care who you are. I'm right. And you know I am. Just because I can't prove every angle doesn't mean I've lost. Every other discovery I've made is spot on. It's not my burden to poke holes in every coverup."

Matthew shook his head in disbelief. "You're so over. You've betrayed this family. This newfound confidence will be your downfall. What a pathetic waste. The consequences you'll face for this will make you wish you'd never done this. And I'll make sure you're put in a place where you'll never find your confidence again."

In an instant, a beam of light shone down from heaven itself. His previous words rang in his head like large dome bell. The final piece of the puzzle, it came to him. "Poke."

The single word perplexed Matthew. "Poke? What the hell is that supposed to mean?"

Peyton reflected on what he could remember about his heat. The experience was agony after he found out he was pregnant. It meant he couldn't get the much-needed relief as planned. His womb was already impregnated. Any intense thrust from a hand or toy that early could have busted the lining inside him, and the pregnancy would have been over. If he was pregnant. "I've gone through a heat procedure three times. The one thing which never happened before was the only thing which did happen."

Matthew swallowed hard. "What?"

"The pin-prick. Veo even said it during mediation. Wolf-God, the nurse told me it was a new routine procedure." He had the answer. It was the only explanation. "You sick fuckers! How could you do this to me?"

"Peyton!" Terrence screamed. "Watch your language!"

"DO WHAT?" Matthew belted.

"He impregnated me, didn't he?" There it was, the guilty look between his parents. "DIDN'T HE?"

Terrence broke first. "Yes, he did."

The growl from Matthew carried far. "Terrence, what the HELL are you doing?"

"I can't do this anymore, Matthew. I just can't. We've touted Peyton everywhere as one of the smartest kids around. And he didn't disappoint."

With sweaty palms, Matthew rubbed his face. "This is madness! How on earth could you even come up with such bullshit? Finding random sperm to inject you is the most laughable thing you've imagined yet. An Alpha can scent his pup on an Omega just weeks after a pregnancy. If Roman scented anyone except his, it'd all be over."

Peyton threw up his hands. "Then, it's not random! It's Roman's!" Matthew stood there and huffed, like a loser in a sports tournament. To Peyton, it was another confession without a confession. "How did you plan on keeping that charade up if the pregnancy didn't take?"

Terrence confessed, "For starters, your 'nurse' wasn't a nurse. He was a doctor. During every routine check-up, we'd just instruct the doctor to do another insemination once he checked the lining of your womb. As long as you were on the drugs, your womb would just be sitting there primed."

With two fingers, Peyton pressed the bridge of his nose with furrowed brows. "So, where did you get his sperm from?" His parents stared at one another but refused to speak. "I said, where did you get it from?" Still nothing. "WHERE DID YOU GET IT FROM?"

***

Roman thought sitting in the conference room with Matthew Whitmore and Peyton felt different—way different. And it was a lot more than just the fact Terrence wasn't there. Whitmore appeared to have been drained of all his energy and his pride. The obvious conclusion of course was his Veo's condition. But the pheromones in the room told a different story.

Jake started, setting the tone, "How is your mate, Matthew?"

With a sober face, Matthew nodded. "His recovery is going well, thank you. He gives his regards and apologizes for his absence."

"None needed whatsoever, of course. However, I am sorry for Adrian's absence. There's a situation at home with the twins so...uh... he's supporting that." Roman avoided the look his father attempted to give him. "Hopefully this will be the last time we have to be here," Jake commented.

A voice of confidence cut through the tension; it shook the room. "It will be." The voice didn't belong to Matthew nor his lawyer. It was Peyton, wearing a look of subtle satisfaction.

Jake continued cautiously, "Right." He adjusted, "Roman and I have discussed it and he is absolutely committed to—"

Matthew held his hand up, which stopped Jake in his tracks. "Before you get too far into this, I need to speak." Surprise fell upon both Jake and Roman's face, but they humored the interruption. A moment came where Matthew closed his eyes and turned his head as he sat, chewing on his words. "Some changes have occurred which we weren't expecting." Matthew swallowed. "In finding out, our family has realized the errors made can only be rectified if the contract between Roman and Peyton is dropped."

The words were clear, but the message was lost in the sea of misunderstanding. Roman spoke first, "What?"

"You're not serious?" Jake sat there in dismay.

"We are," Peyton reassured, "or rather, I am."

The lawyers gawked at one another.

Roman couldn't believe the Peyton before him. He sat there like a pure version of his father, an entirely different person. "I don't understand. Why?"

Peyton scratched his temple. "I guess I've finally seen what was there all along. For a while, I didn't. Then, I decided to ignore it. I can't anymore."

"Ignore what?" Roman asked.

"You don't want to be with me, Roman." Oddly, a smile appeared on Peyton's face. It was the face of a parent confessing to their child they knew a secret all along—but in a good way.

Roman's face turned red. "I—"

"No, it's alright. I've come to terms with that." Peyton checked in on his Sur who was sitting there like an empty shell. "You found your Fated Mate. It's who you are supposed to be with. You knew it from the very beginning we weren't going to work out. And if I swallow my pride, I knew it too. Not that I wouldn't have tried to make us work."

"I would have too," Roman quickly answered.

"I believe that." Peyton folded his hands and leaned in on the table, his face more serious than before. "There's only one thing holding us here."

"The pregnancy." Roman was ashamed of the confession.

"You're going to make a great father one day, Roman," Peyton inhaled, "but it's not going to be with me."

Roman couldn't believe the words coming out of Peyton's mouth. *Am I going crazy?* It certainly would explain this stranger sitting across from him. *How can he cast my right to be a parent aside like that?* "How can you say that? I have every right to be a part of this pup's life—"

"Roman," Peyton interrupted, "I'm not pregnant."

A trick? A joke? A test? Several different scenarios crossed Jake's mind, let alone Roman's. He narrowed his gaze upon Peyton, assessing the appropriate reaction he should take. "What do you mean you're not pregnant? A miscarriage?"

Peyton shook his head at Roman's Sur. "No. An error." He turned his chair and faced his father head-on, signaling for him to continue the discussion.

Matthew looked up from constantly staring at the table. Outside, his pride was bested. Inside was his undeniable rage. But with witnesses here, deviating from the agreed plan carried with the fear—no, fact—Peyton would begin a vivid account. Proven or not, these words were damaging just the same. "From what I've been told," he curled his lips, "there was an error on several reports from the clinic. A systematic error produced several false positives. It's going to create quite the scandal, I'm sure. But since the error was caught early, before our contract, I've decided to let it go. I don't have any plans to prosecute. Doing so is cheap and a waste of time. As one professional to another, I'd understand if you'd want to take action, but perhaps this can just be settled on the fact we're dropping our position."

"Mr. Whitmore," his lawyer spoke, "are you sure this is what you want?"

"Yes, it is, Nathan." Matthew spoke without even looking in his direction.

"I don't know what to say," Jake stuttered.

"So, you were never pregnant?" Roman clarified.

A visual and verbal response came. "No. I never was. You were right all along."

The flood of emotion coming through to Roman made him want to shout from the highest mountain, hurl waves in the deepest ocean, and run across the longest prairie. But he didn't. He felt glued to the chair. "I'm sorry." He laughed nervously. "I don't know what to do."

The admission amused Peyton. "Yes, you do. Go find your Fated Mate. Do what you were meant to do."

A hand reached across the table. With it came Roman's whimpering voice, "Thank you."

"You're welcome. Now, if you could do me a favor, I'd like to speak to you here in private," Peyton requested.

Matthew jerked his head. "Peyton, I don't think—"

"It will only be a couple minutes." Peyton's words carried no trepidation. It wasn't a suggestion.

Nodding slightly, Matthew stood up. All followed his lead. He buttoned the bottom of his suitcoat and held out a gesture. "Jake. Roman." Handshakes ensued.

"Matthew. Thank you," Jake replied.

Roman chose to remain silent.

Matthew returned a nod and led all but Roman and Peyton out of the room, the door shutting behind them.

Staring into Peyton's eyes, Roman couldn't believe what transpired. "Peyton, what just happened?"

"I listened to your advice. Thank you."

"I don't get it. How does a false pregnancy test equal you needing to confront a truth? Was there a plan to not tell me?"

Peyton paused. "All you need to know is you helped me become a person I've always wanted to be. You gave me the strength to make sure the right thing happened in the end."

"Yeah, and how were you able to do that? I didn't know you had this in you."

"Heh, I didn't either. Believe me, my heart was going a mile a minute in here. How I didn't keel over from a heart attack, I'll never know." Peyton laughed.

"You were amazing," Roman complimented.

"So were you. Through all of this, you were sweet, kind, caring, and so much more. Your mate is one very lucky person."

Roman's expression fell. "I did so many things wrong."

"Eh, you weren't the only one. No one is perfect, definitely not me."

"I have to ask: what happened to your Sur? It's almost like you and he switched bodies."

Peyton mulled over the words. "Let's just say he's finally learned he can't always get what he wants. I have a feeling he's going to be dealing with the agony of defeat for a while. It's okay; he needs it. It builds character." He chuckled.

Roman grabbed Peyton's hands in his. "What are you going to do now?"

Now it was Peyton's turn for his emotions to become heavy. "Things are going to be changing for me." He bit his lip. "I wish I could say it's all good things, but it's not."

"What?" Roman asked with concern.

"I'm going away. Separating myself from all this. My Sur has made it clear I'm not exactly a welcome member of this family anymore. So, I'm taking the assets I have and venturing out, away from the safety of my bedroom. Consider it a trade in surrendering the contract."

"Peyton, no."

"Oh, don't worry about me!" Peyton waved him off. "I'm not banishing myself to a remote mountain village or anything. I can't go too far away from the city. After all, I have a foundation to protect and to turn homeless Beta and Omega lives around. Believe it or not, that is a real thing. It wasn't just for my father's leverage on the contract. Mostly—but not all." He sighed. "I will miss you."

A tear formed in Roman's eye. "I'll miss you too." He pulled Peyton into a tight embrace. With one final gesture of affection, he kissed Peyton's head before separating themselves.

As they parted, Peyton's own eyes were glistening too. "Whew! Okay, you blubbering giant. Go find your prince charming!"

Roman walked to door. Before leaving, he looked back one final time. "Goodbye, Peyton."

"For now," he replied.

CHAPTER 26:

A Time to Process

"Did you pack all your device cords? I saw them earlier in your desk drawer," Roman asked.

"Now you're going through all my stuff?" Ryan accused.

"I was just trying to help," Roman pleaded.

"You've done enough, don't you think?"

Roman's head fell as he watched his brother clean some final items out of his room. When Ryan walked out, the room was bare minus some dust bunnies and random bits of trash. His desk—gone, his bed—gone, his clothes—gone. The only notable items left were the window curtains.

A few beats after his brother, Roman followed up the stairs.

The main floor was uncomfortably quiet. Both of their parents were in the backyard. Adrian was a complete wreck, and Jake held him in his arms. Just then, Rixen walked down from upstairs.

"What are you doing up there?" Roman inquired.

"I was just double-checking that Ryan didn't leave anything up there."

Those were the first words Rixen had spoken to Roman since the argument in the kitchen where Roman decided to do a tell all. But Rixen made no effort to stop his one-track mind out the front door to the packed car in the driveway. A moving truck sat on the curb by the property. Ryan was there giving some final instructions before the truck went ahead to deliver the items to the apartment the twins acquired south of the city.

Before Roman knew it, Rixen locked himself in the car and glued himself to his phone.

Ryan walked back up the drive and took notice of Rixen's isolation. He walked up to Roman, noticing his defeated expression. "I guess this is it," Ryan uttered.

"You don't have to do this," Roman stated.

"Tell that to Sur dictator in there."

Roman moaned. "He's upset, Ryan. Give him some time and he'll come around."

"I'm not waiting around to find out." Ryan stood there with his arms crossed, tapping his foot. He wasn't sure if he wanted to stay talking to Roman or run in the opposite direction.

Roman sensed the posture. This was his last chance. "You know I didn't mean to do that, right?"

Ryan huffed. "So, you've said."

"I was so fucking caught up in my own shit, I took it out on you."

Ryan digested the words. "It wasn't all your fault. I was looking for a fight, and you gave it to me." Ryan shook his head. "You know, I never thought we'd be the first to leave. Tradition says the oldest brother leaves first. And now, we're leaving you behind."

"I want you to know that I'm still your brother. If you need anything, just let me know."

Ryan curled his lips and nodded. "Okay."

Roman examined his brother. "Is Garrace meeting you there?"

"He said he'll be there either late tonight or tomorrow afternoon. I guess his parents are hesitant about all this."

"Do they know about...?" Roman gestured a finger back and forth between him and Rixen.

"No," Ryan responded in record time.

"Think this is all going to work out?" Roman was risking a lot by asking the question so casually.

"Like everything else in my life, does anyone care?"

"I didn't say everyone else. I said you."

Ryan paused, considering. "I didn't see this coming. I never planned it. I never thought I wanted it," he paused, "but I want it." He nodded. "Yes. I think it can. Otherwise, I wouldn't have risked being banished from my house for it."

"Will you at least say goodbye to Veo?"

"No. Time for that has passed, and so is my time here." Ryan looked at Rixen who was intentionally looking anywhere but here.

"Remember," Roman leaned in, "I'm here if you need me."

"Thanks," Ryan whispered. He walked down the steps to the car in the driveway. As he opened the door, he looked one last time at Roman. Unable to hold his emotions still any longer, he entered the car and drove off.

After the car was completely out of sight, Roman heard a ping on his phone. A large text message came through. The wind could have blown him over from how weak his knees became.

Roman walked back into the house. Jake saw him first, signaling the twins had left. With an arm wrapped around Veo's shoulder, Jake led his mate back into the house. Adrian with red eyes was still sniffling a bit.

"Why don't you go upstairs, babe? Take a bath. Relax," Jake suggested.

Adrian silently agreed. His misery was held for a second as he acknowledged Roman and then passed by to head upstairs, arms and legs shaking, barely containing the liquid spirits in his hand.

After the bathroom door shut, Jake shuddered. "I never want to see him look like that again."

"Don't you think you contributed to that a bit?" Roman challenged.

"Don't start!" Jake sneered.

Jake walked over to the couch and collapsed. What he really wanted was a glass of whatever could make him forget the picture of seeing his mate in pieces. However, once he sat down, he didn't really want to get up again.

"Are you up for a conversation about the contract by chance?" Roman tested.

Jake's head snapped back up and saw Roman's needy face. The energy to get up found him quickly. He walked over to the bar and poured ice and amber into two glasses and handed one to his son. "That was quite the show, wasn't it?"

"I'm still in shock over it."

"You and me both. I never thought in a hundred years I'd see Matthew Whitmore look or act like that. He was a zombie."

"I'm still reeling from the new Peyton as well."

Jake took a sip and grunted. "Yeah, he wasn't like that any other time I saw him."

"Do you believe everything Peyton and his Sur said was the truth?" Roman washed the words down with a gulp.

"You saw Matthew's face, right? It's safe, I think, to believe him."

Roman cleared his throat. "What about the mix-up about the false positive tests?"

Jake considered the words in his head. "It's not unheard of. Rare, but not unheard of. Why the questions?"

"I want to contract with Mikaél."

It was ignorance to say Jake didn't know it was coming. That's what this entire ordeal was about. "I suppose that was the point." Jake swirled his drink. "You still have to get Dustin's permission. Otherwise, you're waiting until his 18th birthday. And even then, things aren't guaranteed."

"Dad, I'm not asking for permission. He's my Fate. We're supposed to be together, and it's my job to protect him. I'm going to do it with or without your blessing."

"You have mine. Before all this went down, you had Dustin's support. But..."

Roman waited for the ending of the sentence. "But?"

Jake grunted. "There's just a lot involved, okay?"

"Ah, yes. The mysterious wrench that fucked it all up," Roman replied sarcastically. "Are you going to fill me in?"

"In time, Roman, I promise. I need to talk to Dustin again. After I do, consider it a done deal."

Roman huffed. "Whatever. Then I guess there's just one final thing."

"What?" Jake asked, not sure he wanted to hear it.

Answering his father was a pivotal moment. With an instant finish of his drink, he pulled his phone from his pocket and handed it to his Sur. He stood over him, waiting for a reaction. He wasn't disappointed.

Jake thrust himself forward upon hitting the most damaging information in the text. The expression on his face read like seeing a ghost or aberration. "Can you please wait before telling anyone anything?"

Roman nodded without hesitation. He knew its importance.

CHAPTER 27:

A LONG-AWAITED EMBRACE

On the long drive down the highway on the evening of a Friday night in September, Roman sat in the front passenger seat, resting his head on his fist, his elbow pressed against the sill of the glass window. The gesture was supposed to help calm his nerves, but it gave no reprieve. Instead, as the minutes ticked by, the tapping of his foot on the floorboard became louder.

"Are you okay?" Nico asked, keeping one eye on the road and one eye on Roman.

"Yeah." Roman's reply was swift. He ran his finger across his lip.

Nico didn't like seeing Roman in this state. He felt for his friend. "Are you sure you want to do this?"

"More than anything." Roman looked at Nico.

"He's really going to be there? He's really going to see you?" Nico questioned.

Roman's nerves got the better of him. "Look, if he says he's going to be there, he'll be there!" Pursing his lips, Nico chose to look out his window instead, feeling the anxiety pour off Roman. With a sigh, Roman apologized. "I'm sorry. I shouldn't have done that." Nico nodded, and the car stayed quiet until Roman saw the exit to the neighborhood he remembered all too well. "Before we get any farther, there's something I need to talk to you about."

Nico saw Roman's awkward expression. "Go on."

"I'm embarrassed to ask, but I'm not going to be able to live with myself without knowing."

"Knowing what?"

Roman's chest rose. "When we slept together, did we..." He let the words fall away. He hoped subtle hand gestures and facial expressions communicated to Nico that he understood what the final missing word was—like a partner in a silent boardgame.

"What? Fuck?" Nico smiled.

If Roman could have crawled under the seat at the word, he would have. His face cringed, but he held in an overdramatic reaction.

Nico blushed. "No." Roman's expression highly doubted Nico's answer. "I'm serious. No. We didn't."

It was a rush of excitement indeed. But Roman couldn't understand how it was possible. *Is Nico just being nice?* "Okay. But wait. You said we did stuff you wouldn't even tell your grandparents."

Nico laughed. "Yeah, that's still true."

"Ugh." Roman rubbed the back of his head. "Seriously, how did that not happen then?"

Nico relaxed in the driver's seat. "Roman, you're an amazing guy with an amazing body head-to-toe."

Roman's eyes shifted. "Uh, thank you?"

"But you're not perfect."

"Huh?" Roman's expression was absolutely clueless to Nico's angle.

"Whiskey dick," Nico replied.

"Oh." Although grateful, Roman's tone was still deflated.

"Plus, occasionally mumbling Mikaél's name didn't help. So, depression plus booze." Roman thought about the sentiment. "Oh, don't get me wrong, I still had my fun." Nico winked.

"Thanks for that," Roman spoke sarcastically. "Okay, how about this then...Mikaél told me he could scent an Omega on me—a.k.a. you. That usually doesn't happen so easily unless you get pretty hot and heavy."

"True. Unless you get hot and sweaty."

"What?"

"We cuddled for a long time. And when you're drunk, your body apparently becomes a space heater. That was the reason I took a shower." Nico clicked on his turning signal. They were at the Cavenbelle residence. "So, all things considered, you can walk away with at least a semi-clear conscience."

Off in the distance, the house lights were on, though the night hadn't fallen yet. Unfortunately, the sunlight coming through blocked any easy view into the home to see if Mikaél's parents were sitting at the kitchen table near the bay window.

Nico squinted as he examined the property in the cul-de-sac. "Um. Where exactly are you supposed to go? I don't really see a place for a stealthy entrance."

"It's hard to see from here. The rear of these homes back up to extended lots leading into the woods. Mikaél said to just follow the perimeter to the property line."

"Wow, you really are going undercover here. Creeper." Nico snorted.

"Yeah. I guess so." Roman looked at Nico a as friend should, with gratitude. "Thanks for this. You have no idea how much this means to me."

"Of course. That's what friends are for. But I'll say it again, I won't be waiting long here. I'd appreciate a text, so I don't have to worry about you getting shot or something."

"Uh-huh. Funny."

"I'm serious. I'll send you to a taxidermist, hang you on my wall. Ooo, how about attach you to the front of a ship?" Roman soft-punched his arm. "Ow! Just kidding, just kidding!" Nico's eyes went to the backseat. "Hey, don't forget that."

Roman turned. "Oh yeah. Thanks." One final smile and a hug ended his rendezvous. "7:00 AM tomorrow?"

"Hate you," Nico groaned.

"Appreciate you," Roman said as he exited and shut the car door.

It was irrational, but Roman's steps were practically silent as he walked on the property, as if the slight crunch of the grass would tip off Mikaél's parents from inside the house. The well-kept lawn was razor cut with a row of trees going all the way back to the rear property line. As time went on, Roman swore the sloped yard grew twice in size as the butterflies in his stomach fluttered. Feeling insecure, Roman sent off a text to Mikaél to ask if he was indeed still up for this meeting. The text ping back was a heavenly noise. He confirmed.

The manicured yard finally stopped; mission accomplished. The next challenge was getting to the back's center where a carved-out entrance led to a wooded trail. Once again, fate was on his side, and he entered, deciding to optimistically think no consequences would follow.

Newly fallen leaves painted the dirt trail. It began as a fork with a mature tree line separating the sight of the other trail completely. Without knowing exactly where to go, he took the path to the right. Trees of all shapes and sizes shook in the variable light wind. The sun kissed each and every leaf it could. Occasionally, a gold, red, or brown leaf dropped like a feather down to the ground.

Suddenly, the trail curved to the left. The wall of trees disappeared, and the two trails formed back into a singular one. There stood the most beautiful person Roman had ever seen in his life. His black hair cut through the fall colors, and blue eyes shone. His lips were in a neutral position: no smile, no frown. It took all of Roman's willpower to not rush up and wrap his arms completely around him. But Roman wasn't naïve. He knew the last encounter ended like the destruction of a house of mirrors. So, he started conservatively.

Not knowing immediately the best word, Roman presented a rose to Mikaél. He accepted it.

"An orange rose?" Mikaél questioned.

"An exotic seasonal favorite," Roman affirmed. "Apparently, red and white are too cliché and overrated. That's what the florist said anyway." Mikaél broke into a smile. Hearing his words and seeing his face was a gift Roman wanted to record and watch on repeat. "I know I don't deserve this, but it means everything to me to have you talking to me."

Mikaél nodded. "I'd be lying if I didn't say a part of me needed this too."

Roman's expression dropped, and he shook his head. "I was in a contract with a person who I thought was going to give me what I wanted. That man changed my life for a couple weeks. You walked into my home and showed me what I needed. You came into my life and changed it forever. I didn't know what it meant to be a whole person until you showed up. Some people say having a Fated Mate is a dumb excuse just to force people to produce offspring. For me, it's always meant everything. You mean everything to me. I don't want to live without you, Mik. And I am willing to fight until the day I die to get you to accept what you already know is true."

A loud wisp of wind allowed Mikaél an easy opportunity to look away and process the confession. "Roman," he exhaled. "You know how I feel. I've told you before. I know who you are. I know who you are supposed to be. And I know what fate is telling us to do. But fate can only do so much. People change their destiny all the time, regardless of what is written in the stars. You have other responsibilities. They leave me at the short end of the stick, but I can at least commend you on doing the right thing. So, with that, I'll leave you to focus on all you should." Mikaél stepped to the side and headed back to the house.

"Wait," Roman pleaded. Mikaél stopped in his tracks but refused to turn around. "Tell me, what would you do if this wasn't the situation? What if there was no contract with Peyton? What if there was no obligation? With everything that has happened, what choice would you make?"

To have to consider such scenario was pointless, torture in fact. But since this was going to be their last meeting, the request wasn't outlandish. Mikaél turned. "Take a few pills, chug a beer or two, and sleep it off, for starters."

"I'm being serious. Please."

Mikaél shook his head in confusion. "I don't know! I'd stay, I guess."

"You'd stay?" Roman repeated for clarification.

"For Wolf-God's sake, Roman. What kind of question is that? Yes, I'd stay. As you imprinted me, I experienced a feeling I never knew existed. My Fated Mate? It was a dream come true. But I grew up in a house where all my accomplishments and celebrations were dimmed by my brother who saw all of his dreams get fulfilled and more. I may only be 17 but being in that type of situation gives you a lot of wisdom on how the real world works. I wasn't going to wait for my Fate to just walk up one day and make it easy. And now, here you are: my Fate. And damn it, Roman, you didn't make it easy."

"But?" Roman hoped this wasn't the end.

The heart in Mikaél's chest ached to the point to where he made an audible response to it. "But you were worth it." His eyes began to sting. "I can't explain it. This biological pull we have as humans doesn't automatically make a perfect relationship. And if we were together, it still wouldn't be. But when you comforted me after putting me through the most traumatizing event of my life, I knew you were the one. When you spent the night in my bed, I felt safe. When you held me in Tauris Square, I felt complete. When you comforted me in the cafeteria, I felt..." Mikaél stopped himself.

"Loved?" Roman uttered.

"Yeah," Mikaél whimpered as he wiped away a tear.

The air in Roman's lungs was sucked out. *Is this really true? Can this really work?* "That's why I want to be with you for the rest of my life."

Mikaél rolled his eyes. "That's what I want too. It can't happen."

"Yes, it can," Roman countered, walking closer, closing the gap between them.

"How?" This exchange was beginning to be too much for Mikaél. If he was going to leave with any piece of self-worth, he had to go now.

"Peyton isn't pregnant. He never was. It's over; it's all over."

It was a tidal wave to the chest laced with a soft landing on a cloud. Mikaél couldn't comprehend the words. "What do you mean he never was pregnant?"

"What I know right now is it's all a fucked-up situation. But I will do whatever you want me to do to prove it. My intuition, my inner wolf, knew it all along. Peyton and I separated amicably. His Sur isn't going to interfere anymore. I'm free. We're free."

An excitement set in. Trusting it was the hardest part. "Roman, this better not be a trick," Mikaél warned.

Roman pressed his body up to Mikaél. "You look into my eyes. What does your wolf say?"

For Mikaél, it was hard to breathe being this close to Roman again. This was it. Everything was riding on Mikaél's Omega intuition. If Roman allowed himself to be an open soul, he'd know in the matter of seconds whether or not Roman was truly being honest. His eyes would show it, his scent would indicate it, his touch would feel it. Taking in all the oxygen he could, Mikaél stared back into the jade green eyes he'd missed for so long. Mikaél painted a picture of what he sensed. Many scenes flooded his mind: a bright day on a mountain top, a tranquil rush of water down a stream, a still moment in the forest hiding no secrets. From all of it, the truth was clear. Roman was his.

He cried. With a quick thrust up, Mikaél pulled his mate down to press his lips against Roman with a fierce passion. He missed the physical connection to his destiny more than any other pleasure in the physical or spiritual world. Gasping for air like his life depended on it, he took the moment to say what he'd always wanted to say. "I love you, Roman."

An emotional cry came out from Roman's entire being, "I love you, Mikaél." As if by magic, a wind kicked up beautiful fall colors all around them in a swirling column. The breeze was chilled, but the two mates couldn't have been warmer.

* * *

Twilight commenced. Quietly entering the house from the walkout allowed a night of passion long overdue. The light shining in from bedroom window exposed the outlines of two bodies standing next to a bed. Sounds of mouths repeatedly engaging and vibrating moans filled the room.

Like on the majestic trail, Roman's expression of love was soft and slow. However, taking in Mikaél's seductive orange and clove scent pushed his restraints to its limit. The Alpha in him began to do what he was built to do, take control of his mate—his Omega. He pushed Mikaél back, slow at first to see if he'd accept the forced pressure, then quicker when no resistance came. The edge of the bed came fast, and it pushed Mikaél backward flat. Roman pushed his fists down on either side of him, allowing Mikaél to adjust himself.

Without experiencing this before, Mikaél knew he'd been caught in a moment every person's instinct programmed deep into the most vulnerable parts of their brain. No one had to teach him to recognize both he and Roman's bodies were preparing themselves for the most sensual natural act two mates execute in their lives. Like the virginal Omega wolf he was, Mikaél didn't how to take in the situation. He felt his body rush backward on the bed until his head hit the pillows pushed up on the headboard.

The act was futile, for Roman, just like a wild animal, used his four limbs to follow him immediately step for step, his eyes never leaving his. He saw a textbook Omega feeling the situation out, wondering if it was safe. The burn inside him didn't give Mikaél much time to think or consider comforts or safety. He came down and kissed his love again which involuntarily thrust his body back against his. The Alpha in him pushed Mikaél down with his body weight and soon both were in a body thrusting pattern, awakening all their physical senses. Roman couldn't stand to feel Mikaél's clothes anymore. With strong hands, he lifted his shirt off in a swift motion.

Mikaél grabbed his shirt to do the same; it seemed neither of them could do it fast enough. Staring down, Roman examined Mikaél's soft chest. The marks he once scarred him with were faded but not gone. However, this time, he could touch every part and get the full effect of what he wanted. No pain nor protest came. Roman climbed on top of him and pressed their bodies together. That first contact, naked chest to naked chest, could have sent them to orgasm.

Sucking on Roman's lips was fantastic, but Mikaél wanted nothing more to claim his Fate. Knowing at one point Roman belonged to someone else initiated an urgency to declare to the world he was his again. Like last time, Mikaél chose not to be gentle about it. A slight lick of the neck was Roman's warning call before he sank his teeth in.

Roman roared, but he knew he could only be so loud. What he really wanted to do was shout out tremendous feelings of pleasure, like a wolf howling at a full moon. He knew what his mate's intention was. He was going to make sure Mikaél learned going first was a big mistake.

As soon as Mikaél released him and licked his lips, Roman attacked like a viper right where his pheromone gland was. He felt Mikaél's body tense up on him like he was trying to escape. It was a no-go; Roman wasn't deterred. Instead, a symphony of moans and expletives rang into his ear, making him want to do it more.

After the satisfying taste, the act was done. Now, Roman wanted what Mikaél couldn't give him before. Considering what they both had to go through, he wasn't going to wait any longer. Hands pulled pants off in a flash. All that remained between them were two pairs of tight underwear, both leaking hot fluids. It was at this point Mikaél's slick came through. The call of a Fated Mate must have triggered Mikaél's body to go into overdrive in order to attract Roman to him, and boy did it ever.

Not wanting to worry about whether or not Mikaél was self-conscious, he decided to ease into the moment. While in a deep lip-lock, his hand dug into Mikaél's underwear and gripped his already hard manhood. With a couple of good strokes, he felt the sticky pre-cum and used it to help his efforts. Having Mikaél vibrate moans into his mouth was ecstasy. Gliding his hand down the shaft, past his swollen balls, Roman found his lover bathed in his own slick. It was warm. Sticking a finger inside him was effortless so he did another. His body was preparing itself, and it was going to need to in order to allow Roman's girth inside him.

In all of the fantasies Mikaél had about what this moment was going to be like, this blew away any expectation he had. The only thing he wanted was for Roman to do more and more. He pulled his underwear down which gave Roman permission to slip them right off. His gaze fell to Roman's generous bulge. It too had dark splotches which indicated a well-aroused Alpha. He grabbed at Roman's underwear, feeling the massive organ's outline first. Pulses vibrated against Mikaél's hand. Curiosity took hold, and he pulled down the remaining cloth on Roman's body. Seeing this large cock thrilled him.

Roman saw the look of hunger in Mikaél's eyes. In no time, Roman found out what he was hungry for. In slow motion, Mikaél's head came forward and hot breath engulfed his member. Soon, his entire cock head had disappeared. Roman gasped, thoroughly unprepared for the moment. His timid Omega turned into a greedy animal, taking what he wanted, and it was both pleasurable and entertaining to watch. He massaged the back of Mikaél's head. With his eyes closed, he felt a hand grab his swollen orbs underneath his hard cock. The massaging sensation made it unbearable; the result was going to commence soon.

Mikaél tasted hints of Roman's sweet and salty fluid which coated his tongue. He tried his best to use only his tongue and lips to pleasure his Alpha. But while Roman's girth made it a challenge on his mouth, it wasn't going to stop him from his goal. Prepared for an ending he repressed deep within his sexual fantasies, he moaned on Roman's member. The heavy balls he held in his other hand began to move closer to Roman's body, and he knew the climax was near. But without warning, he felt his mouth being pulled off.

"Not yet," Roman panted. With those words, he laid Mikaél back on the bed and lifted his hips. After a gentle two finger stroke inside him, Roman dove his tongue inside his mate, tasting his slick for the first time.

"Nnnh, fuck," Mikaél moaned. Feeling helpless to the pleasure, he laid there, submitting to Roman's every move. He knew Alphas did this to show ownership to the world. His scent belonged to Roman. It felt like forever, but at the same time not long enough. Roman's head came up, and he licked Mikaél's lips. With his tongue, Roman shared his own taste with him. Mikaél had only lightly experimented with such acts, but now it was here in full force.

Finally, Roman rested his forehead onto Mikaél and watched his every movement. "What do you want me to do?" Roman whispered.

"Take me," Mikaél moaned.

Roman's heart raced. "Are you sure? Do you want me like this, or do you want me to wear a condom?"

Mikaél shook his head. "No. Just like this. Please." He ran his hands around Roman's broad shoulders.

"Prove to me you want this," Roman commanded.

It started with a groan. It was a conjuring of sorts. All Mikaél needed to do was put his mind back to when they first met. With shirt torn open and scratch marks on his body, he envisioned the sight of Roman's similar command. Then, the moment he gave himself to Roman came front and center. It was the most beautiful moment he could think of and also the most important one he needed.

Slowly but surely, Mikaél's bright blue eyes dilated to black pools.

Gasping out of the sheer elation it brought, Roman's beautiful jades faded as well. At that moment, both were ready to give themselves to each other. Using Mikaél's slick, now dripping in anticipation, he coated his cock and put himself into position and slowly pushed in.

Once a generous portion of Roman's length was inside him, Mikaél closed his eyes and began to moan in a regular rhythm. Roman's thrusts became fuller, faster, deeper.

Hearing Mikaél's moaning was getting Roman worked up in a way he didn't anticipate. He hoped pressing his tongue into his Fate's mouth would cause him to focus better on the movements versus the never-ending thralls of pleasure. It worked...until it didn't work.

Roman scented it first. He knew Mikaél's palette through and through. He could track him back to the woods if he wanted to. But this scent was new. It was strong. VERY strong. It was a siren's call forcing him to keep going. Beneath him, Mikaél's face flushed and his grip on him became sharp. Mikaél's body was prepping itself. However, this wasn't for an orgasm.

Mikaél's breath became irregular, and his eyes shut tight. He gritted his teeth to try and deal with what was going on inside him. "What's happening?" he whimpered.

"Grab onto me," Roman instructed. Still connected as one, he lifted Mikaél onto his lap and steadied him. He tried to get consistent eye contact, but the new development was making it difficult. Suddenly, the question hit him. "Have you had your first heat yet?" he asked.

A contraction hit hard. Mikaél pressed his face against his mate and muffled a cry into him as heard Roman wince in pleasure from it. "No," he moaned. "Wolf-God, it hurts."

Roman's instincts knew. "It's your heat, baby. It's here. Now."

Mikaél panted. "No. No, it doesn't happen this way. I would have known days ago."

"You're having an emotional heat. It's because we're together. We triggered your first one."

The color drained from Mikaél. Pain and pleasure came in and out in all directions. He couldn't concentrate on either one. They were happening all at once. "Roman, I'm scared. I don't know what to do. How do we make this stop?" Another contraction.

"There's only one way. We have to finish this." He looked at Mikaél's vulnerable expression. He was frightened. "Do you trust me?" No answer. "Do you trust me?!" he demanded.

Mikaél nodded and began to focus on regular breathing, knowing how this was going to end.

Roman eased Mikaél back down and returned to deep pleasurable thrusts. He heard regular intervals of his mate moaning in pleasure and then moaning in pain. Feeling tight contracts on his cock drove him deeper and harder.

"Roman!" Mikaél cried out.

"It's okay, Mik! I've got you." Roman's body continued its physical onslaught, feeling controlled by a primal force. In addition, his inner wolf was going into protection mode. He tried his best to tell himself he didn't need to release the savage beast as he had once before. However, the growing scent and painful moans coming from his mate had two worlds colliding. Only one was going to win.

"Oh fuck, I feel it!" Mikaél whispered.

"I do too," Roman grunted. Deep inside, Roman's cock was hitting a barrier which was undoubtedly moving lower, closer to Mikaél's pheromone and prostate gland. The more Roman hit the flexible barrier, the softer it got and the harder he got. But Mikaél was losing control beneath him.

"You're almost there! Please, I can't take it anymore!" Mikaél's voice became shallow, and his scent turned darker.

Roman felt veins swell all over his body and an intensity raced through his muscles. In a flashback, Roman saw Mikaél standing in his home for the first time all over again. All he could focus on was the unmarked Omega standing in a room full of other strong Alphas. The thought triggered a fire in his eyes he didn't want to return to.

In the agony of both their plights, Mikaél saw the animal inside his Fated Mate come out again. Seeing it sent a shock of fear through him. He didn't know what to do. He didn't know what to say. All he knew was if he didn't do something fast, he was going to be Roman's victim all over again during the most intimate moment they were supposed to share. He forced Roman's head onto his and locked into his eyes. Now Roman himself looked scared, while still panting from the pleasurable goal they both needed.

"Roman, I love you. You're my Fate, my Alpha, and my wolf. I'm going to be here for you. Always."

Fighting against the beast inside was the most difficult undertaking Roman ever had. But Mikaél's words were an enchanted spell. He didn't know he needed them until he heard them. With the few breaths Roman had left before going on a feral rampage, he repeated what he knew in his heart, "I love you, my Omega. I'm going to protect you until the day I die. My Fate."

Like a busted, pressurized valve, Roman felt a hot sensation engulf his entire manhood while deep inside his Fate. In a now deeper, tighter space, Roman felt swollen tissue milk his cock in continuous contractions. He was there, inside Mikaél's womb. The scent of it hit Roman instantly, and he began to feel his reproductive organ swell in a manner he'd never experienced before. His cockhead grew larger than it ever had, and the base of his cock grew wider. Uncontrollably, he felt load after load jet out of him. With every pump, Roman moaned, throwing his head into the pillow to prevent him from shouting at the top of his lungs. Roman didn't know how many times his body forced him to orgasm, but it just kept going, even after he felt the ejaculate end.

Mikaél's experience of euphoria wasn't any less. When he felt Roman break through his womb, a tremendous pressure released inside which took the pain away instantly. He threw his mouth on Roman's shoulder to prevent an echo of pleasure sounding throughout the house. As he felt Roman's seed splash against his insides, it triggered his own orgasms. One of the orgasms happened outside of his body. His prostate pulsed which repeatedly tightened and released his swollen hole at the base of Roman's cock. In addition, his own cock spewed hot cum all over his chest and stomach. The second orgasm came from the now pleasurable contractions closing around Roman's cock which he felt get bigger than it already was. What once was fear turned into comfort as he felt Roman slow his thrusting to a halt and felt his body tense one last time.

Finally, Roman felt a grip from Mikaél's insides which closed tight on his manhood. They were officially locked in a knot—the first for both of them.

Once the intensity stopped, both were finally able to look each other in emotional joy. A kiss sealed their love as the knot sealed their bodies. As the knot continued to contract periodically, sending smaller waves of orgasms throughout them both, Roman held the back of his mate's head, occasionally pressing kisses all over him like an Alpha wolf in the wild protecting their Omega.

CHAPTER 28:

A Dinner for Fate

"Dad, seriously. How long do we have to wait?" Roman paced on a runway of wood flooring between the kitchen and living room. He was attempting once again with his tie, frustration increasing with every mediocre attempt.

"I told you," Jake reminded him, "my contact has been indisposed. He comes back tomorrow. I'll talk to him Monday." Checking for what was sure to be Roman's blatant disapproval for the tenth time, his attention instead went to Roman's failing fingers. "Oh, for crying out loud, let me do it." Jake shook his head. "24 years old and you still can't do a tie right."

"Of all the things to shame me for." Roman stuck out his tongue.

"Right?" Jake laughed.

Footsteps were heard coming down the stairs. "You ready? We probably should be going," Adrian insisted.

"Yes, any longer and traffic will be atrocious," Jake confirmed.

Adrian took one good look at his mate and his oldest son. "You two look stunning."

Walking up, Jake kissed his forever mate. "Not so bad yourself, babe."

"Let's go! They're not going to wait for us forever." Roman strolled to the door.

Jake grabbed the keys. "Then let's do this."

An upscale seafood restaurant wasn't Roman's ideal place. It was Mikaél's request, an accommodation he was more than happy to consider. Besides, all seafood restaurants had some sort of land option. This official doting phase was turning Roman into a submissive Alpha. It wasn't something to advertise, but he thoroughly enjoyed it.

The Cavenbelle family arrived first. They were already seated at the table. Roman wanted to sprint but settled on a brisk walk instead. There was a straight, uninterrupted line straight to his mate-to-be. His soft lips were the goal. When he completed the act, it was winning a championship game in any sport or challenge.

The kiss was conservative, but that didn't stop Mikaél from returning a full-fledged response. "We were getting worried."

Roman hummed. "Friday night traffic. Can't escape it."

"Roman!" Dustin acknowledged with an upbeat expression. He lifted himself and gave him a generous hug. Alec followed.

After Mikaél received his own warm welcome from the Erricson family, all sat at the table. A waiter was quick to hand the new members their menu.

"Hmm. If you couldn't guess this place was swanky from the décor, the prices sure tell you," Jake critiqued.

"Jake!" Adrian sighed. Roman equally disapproved.

"Just kidding! This is your night."

"Still," Roman added, "it would have been nicer to do this after the contract signing."

Jake didn't move his eyes off the menu. "Did you want to wait until next Friday?"

"Nope. I'm good." Roman returned to an attitude of gratitude. He heard his father stifle a bit of laughter.

"So many choices on this menu!" Alec exclaimed. "What are you getting, Mik?" No words came. "Mik?"

"Huh?" Mik was slow to turn his head up. It appeared he was zoned into looking at the options. But it wasn't so.

"I said, what are you getting?"

"I think I'm going to just get some pasta and white sauce," he mumbled.

"Really?" Alec's voiced uttered confusion. "You chose this restaurant. You didn't want seafood?"

"I did. I'm just not feeling it right now."

"Oh. Okay," Alec deflated.

Roman rubbed his lover's leg. His Alpha instinct told him this was more than disinterest.

All ordered their entrées. While waiting, conversations were plentiful from updates on Adrian's private hire jobs, Alec's progress on his studio, Dr. Birowack's business trip, and hearing once more how excited all parties were there was a contract signing binding Roman and Mikaél together forever next week.

The last conversation lent itself to a more serious topic.

"So, Mik...Roman" Dustin observed his son and son-to-be, "there's a conversation we wanted to discuss before the contract next week."

Mikaél searched his parents for their facial read. No hint was given. "Should we be scared?"

"No, no," Dustin chuckled. "Goodness no."

No one else other than Jake even attempted to match Dustin's carefree attitude.

Jake continued, "Just something we wanted to discuss here so when we go to mediation, we're all in the know."

Roman looked toward his Veo. It seemed Roman and Mikaél were the only ones not "in the know." "Any reason we're doing this in a crowded restaurant?"

Jake attempted an answer, "Now, Roman—"

"So, a scene doesn't happen, right?" Roman was seeing an uncomfortable dinner with the Whitmores all over again.

"Nothing bad is going to happen," Jake stated.

Dustin nodded and scanned the room. "Just some precautions is all."

"What precautions?" Mikaél wondered.

"Son. You asked why we weren't letting you and Roman contract? We believe now is the time for you to know."

Roman and Mikaél glanced at each other before giving Dustin their undivided attention.

"I know your father and I have failed you in some ways in giving you support and validation. Drew was a powerhouse sometimes, but that didn't mean you deserved any less. You've always been special to us, Mik. And had I been the father I should have been, I could have realized just how special you were."

"Okay? Special how?" Mikaél inquired.

"You may remember the contract ended with the reading of your Blood-Type verification."

"Yeah. Why?"

"It was because your bloodwork came back in a way we didn't think possible."

"Right. It was a bad test. Something went wrong," Mikaél confirmed.

"No, Mik. Nothing went wrong. We just didn't care enough before to realize."

The constant suspense was losing its effectiveness. "Care enough to realize what, Dad? Seriously!"

"You're a Type 6, Mik."

Mikaél's eyes widened. He waited for his father to show a bluff. None happened. What was worse, none of the parents had any surprise nor hint of disbelief.

Roman, on the other hand, was beginning to breathe harder. He felt all pieces come together in his mind. It all made sense. He was never going to be able to scent any Fated Mate. He was going to scent Mikaél because his Fated Mate was also Type 6. If Mikaél had been put in a room with a thousand Alphas of all Types 1-5, there was zero chance anything was going to come of it. And Mikaél didn't even know it.

It didn't click for Mikaél with the same ease. "A Type 6? I'm not a Type 6. Ridiculous. They don't exist."

"One does, Mik," Dustin corrected. He pointed at his son. "And you're it."

Rubbing his brow, Mikaél tried to settle on the truth. His father's conviction didn't do much to convince him of anything. But he didn't have a choice at this point to not believe it. The contract was once cancelled, and now it was days away from being law. Why would his Sur give his blessing on it now and use this as some fake excuse?

Alec placed his hand on top of his son's. "Do you need a minute?"

Mikaél shook his head. "No, I just need…" He grabbed his water glass and took a few gulps down.

"Mik, seriously. Are you okay?" Alec repeated.

"Hey," Roman whispered to his mate, "it's going to be okay."

Roman's voice soothed a lot more than his Veo's hand.

"Which brings us to the next issue," Jake refocused.

"Oh, what? Seriously!" growled Roman.

"Now, now," Adrian soothed, gesturing for the volume to go down.

Jake continued, "In order for this contract to work, we need you both to abstain from conceiving offspring."

Roman's blood began to boil to the surface. Saying such thing to any Alpha was equal to attacking their Omega or their offspring. "There's no way we're agreeing to that." Realizing the comment was quick, he looked to his Omega. "Mik?"

Still shell-shocked from the previous statement, plus noticing a wave of heat overcoming him, he had to replay the statement in his mind. "I agree. I can't agree to that. That's insane to ask of anyone."

Dustin held up his hands to stop the criticisms softly. "No, sorry. That could have been worded better." He looked a bit irked from Jake's lack of grace. "We're not telling you to not have pups. We're saying it's important to not have them conventionally."

Roman stared Dustin down. "Conventionally?"

He continued, "There needs to be protection or birth control when you two start intimacy. When the time comes for you to consider a family, we suggest alternatives."

Mikaél had a moment of better concentration. "What alternatives?"

"Surrogacy. Use Roman's DNA with an egg donor and use your eggs with a sperm donor."

To Roman, the concept and logistics were unheard of. "Wait. If we did that, our pups would be half siblings. Not to mention, Mikaél and I wouldn't pass on our genes together."

"That is correct," Dustin affirmed.

Mikaél took another drink of water. "Dad, what is going on?"

"Jake, tell them what they need to know," Adrian pushed.

He cleared his throat. "Had either of you found any other Blood-Type for your mate, this conversation wouldn't be happening. But once we discovered the truth about Mikaél, we ran some tests."

"What tests?" Roman asked. The phrase "ran some tests" was never good.

"The same we did for you, son. But with both of your DNA make-ups, we were able to find compatibilities or in this case, incompatibilities."

"Like?"

"The original theory was, should a Type 6 Omega ever be found, the combined DNA could create a powerful era of wolf-descendants.

That has yet to be seen, of course. But the bigger problem is the vitality of the pregnancy."

Mikaél sighed. "In layman's terms?"

Dustin picked up, "If you two choose to have a traditional pregnancy, there's an alarming rate in which the pregnancy will result in a miscarriage. And, unfortunately, there's no real way to know if that would be an early or late term termination."

"Look," Roman hit his fist, "this overconcern is great, but this is a choice and risk Mik and I decide for ourselves. Not you."

"Roman," Adrian began, "we're only looking out for your future."

"We'd never tell you this to hurt your feelings or dictate how to live your lives. We just want you safe," Alec added.

A low growl came from Roman. "Mik and I will do what we feel is best. And whatever that is, I will protect him and help him through whatever he goes through."

"Roman." Jake shook his head.

"How are you going to help and protect him if he's not around for you to help and protect him?" Dustin threw out.

The Alpha in Roman perked up. "Is that some sort of ultimatum or threat?"

"No. It's a reality. The child isn't the only issue. Mikaél's body is equally in danger of not being able to support the pregnancy."

As if Mikaél was in physical danger, Roman looked to his Omega to assess his wounds: his emotional ones. Once again, he appeared to stare off and zone into nothingness. Roman sensed his pheromones changing. "Mik…"

"I know," he whispered back.

Roman retracted his claws. "How bad is it?"

Jake saw Dustin eye him back. It was his turn. "For both the viability of the pregnancy and Mikaél's mortality: 80% chance of failure."

The number struck through Roman's heart. So many hopes dashed in minutes. To never combine his and Mikaél's love in the purest result? It was a wolf's lament to the full moon. "Both of you are beyond help if you honestly thought this was a conversation to bring up here." He couldn't imagine what Mikaél thought.

"The goal was to have a productive conversation. But like usual, you are stubborn beyond belief." Jake rubbed his nose and took a sip of his cocktail.

"Perhaps Roman is right. This wasn't really the place," Adrian commented.

Jake set his glass on the table and stared at his mate. The words were coming. But the food came faster.

Several plates were placed on the table. The aromas filled the room. Different meats from land and sea intertwined, sauces interlaced, temperatures rose. On any other occasion, it was bliss. But now, the whole evening was tainted.

Mikaél groaned and rubbed his temples.

Roman scented a stronger change in his mate again. "Babe, what's going on?"

Alec leaned again. "Mik, you're burning up. Are you sick?"

Roman shook his head. "He's not sick. It's something else." He couldn't put his finger on it.

Suddenly, the room spun in waves for Mikaél. He had to get out. Now. "I need to excuse myself." With one heave, he got up from the table and hurried to the nearest restroom. It couldn't come fast enough. Barely holding it in, his body shook, and pain radiated everywhere. His skin was boiling, and his forehead was beginning to sweat. Entering the bathroom, he noticed a large stall with its door open. Instantly running in, he didn't have time to lock it. With an involuntary movement, his knees hit the floor and his stomach retched into toilet below.

Roman was hot on his heels. It was clear Mikaél had no clue. He walked in to hear his mate gagging and whimpering. He stepped closer as he heard sounds of pain echo in the entire room, luckily void of other people. Finally, he heard the heaving slow down. But it was followed by a stronger scent of sadness. When Roman finally looked in, Mikaél had cleaned himself up but sat on the floor with his head against the wall, tears running down.

"Mik, what's going on? What's wrong?"

With shaking hands, Mikaél held his stomach. He closed his eyes in pain, but it wasn't from being sick. He squeezed his eyes shut. "I'm so scared," he squeaked.

"No, you don't have to be scared." Roman wiped the tears away and sat next to him. "We'll figure it out. We have the rest of our lives to figure out our options for a family. And who knows? It seems every week we get a new update on this shit. I bet next week they'll say 'Oops, we were wrong. Breed like rabbits.'" Mikaél's face was plastered in sorrow; he knew the joke wasn't timed the best, but nothing else was working.

Mikaél slowly turned and looked at Roman. Whatever strength Roman had, he needed it. "I'm pregnant."

Frozen. Eyes, face, body, everything. The words sank into his core. "You're serious?" Roman's heart pounded to the point to where he could feel it in his ears.

Mikaél nodded his head, almost like he was ashamed.

Suddenly, Roman's wolf took over, and he dug his mouth into Mikaél's neck. With Mikaél's already high distress and blood pressure, it didn't take long to get a rush of pheromones back. Mikaél's scent had indeed changed. He knew something was up, but the scent was weak before. Now with the words spoken and pheromones emanating, it was all Roman could smell. There was a combined scent of him and his mate but underneath it there was a new scent. Mikaél was carrying his heir, his pup, his son. Roman was going to be a father.

His mind went to the primal part of every human's mind. Upon hearing a successful attempt at putting their pup inside an Omega's belly, every Alpha had the automatic response of pride and protection. Roman grabbed Mikaél and held him close. "Wolf-God,

Mik. We're going to be fathers. We're going to be a family." His eyes became heavy with tears.

A grim look crept on Mikaél's face. "Roman, this isn't a good thing. Our Surs just said this can't happen. We can't do this."

In a one-eighty turn, a shock ran through Roman's body. "Wait. What are you saying?" The tears fell but the intent had changed. "Mik, are you wanting to stop this? End the pregnancy?" The thought alone made him want to retch just like Mikaél had done.

"No!" Mikaél responded. "Wolf-God, no. I couldn't do that. I wouldn't."

Roman sighed louder than he anticipated himself to do. "Oh, thank you." His senses came back to him, and he realized what the fear was. "This is about the risk, isn't it?" Mikaél nodded. "Come here," Roman nudged. Mikaél's head rested on him. "We're in this together. I'm not going to let anything happen to you. My job is to protect you and I will. Whatever happens, I'm here."

"Thank you," Mikaél breathed.

Roman thought for a beat. "When did you know?"

"I didn't know what was going on. But I guess last week I started feeling funny. It wasn't until tonight with everyone talking about pregnancy that I realized what it was."

"And what do you feel about that?"

With arms wrapped around his mate, Mikaél sighed. "Other than terrified, I couldn't be happier." He stared into his Fate's eyes. "We're going to be a family."

Roman's voice trembled, "I love you."

"I love you, too."

A gentle kiss sealed their trembling emotions. Time stopped in those moments. Nothing else mattered. Roman had his Fated Mate. And now, with the Great Gray Wolf's help, Roman had his heir.

CHAPTER 29:

A Validation for Exploitation

D r. Birowack walked into a quiet, abandoned laboratory. During this time in the morning, several different employees should have been hustling and bustling with samples, orders, diagnostics, supply boxes, and communicating at louder volumes than necessary. But no such activities were witnessed.

Opening his closed office door, Dr. Birowack saw his two constituents sitting in chairs waiting for his arrival. Upon seeing their cold expressions, he stopped a gentleman, unknown to Jake and Dustin, at the door and walked in.

Upon shutting the door, Dr. Birowack smiled cautiously. "Gentlemen, it seems the lab mice have gone missing. I'm sure the correct protocols have been put into place in order to find them? Filing missing persons reports for a dozen of our employees comes to mind."

"We told them to take an extensive morning break," Jake answered.

"Who is that?" Dustin asked, appearing at a closed door like he had x-ray vision.

"All in good time," Dr. Birowack waived them off. "So, shall I hear what has our lab paying for a complimentary breakfast?"

Jake adjusted and centered himself. "My son Roman came into some information from Peyton Whitmore which has me very disturbed. It has haunted me every single minute since I got wind of it. The only way I could do this conversation was in person; otherwise, I would have called you immediately. But I needed to see your face right in front of me." Jake's tone grew more irritated with every word, his Alpha pheromones seeping out.

Dr. Birowack adjusted himself but held his expression steady. "And what information is that?"

Now the hard part. Jake stole a look to Dustin who didn't appear to envy him. He rubbed his face with both of his palms. "Did you give Matthew Whitmore my son's sperm in order to have Peyton artificially inseminated?"

Dustin cringed in his seat.

Dr. Birowack listened to every word as if it was said in slow motion. He could nearly hear Jake's heart pounding in his chest. "Yes."

Jake about exploded from the simplicity. "Yes? That's it? Just 'Yes'?" Jake balled up his fists until his knuckles were white. "How can you sit there and say it so easily? Not to mention, what gives you any right to do this?! I want answers!"

"And answers you shall have." Dr. Birowack nodded.

Both gentlemen stared at the elder, waiting for what must be outlandish reasoning.

"If it means anything to either of you, it was not my intention to interfere with the trivial problems of mating contracts. Your contract with the Whitmores was a great prospect for our future financial vitality. Not to mention, the goal was to anticipate the grand outcome of the intercourse between both young men."

Jake stood and pointed down at the man whom he once considered his idol and cursed the day he ever followed under the direction of this duplicitous snake. "You're going to jail—prison in fact!"

Dr. Birowack snorted. "Oh please. No one is going to do anything to me for giving someone deactivated sperm."

Of all the possible answers Jake anticipated hearing, that wasn't one of them. "What do you mean 'deactivated'?"

Dr. Birowack chuckled. "To study an exceptional Type 5 Omega with your Type 6 Alpha son could have kept research alive for the next ten years while we observed their pup's development. But to study the offspring of a Type 6 Omega with a Type 6 Alpha? That will keep research alive for a hundred."

The clouds became thicker in Jake's head. "I don't understand."

Dr. Birowack rubbed his tufted chin. "It must have been right after you severed the contract with Whitmore that he came to me irate. Of all things, he accused me of somehow playing Wolf-God himself and intentionally suggesting up a phony contract in order to get the funding for the facility and research grants. Naturally, I dismissed such an irrational allegation. But he would not be deterred from such a mindset." He paused and inhaled, preparing himself. "So, as a show of good faith and loyalty, I devised a plan for him to get back into the contract through a pregnancy. Of course, I had no intention of being third party to such conception, let alone endanger this magnificent opportunity we have."

"And how was that supposed to happen exactly?"

"I told him to hire a Low-Type doctor from one of the community hospitals. With Whitmore not caring about money, I'm sure he found some poor soul and paid him enough to cover all his tuition bills. I told him to have the doctor prescribe him the fertility drugs to hide any suspicion I was leading him down a futile path. Then, I said it was up to him to fill the rest of the holes to make sure everything else was legitimized. Whitmore's son was never going to be expectant from Roman, barring any in-person act between the two of them. I made sure of that."

"I can't believe this." To Jake, his superior was one step away from being strangled with his own telephone cord or being thrown out the fifteen-story window. "That is disgusting, not to mention the most foolish plan I've ever heard. I mean, what if Roman had agreed to stay with Peyton? You'd be in no better position."

"It wouldn't have been ideal. I would have accepted such results. However, science in its infancy is about gambling with the variables you know, and I myself am not immune from taking risks."

Jake wasn't going to stand this patronization any longer. It was apparent Dr. Birowack had no limits in getting what he wanted. He and Whitmore deserved each other. "Whitmore could have made any number of mistakes to derail all of this in a blink of an eye: making an error in who to trust, finding an inept doctor, continuous test failures, or a trail leading back to..." An image of an injured Whitmore in a conference room flooded his mind's eye. Next to him, his Omega son looming over him like a prosecutor getting ready to announce the smoking gun evidence. Somehow, the process failed, and Matthew surrendered. Jake rubbed his head and conceded his own theories back to his boss.

Smiling, Dr. Birowack stood and walked around his desk. The sun glistened down upon an unsuspecting city, quite the contrast to the emotional tension in his office. "When you first came to me and claimed Roman had not only imprinted but found his Fate, I started to do some of my own research." He turned. "Dustin, you were right. Back when your son was born, no one other than me was going to tell you your Omega son's blood panel was exceptional. And I didn't know him nor knew to look for him. Still, I was convinced your son must have possessed some sort of mystical quality in order for Roman to discover his Fate. Once again, everything right in front of me but unable to see it."

"But wait," Dustin interrupted, "you showed us the documents of your brain theory only recently."

Dustin's comment was met with a shrug. "Just because I told you it was recent, doesn't mean it was days before. Yes, I spent the previous couple of weeks looking for it. But I was only confirming what I had previously expected months ago. Not ever anticipating Roman to find a Fate, I didn't feel the information pertinent. I saw the blood panel of Mikaél's birth record after you described to me the fating incident. I was certain right away of what the possibilities were. My intent was to sit back and let time do its natural business. Fated Mates are notorious for starting families almost immediately upon recognizing each other." Jake and Dustin gave each other a frustrated look of admission. "Ah," Dr. Birowack marveled, "so the budding couple has already become pregnant."

Dustin grimaced. "No thanks to his aggressive brute of a son."

Jake gritted his teeth. "Last I heard, Mikaél was quite the equal partner in the act. Not to mention, very passionate about keeping the pup."

"Congratulations to you and your families," Dr. Birowack interjected.

"No, no, no. Not 'Congratulations.' This is a nightmare," Dustin insisted.

"Why so?" Dr. Birowack cocked his head. "This is a celebratory time for families and a potential scientific phenomenon."

"We just talked about the poor chances of this pup even surviving the pregnancy. And let's not forget my own son's mortality rate."

"Now Dustin, we have no intention of putting your son in harm's way."

Dustin eyes narrowed. "We?"

"Doctor," Dr. Birowack raised his voice, "will you please join us?"

The office door opened and in came a distinguished man, not any older than Jake or Dustin. He had fashionable glasses covering his naturally narrowed eyes, cultured face, and black hair.

"Gentleman, this is Dr. Ehan Zang. He is from the Western Territory."

Jake was stunned. "I didn't even know there was a research facility in the Western Territory."

Dr. Zang appeared smart in his appearance and confirmed it in his accent. "Our center is very discreet for appropriate reasons." He nodded. "I am very glad to meet you both. Dr. Birowack has praised you both many times. I have been so honored he convinced me to come back with him to meet you."

Jake grew suspicious. "Hmm. What did he have to say in order to convince you?"

Dr. Zang smiled and bowed his head. "Forgive me. I was informed of the situation regarding the Type 6 Alpha and Omega, and it means a lot to me and my medical community to continue our research on the endless possibilities of the Type 6."

"Wait." Dustin held up his hand. "Paul, you said we were the only three doctors working on this project in the world."

"I said no such thing. I said there were only three doctors in the world leading this study. Now, you and Jake are a critical part of my team, yes. However, when it comes to leadership, I'm afraid you two have some growing to do, especially in the realm of teamwork. Thus, I have confidently relegated such titles to myself and Dr. Zang."

Both gentlemen felt a gut punch to their stomach. Egos fell to the floor and broke like delicate eggs.

Jake sighed. "And who is this third doctor?"

Dr. Zang answered, "Dr. Samuel Dasu. He's a brilliant researcher from the Indian Territory."

Dustin put his hands on his hips, understanding how this was all working out. "So, you contrived the whole contract with Matthew Whitmore's son and Roman, hid your own research agenda, deceived countless people in the process, including your now downgraded co-workers, broken several laws—all under the sake of science sealed with a smile?"

"The Devil is in the details, Dr. Cavenbelle. Those who look for him will find him."

A flashback came to Jake's eyes. The words had come full circle. "I'm sure you and your secret trio has discussed all your fun theories on what our grandson could be?"

Dr. Birowack laughed. "Many hours and countless bottles of wine, Dr. Erricson."

Dr. Zang stifled a laugh as Dr. Birowack continued to enjoy his own comment.

Jake continued, "So, what is it? Are you hoping the pup will be the first Blood-Type 7?"

Dr. Birowack scoffed. "Dr. Erricson, you are worse than the students I teach. This is hardly the time to assume childish fantasies of superhuman powers or shapeshifting."

"I'm not implying such things to happen. But once upon a time, critics didn't anticipate Roman to be the man he is. I myself had to protect him as a child from onlookers once he became public knowledge. I can't imagine what will happen once Roman and Mikaél give birth. The doctors alone will sell every piece of information they have once the pup's blood panel comes back. They have to submit to it; it's the law. Not unless Mikaél gives birth under a kitchen table and hides from the government for the rest of his life."

"There's no damn way I'm having my Omega son give birth under a table or in the woods somewhere like an animal!" Dustin growled.

"Rest assured," Dr. Zang began, "we will do everything in our power to make sure your son gives birth safely and that his and the pup's information is kept confidential."

"And where is this exactly?"

Dr. Zang looked back at his partner.

"It is the professional opinion of Dr. Zang and myself that the check-up appointments and birth take place in Dr. Zang's medical facility in the Western Territory."

Dustin nearly fell over as he looked at humorless faces around the room. "You expect me to send my son to the Western Territory?" No faces gave any indication he had the assumption wrong. "I am not sending my son alone on doctor appointments to the Western Territory!"

"We fully encourage the Alpha father to take part in these appointments, especially under the circumstances," Dr. Zang commented.

"Roman?" Jake spoke.

"Of course, Jake!" Dr. Birowack reaffirmed. "No Fated Alpha wants to leave his Omega alone, especially in pregnancy."

"The Western Territory is a five-day road trip," Dustin declared. "The mountain passes are dangerous, even for a professional driver, let alone a casual one. If he takes the six-hour plane ride, no airport is going to let him get on a plane weeks before he's due, not to mention if he falls into labor unexpectedly."

Jake now understood the broader scale they were after. "You don't want Roman and Mikaél just to make appointments in the Western Territory. You want them to move there. Don't you?"

Both superiors eyed one another.

Dustin began showing off his Alpha pheromones and readjusted his stance. "You are not forcing my son to uproot his entire life away from his family, and everything he's known, to live half a year and Wolf-God knows how long after the birth in the Western Territory!"

Dr. Zang shook his head. "Oh, no. We would never force your son to go there."

"But you might want to start convincing him," Dr. Birowack added.

"Why?" Dustin begged.

Dr. Birowack stood at his desk and leaned over. "This single-handedly might be the most important scientific miracle in the last 200 years. And I don't use that word lightly."

Dr. Zang concurred, "Indeed. I'm sure I don't have to remind anyone here of the former views shared by the public regarding Type 6 Alphas once they were identified. It is even more disheartening when evaluating the larger history of our own kind intentionally

exterminating Higher-Types. To have your son's increasing pregnancy pheromones shine a spotlight on his Blood-Type, let
alone the Blood-Type of your future pup, could have devastating
consequences."

Jake furrowed his brows. "I'm confused. A little bit ago, you
said there shouldn't be anything extraordinary to worry about. Now
there is?"

Dr. Birowack turned to Dustin. "These are precautions, gentlemen. Necessary ones, I might add." He sighed. "But our facilities
are not prisons, and our research is not a mandate. We are merely
wanting to give your sons and their future family the best chance
of success in an unprecedented way. Regardless, if this future pup
walks on water or merely blends into the background, it will be
extraordinary."

Dustin relaxed his stance. As a father, his only goal was to protect his son. Seeing him happy was icing on the cake. But no joy
could happen if he wasn't even in existence. Perhaps this was the
best action he could give his son. If nothing else, this might correct some of his past mistakes. He turned to Jake. "I think there is
enough rationale to support this."

"You want to go forward with this?" Jake posed.

"I don't like this anymore than you do, Jake. But I'm going to feel
a lot worse if political extremists think my grandson is the Devil's
offspring."

"You can't force them to the Western Territory."

"I have no plans on doing that. This is their decision. Once
Mikaél turns 18, I don't have jurisdiction anymore. To put him in
handcuffs and ship him off now only results in him running back
here once he's a legal adult. At that point, it would be all for nothing."

Jake nodded. "Then I'll support you."

"Splendid!" Dr. Birowack clapped. "Now come on, gentleman,
turn those frowns upside down. You are going to be first-time
grandparents!"

"Drew is going to have his pup first," Dustin clarified.

"Oh, yes, yes." Dr. Birowack dismissed the comment as if he didn't hear it. Instead, he pulled out a set of four glasses and a bottle of champagne from a small fridge behind him.

"What's this?" Jake asked incredulously.

"Every now and then, you have to celebrate life and success." Dr. Birowack spoke as he popped the cork and filled each flute perfectly, never letting one drop of fizz spill over the outsides. Not hearing any supportive comment in return, he continued, "Now, now. I may be old, and I may be set in my ways, but I'm not a killjoy or cynic. Let's toast this special occasion."

All held a sparkling glass with a matched expression—the first shared by all.

"I'll take the lead, if you don't mind," Jake offered. "A toast to a successful, scientific miracle and even more importantly, a healthy, beautiful baby boy."

All knocked back their glasses for a first congratulatory drink, except for Dr. Birowack, who held his lips back for a moment.

"Or girl," he replied.

Jake swallowed the liquid hard like it was rock candy.

Dustin himself choked on his drink as part of it entered and burned his lungs. He looked horrified as his beet red face snagged looks at both Birowack and Zang in their mildly entertained expressions. He gasped for air. "A girl? What do you mean?" Coughs came immediately after.

"Is this your idea of a joke?" Jake grimaced.

"No jokes, no pranks, no lies, no kidding," Dr. Birowack cooed.

Dustin regained his composure. "A girl?" he repeated.

"Yes, Dr. Erricson and Dr. Cavenbelle. A female. The first female born in 200 years."

Dustin and Jake carried disbelief in every part of their body. Their hands became weak, their eyes became weary, and the floor was starting to feel soft and squishy. This indeed wasn't a joke. This was serious. This is why Dr. Birowack had gone to such great lengths to steer all the game pieces to his favor. He anticipated the outcome all along, including the gender. That is why Dr. Birowack finally unveiled Dr. Zang. It was not a mere curiosity which enticed Zang, it was the assurance the newborn pup would not only usher in a scientific miracle, but a revolution, a revolution easily threatened by closed-minded conservatives seeking to destroy their interpretation of hell on earth. Keeping Roman and Mikaél out of the spotlight was meant to save their lives. With so many broken ties and barely healed wounds as it were, how were these burdened scientists going to move forward and tell their families this pup in question was to bring in a new era? What were the consequences of Roman and Mikaél knowing? What were the consequences of them not knowing? So many questions and emotions circled in their heads and yet only a second passed.

Dr. Zang walked in front of Jake and Dustin, two stone statues, his drink in hand. "Now gentlemen, where should we begin?"

Roman and Mikaél return in *Mikaél's Moment*!

Author Bio:

Lucas LaMont lives near the mountains of Colorado and has been a storyteller since childhood. Throughout the years, he has dabbled in fiction and poetry and in his adult writing, most of his focus has been in gay fiction. Recently, he discovered the Omegaverse genre and is obsessed with it! During the Covid pandemic, he found his favorite series to read: *The Adrien English Mysteries* by Josh Lanyon (But he is very much a fan of several noteworthy Omegaverse authors). When he's not writing and reading, Lucas loves traveling to fabulous Las Vegas to gamble or staying near the rustic lakes of Minnesota to go fishing. His current focus has been the creation of Boy Love Visual Novels, starting with his first one *Fated: Type 6*. The goal of his writing has always been to focus on the power of relationships and the journey they take. You can find Lucas Lamont on Facebook, Twitter, Instagram, and Wix.